D0451776

How to Knit a Wild Bikini

CHRISTIE RIDGWAY

BERKLEY BOOKS, NEW YORK

THE BERKLEY PUBLISHING GROUP
Published by the Penguin Group
Penguin Group (USA) Inc.
375 Hudson Street, New York, New York 10014, USA
Penguin Group (Canada), 90 Eglinton Avenue East, Suite 700, Toronto, Ontario M4P 2Y3, Canada
(a division of Pearson Penguin Canada Inc.)
Penguin Books Ltd., 80 Strand, London WC2R 0RL, England
Penguin Group Ireland, 25 St. Stephen's Green, Dublin 2, Ireland (a division of Penguin Books Ltd.)
Penguin Group (Australia), 250 Camberwell Road, Camberwell, Victoria 3124, Australia
(a division of Pearson Australia Group Pty. Ltd.)
Penguin Books India Pvt. Ltd., 11 Community Centre, Panchsheel Park, New Delhi—110 017, India
Penguin Group (NZ), 67 Apollo Drive, Rosedale, North Shore 0632, New Zealand
(a division of Pearson New Zealand Ltd.)
Penguin Books (South Africa) (Pty.) Ltd., 24 Sturdee Avenue, Rosebank, Johannesburg 2196,
South Africa

Penguin Books Ltd., Registered Offices: 80 Strand, London WC2R 0RL, England

This is a work of fiction. Names, characters, places, and incidents either are the product of the author's imagination or are used fictitiously, and any resemblance to actual persons, living or dead, business establishments, events, or locales is entirely coincidental. The publisher does not have any control over and does not assume any responsibility for author or third-party websites or their content.

HOW TO KNIT A WILD BIKINI

A Berkley Book / published by arrangement with the author

PRINTING HISTORY
Berkley edition / June 2008

Copyright © 2008 by Christie Ridgway.
Excerpt from *Unravel Me* copyright © 2008 by Christie Ridgway.
Cover illustration and handlettering by Ben Perini.
Cover design by Rita Frangie.
Interior text design by Laura K. Corless.

ISBN: 978-0-425-22193-8

BERKLEY®
Berkley Books are published by The Berkley Publishing Group,
a division of Penguin Group (USA) Inc.,
375 Hudson Street, New York, New York 10014.
BERKLEY® is a registered trademark of Penguin Group (USA) Inc.
The "B" design is a trademark belonging to Penguin Group (USA) Inc.

PRINTED IN THE UNITED STATES OF AMERICA

10   9   8   7   6   5   4   3   2   1

Sabrina fair
Listen where thou art sitting
Under the glassie, cool, translucent wave,
In twisted braids of Lillies knitting
The loose train of thy amber-dropping hair . . .

—JOHN MILTON, *COMUS: A MASQUE*

One

A good cook is like a sorceress who dispenses happiness.

—ELSA SCHIAPARELLI,
FASHION DESIGNER

Slowly threading through the tables of the darkened restaurant, Nikki Carmichael refused to let a single tear fall. No, she wasn't going to cry, though the night's last entree had been plated and served two hours before and the last patron escorted out the door thirty minutes ago. For the final time, she'd heard the clear-bell clink of the wineglasses greeting their partners as they were slid into their nightly resting place in the rack over the bar. The kitchen's enormous stockpots that had simmered broth all through the dinner service were now clean, their steam no longer able to corkscrew the baby hairs that escaped her braids.

Pausing beside a table, she tweaked a white linen napkin already folded in the signature Fleming's twist, ready for the next day's dinner rush.

The dinner rush Nikki wouldn't be here to see, sweat over, or even swear about, as from now on a different souschef was responsible for the production of the restaurant's elegant meals.

Still, she wasn't going to cry.

After all, she'd been the one to turn in her resignation. And she'd had plenty of time to accustom herself to the idea of leaving the place where she'd worked since cooking school.

Not to mention that she never cried—not since she was fourteen and her father told her at her mother's funeral that crying was something big girls didn't do. *Don't let anyone think you're weak.*

At the locked door of the employee break room, with nothing left to do but gather her things and head home, she keyed in the pass code and then pushed it open.

"Surprise!"

Startled, Nikki took an instinctive step back and felt that familiar, dangerous doughiness in her right knee. Her leg almost gave way, but she gritted her teeth and fought for balance. The small crowd in the room didn't seem to notice, and then she was being dragged inside.

Colleen, the youngest member of Fleming's full-time waitstaff, grinned at her. "You didn't think we were going to let you go quietly, did you?"

Nikki had really hoped so. She didn't know how much longer she could remain upright on her listing leg.

But slices of the pastry chef's celebrated Chocolate Can't Kill You cake were already set on a rolling cart beside champagne glasses filled with bubbly. The dishwashers, grizzled Joe and his baby-faced sidekick, Carlos, passed out forks. Colleen danced around with the champagne.

"To Nikki!" she finally said.

And everyone there, from the bartender, to the waitstaff, to her favorite prep cook who must have made a return trip just for the occasion, echoed the words, their glasses held high. The enthusiastic goodwill surprised Nikki all over again. She'd inherited her keep-your-distance DNA from her dad, so she didn't get too friendly with people, not even coworkers.

In the convivial atmosphere, though, Nikki did okay through the next few minutes, sipping at the champagne she hoped would work like ibuprofen. Then Colleen asked her about her future plans.

"Do you have your next chef job lined up? You said you had prospects."

It took a moment for Nikki to clear her throat of her latest swallow and her sudden awkwardness. "Not, um, yet. I'm still, uh, sifting through those prospects."

"I have a friend—"

"What about—"

"Why not—"

The room filled with suggestions. Wearing a polite smile, Nikki listened to each of them. Her excuse for leaving Fleming's was creative burnout, so their ideas ran the gamut from Japanese to Egyptian to a place that touted a Swiss-Argentinean fusion cuisine.

That last gave her pause. Swiss-Argentinean fusion cuisine. What would that be, exactly? Reuben sandwiches?

After the cake and champagne were consumed, the well-wishers walked her out to her car. She was forced to smooth her gait as she headed across the blacktop, pretending for the crowd she had two completely functional legs. She'd never wanted pity, or worse, the inevitable questions: Why not see a surgeon? Surely some doctor could . . . ? There were reasons that wasn't going to happen.

Once home, in the smallest rented condo Santa Monica had to offer, she called out, "Fish, I'm back," then limped about to gather a 32-ounce bag of frozen baby peas and a week's worth of unopened mail. With a sigh of relief, she perched on the recliner in the living room, setting the envelopes on the small table bearing a lamp, her answering machine, and the goldfish bowl.

Nikki switched on the light to cheer the early A.M. gloom, then tapped the aquarium with her fingertip. "How you doing, Fish?"

In seconds, she'd popped off her cooking clogs and shimmied out of her black-and-white baggy chef's pants.

Sucking in a breath, she stared at her knee. Swollen to the circumference of a summer melon, it throbbed with each one of her heartbeats. She slapped the bag of frozen peas on it, then pushed back on the chair to elevate the aching joint.

"I'll take the anti-inflammatories before bed, Fish," she said, glancing over at her finned roommate. Her eye caught on the top envelope in the pile of mail. Her name was written in a beautiful hand and the return address was Malibu, California, the famous seaside enclave just over the Santa Monica mountains.

Curious, she picked it up. Leaving the hectic, ever-active restaurant business had become a necessity, thanks to her injury, but doing something else besides cooking—well, she wasn't trained for anything else besides cooking. With a wonky knee and a decidedly private personality, she'd hit on the idea of working in a home kitchen where her work space and her contact with others would be limited.

So she'd advertised in L.A.-area neighborhoods where households might be interested in a private chef.

Bel-Air.

Beverly Hills.

Malibu.

Nothing had come of it . . . until now? Her pulse quickened as she tore open the seal—and then it slid back to a slow thud.

This piece of mail wasn't what she needed. It was an advertisement—granted, a beautiful advertisement—for a yarn shop, address on the Pacific Coast Highway in Malibu.

Join us each Tuesday for
Knitters' Night at Malibu & Ewe!
Make a Connection!
Make something beautiful . . . friends, too.

An enclosed brochure showed the exterior of a cottage-styled shop overlooking a golden beach and an endless ocean. Other photos captured the displays of yarn and a cozy, comfortable-looking seating area filled with women chatting and knitting. There was an open spot on a particularly inviting sofa.

Shaking her head, Nikki tossed the papers back on the pile of mail. What she needed was a job, not a hobby.

"And who needs friends, Fish," she murmured, glancing at the aquarium as she pulled the bands free of her braids and untangled her gold and brown hair, "when I have you?"

With a frown, she noticed his tail sinking southward and used her fingers to spoon him out of the water. Then she wound the tiny screw on his side and tossed him back in, gratified as he whirred around his little pond just as if he was a real, live pet.

He was perfect, wasn't he? Perfect for her, anyway. She didn't have a good track record keeping things that lived and breathed. And a twenty-seven-year-old woman with culinary school loans and without a job couldn't afford to feed another mouth anyway.

"Yes, you *are* perfect, Fish," she said aloud.

And she wasn't going to cry, even though her knee was still throbbing like a bitch.

It was then she noticed the light blinking on her answering machine. Who would be calling? Her parents were dead and her social life was practically nil. Was *this* something about a job? Her heartbeat picked up again, even as she remembered how disappointing the envelope from Malibu & Ewe had proven to be.

Make a Connection!

She needed a way to make a buck or she wouldn't be able to afford the water to fill Fish's bowl, let alone the rent on her condo.

Crossing the fingers of her right hand, she reached over with her left to press Play. A man's voice rumbled into the air.

"Yo. Nancy? Nellie? Whatever. Your friend Sandy gave me your number. Said to call. This is Jay Buchanan."

Nikki crossed the fingers of her other hand. "Fish . . ." she breathed. Jay Buchanan. Editor for the hip men's magazine *NYFM*, L.A.'s man about town, and former employer of her fellow cooking school student Sandy Bivers. For two months, Sandy had worked for him while he wrote a journal-style account of the bachelor joys of having a woman in his kitchen who wasn't also warming his bed. The attention had garnered Sandy a gig on *Oprah* and from there a deal with the Food Network.

Nikki's mind flashed on what her fellow chef had told her about the man. Like that yarn shop, Jay Buchanan was a resident of Malibu, and though he was credited with the magazine's sexist signature tagline, "Men are boys and women are toys," Sandy claimed the worst thing anyone had ever said about him was that he was born under a lucky star on a sunny day at a Southern California beach.

"I've seen him charming water from the devil," Sandy had gone on to say, "at the same time he was slipping the panties off an angel." Nikki had caught a glimpse of him herself, in a pictorial layout in *NYFM*. Leaving a charity function at an L.A. club with a starlet on his arm, he'd appeared both classy and capable. A guy in black tie who looked as if he could make a mixed drink or change a car tire with the same aplomb.

"I need a cook—a chef," the man was saying now. "Just for August. I've got a houseguest for the next few weeks and then a big event to host at the end of the month."

Her heartbeat ratcheted up another notch. Okay, it wasn't long-term, but it was something, not to mention a likely way to make future contacts. And anyhow, she'd do whatever she had to if it meant cooking and keeping off her knee at the same time.

"If you're interested, come by tomorrow. Ten A.M." The address he gave was on the Pacific Coast Highway. "We'll talk."

Her gaze flicked to the time. Given the late hour and the

traffic she'd likely encounter heading to the beach on a summer morning, if she went to bed now, she'd have enough time to get four hours of sleep. Her knee needed at least seven, but she'd make do.

"Oh, yeah," the male voice added. "And bring your best batch of cookies."

Two hours of sleep.

Optimism would keep her awake, though, and maybe work as an analgesic as well. "Jay Buchanan, you're the answer to a prayer," she said, though still not allowing herself even a single grateful tear. But God, how much she needed—

The chance. Not him.

No, not him.

She might be in a tight spot, but long ago she'd learned the hard way what it was to need a man and she wasn't about to make that same mistake again.

Bleary-eyed and fuzzy-brained from lack of sleep, Jay Buchanan yanked on a pair of shorts and stumbled barefoot toward the front of his beachside house, where someone had the annoying gall to knock on his door at the early hour of—

He paused, then leaned back and craned his neck to read the clock on the coffeemaker in the kitchen. Why, oh why, was the carafe empty when he needed it full, and why did the digital numbers claim it was almost 10:00 A.M.? He'd just woken up and . . . oh, yeah. He'd just woken up because he hadn't hit the sack until after 4:00. An idea for a couple of ManTalk columns had nagged him until he'd stopped tossing and turning around midnight and headed for his computer instead.

The idea was worth it. It was all about New Year's resolutions and he'd had a sufficient number of words on the subject to fill the required inches for *NYFM*'s print edition with enough left over to offer a slightly different slant for the online version.

Not so different, actually. They were both about giving up women for the forthcoming three hundred sixty-five days. The columns were for the January issues because magazines worked ahead—and Jay did, too.

While in his latest writing for the magazine he resolved to give up the fairer sex in the new year. Though it was only August, he'd already made that commitment to himself.

As of today, no females.

No how.

It was going to put a hiatus on his popular "In Search of the Perfect Woman" articles, a series inspired by his discovery of his grandparents' old Broadway cast album of *My Fair Lady* in the back of a cabinet. Rex Harrison rapping his way through "A Hymn to Him," which asked the immortal question, "Why can't a woman be more like a man?" had sent Jay on the hunt for just such a one—and his readers voraciously feasted on every account of his failures. So while he'd yet to find a breezy, sexy, sloppy-emotions-unnecessary female, now he was determined to go without looking for the rest of this year and all of the next.

There was that irritating *bam-bam-bam* on his door again. Obviously, the irritator wasn't giving up. Fine, he'd send them on their way and return to bed.

The soles of Jay's feet registered the rug in the entry, then his hand found the knob and he wrenched open the door. Heat wafted over him, as well as the scent of car exhaust and hot asphalt mixed with something sweet. The Pacific Coast Highway was as close to the house's front entry as the ocean was close to his back one and the four lanes were already bumper-to-bumper with Angelenos out for their sand-and-surf fix.

He blinked against the bright sunlight, his gaze now taking in the leggy teen on the doorstep, her hair in two loose braids and her hands clutching some kind of lunch pail.

"Fern's out," he said, making the assumption about his young cousin since she hadn't answered the knock herself. "Don't know when she'll be back." Without waiting for a response, he swung shut the door.

It bounced off the toe of a bright yellow rubber clog. "Mr. Buchanan?" the braided girl said. She had a curiously low, intriguingly husky voice. "I'm here to see *you.*"

He'd written a ManTalk column last year debunking the myth of the hunch, so it was ridiculous of him to feel cold, webbed feet goose-stepping down his spine. Ignoring the sensation, he inched back the door and peered again at the intruder.

Leggy. Braids. Now that he looked more closely, she wasn't the teenager he'd first thought. He made a vague gesture to his right, still hoping he could shoo her off. "No, you can't use the bathroom. And the public beach access is three doors down." He couldn't hold back a little grin. "Right between Geffen's mansion and that equally over-built monstrosity next to it."

Her brows, he noticed as they came together over her small nose, were a shade darker than her brown hair that was heavily laced with lighter streaks. "What?" she asked.

It was one of Malibu's longest-running feuds—the privacy-obsessed celebs versus the public's right to beach access. Newspaper articles and court battles had proven that some of Hollywood's most liberal were anything but when it came to sharing the sand in front of their homes. Jay wasn't entirely unsympathetic. In the summer, he'd had his share of sun worshippers trespassing while in search of showers and toilets. But even when his grandparents had built this house in the 1950s, they hadn't assumed the beach bordering it was theirs and theirs alone.

"It's the price of privilege," he explained to the girl. "You get the incredible property, but you have to share it from the high-tide line to where the surf breaks. There's a public path to the water two hundred and fifty feet down that way."

Leggy with Braids frowned at him. "Mr. Buchanan, I said I came here to see *you.*"

He hadn't missed that, not really, he thought, rubbing his hand over his bare chest. But as his mother always said, Jay was a hoper, and he'd been hoping to get back to sleep.

Yet he should have known better, because nothing was ever simple when there was a woman involved. Why did they always have to complicate everything? Leggy with Braids even *looked* like a complication. A man just couldn't ignore that sweet, full mouth and she had an interesting sprinkle of freckles across her nose that—

Crap. There he went again, heading off into muddy and probably mined female territory. "What, then?" he demanded, sounding surly even though he was mostly mad at himself. "What is it you want?"

To wring his neck, if her expression was anything to go by. But she gave him a tight little smile, not a slice of teeth showing. "I want to talk to you about the private chef position. Remember, you called me yesterday? I'm Nikki."

"Oh." He let his gaze run down Leggy with Braids. Nikki. Nikki of the cute freckles, the slim body, that pretty, earth-and-sunlight-colored hair. "Sorry, you won't do."

Without a whiff of remorse, he shut the door again.

Again, it bounced off a rubber toe.

Jay sighed. This was what was wrong with them. Women. They were tenacious and stubborn in the most troublesome ways. You tried to let them down easy, but they would never take the hint. Why couldn't they appreciate fun and games? Why couldn't they accept when the fun and games were over? But no, they'd always come back—

"Mr. Buchanan," her low-pitched voice was forced to find its way through the narrow crack in the door, yet still he could hear it over the rumble of the traffic on the highway and the surf's shush-and-crash at his back. The goose made another march down his spine. "*You* called *me*. Remember?"

Right. There was that. With a sigh, he pulled back on the knob to gaze on her again, girly as all get-out. "Look," he said, "it's nothing personal. It's just that I've sworn off women."

His last chef had worked out great. Sandy was businesslike, quiet, and a lesbian to boot. When she'd recommended her friend Nikki, Jay had assumed—which reminded him of one of his grandfather's favorite old saws, "Assume makes an ass out of u and me"—that she'd be of the same sexual persuasion.

But after studying the woman on his doorstep . . . well, to put it bluntly, this leggy darling was no dyke.

"Mr. Buchanan—"

He held up his hand, once again wishing like hell he'd had a cup of coffee waiting for him when he rose, which was just another reason to regret this pretty chef person wasn't an ardent fan of *The L Word*. "I've got enough trouble right now, okay? Believe me, I've sworn off women."

Those eyebrows slammed over her nose again. "Then we're even, because I don't like men."

Jay stared in surprise. Could it be? Could his lack of caffeine have impaired his usually impeccable, spot-on radar? "You . . ." He shook his head, because now he noticed something even more remarkable about her. Pretty chef person, Leggy with Braids, Nikki-who-said-she-didn't-like-men had the most amazing eyes. One was blue, and one was green. Like a mermaid, like a witch, like a . . . ?

Could it really be? He frowned. "You don't like men?"

She took a breath.

He leaned forward so as not to miss her answer.

Another female's voice found him first. From the vicinity of his back door floated a light, sugary voice that he was painfully familiar with. "Jay? Jay, darling. I can't go another minute without seeing you."

Tension tightened a strangling hand around his neck. He closed his eyes, opened them, and was distracted for a second from the sticky problem coming up behind him by Nikki's pretty, pretty face and those witchy, witchy eyes.

Hmm. Was she or wasn't she?

"Jay?"

Uh-oh. The sticky problem was getting closer.

"Jay, honey, where are you?"

Nikki's bi-colored eyes were big and full of questions. Jay had one of his own, of course. Did she really dislike men or didn't she? But there wasn't time to speculate, not with the minty breath of his worst double-X chromosome mistake bearing down on him.

And then, *bam*, it hit him. Call it an impulse, call it a brilliant idea, call it both. He kicked aside the unsettling warning that not all his impulses or even his brilliant ideas had panned out to be oh-so-successful.

Like Mom said, Jay was a hoper.

And now he hoped to kill two birds with one stone. A single, simple move—and oh, how he liked things simple—could clear up one little question as well as one big problem.

As high heels clacked on the tile behind him, he grabbed Nikki-who-might-not-like-men, yanked her across the threshold, then pulled her close for a kiss.

Two

Life is a series of commas, not periods.

—MATTHEW MCCONAUGHEY,
ACTOR

Jerk, was Nikki's first thought.

Jerk away, was her second.

Her third thought fizzled as Jay Buchanan's hands tightened on her upper arms and his mouth softened against hers. He smelled good, the scent of sun-dried cotton sheets was wafting off the warm skin of his bare chest. He tasted faintly of toothpaste.

Not that he poked his tongue into her mouth. No, he seemed content with a thorough lips-to-lips kind of kiss, one that belonged in the last row of a movie theater or in the spotlight on the prom dance floor. It was the kind of kiss she'd fantasized about at fifteen and had—biggest blunder of her life—gone looking for in all the wrong places with all the wrong boys.

Then it was over, and he was half smiling at her, bemusement—or was it amusement?—in his gray-blue eyes. He shook his head, causing straight, dark blond hair to fall over his brow. "Hellooo." The one word carried with it surprise, laughter, and a nearly lethal dose of charisma.

Sandy's words rushed back. "I've seen him charming water from the devil at the same time he was slipping the panties off an angel."

Nikki slammed her mouth into her fiercest frown. Lord knew she was no angel, but he *had* to be the devil. A blue-eyed, blond-haired devil. Kissing wasn't any way to conduct an employment interview. And what was with that soft "Hello"? That was all he had to say for himself? She should raise her knee and return a greeting directly to his family jewels.

And she would, she promised herself, if his job wasn't so perfect for her and how she found herself at the moment—broke, broken, and just a little bit desperate.

His smile grew wider, as if he read her mind and was appreciating his narrow escape.

Which made her want to knee him all over again. But the restaurant business was notoriously male-centric and she'd held her professional own with men who'd chosen all sorts of ways to test her.

So the kiss didn't matter. What mattered was getting the job so she could pay this month's bills. Straightening her spine, she stared him down and remembered her father's advice. *Don't let anyone think you're weak.*

His expression changed. A trace of concern cooled the laughter dancing in his eyes. "Hey, now . . ."

"*Jay?*"

They both started, but he recovered first, and in a smooth move turned toward the female voice even as he slid his hand around Nikki's waist. Without his wide shoulders blocking the way, she saw another woman standing a few feet off, poised as if she didn't know whether to run or cry.

The easy expression spreading over Jay's face was belied by the steely tension in the arm circling Nikki's back. "Shanna. What's up, sweetheart?"

His "sweetheart" pasted on an awkward-looking smile. She was older than Nikki, thirty-something, but had the kind of Hollywood curves—large breasts and sleek thighs—that shouted plastic surgery and private pilates sessions. Her manicured nails flicked the ends of her bleached platinum and iron-straightened hair as her glossy lips curved in another embarrassed smile.

"I'm, uh, okay," she said, her gaze flicking to Nikki. "I didn't mean to interrupt . . ."

Oh. Embarrassment explained. This beautiful woman thought she'd interrupted an intimate moment.

Nikki started to edge away from Jay. "No—"

"Problem," he finished for her, his lean fingers pulling her close again even as they gave a warning dig to her waist. "We were just saying good-bye."

Nikki swung her head toward him. "*Good-bye?*" No. No way. She'd come for an interview. She'd stayed up late and ignored her screeching knee to bake Mr. Uninvited Kiss some cookies. Her best cookies, just like he'd asked. So he wasn't going to scare her off, kiss or no kiss. "I'm not going anywhere."

The other woman shuffled one step back, swallowing hard. "I-I didn't realize you'd had an overnight guest, Jay."

Nikki shook her head. She was no overnight guest. "I—"

Mr. Kiss stepped over her words again. "Please, let me perform the introductions. This is Shanna Ryan. And Shanna, this bewitching woman is, um, N . . . uh, N . . ." His shoulder gave hers a subtle nudge.

Oh, geez. Apparently his memory wasn't as good as his make-out technique. "Nikki." With a polite smile, she nodded at the other woman. "I'm Nikki Carmichael."

"I'm happy to meet you," Shanna murmured, looking anything but happy.

"Shanna's my neighbor," Jay added. "She's been my neighbor for . . . God, who knows how long? Since we were kids."

"Yes. His neighbor," the other woman repeated. She cut her gaze to Nikki again. "And you're his . . . ?"

"Chef," Nikki piped up, before Buchanan could say any different.

Shanna brightened. "Oh—"

"*Private* chef," Jay interjected. He cuddled Nikki closer and his mouth brushed the top of her head. "You know. My chef with benefits."

Nikki turned to stare at him again. Oh, good God. Now she got it. Finally.

The kissing, the arm that still had her tucked against his warm, great-smelling chest, the now-decidedly bereft look on Shanna's face. Jay was using Nikki to announce himself as—temporarily at least—unavailable.

Though she doubted a man like him would ever want to declare himself "taken," at this moment it was quite clear he was giving his neighbor, Shanna, the big back-off, and using Nikki to do it. It completely explained his come-on at the front door. His kissing her had been for his convenience, not for any authentic interest in finding out what it might be like.

She decided not to think about why the idea made her even more pissed off.

Instead, she considered what she was going to do about the situation, even as she sketched a wave at the disappointed Shanna, who was retreating while mumbling an excuse about something in the oven.

As if a woman who looked like that baked, let alone ate.

Jay switched his hold from Nikki's waist to one hand, and pulled her in the wake of his disappearing neighbor. They ended up in a living room filled with sunlight, thanks to expansive windows and the ocean-facing wall that was floor-to-ceiling glass sliding doors leading to a narrow deck, forty-feet of sandy beach, and then the dark blue ocean.

Dazzled by the incredible view, Nikki barely took in that he was watching Shanna as she disappeared around the corner of his house. When she was gone from sight, he dropped Nikki's hand and rounded on her, his arms folding over his tanned chest. She took in the fact that he was muscled in all the right places and lean and tight everywhere else.

Sandy was right. With those golden, beach body looks, he was born under a lucky star.

At the moment he didn't look like he felt lucky, though. "What do you have to say for yourself now?" he demanded.

She blinked. The laughing guy who'd kissed her was gone. His expression held only unmistakable annoyance.

"What?"

"Don't go blaming me," he said. "Yeah, I slept with her. Once. And yeah, it was a big mistake because she can't seem to let go and I hate that I'm hurting a woman I've known my entire life."

His hand lifted and he aimed a forefinger straight at her nose. "But this is all on you. It's your own damn fault that you've just signed up to be my lover."

While people might equate day-to-day cooking with women, *cuisine* was the provenance of men. Creative, cantankerous, oftentimes crazy men.

Nikki had learned long ago how to cope with their uneven tempers and their off-putting idiosyncrasies. She ignored what she could and distracted the crazy men when she couldn't. Now she went for the second strategy.

"Well," she said, turning on the sun-drenched hardwood floor to run her gaze around the room. The wall on her right was white-painted brick that enclosed a well-used fireplace. Other walls that weren't taken up with glass had been paneled with wood finished in a warm oak color. It only made her small dark condo seem more dreary by comparison. "This house is incredible."

His pointing finger dropped. "You like it?"

She hid her smile. Good. He was already off the lover thing, thank God, and she'd work him around to what she was really after—the private chef position. "I love it."

Not that she didn't mean the compliment. The uncomplicated style of the large room didn't take anything away from the out-of-this-world view. On the other side of a short counter to her left, she glimpsed the narrow kitchen with an adjacent small breakfast table positioned near more glass.

Over her shoulder, she could see the atrium they'd passed on the way to the living area. A banana tree was growing inside and more sunlight fell onto a plain-styled dining room set. Tucked in the farthest corner were two reading chairs surrounded by white-painted shelves of books.

The whole place had a straightforward, unpretentious ambience, reminding her of a man comfortable in his own skin. But a mature man, because there was a definite 1950s vibe to the paneling and the built-in cabinets in that sunny dining area.

"I thought your magazine was going to make over your place into the ultimate bachelor's It Pad. You know, the supreme destination for all of L.A.'s It Girls."

He shook his head. "I nixed that idea. My grandparents built the house in 1955 before they called this stretch of sand Millionaire's Beach, which was before they had to change *that* to Billionaire's Beach. It's bad enough that the dealmakers are buying up as many as three or even four adjacent homes. They scrape them and then build compounds totally out of character with what Malibu once was. I've decided to keep what I have just as it is."

His eyes glinted with a renewed sparkle and an eyebrow rose. "So . . . you read *NYFM*?"

NYFM, short for Not Your Father's Magazine—the symbolic "father" in this case rumored to be the one and only Hugh Hefner—was a magazine not quite as skincentric as *Playboy* yet not as New York–styled as *GQ*. After Sandy had mentioned possible employment, Nikki had flipped through a few copies. Though it featured pictorials of half-naked women, there was also information on cars, work, and relationships, as well as well-regarded, in-depth writing on global issues.

She shrugged. "I like the articles."

"Admit it. You buy it to check out the girls." He was grinning.

God, he was attractive, she had to admit it. That wide, white smile and tumble of golden hair topping his high-cheekboned face, the strong column of his neck, his bare chest. He was still shoeless and half-naked and she remembered his delicious smell. Somewhere nearby was a bed of those tumbled sheets that might still hold the heat of his bare skin.

Her skin prickled with goose bumps and in her head an internal movie screen blazed to life, flashing the image of a woman's body stretched out on the wide mattress, waiting for a man. Though it didn't happen often, it was her typical fantasy vehicle—her imagination conjuring up a scenario between two strangers.

Except, unprecedented and a little alarming, in this mental film the starring roles weren't played by strangers. It was her own eyes she saw opening as Jay Buchanan entered the room, their blue and green turning slumberous as he loosened the fastening at his waist and dropped those low-slung shorts—

You buy it to check out the girls.

The words echoed in her head, and the sexual chills racing over her skin stopped mid-dash.

A flush burned her cheeks. Obviously he thought . . .

"I do not buy it to check out the girls." She'd said she didn't like men—when she'd only meant that at that particular moment she hadn't liked *him* for trying to get rid of her—and he'd taken it completely wrong.

He didn't stop grinning as he stepped closer. Too close. She held her breath so she wouldn't start thinking of beds again. Of her on his bed and his naked body against hers.

One of his lean fingers chucked her under the chin. "Hey, it doesn't matter to me. I like girls, too."

She opened her mouth to set him straight—and then closed it. What had he said when he'd tried to shut the door on her? "I thought you'd sworn off women."

He grimaced, then shot a look in the direction in which his neighbor Shanna had disappeared. "What a damn mess." His gaze switched back to Nikki again, his eyes narrowing. "Which reminds me that you—"

"Can really do a great job as your chef." As she went for distraction again, she made a hasty shuffle backward and had to ignore the answering twinge in her knee. "Do you mind if I check out the kitchen?"

He trailed behind her. "Could you make a pot of coffee?"

The pitiful note in his voice only gave her more hope. "Absolutely."

The cooking space had been recently remodeled. State-of-the-art appliances were built into cabinetry with open shelves and included a warming drawer, a sink with instant boiling water, and a refrigerator large enough to defrost two turkeys—or hold three cases of beer, which was the situation now. She set down the pail of cookies, then frowned as she peeked in the freezer and found a bag of coffee beans.

"These shouldn't be in here. And don't you have any actual groceries?"

"I think there's some leftover steak around. Check in the lettuce crisper."

"Don't tell me," Nikki answered, moving away from the fridge to locate the bean grinder. "Your favorite food group arrives on your plate still bleeding."

"Yep. And if grilled by me, charred black on the outside."

While she finished preparing the coffee, she got him talking about what his expectations for the chef position were. His teenage cousin was staying with him until September, so he wanted decent meals for her. There was an anniversary party he was throwing for his parents at the end of the month. And though he was taking August off, on Monday mornings the *NYFM* editorial staff would meet at his house for breakfast.

But when she put a tall mug of coffee in front of him at the breakfast table, as well as a quick snack she'd made with the one egg, the one-half avocado, the wedge of hard cheese, and the frostbitten croissant she'd found in the freezer, he quieted down. Nikki leaned against the counter to give her knee a break and thought over the situation as he ate.

If she got the job, she could drag one of the bar stools sitting on the other side of the counter to the chopping area and keep off her feet even during food prep. And though she didn't know anything about the markets nearby, surely she could find ingredients for the meals Jay liked. He wasn't picky.

And then there was Malibu itself. Her gaze drifted out the glass to the curve of white-hemmed blue ocean that kept tossing itself against the sugary sand. Who wouldn't want to work here?

Though she'd have to fight traffic getting to and from, she couldn't fault people for swarming to this spectacular place. Craning her neck, she took more of it in.

The houses along this stretch of beach were built shoulder-to-shoulder. As she followed the curve of the sand, she understood what Jay meant about the out-of-character compounds. From here she could see some houses that looked like small resorts rather than actual homes. Right next door—Shanna's house?—was a place that looked to be built with gleaming marble. A pool stood between it and the beach, and inside a threatening fence, a sun-hatted gardener was squeezed behind a Grecian-styled statue, manicuring an already perfectly trimmed box hedge.

To her surprise, though, the beach itself wasn't crowded in front of the houses, maybe because of the public access controversy that Jay had spoken of when she'd first arrived. On her way to his address she'd passed the packed state and county beaches, but here there were just a few towels and paraphernalia scattered in front of the homes, and those were set close to the waterline. No one seemed inclined to park themselves any nearer to the private residences.

At that thought, a young couple came into sight and paused on the sand at the corner of Jay's deck. The girl couldn't be long into her teens. She had a gentle curve up top, but her string bikini was tied on either side of narrow, almost childish hips. What she lacked in womanliness, she made up for in mascara, however. Though her natural hair color was nearly as blonde as Shanna's bleached stuff, her eye makeup was closer to Cleopatra's. Her mouth was glossed the color of a raspberry lollipop.

The black-haired boy with her leaned down to take a taste of it.

The girl made an instinctive move away, and the boy's eyes narrowed. The skin on Nikki's nape crawled as she watched his lean fingers grab the girl's chin. A memory reared from her subconscious.

Dark party. Loud music. Dim lights. She had on the clunky black shoes she'd worn to her mother's funeral and a skinny boy with thin hands was holding a glass to her mouth. The liquid inside it smelled like medicine and she hoped it would cure the cold, lonely sickness inside of her.

The sound of Jay's chair scooting against the floor yanked her back to the present. As he approached the coffeemaker with his empty mug, though, her focus drifted to the teen couple again. The girl looked both attracted and repelled by the boy, and Nikki could remember that same sensation, too.

"What do you think?" a voice asked.

"It has the feeling of a train wreck," she murmured.

"What?"

Nikki started and turned to look at Jay. "I'm sorry. You were saying . . . ?" Despite herself, she flicked another glance out the window. She wasn't one to insert herself into someone else's business, she of the keep-your-distance DNA, but the dynamics she read in the body language of the two on the sand unsettled her.

Once upon a time she'd been young like that, with the intense, older boyfriend whose demands had for a while made her feel safe and loved.

Until they made her feel small and afraid. Weak.

She wiped damp palms along the sides of her pants and forced her attention back to Jay.

He was studying her face as if he didn't have anything better to do with his time. Thoughts of the teen couple, her past, anything but the way he was watching her evaporated in the sudden heat in the air. Nikki's cheeks flushed at his still-lazy perusal and as the burn traveled down her neck toward her breasts she dropped her gaze from his. Naturally, it first landed on his bare skin and she desperately jerked it farther downward, seeking cover.

There. The waistband of his shorts. Secure territory.

But the loose garment was even looser now, hitting just below his hip bones to reveal the saliva-stealing sight of the lines that traced from his lower hips toward his lower groin. Thanks to Colleen and one rainy, dead night at Fleming's, Nikki knew those were the inguinal ligaments. A clunker of a label for the part of a man's body that drew one's eye from his lean hips to his . . . well.

In the break room, Colleen had called up on a laptop the infamous, naked-to-there photo of the pop star Usher. Her forefinger had followed the interesting pathways. "A glimpse of these make my nipples go hard every time," the younger woman had confessed.

Nikki now couldn't disagree. Hers were tightening in a way she didn't—

Jay cleared his throat.

Oh, God. Embarrassment burning her neck, she glanced up, because his eyes had to be a safer place to look.

But the expression in them only made the heat in the room spike. It tasted like ozone, and incongruous chills broke over her skin again. She was aware of her mouth like she'd never been before—he was staring there—it felt swollen and her lips stung as more goose bumps chased across her skin. Her heart sped up, drumming in her chest to spread the astonishing news throughout her body: *Hey! Look at this! That fantasy thing a few minutes ago wasn't a fluke. The girl's getting turned on.*

But she never got turned on—never like this.

Jay spun back toward the counter, clearing his throat again. "You'll have to leave your Doc Martens at home," he said, his voice abrupt.

"Huh?" She stared at his back as her head gave a woozy revolution, rattled by her body's response and his sudden snap of the sexual connection. "What?"

"You want the job, don't you?" He named a sum that was in line with what she'd expected. And more important, what would keep her solvent for the next thirty-one days.

Relief tasted sweet, but she quickly swallowed it down. "Yes, I want the job . . ." It was what she'd come here for, what she needed, but there was that kiss, his attraction, the way two minutes ago sex had seemed to bubble up between them without the slightest effort on her part. And sex had always meant effort—if not satisfaction—on her part.

The last thing she wanted in her life right now was a man, even the temporary kind that he obviously was and the only kind she let herself sample when she felt the need to prove she was at least semi-normal. She heaved in a calming breath. "But . . ."

His back still turned, he toyed with his coffee mug. "It's only until the end of August."

"The end of August," she echoed, sounding stupid.

"It should be enough time to take care of that other problem."

What was he talking about? What other problem? Her mind wasn't keeping up. But the month was doable, wasn't it, no matter what her worries?

"Like I said, though, Doc Martens and such are out. I'm going to insist you dress like a girl."

Nikki glanced down at her plain shirt, khaki pants, soft rubber clogs. She'd chosen them because they were close to a cook's uniform without being one. She hadn't wanted to presume. But now it seemed he was presuming—

"Shanna will never believe I'd go into even a casual thing with a girl who dresses like a guy. That might be how you signal your sexuality, cookie, but that's not the signal to be sending when you're with me."

"Oh, no—"

"Oh, yes. When she showed up I tried to rush you out as a one-night stand, but it was you who implied we had something more."

"As your cook!"

He turned around. "So cook up something a little spicier. Surely you can fake it."

Fake it? Did he think she'd faked the way the temperature had jacked up fifteen degrees when he'd been looking at her a few minutes before? She swallowed. "Come on. You're telling me you think . . . you didn't feel—"

She shut her mouth. Maybe he *hadn't* felt the heat the way she had. Maybe it *had* been completely one-sided. She was sexually handicapped enough, she had to admit, not to be certain.

Seriously, though. Even if the attraction didn't run both ways, surely, surely he didn't believe . . .

Footsteps pattered on the wooden deck. They both turned to see someone—that young girl Nikki had watched on the beach—let herself into the house through the sliding glass door. She looked at the two of them, one over-plucked eyebrow rising.

"Cuz." Jay acknowledged the newcomer with his coffee cup. "Just in time."

The girl shrugged one shoulder with the universal nonchalance of teendom and came into the kitchen to reach for a juice glass beside the sink. The contents of Nikki's stomach curdled as she noticed a dark bruise on the girl's slender wrist.

"Nikki, this is my cousin, Fern, the one I mentioned was living with me while her parents and mine are on a cruise through Europe."

Fern filled her glass with water.

"And Fern, meet our latest lesbian chef." He threw Nikki a smile. "Who's coincidentally my new girlfriend."

Fern showed no sign of surprise, though Nikki was rendered speechless by the no-frills, all-chills introduction. There it was. Nikki Carmichael, professional bachelor Jay Buchanan's new lesbian chef girlfriend.

Okay.

Well.

Apparently she'd gotten the job she needed—and way more than she'd ever anticipated.

Three

Move to California. Malibu is paradise.

—DAVID GEFFEN,
RECORD EXECUTIVE, FILM PRODUCER

Jay carried out to the deck a second round of long-necked beers. Lifting his foot, he popped off the tops with the bottle opener the shoe manufacturer had conveniently embedded in the arch of his beach sandal. Then he dropped into a chair and passed a beer over to the man seated beside him.

"*Gracias*." Jorge Santos took a long pull, then slouched lower in his chair and propped his ankle-length work boots on the railing in front of him.

Jay followed suit, closing his eyes against the rays of the setting sun that were washing over his right shoulder and the right side of his face. Malibu's coastline faced south, allowing the waves generating from the southern hemisphere to reach shore with organization and power, contributing to half its status as the West Coast's surfing mecca. The other half was thanks to the goofy *Gidget*-style movies filmed here in the 1950s. Just up the way and past the pier was the Surfrider Beach Hollywood had made famous, and today there were dozens of modern

Moondoggies out on the water making their California dream come true.

It was summer in paradise and it didn't seem right that a single guy had to spend even a single second being so pissed off at himself.

And Jay had been pissed off at himself all morning and all afternoon. He guzzled down a quarter of his beer.

"I've got a question for you, Jorge," he said.

"Mexican men only talk about their kids and soccer."

"Neither one of us has any kids."

"Bringing Beckham to the L.A. Galaxy doesn't mean the U.S. will ever take professional soccer any more seriously," Jorge replied in his precise English.

"Do I seem stupid to you?" Jay asked, ignoring the soccer gambit. He opened his eyes a slit, but couldn't see the other man's expression beneath his wide-brimmed straw hat, the same as the ones worn by the lifeguards in their blue-painted towers.

"Stupid? Only, *hermano*, if you think marriage to Posh Spice has improved Beckham's game."

Jay continued ignoring the smart-ass. "I hired myself a new chef today."

"*Bueno*. There'll be better leftovers for me to mooch in your refrigerator. I'm tired of gnawing on steak bones."

"I think I made a mistake, though. You should have let me hire your sister like I wanted after I tasted her tamales."

"Sorry, but I wouldn't let you within twenty feet of my sister, and she's forty-five and shaped like a burrito."

Jay frowned. "Should I be insulted?"

"You're the one who made me swear to keep you away from women, remember?"

"Yeah." Shit. Jay picked at a corner of the label on his beer bottle. "And it's definitely a woman I hired to cook for me."

"Uh-oh." Jorge straightened in his chair and pushed back the brim of his hat to squint in Jay's direction. "I take it she is not shaped like a burrito."

"One of her eyes is blue and the other is green."

"Ah." The other man slouched in his seat again. "A *bruja*."

Witch. That's what Jay thought, too. She sure as hell wasn't a lesbian, even though he'd played out that little farce with her. He couldn't believe she'd fallen for it, really. There'd been that melting-sweet kiss they'd shared, one of his best, if he did say so himself, and then that moment in the kitchen when they could have cooked up something piping hot just from the sudden sexual heat sparking between them.

When he considered that, Christ, maybe he'd been right to hire her. By doing so he could consider himself a kind of good Samaritan. A woman who didn't recognize the scent of that particular smoke obviously needed more exposure to the fire of mutual sexual attraction.

Yeah. Jay wouldn't mind striking a match or two, just for the sake of her education.

Then he groaned aloud, bemoaning the direction of his thoughts. "That's what got me into trouble in the first place."

Listening to his cock instead of his common sense. He really, really had to quit doing that.

"Quick," he said to his friend. "Give me an incentive. Make me a bet about the chef."

"Okay." Jorge tapped the mouth of his bottle against his lips. "Let me think a moment about the terms. What does the *bruja* look like?"

Jay thought about his first look at Nikki. "She wears braids. Two of 'em, one on each side of her head." There was nothing in the least appealing about those, right? They'd been tied loosely enough that she'd still had to tuck strands of hair behind her ears. "She hasn't pierced her earlobes." He didn't even realize he'd noticed that until now. "Though there's a tiny diamond high in the rim of the one on the left."

Jorge gave a noncommittal grunt. "And her figure? You said she's not shaped like a burrito, but she probably likes to eat, since she's a cook."

"I can't tell you much about that." His shoulders relaxed.

Surely he would have noticed if she was built like one of the magazine's models. Imagine dealing with *that* in his kitchen every day! "She was wearing pants and a shirt. Her legs are long."

And her ass was supreme, not that he would mention it to Jorge. When he'd been standing behind her while they talked to Shanna, its high, luscious curve had bumped his hip bone. Yeah, the chef baby had back. Mmm-hmm, there was definite junk in the cookie's trunk.

Oh, hell. This was bad. Here he was, waxing as poetic as a Def Jam Records rapper. "Jorge. C'mon. Help a man out here." It didn't bother him that he sounded panicked.

"Tell me about those witchy eyes again."

Jay's head clunked against the back of his chair. *Those eyes.* Between thick, dark lashes were those incredible eyes of hers. One as blue as the summer sky, the other the sea-green of shallow Pacific waters. In the hour they'd spent together he'd seen a multitude of expressions caught in them: irritation, surprise, craftiness, attraction.

Lust.

She'd kept those eyes open when he'd kissed her. He remembered that now, remembered being unsettled by the contrasting glint of colors as he became acquainted with the pillowy softness of her full mouth. That goose's tap dance had drawn shivers down his back and he'd wanted nothing more than to warm himself against her skin.

Her bare skin. Breasts to his chest, his hands cupped around the curves of that luscious ass.

Instead, he'd been smart and pulled away, but hadn't gone far. No, he'd been laughing at himself, and at her, and at how damn startling and unpredictable sexual chemistry could be.

But it wasn't funny now, was it? He sighed. "She has a dimple in her right cheek and she smells a little like vanilla and tastes like cherries."

"Okay." Jorge took a sip of his beer. "How's this? Fifty bucks says you get the *bruja* into bed by Saturday night."

Oh, yeah. Jay smiled, drifting away on the thought.

Then Sunday brunch in bed, too, with those summer eyes of hers gleaming down at him from her position on top while he lifted his head to take a suckle of her mystery breasts . . .

"Oh, hell. I *am* stupid." He shot a disgusted glance at Jorge who was snickering through his next swallow of beer. "You know damn well you were supposed to bet me *not* to bed the *bruja*."

Jorge was still laughing as Jay fished in his pocket for his cell phone. "That's it." On Mondays, the editorial staff could hump in bags of Sausage McMuffins and maybe Fern could at least learn to make a good cup of coffee—though so far it appeared to be a familial defect. Nikki was too big a risk when he had sworn off women. "I'm telling her I changed my mind."

"Telling who you changed your mind about what?"

Jay's feet dropped from the railing to the deck with a clunk. "Shanna," he said, guilt jabbing him in the gut. Hell. *Shanna.* She'd come up along the beach, the sand muffling the sound of her approach.

He tried to make his expression pleasant, yet noncommittal. "Hello, neighbor. That makes it two times in one day."

Which didn't come close to her record. Last Saturday she'd made three impromptu visits and called him four times on the phone. She shoved her hands into the back pockets of her white jeans, then cleared her throat. "I . . . I wondered if the mailman delivered my *TV Guide* to you by mistake."

"Nope. Sorry." God, he was so damn sorry. Six months ago he'd shared a bottle of wine with Shanna by her pool. And then a second bottle. They'd started on a third and that's when she'd suggested they finish it . . . in her bedroom.

What had there been to worry about at the time? Two healthy, single, consenting adults. He'd accepted her offer at face value—and that's where he'd gone wrong.

You'd think he would have been smarter, being a man

who'd sifted through dozens of letters to *NYFM*'s relationship expert that all began with this same lament: "What did I do? Saturday night's casual hookup now thinks we're going steady."

He didn't have the answer for his brothers-in-the-wrong-arms, nor had he been wise enough to keep himself out of their ranks. But by messing around with someone who not only lived next door but who was pictured in Buchanan family photo albums going back dozens of years, he'd made himself the General of the Bad Decisions Brigade.

The fact was, you couldn't take out a restraining order on, let alone be in-her-face rude to a woman you remembered attending your seventh birthday party wearing a polka-dot hair ribbon.

A polka-dot hair ribbon and the identical fragile smile that flickered across her face now. "And my kitchen faucet is dripping."

See, that's where the restraining order would be helpful. Day after day since the night he'd stumbled back to his own bed after a drunken romp in hers, there'd been dripping faucets, missing mail, back zippers she couldn't reach, heavy boxes on high shelves that only he could retrieve for her.

And every response of his, from brotherly warmth to distant politeness, hadn't kept her from returning to his door.

Over and over and over again.

He swallowed a sigh. "Shanna . . ."

"I know, I know. I shouldn't have asked."

Jay stared. "What?"

"I shouldn't have asked."

Hallelujah. Praise God. Just as he was wondering if Shanna would never accept reality, she said this. On high, angels began to sing.

If Shanna had finally moved on, then paradise would return to Billionaire's Beach. Jay could go back to his single, carefree life.

Still, his fingers tightened on the cell phone he'd located in his pocket. Even though it looked as if he might be out of the frying pan, he had to be careful about setting any new fires. So yeah, his decision was a sound one. Nikki wasn't going to work out.

And a little more celibacy wasn't going to kill him.

"I can help with this faucet, Ms. Ryan," Jorge suddenly said.

Jay and Shanna turned their gazes on the other man. He'd gotten to his feet and was fumbling with the buttons on his shirt to cover the tattoos that were sprinkled across his chest.

Shanna shook her head. "I couldn't . . . aren't you my gardener?"

"*Sí,*" Jorge answered, ducking his chin.

Jay rolled his eyes. "Jorge is the *owner* of the landscaping company that takes care of your property."

"No, no," Jorge corrected, his accent thickening. "She is right. I am a gardener. Today, when one of my employees went home to his mother in Tecate, I worked on Ms. Ryan's hedge."

Jay narrowed his gaze, trying to figure out his friend. The six-foot, strong-as-an-ox businessman he'd known for the past five years looked as if he'd keel over if Shanna did so much as sigh in his direction. He shrugged. "If he can fix a sprinkler system, I'm sure he can tackle your faucet problem just fine."

"*Sí, sí.*"

Shaking his head, Jay watched the other two head off in the direction of the marble palace next door. He pulled out his phone and flipped it open with his thumb, prepared to make his call to Nikki once he was alone. Then Shanna paused.

"Jay," she called over her shoulder.

Uh-oh. That goose was back, climbing up the ladder of his vertebrae.

"Now that you have a new girlfriend—well, I'll try not to bother you so much anymore," Shanna said. "But tell

Nikki I was happy to meet her and I plan on visiting her in your kitchen very soon."

Hell. His cell clicked closed with a sharp finality. Neither he nor his new cook girlfriend were going to get off so easily.

His lashes drifted shut, thinking of Nikki's witchy eyes, the wink of dimple in her cheek, the amusing little trick he'd played on her. Lesbian. Hah.

But he was sticking to that story. If she was destined to spend her days in his kitchen, then he was all for coming up with obstacles to the two of them heating it up together.

On her first day of employment, in the quiet of Jay Buchanan's kitchen, Nikki measured out coffee grounds then added a dash of freshly grated cinnamon stick before sliding the basket into the maker. As instructed, she'd let herself into the house and gone straight to work on breakfast preparation. If his bed-tousled look of the other day was any indication, he was a late sleeper and she decided to dislike him for it, even though she appreciated getting started without his presence to distract her.

The day of the interview she'd been broke, broken, and a little bit desperate. Today, she was broke, broken, and more than a little determined. With only a month to build the foundation of a new career, she refused to be diverted from that goal, no matter what Jay Buchanan threw her way. Though she was committed to acting both gay and girlfriend—and wasn't that enough to make her brain reel—she was his chef first and foremost. Fact was, she worked for the man and no matter what other parts she was called on to play with him, she planned on maintaining a professional distance.

A businesslike detachment.

A private chef didn't mean a personal anything—just the way she liked it.

At the thought, more of her tension loosened, easing out

of her like a deep sigh. She closed her eyes. Even her bum knee seemed less painful than before, as if Jay's seaside kitchen and the decision she'd made to take this job in it calmed her old injury as well.

"Morning," a male voice said.

The interruption yanked the serenity from beneath her feet. Her eyes flew open and her leg wobbled as she spun toward the sliding glass doors at her left. The knee restarted its own painful heartbeat.

"You scared me," she accused.

Jay Buchanan's eyebrows rose. "Jumpy, much?"

Not that she wanted him to notice. Not that she wanted to notice *him*, but God, who could look away from a man so blond, so gorgeous, so ripped? He stood in the open doorway, shirtless again, his hair wet, his board shorts dragged low on his hips by the weight of the water they'd absorbed. One of his tanned forearms was braced on the jamb, and the pose made him look like a living, breathing ad for Hawaiian Tropic suntan oil or some exotic brand of rum. She swallowed, the movement as slow as the drop of saltwater rolling over his pumped pec and copper nipple. Dragging her gaze off it, she noticed the kayak and paddle he'd propped against the deck railing.

So he hadn't been in bed after all. People who left their sheets at the crack of dawn to engage in athletic endeavors were more dislikeable than people who spent their mornings lolling between them.

But even a dislike was more personal than she wanted to get with him, so she tucked away her annoyance and reached for a mug. "Coffee?"

He wrapped a beach towel around his hips before stepping off the deck and into the house. "I thought I told you to dress like a girl," he said, eyeing her from across the bar separating the kitchen from the living area.

"This from a man in a striped terry cloth skirt," she murmured.

"I heard that." He picked up the coffee she slid in front of him and sniffed at it, sipped, then took a longer swallow as he hitched a hip onto a barstool. "But great coffee isn't all I need from you, cookie."

She decided to ignore the nickname. In kitchens where she'd worked, she'd been called much worse.

"You can't have forgotten already that you're my woman."

"Of course not. Last night I wrote a long entry in my diary about it in pink ink. With little hearts like champagne bubbles surrounding your name."

He ignored the sarcasm. "Pink is exactly what I'm looking for, cookie. Tomorrow ditch those black-and-white checked pants and that starchy white tunic thing."

His order irked her. It was as if no one had ever stood up to the man. Though, looking like that, probably no one had. Probably women fell all over themselves to make him happy. "There's nothing wrong with what I have on. This is chef-wear. I'm your chef."

"About that . . ."

Her stomach clenched. "Okay, I'll wear pink. Fuchsia or baby?"

He seemed to consider. "It doesn't really have to be pink, but it does have to show off your tits."

Her mouth dropped.

"What?" he asked, as if surprised by her shock. "You're supposed to be my girlfriend. My girlfriends like to show off their bodies to me. Are you telling me lesbians don't look at each other's tits? *NYFM* did a survey—"

"Let me guess. Ninety-eight percent of your readers, 98 percent of your readers who are *male,* are certain they know exactly what lesbians like to look at, or at least they're certain they'd like to watch lesbians 'looking' at each other."

His mug was halfway to his mouth and he toasted her with it. "You *have* been reading the magazine."

Rolling her eyes, she turned away to face the cutting board. Her plan was a modified huevos rancheros using scrambled eggs and fresh mango salsa. "Will your cousin want breakfast?"

"I don't know. She's not here."

"What?" Nikki tried ignoring the morning's second little jumpstart to her heart. "Why?"

There was the sound of a shrug in his voice. "She's already hanging out with her friends. I saw her on the beach from my kayak."

"Oh. Well, then." It wasn't any of her business. Really, it wasn't. Professional detachment, remember? But words were already tumbling out of her mouth. "Shouldn't she be better supervised?"

She found herself facing Jay again, knife in hand.

He glanced from it to her face. "Um . . . Fern's seventeen."

She looked much younger. "Still, it's so early to be already at the beach . . ."

"It's Malibu. It's summer. That's the whole point of living here when you're a teenager."

Nikki forced herself to return to chopping mango. "Her parents must really trust you."

He laughed. "Everyone in the family knows Fern is plenty responsible. As for me . . ."

She remembered the magazine's motto. "Men are boys?"

"I'm the oldest and the only male cousin in the family. We're a close-knit group. Fern's mother and mine are twins who married brothers. Between the two families there are six girls—and me."

"Which so explains your fabulous rapport with females."

She heard the legs of his stool scrape against the floor. Then she felt him at her back as he came to stand before the coffeemaker. As he reached for the carafe, his elbow brushed against her arm and she abruptly shifted away, her starched cotton tunic tickling the sudden goose bumps it hid.

"I don't seem to do that well with you," he said.

"But that's no cause for sulking, handsome." She pretended to be kind as she ignored the wayward tingles. "We've determined I play for the other team, right?"

He was silent for such a long moment, she wondered if she'd pushed him too far. Damn, she knew distance and detachment were a better plan. She busied herself removing items from the refrigerator, then turned, only to find him blocking her way, his chest in her direct line of sight.

A smattering of golden hair glinted between his tanned pecs, and suddenly she imagined touching them, feeling them beneath the curve of her palms, the skin hot and smooth. Her fingers flexed and she started, realizing she'd nearly cracked the eggs she'd taken from the fridge. Flushing hot, she jerked her gaze away from his naked flesh. Lord, she thought, if she swore to showcase her own chest would he promise to cover his?

"Excuse me." She sidestepped him, her shoulder grazing his biceps. Goose bumps prickled beneath cotton again and she coughed to clear her suddenly thick throat. Had her body betrayed her by unconsciously creating that "accidental" touch? There'd been plenty of room to bypass him, but he seemed to exert some unprecedented magnetic pull on her.

On her, his lesbian chef. Great.

"Are you all right?"

"Hmm? Fine." Keeping her head down, she drew a bowl closer.

He leaned his hips against the counter a few feet from where she stood. "So tell me about you, cookie."

"Why?"

"I shared something about myself. I told you about my family."

She flicked him a glance. "And about how you screwed your next-door neighbor."

"Ouch, that hurt." Though he sounded more entertained than pained. "Are you saying you've never made a . . . uh . . . romantic mistake?"

Nikki had made plenty of mistakes, starting at age fifteen. "Well . . ."

"You've never gone to bed with the wrong woman?"

She could look up and meet his gaze without flinching. "I've never gone to bed with the wrong woman."

A little smile played at the corners of his mouth.

It made her uneasy. Looking away, she used her right hand to crack the eggs into the bowl.

"Now there's something I've always wanted to do," he said. "I've never gotten the hang of using just the one hand."

"If you weren't so satisfied by the ladies, you could practice in the shower."

There was another moment of silence. "Which I suppose is the only option open to me, now that we're a couple. When I have a girlfriend, I'm sexually monogamous and you're—"

"Sexually unavailable. To you."

"But that has to be our secret, cookie. You can't be traipsing around Malibu flirting with girls, since I don't want my fellow residents to suspect we're a sham."

"I'll tell them you're into threesomes. That should up your cachet." She wondered where all this mouthiness was coming from—and then she didn't. Despite her desire to stay impersonal, a man like this deserved to be taken down a peg or two, and she was in a unique position to do it. It was practically a noble—if not holy—purpose. As a lesbian, she could act unimpressed by him even though Hetero Nikki would have found his masculine beauty downright intimidating.

He chuckled. "All right, then. Flirt away."

Deflecting more of his questions, she managed to finish his breakfast and place it before him on the bar at the place she'd set. As he took his seat, he looked over the eggs, the crisp hash browns she'd shredded along with a smattering of onion, the creamy green avocado slices she'd fanned along the side of the plate. "Looks great, smells great. You won't join me?"

She blinked. "Of course not."

"Why?"

"I'm your chef."

"With benefits, at least as far as the public's concerned. And if you're going to play my girlfriend, I really do need to know more about you."

"I grew up in L.A., I went to culinary school in L.A. I'm

still in L.A." What else was there to say? She'd never acquired the knack for chitchat. Her father had been a taciturn man who could go for days without talking. Nikki had grown accustomed to quiet, and later, it developed into a self-contained remoteness that had offered her some protection in raucous restaurant kitchens.

In silence, she watched Jay take a bite of the huevos and could judge his approval by the expression on his face. Though she had plenty of confidence in her cooking skills, it was always gratifying to please the person for whom she'd created a meal. Satisfied, she turned back to the sink to take care of the cleanup.

"You won't even stay still long enough for the compliments?"

She filled a pan with soapy water and gathered closer the utensils she'd used. "Your empty plate will be compliment enough for me."

She felt him staring at her. "It can't be this easy," he finally declared. "It just can't."

"What?" She turned to face him.

"Seriously. I've devoted my life to finding a woman who makes things as simple as that."

She'd read a couple of *NYFM* articles with his byline—the last a scathing exposé of the wasteful spending of one of the departments of the federal government—and so she doubted the only thing he was interested in was simplicity. But then she remembered those pictorials. "You've got women who fit that requirement plastered all over your magazine, my friend. A simple two digits for breasts, waists, hips, and brain."

"That's the fantasy, cookie. But in real life . . ." He interrupted himself to take another bite. "This meal is incredible."

As she dumped the knives and the spatula she'd used into the suds, she discovered she was smiling. "Thank you."

"So tell me, what inspired you to create good food?"

The answer flew to the tip of her tongue. "My mother's spaghetti. Store-brand tomato sauce dumped over browned ground beef and limp sticks of noodles. Not a spice to speak of."

With her grim father at the head of the table and plates of such banal food on top of it, Carmichael family meals had been mostly wordless and mercifully quick. All three of them had been thin.

Then her mother got thinner.

"And the first real meal you ever made was . . . ?"

Jay's casual prompt sent her to the past again. To when her mother was sick and Nikki had learned to do laundry and be her father's silent partner on runs to the grocery store. During one of those runs she'd remembered a recipe she'd seen on TV or scanned in one of her mother's unread magazines or maybe merely dreamed about after finally dropping off to sleep at night.

"It was pasta, too," she said, recalling it with perfect clarity though it was years away from the Malibu kitchen. "I was fourteen years old and I put together fresh fettuccine from the refrigerator section, grated Parmigiano Reggiano, heavy whipping cream, butter, fresh mint, and basil."

She'd made the dish with deliberation, as if each ingredient was an important element of a magic spell. And then she'd added a final, uncalled-for component: the salt from her very own tears. Never again had she cried with such abandon.

"My mother asked for a second helping. It was the only time I saw her eat like that. She asked for a second helping, smiled with more energy than she'd had in months, and told me I had a marvelous talent. And then . . ." Never mind about that.

"Then what?" When she didn't answer, he prodded again. "Then what?"

"Then she was hospitalized the next day. She had cancer and she died." The words came out cool and matter-of-fact, just how she'd wanted them to.

Still, the pain of the memory was sharper than anything her knee could deliver. She cried out, and staring down, was shocked to see blood floating in the sudsy water.

"You've hurt yourself." Jay was beside her, his long tanned arm pulling at her wrist. He put her thumb under a cool stream, then dried it on a paper towel and took an elastic bandage from a cabinet.

Embarrassed, she grabbed it.

"Nikki," he protested. "Let me take care of you."

Let me take care of you? The words screeched in her head. No one could be relied upon for that. Backpedaling, she jerked out of his range, ignoring the puzzled expression on his face and the objection from her knee.

"What's wrong? I said, let me take care of that for you." He nodded toward the elastic strip she held. "The Band-Aid."

"Oh. Of course. The Band-Aid." *Let me take care* of that *for you.*

Her heart still pounding too fast, there was nothing she could do but let him wrap the sticky bandage around her thumb. As soon as it was over, however, she found herself scrambling to the other side of the room.

His eyebrows rose. "Are you all right?"

No, but she was halfway to the front door and the distance made her breathe easier.

"I forgot something at the market," she said, speaking nearly as fast as her racing pulse. How could she have told him that stuff about cooking? And about her mother? It only made her feel vulnerable. Exposed. Weak.

What she'd forgotten was her good sense. But her vow to stay detached—that she wouldn't forget again.

Four

> The sea does not reward those who are too anxious, too greedy, or too impatient.... One should lie empty, open, choiceless as a beach—waiting for a gift from the sea.
>
> —ANNE MORROW LINDBERGH,
> AUTHOR

The main road through the twenty-seven miles of coastline that made up Malibu was clobbered with cars. But Nikki didn't mind the slow speed she was making northward. It gave her a chance to lookie-loo through the dark lenses of her sunglasses. On the beach side of the Pacific Coast Highway were mostly residences, but there was little to see of them besides generic garage doors and mysterious gates. With so much endless ocean to face, the homes were designed with backsides turned to the road's vehicle noise and public commotion.

The inland side was more interesting. Here was where most of the commercial establishments were congregated: surf shops with sidewalk displays of rubbery wetsuits and rental boards, as well as small clothing boutiques tucked between restaurants and real estate offices. But then the businesses petered out to expose stretches of undeveloped land that lent the place a decidedly rural feel. Looming over it all were the shrub-and-dirt faces of the Santa Monica Mountains that provided a natural barrier from the rest of L.A.

Nikki flipped off her A/C and rolled down the windows of her secondhand Jetta to let in the summer air. The salty smell was laced with car exhaust, but it tasted fresh enough to a SoCal native who'd been sucking in smog since birth. She took another long breath and let it out again. Then she glanced down at her bandaged thumb and shoved her fingers through the open window so the wind could whip away any of Jay's touch that might still linger.

Don't stick your hand out too far, it might go home with another car.

Her mother's singsong warning popped suddenly into Nikki's mind. She smiled for a moment, remembering another summer, another car ride, hands, head, even bare feet poked into open air as relief from the sticky confines of a station wagon with an unreliable cooling system. She could see the sunburned back of her father's neck as he drove and how the wind caught the ends of her mother's hair, creating a little golden-brown tornado that entertained Nikki on yet another leg of their family vacation.

The last time there had been a family.

Her smile dying, she brought her hand back into the car and tucked her thumb inside her fist as she deliberately turned her thoughts away from the past by taking in more of the Malibu sights. A public beach, flanked by a full parking lot, was teeming with towel-by-towel bodies. A pier stretched into the bay like a finger pointing to the horizon. A monster of a house poised dangerously on the hillside to her right, wearing an apron of yellow tarp to cover the dried mud that had probably slid in last spring's late rains.

Malibu was always one season away from disaster, she knew, whether it was the mudslides of the wet months or the devastating fires of the dry ones. Nikki quickly moved her gaze off the mansion that now looked too much like a desperate creature contemplating a suicidal leap. She was practiced at putting unpleasant thoughts from her mind.

Look how brightly the bougainvillea bloomed.

And wasn't that a sight—a boy on a bicycle complete with a surfboard in a side-mounted carrier.

Up ahead, a string of Malibu teens, who looked like the cast of an MTV reality show, single-filed along the highway. Two of the guys were setting volleyballs overhead as they walked while the girls were passing around a tall bottle of water. At the rear of the pack a couple was linked by clasped hands. A boy, tanned and dark, the girl—

The girl was Jay's cousin Fern.

Nikki jerked her gaze away—and lucky she did, because the car in front of her suddenly braked. She managed not to smack its bumper, but as she waited for the traffic to pick up again, her attention swerved back to the young people.

The leader with the volleyball picked his way between two boulders alongside the road and descended a well-worn path that took him below the level of the highway. The others followed like ducks after their mother even as that plastic bottle continued to be shared. Over the sound of the slow crawl of car tires heading in the opposite direction, Nikki thought she heard the wild giggle of one girl as she tossed that water back to Fern.

Or was it water?

Vodka was colorless. Gin. Everclear.

Of course, Nikki had no way of determining what it was beyond none of her business, yet still she watched as Fern squeezed a stream into her mouth. When the boy she was with grabbed the container out of her hand and directed yet another blast between her lips, a shiver tracked down Nikki's spine.

A horn tapped behind her, she saw the car in front of her was long gone, and then the last two teens were gone, too, following their friends to the beach that was situated below a parking lot shared by a café and another adjoining business. Pressing on the accelerator, Nikki left it all behind. Shifting her shoulders to shake off her sudden tension, she wiped at the slate of her mind and proceeded toward the next stoplight.

Where she found herself making an impromptu U-turn.

Her fingers tightened on the steering wheel. What? Stop! Don't! Yet her body wouldn't heed her brain's commands as she steered into the parking lot for the businesses that overlooked the teenagers' destination. Her car passed a metal sign ordering ABSOLUTELY NO BEACH PARKING! and was signed by Gabe Kincaid, Owner, but the grumpy tone was mitigated by the cartoon sticker of a crab plastered below his name at a cheeky angle.

Pulling into a narrow spot, Nikki gave a guilty second glance to the sign. It was not the beach, she told herself, but the café that was her destination. Especially now that she could see it was also part fish market, which was certainly well within the realm of her chefly interests. Yet her clogs headed over the gravel to another door, and it wasn't until bells rang out as she pushed on it that she noticed the sign arched over the top: MALIBU & EWE.

Which rang another bell, this one in her head.

Join us each Tuesday for
Knitters' Night at Malibu & Ewe!
Make a Connection!
Make something beautiful . . . friends too.

The business sharing the parking area was the yarn shop that had sent her the eye-catching invitation. And while she didn't know anything about knitting or even why she'd been targeted for the shop's advertising, Nikki stepped inside. The first thing to snag her attention was the glass back wall and the wide sliders that opened to a deck overhanging the beach Fern and friends had been heading toward.

Those back doors were open and she made her way to them, passing built-in bins filled with yarns as colorful as the produce aisle at her favorite market. In the middle of the store was that seating area of sand-colored, softly uphol-stered furniture draped with textured throws in the colors of the ocean: blue, gray, aqua, green. Nikki skirted the furni-ture on her way to the deck, only half-registering a few browsers. Knitted pieces displayed high on the walls were less easy to ignore. A silky shawl, a woman's teddy crafted so delicately that it must be spider-designed, child-sized striped socks, a bra and panties knit from . . . red shoelace licorice?

These last garments warranted further inspection, but she didn't halt her forward motion until she noticed a couple standing on the wooden deck. The man was bent low, inspecting a white-painted railing while the woman leaned near him, holding back a long fall of rippling brown hair in a fist. "It wobbles," she said. "I'm certain it wobbled yesterday during my How to Knit a Wild Bikini class."

Nikki blinked. *How to knit a wild bikini?*

The muscles in the man's forearm flexed as he tried to make the wooden structure move. "It seems fine now." He straightened, then crossed his arms over his chest and frowned down at the woman who looked to be around Nikki's age.

She lifted her slender hands. "Really?" Her big blue eyes lent her an innocent air as her lashes fluttered. "I'm just sure there was something wrong."

His scowl was distinctly unfriendly. "Like you were just sure there was something wrong with your porch light? I checked that this morning on my way into town and it seems to be working fine too, Cassandra."

"Oh. Well." Cassandra didn't appear the least repentant. "Thanks, anyway."

"For nothing. You got me to your house and then over here for nothing."

Cassandra stuffed her hands in the back pockets of her faded, low-rise jeans. She was wearing a knitted tank top and the movement thrust her chest forward a little. The man's eyes didn't drift from Cassandra's face, Nikki noticed, and she got the idea that his imperviousness to the spectacular chest on display—and she figured as a pretend lesbian she had the right to judge—annoyed the other woman.

"You don't have to sound so crabby," she said.

"About that, too . . . I saw what happened to my parking sign. Would you happen to know how that sticker got there?"

So this was Gabe Kincaid. And though Nikki wanted to get out on that deck and get a gander at those teenagers, it didn't seem like the time to interrupt. So she leaned against the doorjamb, bemused by the little show.

Cassandra had the innocent look down pat. "How what got where?"

"The stupid sea creature currently slapped over the line on my sign that specifies the two-hundred-dollar fine for violations."

"I've always thought that two hundred dollars is a bit excessive, haven't you?"

He wasn't taking the bait. "The sticker, Cassandra. What's up with that crustacean cartoon sticker?"

His growling tone didn't deter her from offering a teasing smile and a quick poke to his hard belly. "That's no ordinary animated character, but none other than Mr. Krabs, proprieter of The Krusty Krab. Don't you know anything?"

"I'm quite familiar with SpongeBob SquarePants, Cassandra." Pain flashed across his austere, yet handsome face, then was gone. "So what's this all about? Why the sticker, why the calls? Why are you provoking me?"

Her expression had sobered with his mention of the cartoon show. She shoved her river of hair behind her shoulders and tucked her hands under the opposite arms as if she didn't know what to do with them. The teasing light was gone from her eyes. "Gabe, no one had seen you around in a while and . . ."

His mouth tightened. "I'm not one of your wild cats, Cassandra, the ones that you go against our rental agreement to feed. I don't want or need to be lured into your little circle of caring, okay?"

"Speaking of feeding, how about an organic bran muffin? I picked up a couple at the bakery before work."

Gabe shook his head. "I should have known. This is about my breakfast choices."

"Okay, I'll admit it. Peanut brittle before noon offends me."

"That was once. One time."

Cassandra rocked back on her heels. "Twice that I caught you. So then when you disappeared into your bat cave for several days, I felt it was my compassionate duty to make sure you weren't lying on your back somewhere in a sugar-induced stupor."

He ran a hand through his short dark hair. "Did it occur to you I might be lying on my back somewhere perfectly content not to be disturbed by you?"

"I hope you're not trying to suggest you were with a woman."

His half-step back was hasty. "I wasn't with a woman."

"Well, that's good news," Cassandra replied, her tone smug. "Because if you'd said 'yes,' I'd be forced to call Dr. Hastings and have you put away for delusions. There's not a female in town who'd have you. Out of town for that matter, either."

Since Gabe Kincaid was good-looking in a lean, angry sort of way, Nikki couldn't quite believe this was true. She wasn't sure what Gabe believed, but he stepped up, going toe-to-toe with the woman. He took a fistful of her rippling hair and yanked, forcing up her chin so she had to meet his eyes. "Is that so?"

She didn't flinch. "That's so."

"Next time I want an opinion on my sexual prospects with a celibate, meddling Froot Loop, I'll give you a call. And maybe you'll do me a favor and hold your breath until that happens." He let go and turned away.

"You don't think I'm going to let you have the last word, do you?"

He paused, his back to her. "I don't suppose I do."

"The celibate, meddling Froot Loop's bathroom shower is dripping. My house, seven o'clock. I'll have a nutritious, organic meal waiting. You bring the beer."

The man didn't bother answering, probably because he was too smart to invite Cassandra's next last word. Without a glance back, he passed Nikki and strode out of the shop. The bells on the door rattled like a bad mood as he shut it behind him.

With the show over, Nikki remembered she needed to check on Fern so that she could get back to her regularly scheduled—and nonnosy—life.

She stepped onto the deck.

Cassandra started, then recovered and pasted on a gracious smile. "I'm sorry, I didn't see you there." Her eyes cut to the front door and then back to Nikki's face, and her smile turned apologetic. "Please excuse our little drama. We've been playing it out a couple of times a month since Gabe bought both the building that houses my business as well as the home that I rent."

"Ah." Nikki nodded, struck by a sudden feeling that she knew her. But as familiar as Cassandra seemed, Nikki had never met anyone with such beautiful waves of long brown hair that nearly reached her waist. "If you ask me, I think 'meddling Froot Loop' is pretty harsh." She wasn't touching "celibate" with a ten-foot pole.

Cassandra grinned. "And doesn't it just prove he's nutritionally challenged? I haven't tasted a Froot Loop in my entire life. Meddling granola girl would make more sense."

"Raw food rah-rah."

"Fresh food foodie."

They smiled at each other and Nikki was struck once again by that odd sense of familiarity. Which didn't make any kind of sense at all.

Cassandra tucked her hair behind her ears. "So, can I help you with something?"

Nikki remembered why she'd entered the place. "I'm, uh, just curious, I guess." Though she couldn't exactly admit she was curious about her employer's teenage cousin. Edging toward the railing, she glanced down, looking for Fern on the beach below. Though she still wore her sunglasses, she had to squint a little against the glare of the sun on the ocean. In moments, she spotted the girl sitting on the sand, the boy's head in her lap. "I've never knitted anything."

"It's probably a lot like cooking," Cassandra said. "You take ingredients—like yarn—and use them to create something beautiful and useful. When I make a sweater or a purse or a scarf I'll bet it's the same kind of process you use to create a meal."

Nikki glanced at Cassandra, surprised. "You know I'm a chef?"

"My Froot Loop ESP is working well today." Then she laughed. "What you're wearing gave you away."

"Oh. Duh me," Nikki responded, glancing down at her pants and tunic. She returned her gaze to the beach. The kids were horsing around, laughing as one of the boys bounced a volleyball off his friend's head over and over. Fern wasn't smiling, though, and Nikki's stomach gave a queasy roll as that plastic bottle was passed to her once again.

"Would you like to give it a go?"

Nikki looked over at the other woman. "What?"

"I have some needles with stitches casted on, ready for a quick lesson. You could sit out here," she motioned to the line of deck chairs on the right, "and see if knitting interests you."

As far as Nikki knew, knitting *didn't* interest her. But neither did getting involved in other people's lives, including becoming a man's lesbian girlfriend or the reluctant watchdog of his young cousin. "Sure," she said. At the very least she'd have a good cover if Fern looked up and caught her spying.

I was just indulging in my new hobby. Not that I didn't notice you weren't all that thrilled with the possessive way that boy is touching you.

She was settled into the nearest deck chair when Cassandra came back with a pair of needles and a ball of yarn the buttery color of the middle of a good crème brûlée. "You've never knitted at all?" she asked.

Nikki shook her head as the other woman crouched close and then showed her how to make the first couple of stitches. "Now you try it," Cassandra said.

Nikki tried copying the nimble movements, but she seemed to have grown four extra fingers. Making a little grunt of frustration, she shoved her sunglasses to the top of her head and frowned at the woman beside her. "I can take a radish and make a rose, for goodness sake. You'd think I could do this."

Cassandra stared at her. "I . . ." Her voice died and she grabbed the arm of Nikki's chair as she seemed to wobble on her feet. Pushing to a stand, she cleared her throat. "It . . . it takes some practice."

"Or some talent that it looks like I don't have." Nikki tried handing off the items as Cassandra sank into the seat beside her.

The other woman pushed them back into her grasp. "Time," she said, her voice husky. "It takes time, too."

Nikki frowned. "Are you all right?" Cassandra seemed to have paled, and she was now rubbing her arms with her palms.

"I'm good. Fine. Try it again," she encouraged with a little scoop of her delicate chin in the direction of the yarn. "It's really not that hard."

Movement on the beach distracted Nikki for a moment. Fern was trying to get to her feet, but the boy kept dragging her back down to the sand. When the girl glanced about, Nikki ducked her head and tried another stitch. "Maybe it's like skiing. You need to learn when you're little or you'll never get the hang of it."

Cassandra responded with an abrupt, off-topic question. "What are you doing in Malibu?" she said.

Nikki flicked her a glance. "I'm a private chef. For Jay Buchanan."

"Ah. Jay." Cassandra leaned into the back cushions of her deck chair as if forcing herself to relax. "Malibu's own über bachelor. Known to all as Hef Junior."

"No kidding." Nikki wasn't surprised. "You're acquainted?"

"We have a population of 13,000, which feels a lot more like 300. Our regularly occurring natural disasters band us together. For example, when I and some others couldn't get home last month due to the latest fire, four of us stayed at Jay's for a couple of nights."

Nikki took another long look at Cassandra. Knowing Jay's reputation—and hadn't it just been confirmed that he was an out-and-out player?—surely he would have made the moves on this beautiful woman.

She raised both hands as if she heard the unspoken question. "I spent those nights in the guest bedroom. We're just friends."

Nikki cleared her throat and didn't plan the next words that free-fell from it. "Well, um. So you know, we're not. Just friends that is." Why the heck was she saying this? It couldn't be that she was staking a claim. "We're dating. Um, exclusively."

"You and Hef J— I mean, Jay?"

It wasn't as if she could deny it now, though she felt miserable, and like a traitor to the IQ of her sex with the admission. No smart woman would think professional bachelor Jay Buchanan would become exclusive with anyone. "Yes."

The other woman's arched brows rose. "Well, well, well. You'll have to tell Jay that Cassandra Riley expects a sooner-than-later invite to dinner, then. We should get to know each other better, Nikki."

"May—" Movement caught the corner of her eye and she returned her attention to the beach. Both Boyfriend and Fern were on their feet and plastered together in a kiss that took the summer temperature up another ten degrees. Nikki started to look away, uncomfortable with the intimate display, but then Fern broke the embrace. Boyfriend tried to yank her back, but the teen broke off again, despite his obviously displeased reaction. When she turned to run up the beach in the direction of the path Nikki had seen the teens scramble down earlier, the boy took off after her.

Still clutching the knitting experiment, Nikki ran, too, exiting the store on unchecked impulse, her instincts compelling her to intercept and . . . do something as completely out-of-character as get herself involved in someone else's personal life.

"Nikki!" Cassandra called after her.

But she kept on going, even as the odd thought struck that she didn't remember telling the woman with the rippling hair her name.

Gritty dirt dug into the soles of Fern Daley's bare feet and her bag thumped against her hip as she hurried up the path leading to the highway. The minor discomforts didn't slow her down. She had to get away from Jenner.

Up ahead, a car hesitated at the exit from the fish market parking lot. In the driver's seat was Jay's new chef . . . Nikki? Yeah, Nikki. She gave Fern a little wave and called over the sound of the traffic. "Need a ride? I'm heading back to your cousin's."

Fern didn't hesitate to take her up on the offer. As the car turned onto the highway, over her shoulder she watched Jenner reach the head of the path. His scowl said he was pissed, but she was, too. She hoped he understood that . . . God, he didn't think she was running away, did he?

But she'd told him to cut out the PDA and still he kept up with the too-public displays of affection, no matter how many times she said, "Not here," "Not now," "Not in front of everybody."

She drew her bag onto her lap and hugged it against her chest as goose bumps broke out on all the skin between the top of her bikini and the low-rise waist of her denim miniskirt. The blast of cool air from the car's vents was downright frosty in comparison to the heat of her flesh after Jenner's full-body contact. That was the part about sex nobody explained to you, whether it was your mom discussing "special" feelings or your fifth-grade teacher diagramming female organs. Nobody told you it could be like the sun, melting and burning you all at once.

"You're a brave girl," Nikki said, glancing over at Fern.

Because she was playing with fire? But this woman didn't know anything about her. "What do you mean?"

"Living away for the summer."

"Oh. It's only for August. And this isn't really 'away.'

Over the years we've spent plenty of time at the house that used to be my grandparents'. I know a lot of the local kids from other visits."

"Still, I bet you miss hanging out with your friends at home."

"Janice is on a two-week college scouting trip. Marissa's a counselor at a sleepover camp. My best friend, Emily, well, she's . . . not really available." Their whole group, the "Two Shoes,"—a name they'd adopted after being teasingly taunted with "Goody Two-shoes" for, like, the bazillionth time—were in different places. Fern had to wonder if they'd ever be back to the old place again.

Probably not. Not for Emily, anyway.

"So you have a cute boy to spend time with instead."

Fern frowned. Was this woman just making idle conversation or was there more to it? Had her parents said something to Jay and had Jay then said something to his chef . . . ? Nah. Jay had hired the chef just days before. His lesbian chef, she remembered him saying. And his girlfriend.

Fern's eyes narrowed. Nikki didn't look like any lesbian she knew, but then again, the only lesbian Fern knew was Cher Brooks, who'd cut her hair Marine-style and started dressing in hiking boots and oversized sweatshirts after they'd arrested her stepfather for molesting her. It seemed to Fern that Cher—and maybe Nikki, Jay's lesbian girlfriend—might be as confused by sexuality as she was.

"What's the boy's name?" Nikki asked, glancing over again.

"Jenner." He was nineteen and starting college in the fall. She didn't really know what had happened to the year after he'd graduated from high school, but the mystery of that only made him more attractive. It was stupid of her, and stereotypical—she'd read the S. E. Hinton novels, and just think how teenage Lydia Bennet had been taken in by the disastrous Wickham in *Pride and Prejudice*—but when it came to Jenner . . . Well, the bad in that boy was something Fern found irresistible.

It was because of Emily in some part, she knew that. And because of Jenner himself. Of the way he made her feel when he kissed her and touched her. That's where her confusion came from. She never could figure out, from minute to minute, whether she wanted him to stop or whether she wanted him to take it further.

It's what came from being one of the Two Shoes, she thought in disgust. From being smart enough to figure out you could become popular by being the one to say no to the offers of booze and weed and wild sex. Everyone might like you, from your peers to their parents to the high school principal, but when the day came that you were truly tempted . . . When the day came when you were truly tempted and you discovered inside yourself a reckless streak that would freak out your family if they only knew . . .

Well, then you didn't have enough practical experience to know how far you could edge your toes over the brink before falling completely into the abyss.

If Fern was as smart as her SAT scores said, she'd find a way to go back home for the rest of the summer or at least call it quits with Jenner. But when Emily had returned from her weekend visit to her brother at college, a deep, scary hole had opened inside Fern. Jenner with his dark moods and sullen looks, with his nimble fingers and insistent, sometimes stinging kisses, overwhelmed her fears and let her forget that frightening chasm by making her aware of other things—her skin, the blood running through her veins. Each and every cell.

Chef Nikki was filling the silence between them with questions again. What were some of her favorite foods? "Strawberries and vanilla yogurt." Did Fern have any allergies? "No." What did she plan to do with the rest of her day?

What *did* she plan to do with the rest of her day, now that she'd left Jenner and the other kids at the beach? More to the point, what would Jenner do?

A new Beetle convertible passed in the lane beside them and Fern caught sight of Shelby Templeton, her dark hair swirling like a vampire's cape around her shoulders. Her gaze caught Fern's and she rolled her middle finger up her cheek. *Beeyatch*. She'd had her eye on Jenner, rumor had it, but he'd switched his attention from the pampered Malibu princess to Fern.

And he could switch it back again just as easily.

Her lungs shut down and something that felt like panic twisted her stomach. It was stupid to like a guy so much. It was stupid to worry he'd forget about her just like that. But without Jenner, what would there be to do, to focus on? Without him, it would be thoughts of what happened to Emily, playing in her head 24/7 like some crazy cable news channel fixated on the latest white girl tragedy.

Her hand scrambled in her purse and then closed around her cell phone.

Speed dial #1.

He picked up immediately. "You shouldn't have run out on me."

"I didn't!" That wasn't what she'd done. This was all about *not* running. It was about staying and it was about the lure of sex. "But I'm sorry anyway. Can you come to the house?"

Five

The interesting thing is how one guy, through living out his own fantasies, is living out the fantasies of so many other people.

—HUGH HEFNER, FOUNDER,
PLAYBOY MAGAZINE

Mid-morning, on the Friday of Nikki's first week of employment, Jay found himself wandering into the kitchen, as was his new habit. His chef had cleared away the remains of the zucchini-walnut pancakes she'd served him and Fern along with a citrus and coconut salad. But the coffee carafe was still more than half-full.

He told himself that's what drew him. Caffeine.

It couldn't be the chef. Not only had he sworn off women, but sitting on a stool pulled up to the bar, iPod headphones stuffed in her ears, this particular woman steadfastly ignored him as he filled his mug.

The coffee went down hot and smooth as he watched her fill out a shopping list. He'd been doing a hell of a lot of that lately, too—watching Nikki. It was wreaking havoc on the work he was trying to do from home, since more than once he'd dragged his laptop out of his home office to the living room with its closer proximity to the kitchen.

Of course, it meant that on occasion she offered him tastes of the things she was prepping or baking, but it was getting hard to deny those weren't exclusively the kinds of tastes he was truly after.

Strange, that. She didn't appear to like him much, her attitude decidedly take-him-or-leave-him, with emphasis on the leave-him, and he wasn't accustomed to a woman so intent on stamping out the sexual sparks that continued flaring up between them. Yet still, he was drawn to the kitchen and to her. Yeah. Strange, that.

She stood, and he remembered why it wasn't so strange after all. The girl had a body, he'd discovered, now that she was out of that chef shroud she'd been draped in the first day. This morning he could see her true form, thanks to the bright turquoise T-shirt she wore tucked into a pair of hip-hugging white jeans that were cropped at the calf. The tee exposed her delicate collarbones, some of her smooth-skinned shoulders, and was tight enough to advertise a nice set of breasts.

But his favorite part was on the other side of her. She had the most enticing sway at the small of her back, a pronounced dip that was just begging for the flat of a tongue. It sloped to a sweet curve that was the round little swell of her perfect ass.

He admired that in profile as she gathered up her purse that was perched on the end of the counter. As was usual for her, it looked as if she was headed to the market now, and so he let himself indulge a few minutes longer. She'd be off soon enough and then he'd boot her from his mind and get back to the business of editing *NYFM*'s online edition.

Her head turned toward him. She frowned.

He loved her frown. Her bottom lip pooched out and somehow her eyebrows turned all bristly over her two-color eyes. Who could take the disapproval of a pouting mermaid seriously? He smiled at her.

She hooked her pinkie around one earbud and pulled it free. "Don't you have to work . . . not to mention wear a shirt?"

His grin widened. She'd threatened to put up a sign in the kitchen stating "No Shirt, No Service" until he pointed out that these days he made up the rules and that how he wanted to be serviced was her sole consideration. Just to remind her of it, he let his palm rub a slow path from his heart to his hips, and watched her eyes track the movement. When his thumb hooked inside the waistband of his low-riding 501s, her gaze jerked back to his face, and then away from him altogether.

There she went again, tamping down those little flares of sexual heat, and it bugged him how good she was getting at it. She muttered something as she retucked the earbud.

"What's that?" he called. "I didn't hear you."

"Never mind." She tugged both headphone wires free and curled them into her hand, then withdrew her slim music player from her front pocket. "I'm going to the store. Can I get you anything while I'm gone?"

He shook his head, gesturing at her iPod with his coffee mug. "What are you listening to?"

"A self-help book. I'll let you borrow it when I'm through."

"*The Kama Sutra? Tantric Touches for Dummies?*"

She looked up, unbalancing him with her cool regard from the polar shades of her sky-and-ocean eyes. "*The Expert's Guide to Strap-on Sex.*"

His last swallow of coffee bubbled back up his esophagus. He choked. "You didn't just say that."

Leaning toward him, she repeated the words. "*The. Expert's. Guide. To. Strap-on. Sex.*"

He cleared his throat again, at the same time clearing away the images that had sprung to his mind. "Really. You didn't just say that."

"What you truly want to ask is if I didn't just *do* that."

"Not just now you didn't." Those images were back, but hey, he was a guy, and *NYFM* had done a study that proved his girl-on-girl flights of fancy put him squarely within the heavy majority.

Shaking her head, she tucked her purse under her arm. "No, Jay. Not just now. There's no woman hiding in the broom closet. However, last night . . ."

It was a joke. She was yanking hard on his leg, because she didn't really like girls. That was just their little game, right? Right? But hot damn, if the woman wasn't playing it to win.

She started out of the kitchen, then paused. "Are you okay? You seem a little, I don't know, poleaxed by the idea, which seems an overreaction from the hot stud of Malibu known to his friends far and wide as Hef Junior."

He winced. "Don't go there."

"Why not?"

"First, because the one-and-only Hef—may he continue resting in a bed of infinite sexual bliss—likes to consider himself an original. And second . . . well . . ." Suddenly he didn't want Nikki viewing him as some randy alley cat always on the prowl. "You don't see a bunch of women traipsing in and out of here as if it was the Playboy mansion, do you?"

"Only because I scare them off."

She threw a mean curveball. "You did? How? Who?"

"A brunette named Alicia. Another one with black hair who calls herself M.K. And there was a Trudy, who teared up when I told her you weren't home—and that you're currently taken." Her blue and green eyes were wide with innocence. "I did the right thing, didn't I?"

Oh, yeah, if she wanted to make him feel like a dog as well as look like that alley cat he'd been thinking of. "Sure. Great. Fine," he mumbled.

Wait a minute. He didn't remember any Trudy. And wasn't M.K. the fifty-something Judi Dench duplicate who picked up his FedEx packages? "Hey, hey, hey. You—"

"Not to forget Shanna. Your neighbor came over yesterday afternoon while you were out surfing and explained to me all about your single night of sin."

Guilt pierced him as deeply as Nikki's knowing gaze. Shit. While he'd had a few affairs-gone-bad and one-night stands he wasn't so happy to remember, he'd never botched it so badly as he'd done with Shanna. Sin was the right word. What for him had been the simple act of scratching an itch had wounded the woman who lived next door. A woman he'd known his entire life.

It meant he had a hell of a lot to make up to the fairer sex, even as he resented the hell out of them that they couldn't look at things as light and loose as a man. Running his hand over his hair, he trailed Nikki toward the front door, resenting her just a little bit, too.

She'd shut him up, hadn't she? And she did it every time: turned him upside down with her little gibes, turned off the sexual heat between them with the flick of an eyelash, turned away without a second glance, even when he was following like a goddamn puppy at her heels.

She opened the door, her every move casual and relaxed.

Easy.

Breezy.

It made him nuts and he was glad she was leaving the house, by God.

"Oh, damn," she muttered, her back turning stiff.

He peered over her shoulder. "What?"

"My car's boxed in."

Sure enough it was. Her Volkswagen was parked close to the curb, with both her front and back bumpers just a kiss away from cars that were more massive than hers and very expensive to fix. She sighed and lifted her palm over her shoulder. "Give me your keys."

He stared at the back of her head. "What?"

Turning, she spoke to him like a kindergarten teacher. "Your car is in the garage. The driveway is not blocked. If I take your vehicle, I'll be able to get to the market and buy the milk and graham crackers you requested for your afternoon snack."

So snarky and cool. So unruffled, even though they stood toe-to-toe. Her hand was still proffered, waiting for the keys, and he could smell on her fingers the grapefruit and oranges she'd cut that morning. Fresh. Sweet as well as tart.

He imagined himself drawing a digit into his mouth and sucking on a fingertip. Her nails were unpainted and short, not the long, elaborate canvases of most women he knew. What would she do if he took her littlest finger between his lips, teasing it by running his tongue along the inner skin of her pinkie until he could tickle the pale web at the juncture of her palm? How would she react if then he wet each of the whorled pads of her fingers and drew them down his chest to cool his hot skin before making introductions to the other heat she fired in him? Would she greet his happy cock with five warm welcomes? The idea only made him hard.

But knowing Nikki as he was beginning to, she'd likely look at him just as she did now, her bi-colored gaze revealing nothing as it stayed patiently trained on his. Unaffected. Undisturbed.

Or not. Because then his own gaze managed to escape the snare of hers and drop. The pulse at her throat was throbbing, the thin skin over it trembling with each beat. Lower down and three inches away from his chest were her breasts, and topping those luscious handfuls like berries on top of ice cream were her nipples. Her hard, aroused nipples.

Hard and aroused like him.

He had a boatload of work to finish in his home office. He was minutes away from a peaceful house without a distracting, attracting faux-lesbian in the kitchen. All he had to do was hand her his keys and get that caffeinated, quiet atmosphere he was after. But right now work happened to be the last thing on his mind.

So sue him. It was high summer in Malibu and what man could resist playing hooky with a woman who smelled like citrus and who was doing her damnedest to resist sex?

It was like waving a red flag in front of an angry bull.

"As if I'd let you drive my Porsche," he scoffed. "C'mon, cookie, I'll play chauffer and you can take the role of the rich missus who'll later lure me into the master bedroom before hubby arrives home for his martini."

She didn't blink. "Just as long as I get to use my strap-on."

Good God, Jay thought. It was almost as if the woman could read his mind. Because though Nikki hadn't taken the bull that was him into a china shop, what she had done was close enough. Ten minutes after leaving his house she had him escort her into a *yarn* shop, Cassandra Riley's Malibu & Ewe.

He might have suggested he wait in the car and while away her errand listening to his favorite Sirius satellite channel, but for the first time Nikki's composure cracked a little. She bit her bottom lip—when he wanted to do that—and white-knuckled her leather bag.

"It's embarrassing to ask, but will you come in with me?" she said, not quite looking him in the eye. "You know her, I believe, and I kind of, um, shoplifted the last time I was here. You can vouch for me."

Shoplifted? She continued to surprise the hell out of him. He pretended to hesitate. "I don't know . . ."

"Please?"

He considered another long moment. "Well, okay, but only if you promise to let me break out the fur-lined hand-cuffs when we get home. That way I can honestly tell Cassandra I'll punish you myself."

Shaking her head, she ignored his clever riposte, but still he followed her as she moved slowly—reluctantly?—across the parking lot. He just *had* to figure this woman out. Had she actually shoplifted? And could she possibly get more fascinating?

Bells jangled as he held open the door for her. Inside, a gaggle of women were gathered on the couches in the center of the shop. A swift attack of TP allergy—a phrase coined by the editors of *NYFM* to refer to the well-documented male aversion to all-female gatherings like the ubiquitous Tupperware Party—prodded Jay to make a hasty retreat, but

then Nikki beat him to it, her butt bumping his groin like a
practiced grind of a Pussycat Doll.

Her hesitance only made him more interested in getting into the shop—not to mention he needed to limit
their body-to-body contact before things got any harder.
So with his hands on her shoulders, he guided Nikki forward, speaking to Cassandra in his best Joe Friday when
she looked up. "I've brought in the perp, ma'am."

Nikki flashed him a quick I'll-kill-you from her amazing eyes, then walked out of his reach to approach the shop
owner. From her purse, she pulled out a ball of yarn and a
pair of knitting needles. "I can't believe I left the other day
without returning these first. I'm so sorry."

Cassandra rose from the couch and met Nikki halfway.
The smile on her face looked welcoming, but she watched
the other woman as if she was a skittish animal. "There's
nothing to be sorry about. Can you stay? We're having an
impromptu klatch."

Nikki didn't hesitate now. "Oh, no. I'm on my way to
the grocery store and, to be honest, I didn't really get very
far"—she looked down at the items in her hands and held
them toward Cassandra again—"with these."

"You can give it another try."

"Jay wouldn't have the patience to wait for that," she
said, without looking at him. "He's already tapping his toe
over there."

He was not. Well, not now, not now that everyone in the
knitting circle was looking at him with the identical question on each of their faces. *So when did you stop beating
your wife?*

"You go ahead," he said, trying to appear charming and
accommodating and not like he was afraid to offend more
women in his world. "I'll just hang over here for a while
and, um . . ."

"There's coffee in the kitchen around the corner," Cassandra said, giving him a bright smile even as she tugged
Nikki toward the center of the room. "And Gabe Kincaid's
someplace nearby puttering."

Jay didn't go looking for either coffee or male company. Now that he'd made it past his initial knee-jerk, let-me-outta-here, he thought he'd take a look around, not to mention a listen-in. One of his sisters used to cross-stitch, but lately she'd been yakking about the size of her stash and wailing about the stitch she'd dropped two Wednesdays before. The ladies on the couches could probably clue him in to what that meant.

And he could clue in to Nikki. It was maddening, how damn hard she was to read. As a journalist, he had an idle interest in almost everyone, and when it came to her, his idle was running fast. It could prove enlightening to eavesdrop.

Except she dropped next to nothing. Maybe learning to knit was more difficult than he thought—and to be fair, one woman on the couches was making something that looked very complicated and required a dozen needley needles and several small balls of thread—because Nikki stayed focused on the materials in her hands and was monosyllabic when pressed.

And Cassandra was pressing.

That also seemed strange to Jay. Not that he was surprised that Cassandra was chatting up a customer—she was an outgoing person and he'd heard she was passionate about her craft—yet this seemed like something more than friendly interest. But thanks to her unflagging interrogation, he did learn a few bare bones about his personal chef.

Any brothers and sisters? None.

Father? Passed away from a heart attack two years before.

Mother? More than ten years before that.

Jay—who to this point had been loitering by the deck and faking a fascination with the view—couldn't stop himself from turning toward Nikki. Nothing about her demeanor hinted at an inner wound—the same as when she'd told him about preparing her first meal . . . and her mother's last. She sat on the couch as composed as ever, her down-turned eyes allowing her lashes to hide their incredible colors.

And any reaction to the memory of her mother's death.

But she'd only been fourteen! Younger than Fern. A child, really, who unexpectedly became a motherless child.

He found himself rubbing his chest as if to quiet a phantom pain. Her mother was gone. Her father, too.

Nikki didn't have anybody.

Cassandra was talking at ninety miles an hour now, perhaps as thrown by Nikki's calm as he was. Other women joined in the general conversation as well, yet Nikki, no longer being questioned, retreated into a silence that surprised him yet again. He'd never met a woman who wouldn't open up like a bachelor's wallet at a lap dance table when welcomed into a group of other friendly, chattering females.

He was still mulling over the enigma that was his chef when he was joined by Gabe, a tool belt at his waist and a smattering of what looked like sawdust in his hair. He braced his shoulders against the same patch of wall that Jay had found. "What's up with Cassandra?" he asked.

"Huh?" Jay switched his gaze from Nikki to the other woman. "What's wrong with her?"

"That's what I'm asking you. She's all revved up."

"Don't know," Jay replied with a shrug. "Maybe it's the subject matter. One of those women just related a story about her bad blind date."

Gabe snorted. "Did Cassandra set her up? For a woman with zero romantic life herself, she's damn quick to badger everyone else into having one."

Jay's gaze drifted to Nikki again. He didn't know what she did on her evenings off, did he? That she'd agreed to play his girlfriend didn't mean she was without a real lover of her own. Though it was hard to picture prickly Nikki opening herself up to any man. Or maybe he just didn't want to picture it.

"I edited a piece for the magazine last week," he told Gabe. "It posits that women who are the most skeptical about romance end up with a better caliber of mate."

Gabe snorted again. "Then Cassandra should find herself a prince of a guy, because she's celibate."

"Really?" Jay's eyebrows rose.

"That's what she tells me," Gabe grumbled. "Often."

Jay swallowed his smile. He didn't know the other man well, but he certainly wasn't stupid, so Jay didn't need to point out that a woman "often" flaunting her celibacy at a particular person might have something other than celibacy on her mind. Gabe would figure it out sooner or later.

"Well," the other man went on, "don't say I didn't give you fair warning."

Jay looked over. "What?"

Gabe's tone was matter-of-fact. "But if you do somehow get in her bed, and then you make her unhappy, I'll have to kick your ass."

Clearing his throat, Jay glanced over at Nikki. How had she come to make a conquest so quickly? He glanced back at Gabe and noticed he was focused not on Jay's private chef, but the yarn shop owner instead. Oh. "I'm not after Cassandra," he said.

Gabe's expression didn't betray any kind of relief—it didn't betray anything at all. "Then why are you here?"

"I . . . uh . . ." He shrugged, helpless to explain how his fascination with his cook had become so damn compelling. "I just had to get out of the house," he offered. "I've been going a little stir-crazy and my chef—that's the woman next to Cassandra—needed a ride."

"You should come to the opening of that new restaurant tonight, then," Gabe said. "Somehow Cassandra made me promise I'd escort her there." His gaze moved off Jay's face and settled on the women again. "Bring your chef with you. Cassandra seems fond of her."

And wasn't that just the oddest thing, too? This whole episode in the yarn shop had that goose Jay'd discovered on the first day he met Nikki traipsing up and down his spine again.

"A restaurant opening," he said slowly. Why not?

"Cookie and I wouldn't miss it." He'd make it a condition of her employment, and just like his demand that she wear more revealing clothes, he figured she'd capitulate.

He didn't feel bad about it, because he was done with even the pretense of keeping his distance from her. Nikki was only growing more intriguing by the moment, arousing his curiosity almost as much as his sex. Both were equally demanding, and he decided at least one of them must be satisfied.

Six

A woman is never sexier than when she is comfortable in her clothes.

—VERA WANG,
DESIGNER

"A deal is a deal," Nikki muttered to herself as she readied for the restaurant opening in Jay's guest bathroom upstairs. It was the exact wording he'd used on her when he'd announced earlier that they had a social engagement for the evening. And he was right, she'd agreed to play his girlfriend as part of her job as his private chef.

She just hadn't considered it would mean playing his girlfriend to such a large audience. But she'd make it work, she would. After all, tonight's event also gave her a chance to mingle and make contacts with others who could use her services. She'd need a new job at the end of the month, even if she managed to successfully play gay for the remainder of this one.

"You'd better not be in commando boots," Jay called from the bottom of the stairs. Nikki inched up her ankle-length skirt to inspect the kitten-heeled sandals she'd borrowed from Cassandra. They were stable enough to provide her knee the support it needed, yet pretty enough to go with the dress that Cassandra had created.

Nikki had borrowed that, too. After Jay's party pro-
nouncement, she'd returned to Malibu & Ewe following
lunch preparations. Surely the shop owner could direct her
to a local boutique and save her from fighting the afternoon's beach traffic to get home and back again with the
right kind of partywear.

"I have just the thing," Cassandra had offered. "It's
hanging in my office. I was planning to display it in the
shop, but you can wear it first."

"No! I couldn't . . . The size—"

"Will be perfect," Cassandra had put in. "I made it to fit
my measurements, and haven't you noticed we're a similar
height and weight?"

Now that she mentioned it, Nikki did notice, though the
other woman had it way over her in the chest department.
Cassandra had waved that objection away, too. "Won't
matter. You'll see."

And when Nikki did see the dress . . . Well, something
so beautiful was harder to resist than a plate of homemade
potato chips topped with crumbled, smoky bacon and
melted blue cheese—the decadent concoction she'd promised Cassandra as payment.

So instead of scooting around Malibu seeking something suitable to wear, she'd sat on the shop's deck and
fumbled through more rows of her very first swatch of knitting. Cassandra had joined her when she could, and laughed
as Nikki complained her stitches were reproducing like rab-
bits. In frustration, she'd taken to counting the number on
the needle each time she finished a row. By the time she'd
left the shop, she'd become confident enough to count the
stitches only every *other* row.

"Nikki?" Jay's voice traveled up the stairs again. "Just
so you know, I found Fern's mascara and I'm not afraid to
use it."

Nikki dropped her own tube of Maybelline into her
makeup bag and pressed her top and bottom lips together,
setting her twenty-four-hour lipstick. Her afternoon outside had left a pink flush across her cheekbones, and the

highlights around her face appeared a shade lighter. She'd taken her hair out of her usual working braids, and it waved in a tousled tangle around her shoulders.

With one last adjustment of the spectacular dress, Nikki reminded herself she had a job to do. Making Jay happy on the social circuit was as much her obligation as it was to make him breakfast, lunch, and dinner. "A deal's a deal," she murmured to herself once more.

She ignored the twinge in her knee as she made her way to the top of the stairs. There, she paused a moment, her hand gripping the railing for support before taking the first step down.

Jay was slouched against one of the banisters below, his hands in the front pockets of black linen trousers. He wore a white, thin cotton shirt with a thousand tiny pin-tucks in front. It looked like something a Miami drug lord would wear if you transferred him to Malibu and made him a golden-haired surfer.

He glanced up, froze, then his spine straightened as he slowly turned to stare at her.

She felt her sunburn heat and flow down her neck. "It's Cassandra's dress. She . . . she said it was okay for tonight."

"Christ," he said after a moment. "Well, at least I can be fairly sure you left your strap-on at home."

Her free palm slid over the soft, knitted fabric that covered her left hip. He was right—if crude, as usual. Cassandra's dress didn't leave room for anything besides the skin it covered.

"What . . . How . . ." Jay broke off and made a vague gesture, his gaze still glued to her form as he slowly ascended the staircase. "Is that thing truly going to stay on?"

Nikki shrugged. Most of the dress was a delicately knitted tube of a lightweight, seafoam-colored yarn. She'd had to step into it and shimmy the garment up the length of her body, then dip her head to slip the keyhole in front over her neck. It was halter-style, but the keyhole dipped halfway down to her belly button. A string running beneath the blue-and-seafoam crocheted cups that were the bodice tied at the center of her body, leaving plenty of exposed skin above, below, and between them.

On Cassandra, with her more generous breasts, the dress would present a wealth of naked flesh. With Nikki's more modest cleavage—well, she felt plenty bare, thank you very much.

Jay reached the step below hers, leaving them eye to eye. But it wasn't her face he was surveying. "Christ," he said again. "You're not actually wearing that dress, you're drizzled in it."

Drizzled. There was a word that fit. With Jay's focus on her, with the heat of his body so close, everything inside her melted. Her hand tightened on the banister and she hoped he couldn't see beneath all that naked skin to the way her blood was moving like heavy sugar syrup through her veins.

"What are you doing?" she asked, as he put a finger beneath her chin to nudge it higher.

"Those amazing eyes of yours," he said, gazing at them now. "When I look into them I don't know whether I'm going to sink or fly."

Oh, God. Everything female inside of her went more liquid, even as she tried to move her mouth into a sneer. "Does that line work well with the hetero chicks?" *I don't know whether I'm going to sink or fly.* As it echoed in her head, *both* of her knees felt weak. "Because it seems just short of 'What's your sign?' to me."

"Shut up, cookie." His head drew nearer. He was wearing a subtle, spicy scent that seemed to drug her with each inhalation.

She closed her eyes as if that would keep him away. "Jay—"

"Just shut up," he said against her mouth.

It was that first, movie-theater type of kiss all over again, tender and warm. She could have resisted aggression or turned her cheek to blatant seduction, but this was something else altogether. This was a timeless, all-the-hours-in-the-world kind of mouth to mouth that lured instead of demanded, that showed more patience than outright passion.

The melt happened all over her, all over again. Her lips softened against his and he licked across her bottom one, then tugged it gently with the edges of his teeth. She shivered, and his palms closed over her wrists then slid to her shoulders and drew her against him.

Her mouth parted—for air? to protest? to plea?—but he didn't give her time for any of that before he slid his tongue inside. At the silky touch she shivered again, and liquid warmth rushed between her thighs.

He slid one large, heavy hand to the small of her back, and heat prickled across her flesh. His mouth tilted to adjust the fit of their lips even as his tongue circled hers, dizzying her with desire.

More vertigo made her head spin when he retreated from the kiss, only to draw his lips along the edge of her jaw. She swayed closer, and then she froze as she felt his fingertips graze the bare skin of her midsection that was left naked by the deep keyhole of the dress. At the slight stroke, her nipples tightened in an aching rush that was mirrored by another wave of wetness between her legs.

Her instant response made her giddy with both embarrassment and excitement. She shouldn't react to him for so many good reasons . . . but right now she couldn't remember what any of them were.

Her head fell back as he continued to explore her neck and shivers had her body quaking inside and out. *Oh, God.* Arousal had never been like this before, this quick, this intense, this uncontrollable, not when she was drunk on sadness and vodka at fifteen, and certainly not on the rare occasions since, when she'd forced normalcy on herself and taken a man to bed.

With her goose bumps leading the way, Jay's drifting hand trailed upward, tripping over the narrow string that kept the cups of the bodice from springing outward. His mouth moved back to hers as he twisted one forefinger in the crocheted string. He thrust his tongue between her lips, sure and hot, and at the same time he tugged on the cord, pulling together her breasts as if they'd been palmed by unseen hands.

With a gasp, she broke their kiss. "*Jay.*"

He tugged again, his mouth wet against the side of her neck, and she moaned. Jay stilled, then gently freed his finger from the string.

"Nikki. We need to talk a minute." His hands cupped her shoulders and squeezed. "Look, you've gotta see . . . You've gotta realize this isn't going to work."

Her lashes shot up as panic dashed over her like icy water. What? What did he mean? This had to work. She didn't have another employment prospect, she had a pile of bills, and this job was supposed to tide her over as well as provide her with new contacts.

But he'd taken her on, assuming her sexual interest was girls, and that fact would keep his kitchen uncomplicated. Now, though, she'd messed that up by making out with him.

Taking a hasty step back, she wiped away his stupid, drugging kiss with the back of her hand. It was all his fault. He was too good—too golden, too tender, too subtle and sneaky where most men were in-your-face and blatantly aggressive.

Below, the front door swung open. Fern ambled in, her gaze traveling upward to find the two of them at the top of the stairs. Jay turned toward his cousin, his expression as casual as if they'd been interrupted discussing desserts. "Hey, there."

"Hey." The teenager looked at them a moment longer. "Nice dress," she told Nikki.

She managed a smile for Fern, using the moment to gather herself together. "Thanks, I'm wearing it to a restaurant opening." A couple of kisses weren't going to ruin what she had going here, she promised herself. All was not lost— at least not yet. "And we'd better leave or we'll be late."

Without looking at the man, she breezed past Jay. "Let's go, Sonny."

He followed, she knew, because his question came from a step behind her. "Sonny?"

She threw him a look over her bare shoulder. "That's who you're going as, right? I figured from the looks of you we're both acting tonight. I'm playing straight, and you're Sonny Crockett from *Miami Vice*."

He did have a sort of Don-Johnson-in-the-eighties vibe, and she couldn't tell from his expression whether the comparison amused or annoyed him.

She kept on talking. "So how'd I do with that, um, kiss? I tried to make it work by closing my eyes and thinking of Madonna. Are we two partners going to make it through tonight's undercover assignment with flying colors? Did I pass your test?"

She held her breath as he pulled the front door open for her. "You aced the thing," he said, his voice dry. "Just don't tell Tubbs I said so. That dude has a jealous streak wider than the wake of the cigar boat we used to ride around in."

Jay blamed the damn dress. If Nikki's body hadn't been wrapped in an ocean-colored garment that was as tight to her skin as a mermaid's scales, then he wouldn't have to glue himself into a corner of the restaurant's glassed-in, ocean-view deck in order to keep his hands to himself.

He'd decided to go to the damn party to satisfy his curiosity about her and now he was at the party and reluctant to get within ten feet of her. She was that bewitching.

How in hell had she gotten so far under his skin so fast? The kisses on the stairs had rattled him, and her bullshit response to it—*I tried to make it work by closing my eyes and thinking of Madonna*—only pissed him off. Instead of being honest enough to acknowledge they rattled her, too, she'd tried instead to prick his ego.

Okay, she *had* pricked his ego. The mind-blowing little

episode had left him edgy and angry while she appeared perfectly calm and self-contained as she inspected the food offerings set out on long banquet tables.

The air around him shifted, but he didn't look away from Nikki.

"Hi, Jay. How are you?"

It was, perhaps, the only voice that could break his concentration. Cassandra's voice. He turned toward her, narrowing his eyes. "You," he said. "You should know that dress needs to come with a warning label."

Cassandra had the innocent eyelash flutter down pat. "I don't know what you're talking about."

He took her by the arm to face her in the right direction. "Just look what you've done to my chef."

Across the deck, Nikki brushed her sun-streaked waves of hair over her sleek, bare shoulder. He'd had that smooth skin in his hands, cupped it in his palms, and Christ, he wanted that again. He wanted to caress her skin and suck on her nipples and bury his fingers knuckle-deep in the creamy center of her body.

"She looks like she should be lying on a treacherous rock somewhere singing siren songs to sailors," he muttered.

Cassandra made an amused sound. "Well, if anyone can handle navigating such dangerous waters it would be you, Hef."

"You'd think." He *had* thought. He'd thought their gay charade would work to keep their mutual attraction under control. But he was tangled up with Nikki just the same. Then Cassandra's last word sank in. *Hef*.

He turned to her again. "So it's you who's been telling her stories about me."

"Sorry. At the time, I didn't realize you two were dating."

"She told you that?"

Cassandra gave a little smile. "Fairly emphatically, as a matter of fact."

"No."

"I thought I was being warned off," she said, shrugging a little.

No. He swung back to watch Nikki, only to catch sight of a pair of men on the approach, their lustful intent obvious. "That damn dress," he muttered, starting forward.

Cassandra slowed him by a touch to his forearm. "Look. She sees, she flees."

Huh. Cassandra was right. Without betraying an outward sign of noticing the circling wolves, Nikki moved away, her gaze skipping past the lotharios as if they were invisible.

Her patent disinterest stopped the guys in their tracks. They looked at each other and shook their heads, as if baffled by her cool.

The fact that he wasn't the only man she could brush off didn't make him feel the least bit better. But as long as she wasn't being bothered, he could stay where he was, which would make *him* less bothered. Or so he hoped.

"Where'd you find her?" Cassandra asked.

His gaze followed Nikki as she sampled an appetizer. "Through my *NYFM* feature on private chefs. The woman who cooked for me went to culinary school with Nikki. I don't think they were friends, exactly, but Sandy passed her name and number along to me."

Cassandra took a sip from the glass of white wine in her hand. "So what's her story? Nikki's."

"You found out as much as I know at the yarn shop this morning."

"There's nothing else you can add? Like was she close to her parents? Does she have a large circle of friends or an extended family that she depends upon?"

That goose along his spine was practically honking in his ear now. "She seems the type to keep to herself, I guess, and she hasn't spoken of any friends or family besides her parents, who are gone." He cocked an eyebrow in Cassandra's direction. "Why the questions?"

One shoulder lifted, fell. "Just nosy, I suppose. And interested in other people's origins."

When he kept looking at her, she shrugged again and added more. "I was raised by a single mother. Product of Mom's ménage between herself, a sperm bank, and something she said resembled a turkey baster."

"Really?"

"Really. Mom thinks women don't need a man to make a family. Problem is, a family of two can be a pretty lonely little group. I've always been envious of the kids with the squabbling cousins and gabby great-uncles who overcrowd their holiday tables."

Jay's life to a tee.

All at once, Cassandra's wistful expression reminded him of Nikki. There'd been that same look on her face when she told him about the first meal she'd made. Pasta. For her mother. The goose started dancing and honking again.

"Cassandra . . ." He didn't know what the damn bird was warning him about, but something odd was happening here. "Cassandra, what—"

"Will a man have to do to apologize?" A stone-faced Gabe Kincaid broke into their conversation.

Cassandra whirled to face her landlord. For the first time Jay noticed what *she* was wearing. Another one of her creations, he supposed. Sleeveless, scooped-neck, slinky, the dress was pale yellow with a tangerine color knitted around the neckline and then in tiered rows on the skirt.

Gabe was staring at the spectacular rack the dress did nothing to hide, as if he'd never seen breasts before.

"What are you looking at?" Cassandra demanded.

Poor Gabe. But then Jay's sympathy evaporated as the other man's unflinching gaze moved up to Cassandra's annoyed face. He didn't appear the least concerned that he'd been caught. "I'm looking at what you want me—and every other man—to look at, Cassandra. Otherwise you wouldn't be wearing that scrap of provocation."

Whoa. Jay didn't know whether to applaud or take cover. Cassandra didn't seem to know what to do either. She inhaled a breath so deep it further proved the elasticity of her designs.

"Insulting me won't get you out of explaining why the hell you stood me up," she said.

"You shouldn't have tricked me into agreeing to escort you in the first place," he retorted.

She slammed her arms over her chest, doing even more for it than that previous deep breath. Gabe—God, the guy must be a saint—didn't take the bait this time. His gaze remained trained on her flushed face.

"What's your excuse?" she asked. "Drunk again? If so, you shouldn't have gotten behind the wheel, Gabe."

"I'm not drunk. You want to smell my breath?" He leaned forward.

She shoved him away with the flat of her hand. "Talk about tricks. I'm on to you and your Altoids." Her shoulders drooped and she looked away, then back again, to focus somewhere on the other man's collarbone. "You shouldn't drink and drive, Gabe." Her voice was just a notch above a whisper. "Please, please, don't."

Yeah, because think how that worked out for ol' Mel Gibson, Jay said to himself.

But then that thought skittered away as he noted the bleak look that overtook Gabe's usually noncommittal expression. "Cassandra . . ." He cupped her chin in his hand to bring her eyes level with his. "I might be on self-destruct, but I don't plan on taking anyone else with me."

The air between them filled with tension, and Jay was forced to look away, as if they'd suddenly stripped in front of him. And there, in his direct line of vision, stood Nikki, presenting the sleek line of her back to the crowd as she stood alone, observing the ocean through the glass.

She had every right to be as angry with him as Cassandra was with Gabe, he realized. Sure, he'd brought her to the party, but then he'd promptly dropped her.

Before he had a second thought, he was standing beside her. "Okay, I'm sorry. I wouldn't blame you for being mad that I abandoned you."

Her eyebrows rose as she turned her head toward him. "I'm not mad at you."

"I left you alone."

"I'm perfectly fine alone." She seemed sincere.

Which made him want to gnash his teeth. "I don't believe it. No woman is this easy. You can't possibly be that undemanding."

She blinked at him, her two-colored eyes unbalancing him as they so often did. "I'm that undemanding." A cat's smile curled the corners of her lips. "Or then there's the other explanation—that I'm just not that into you."

Leaning toward him, she lowered her voice to a whisper. "And you know which one's closer to the truth, handsome, and also exactly why."

It was their game. The one she didn't realize he knew they were playing. But that was good. That meant he had control as the rule maker, as the master of what was happening between them.

Which was nothing, of course. He was sworn off women. And she was so against getting involved with him that she was willing to fake liking girls to avoid it.

So why did that annoy him so much? Hef Junior should be able to handle this better.

But now he only wanted to handle *her*. There was a dance floor set up in one corner of the deck. Couples were swaying to the band's California cliché of a tune. But a lousy cover of the Beach Boys' "In My Room" was fine for what he was after.

His hand circled Nikki's wrist. She glanced down at his fingers, up at his face.

"Shanna's here," he said. No, she wasn't. "Let's dance."

He hadn't completely lost his wits, however. Though he took her in his arms, he didn't bring her too close. Her hand was passive in his, the skin cool at the middle of her bare back.

"I saw you talking to Cassandra and Gabe," she said.

"Yeah." There was enough room for a stout fence to be built between them, and it allowed him a view of the fine skin over the swell of her breasts. He remembered the hard outline of her nipples at his front door that morning and then again when he'd kissed her on the stairs. And as if she remembered, too, he glanced down to watch them harden once again.

Christ, did women know how the sight of that affected a man?

She cleared her throat. "Getting cold out here."

He looked up. Her face was flushed and as he watched, she licked her bottom lip. Just as he'd done on the stairs. He'd licked it, bit it, savored its pillow softness before sliding his tongue into her mouth.

Without thinking, he pressed against her back to draw her closer against him. Through their clothes, his cock brushed the tautness of her belly. Her breath hitched in her throat and her bi-colored eyes darted to his.

"There's a woman over your left shoulder," he said, to prove that despite being horny as hell he could play the game, too. "Black hair, brown eyes." Nikki stumbled as he swung her around.

"See her there now, the one in the blue dress?"

"Um, sure."

"She looks like your type."

Nikki tripped again.

"I can introduce you," he said, smiling to himself. This was how he'd regain the upper hand with her. If she'd admit it was him and not other women that revved her engines, then he could back away, satisfied. "Want me to?"

"Well, uh . . . I don't know."

He couldn't swallow his smile now. Goading her felt good, and any minute now she'd give up the game and leave him the clear-cut winner. "Don't be shy. I'll be happy to help you make the first move—as long as you give me a blow-by-blow of the private ones."

She made a choked sound.

"Can you blame me? All that talk of strap-on sex has me firecracker-hot."

He swung Nikki around again, glad to see that the

stranger in the blue dress wasn't blowing his story by cuddling up to some guy. Another turn, and Nikki was facing her potential date once more. "What do you say? Shall we dance her way?"

Surely she wouldn't take the charade that far. He held his breath in anticipation of her confession and his freedom from her unprecedented hold over him.

"Jay . . . I don't know. To be honest . . ."

Yeah. Honesty. Finally.

A line drew itself between her brows. She frowned and it was that adorable, heterosexual frown of hers that he couldn't resist. He started to lean down to take a nip out of that pouting bottom lip.

Then her eyes widened and her mouth moved into a bright, anticipatory smile. "Oh, Jay. I was going to say no, but now . . . well, now, how can I? You big meanie, teasing me like that. You should have told me from the start."

His shuffling feet slowed. "Told you what?"

"That right over my shoulder is my deepest, darkest fantasy come true."

He knew he was walking right into it. He felt the blood rush to his face as he repeated, "Fantasy?" and this time she took the lead and swung him around.

"You should have told me from the start there's two of them—that they're identical twins!"

Seven

I don't know what sex appeal is. I don't think you can have sex appeal knowingly. The people who seduce me personally are the people who seem not to know they're seductive, and not to know they have sex appeal.

—OMAR SHARIF,
ACTOR

Nikki felt Jay's hand close tightly over hers. "That's it," he said, and dragged her off the dance floor. "I'm done here."

Her knee protested as she pulled back to halt his movement. "What's wrong?"

"I told you earlier tonight this wasn't going to work, Nikki." He kept tugging her toward the doorway leading into the restaurant.

"I wore pink," she said, struggling to stay calm. "I told people we're dating. I've done my part, Jay."

"Played a part, you mean," he muttered.

"But that's what you wanted." She knew her voice was reedy with dismay, and she hated having to beg him, but she was getting very close to it. There were bills to pay, a car to feed, a knee to nurture. "And you like my cooking, you can't deny that."

"Your cooking rocks." He continued onward, and too soon they were standing beside the valet's stand, waiting for his car to be brought around.

"You haven't experienced all I have to offer yet," she said.

He turned his head to stare her down. "I'm quite aware of that, cookie."

"Listen to me. Stuffed hamburgers. My famous margarita muffins. What I can do with a pork tenderloin has been known to make grown men weep."

"I'm not much of a crier."

"Me neither. See? We have so much in common. And I can be, uh, nicer. Is that what you want?"

I can be whatever you want. Her younger voice, slurred by booze and by loneliness. *I can be whatever you want, I'll do whatever you want. Just don't leave me alone.*

Nikki shoved the memory underground, where it belonged. She wasn't fifteen. She wasn't that desperate.

Not quite yet, anyway. She cleared her throat as a little white sports car pulled up to the curb. "Jay?"

"You know what I want, Nikki? I want—" He broke off as his beautiful, Botoxed neighbor emerged from the driver's side. "Oh. Shanna."

The other woman gave Jay a tentative smile, her gaze darting to Nikki and then back again. "You're leaving already? I was hoping to run into you here, Jay. I could come over tomorrow, I suppose, or if you have a moment now . . ."

That sounded like a fine idea to Nikki. Shanna was another reason why her employer needed her, maybe even more than her meal preparation, and this would remind him of it. Sidling closer, Nikki slid her arm around his waist and gave the other woman an encouraging smile. "We're in no hurry."

Jay glanced down at her, his expression unreadable.

She pursed her lips, sending him an exaggerated yet silent smack for the other woman's benefit.

His nostrils flared, and he placed his warm palm on her bare spine, two fingers insinuating themselves underneath the back of the dress. A little shiver wracked her body, and he gave her a secret caress with his fingertips as if he'd noticed.

"All right," he said. "What's going on, Shanna?"

"Well, I . . . I don't want to hold you two up," the other woman answered, shifting on her tippytoe Barbie pumps so that the light from the tiki torches decorating the entrance caught in the sequins of her white minidress. Her gaze darted to Nikki again. "Are you sure you don't mind?"

It was hard not to feel sorry for the woman. What she had in the Hollywood looks department she obviously lacked in self-confidence. "It's okay," Nikki said. "We have all the time in the world."

Jay's hand pressed her back. "Not so much time, cookie. You know how anxious I am to get you alone."

Get her alone so he could fire her. Rather than showing her alarm, Nikki pressed a kiss along his hard jaw. "Now, handsome, you know I'll give you all the time you need later." With her free hand she smoothed the placket of his shirt, slowing as she neared his waist. She hooked a forefinger in his belt loop and redirected her attention to the bleached blonde. "Why don't you tell us what's on your mind."

Jay's hand slid deeper beneath her dress. Her skin prickled, goose bumps bursting over her nakedness. "Tease," he murmured, loud enough for the other woman to hear.

Shanna's smile flickered again. "Maybe I *should* come over tomorrow. You two look as if you want to get on your way."

Leaning toward the other woman, Nikki lowered her voice to a whisper. "I know, I think he's fallen hard for me. And I have a feeling this might be the real thing, too. As a matter of fact, I wouldn't object to you spreading the rumor to everyone tonight that I've marked my man."

Jay pulled her upright by moving his wandering hand from her spine to her hip and pressing her back against his front. He felt hot. And big.

"*Cookie* . . . " The word was definitely a threat.

A couple came onto the portico and headed for a waiting Mercedes. They greeted Jay and Shanna by name, and gave Nikki a curious look. She managed a jaunty two-fingered wave.

"I'm Nikki," she called out. "And yes, it's just what you're thinking. Jay's got himself another girl. But you heard it here first. This one's sticking."

"Sticking?" he scoffed as the couple drove off. "They're going to think you've been drinking."

"As long as they think of me when they think of you," she said, sending him an upward glance. "Like a couple. Like an inseparable twosome."

He bent his head to her ear and whispered, his breath hot against her neck. "Like a man who must be out of his mind saddled with a woman playing with fire."

"Did you say saddled?" She shook her finger at him, ignoring the new set of sex chills that were rushing all over her body. "Be patient. I'll get out my riding crop later."

He rolled his eyes as Shanna let out a startled sound. "Don't let cookie here fool you," he started.

"I'm much stricter than I look," Nikki finished. "But enough about our sexual practices. What is it you wanted, Shanna?"

The other woman looked as if she wanted to run away. "Um . . . well . . ."

"She's teasing, Shanna," he said, his voice tight. "Now, what's up?"

She hugged her tiny purse so close it tucked into the valley between her silicone breasts. "It's about the gardener."

"My friend Jorge? I told you, he owns the landscaping business. It's his employees who take care of your gardening."

"Yes, well, I realize that. Are you sure he's reliable?"

"I'm positive. You should know. He's taken care of your house for several years."

"But Daddy handled it. This time I'm sort of in charge. My father bought the place next door."

Nikki tried to give herself a little breathing room, but Jay's hand tightened on her hip when she tried to move away. "The Pearson place?" he asked.

Shanna nodded. "Daddy's going to tear it down to enlarge our pool house."

Jay groaned. "Good God. I know that old place is pretty beat up, but isn't your property big enough as it is?"

Shanna didn't answer that question. "My parents are going to Nice for a few months and I said I'd do what I could to ready it for Daddy's plans. There's a bunch of overgrowth that needs to go."

"Then by all means use Jorge," Jay said. "But damn, I'll hate to lose another of the older places. Remember when we were kids, Shanna? All the casual bungalows and the communal beach barbecues? Now everyone is locking themselves away behind thorny hedges and privacy walls."

The blonde shrugged. "It will never be like it was when we were kids, Jay. But thanks." She started toward the restaurant's entrance, then paused. "Thank you, too, Nikki, for postponing your, um . . . evening."

For postponing the inevitable, Nikki worried as she and Jay watched the woman walk away.

Before she disappeared, he turned her into his body. "Finally." His head bent toward her mouth.

Nikki leaned back. "What are you doing?"

"Shanna's watching," he said. "Act accordingly."

His hand speared through the hair at the back of her head to bring their lips close. Breath-minglingly close. She didn't have to act at all as he swooped in to press another burning yet tender kiss upon her mouth. Instead, she did what came naturally, she leaned into him and let herself savor his flavor and the hot, hard sensation of his body against hers.

He murmured something against her mouth—witch?—and slid his hands down her back to the swell of her behind. He palmed the globes as he lifted his head. "That punishment can go both ways, cookie. You've asked for a spanking, but I don't get into the kinky stuff until I've exhausted all the more traditional possibilities."

She blinked, the sexual intent in his eyes and the impossible-to-ignore, powerful thrill of his arousal against her stomach blanking her mind so that no snappy comeback presented itself. A knot of people separated to stream around their conjoined bodies and a woman said, "Jay!" in a scolding tone. "What are you doing now?"

Nikki found her voice. "Proving he's a one-woman man, and I'm that woman."

Too late, Jay clamped a hand over her mouth.

At the touch, old terror rose up. Pain in her knee, fumbling at her thighs, a palm bruising her lips. She jerked away from him, nearly falling on her butt as she stumbled back. Jay lunged for her and caught her elbow, keeping her upright. She yanked from him again, her heart thumping like the feet of a fleeing rabbit.

His brows slammed together. "Nikki?"

His car was at the curb, one of the valets just clambering from the driver's side. Without answering, she headed for it. Once inside, she tucked away the memories, careful to bury them six feet deep again. Jay got behind the wheel, then started off, only to pull into a dark corner of the lot.

"What's going on?" she demanded, willing the last of her fear away.

"I think that's my line," he answered. He turned off the car and shifted toward her. "Nikki—"

"I'm sorry I called you Sonny," she said, as quickly as she could. "And I promise I won't ever let it slip that I have a yen for female twins in my bed."

Even in the darkness, she could tell he was shaking his head. "Nikki . . ."

It couldn't end like this. She didn't want it to end like this.

He shook his head some more. "I told you this isn't—"

Her mouth stopped the words coming out of his. It was the only thing she could think to do to halt the conversation. And it worked, because his mouth instantly opened under her assault and her tongue found its way inside him.

He tasted like Jay, like sophistication and experience and the sun, blazing against the sand. A dark sound came from his throat and his hands closed over her shoulders. She felt frantic . . . but whether it was to keep her job or for him to keep on with the decadent, hot, drugging kiss, she didn't know.

But she was his lesbian chef!

. . . and then the thought drifted away as his hand covered her breast. Her skin rose in goose bumps and her nipples rose even higher. He had to notice.

He did. His tongue slid past hers to fill the cavern of her mouth as his thumb brushed across the tip of her breast.

Good Lord, he was good. He could move that lazy thumb over her peaked breast in the same rhythm that his tongue played in her mouth. It was the slow, lazy beat of an R&B song, and she went over as easily as if she had Marvin Gaye or Al Green humming in her ear. Her blood, her body, throbbed, caught in the sweet, exotic, erotic music.

When Jay's fingers found the bow that kept her bodice together, her heart seized, and only started back up again when it was loose and he was peeling away the cups that covered her breasts. Her naked breasts. Naked to him.

He looked. He thumbed both taut crests. He made her squirm against her seat and watched her swelling flesh demand more of him. But he didn't seem put out by the unspoken plea. Not him. Instead, he laughed, soft and seductive, then bent his head to cover her left breast with his mouth.

Oh, God.

Her back arched, her shoulders pressing against the seat, and she heard him groan as he sucked, the sensation shooting pleasure from her breast to her womb. His hand played with her other nipple for a moment, then it dropped to her thighs and made a place for itself, the edge of his palm sliding into the cleft of her sex.

He sucked, harder now, and her thighs opened for him, heat and wetness trickling from between them, an invitation for more. She found herself gripping his leg, just above his knee, trying to ride out the exquisite, erotic torture. And then wanting so much more of it that she leaned into the pressure of his heated mouth.

Somewhere close, a horn blared. Oh. Oh, no!

She jerked back, her nipple unlatching from his avid lips with an audible pop. The sharp pull, even the sound of it turned her on more, though she pressed back against the seat. His hand moved away from her thighs. "What—what are we doing?" she asked.

Surely it was the question his lesbian chef would have asked.

He slowly straightened, though his gaze was like his hands had been, hard and hot against her naked breasts. "We're getting a couple of things out in the open, Nikki," he said, his voice tight.

Avoiding his eyes, she yanked the crocheted string of the dress together to tie a clumsy bow between her breasts. Her actions were so inept, that she didn't realize her right nipple was still mostly exposed until his fingers reached out and tugged the fabric toward the center. At the touch of his knuckles against the hollow of her breastbone, her skin jittered from both areolas to her bellybutton.

"This isn't right," she whispered, resisting the reaction with everything she had. Her shoulder blades dug deeper holes in the leather seatback.

"It's damn right, and it's damn time," he retorted, settling back in his seat with an uncomfortable grimace. "Okay, maybe not the right place, but the truth is, you're no lesbian, Nikki. And if I have my way, the only one in the near future climbing into a bed with you is going to be me."

Shanna stepped over the graying, splintered railing that surrounded the deck of the Pearsons' former beach bungalow and pulled a set of keys from the front patch pocket of her pale pink yoga pants. A pile of broken patio furniture stood between her and the back door and she skirted the mass, remembering when the torn, faded canvas of the chairs and umbrellas had been a dark nautical shade instead of the bleached, bluish color of nonfat milk.

The key slid easily into the French door and she swung it

open, stepping into the rectangular room that encompassed the entire back half of the house. Paint cans were stacked in one corner and an old porch swing had been pushed into another. Shanna remembered playing on the contraption as a kid, and she found herself drawn to it now. The springs squeaked like a family of disgruntled mice when she pushed at the seat with the sole of her foot.

"Good morning," a deep voice said.

Shanna turned, startled. The swinging seat smacked the back of her calves, shooting her forward.

Jorge Santos winced for her. "Are you all right?"

No. She'd meant to present herself as calm and in charge—a woman of business—and already she was scampering around like one of those squeaking mice. Her hand pressed against her jittering heart, the same reaction she'd had around him the other day when he'd fixed her faucet.

"You startled me."

He looked away. "I'm very sorry. I was having coffee at Jay's and saw you come this way."

She felt better with his gaze off of her. His face was handsome, a fact she'd noticed when he'd been in her house, and he had dark eyes made only more riveting by the inky lashes that surrounded them. Today, he was wearing a pair of khaki pants with pleats straight from a dry cleaner's, and a polo shirt with *Santos Landscaping* embroidered on the chest. He was broad-shouldered and his arms were heavily muscled—she'd noticed that last week as well—but today she could smell the freshness of soap instead of the salty tang of honestly earned sweat.

His sweat had smelled good, too.

Running his hand through his glossy black hair, he cleared his throat, then darted her an almost-shy look. "You said on the phone yesterday you wanted an estimate?"

She cleared her throat, too, and ran her palms along the soft velour covering her thighs. "Yes. Um. Well. The thing is, my father is ultimately going to scrape the house."

"Your father owns it?"

"Yes. Bradley Ryan." She waited a beat for the man's re-action. Her father was one of the most prolific television producers in history, second only to the late Aaron Spelling.

Jorge shrugged, which surprised her for a moment, and then she realized that as a businessman in Malibu, he likely worked for any number of L.A. legends. "But you have the authority over this project?" he asked.

She nodded. "He's out of the country for a few months and wants me to do what I can to get it ready for the bull-dozers." Shanna supposed her father's expectations of her were pretty low on that score, but she wanted to prove him wrong. Six months before, she'd turned thirty-three and the woman she'd seen reflected in her mirror had fright-ened her. She'd been the Paris Hilton of her generation, but the apex of her fame was ten years gone, leaving nothing behind but a woman who'd never really worked, who'd never wed, and who now hadn't a single serious reason to get up in the morning.

Obsessing over Jay was yielding her nothing. He looked as taken by his private chef as she'd been with the idea that they could be a couple, and at the moment she felt as empty and lonely as this neglected old house.

"What can I do?" Jorge asked.

"Nothing—" Shanna started to say, but then stopped herself, flushing. Of course he couldn't fix her, but there was a reason she'd called him. "I mean, there's a bunch of overgrown brush between this lot and the next and in the front courtyard a couple of palm trees that might be worth saving. Can you take a look?"

"*Sí.*"

With a hand, she gestured toward the narrow hall. "Let's go out the front."

Framed photographs had been left hanging in the hall-way, and Jorge slowed to look them over. "No one wanted these?"

Shanna shrugged, then glanced at them herself. "Some-one in the Pearson family planned to fix the place up but then lost interest when my father made his offer." It had

been an offer generous enough for them to leave behind
cans full of new paint and what looked to be photos of a
Malibu long gone.

Some black-and-white, others colored, they centered
around life at the beach. Adults and children gathered by
firesides, stretched on beach blankets, built sandcastles and
human pyramids a few feet from the frothy surf.

Jorge halted in front of one of the photos. "This is you,"
he said.

"What?" Shanna stepped close to him and followed his
long, tanned finger to focus on a photo from . . . Fourth of
July, maybe? In the background was a reasonable sand fac-
simile of the Statue of Liberty and in front of it a passel of
kids wearing red-white-and-blue bandannas and wide grins.

There was Jay, one of his sisters, a couple of the Pearson kids, and some others she didn't recognize. Standing
front and center, her arms almost outstretched as wide as
her smile, was a white-haired urchin covered with so much
sand she looked like a piece of chicken ready for frying.
Shanna inhaled, taking in another breath of Jorge's soapy-
clean scent. "You really think that's me?"

Had she ever been that full of happiness?

He bent down and brought his face near the photo for a
better look. *"Sí,"* he said. "I think so, yes."

From the corner of her eyes she watched him inspect the
picture. His dark lashes were unfairly long and curled at
the very tips and she remembered the soft, curling hair of
his chest that she'd glimpsed last week before he'd but-
toned his shirt. There'd been tattoos on that wealth of dark
skin and at the memory of them, and of all that hard, masculine flesh that had taken the artist's needles, her heart jittered again.

She took a quick step away.

His gaze jumped to her face, and he straightened, shuffling back. For a moment she thought he looked as embarrassed as she felt. "Those palm trees?" he prompted.

"Sure. Yes." She practically ran through the front door.

He took his time studying the trees and the other growth

that had been allowed to overrun the courtyard. With a frown, he pulled out a notebook and pen to jot down figures and a few words.

"Spanish," she said out loud.

Jorge looked over at her. A smile crossed his face and she couldn't help but admire his strong, white teeth. Oh, yes, he was a good-looking man. "You thought Swedish, perhaps?"

She laughed. "I'm not *that* silly. I was just commenting that you write things for yourself in Spanish."

"I was born in a little village outside of Mexicali, which is just over the border in Mexico. Still have many relatives there. It's where I started school, too, since we didn't come north until I was nine."

She'd lived in the United States her entire life and probably didn't speak her first language as well as he spoke his second. "And yet you've gone on to build a successful business."

He looked away again and his hand went to the buttons that kept his polo shirt closed. "I had my share of trouble. We moved to the *barrio* in East L.A. when we first arrived and it wasn't always a good place for children. Especially teenagers."

"And you think Malibu is?" Shanna shook her head. "Too much can be almost as dangerous as too little."

"Then maybe we have more in common than first appears," Jorge replied.

Yeah, right, Shanna thought. They were about the same age, but that was the beginning and the end of what they had in common. He was a successful, self-made man, and she was the spoiled, do-nothing daughter of another. Without knowing what to say, she picked at the peeling paint on the trim around the front window. It fell to the cobblestones, as thin and brittle as her heart felt in her chest.

"Ms. Ryan . . ."

Her head jerked around. "Shanna. Please call me Shanna."

"It's such a pretty name."

Embarrassed, she laughed again, and lifted another shard of paint from the sill with her fake nail tip. "It came from one of my mother's favorite romance novels."

"Ah. Like all parents, she hoped her daughter would find love."

But what had Shanna found instead? When she was younger, there'd been men who made appropriate playmates in the world of the L.A. clubs and red-carpet parties. But they'd drifted on to ever-younger Hollywood women and the ones who phoned her now had more in common with her father—their age, anyway—than they had with her.

For a few months she'd thought, hoped, Jay . . . Tears stung the corners of her eyes and she squeezed them tight, holding in the pain.

"Shanna. Shanna." Jorge's hand landed on her shoulder. It was warm and gentle. "Can I help?"

Scooting away from his steady touch, she rubbed the back of her hand against her cheek. "You are helping. I could really use that estimate."

He was silent a moment and she wondered if she'd offended him somehow. "*Sí. Sí,*" he said, his voice stiff. "The estimate. I'll get back to you tomorrow."

"That would be great," she said, though she sounded miserable. She felt miserable. Lifting her head, she looked next door at her house—no, the house she lived in . . . it belonged to her father, of course—and tried to imagine herself inside her deep marble bathtub, hot water penetrating its slick cold surfaces, hot water finding a way to warm her inside, too.

But the place next door was never warm, not really. And she rattled around it like an ice cube in an empty highball glass. More loose blue paint floated through the air as she ran her finger over the Pearsons' sill.

A memory burst into her mind. That Fourth of July, the one pictured in the hallway. That had been her, she remembered now, wearing that banana-yellow bikini and grinning like a happy, sand-encrusted goblin. She'd been a happy, sand-encrusted goblin that day. The Pearsons had a tradition, she recalled. The kids invited to their party put on a Fourth of July parade on the beach, marching through the sand dragging wagons or riding thick-tired bicycles, accompanied by dolls, dogs, and whatever else they could decorate in red, white, and blue. Jay had dragged his youngest sister behind him on a boogie board, while Shanna spun in cartwheels beside them.

Unlike a lot of Malibu celebrations, the Pearsons' party hadn't been martinis and hors d'oeuvres, but beer and hot dogs burned by real dads and served by real moms and not by butlers and nannies. She couldn't remember another quite like it—had they started going to Maui in July?—but that day, that day had been so perfect.

"It's going to be a shame to tear this home down," she said aloud. "It was a very happy spot."

"Does your father really need it?"

"My father doesn't *need* anything. But what he wants . . ." She shrugged.

"What do you want, Shanna?"

To feel warm. Needed. Important.

To be a person, and not a sponge.

To have a home. Her own home.

"I could buy this place," she heard herself say.

His eyebrows rose. "*Qué?*"

"I have money. I used to model on occasion, believe it or not. I did a commercial or two."

"For that candy bar. Decadence."

Heat climbed up her throat. It had run for three or four years. Shanna between satin sheets with chocolate melting on her chin and running toward her barely covered cleavage. Her head tilting back, her mouth open for the phallic-shaped candy bar.

Jorge shrugged. "They played it on the Spanish language stations, too. 'Take a taste of sin.'"

Her face burned hotter. "I made money from that." She knew she sounded defensive.

He shrugged again. "*Bueno*. Especially if it's enough to buy this house from your father."

Would he sell? Maybe, if she showed him how nice it could be again, even though not up to the standards of the marble monstrosity next door, of course. "But it's not enough to pay for all the work it needs, too."

"It's a small house. What it needs doesn't look major to me. Do it yourself."

She stared at him. "What?"

He cocked his head toward the house. "There are paint cans inside. Start with them. Go to the hardware store and buy some paint scrapers and brushes."

"But I . . ." Have pilates classes and nail appointments and . . . and . . . nothing. *I have nothing. I know how to do nothing.* Tears stung her eyes again.

But she was supposed to be calm and in charge. A woman of business.

A woman of value.

Yet she'd felt as empty as this old house for so very long that even Jorge Santos's beautiful eyes and steady gaze couldn't change that.

Eight

Cooking is actually quite aggressive and controlling and sometimes, yes, there is an element of force-feeding going on.

—NIGELLA LAWSON,
CULINARY WRITER

Monday morning, Nikki was back in Jay's kitchen, cutting a pineapple for the massive fruit salad she planned to set out for the scheduled meeting of *NYFM*'s editorial staff. She'd already served Fern one of the granola and yogurt parfaits she'd prepared, and then overheard the teenager on her cell phone telling her boyfriend, Jenner, that she was shopping with the girls that day.

Nikki blew out a sigh. She could put away at least one worry for the moment.

Then Jay appeared on the back deck, shirtless and wet, a half-naked reminder of all the other worries that were front and center in her mind—as they had been all weekend she'd been home alone with Fish.

Jay knew she wasn't attracted to girls.

Worse, he knew she was attracted to him.

Worse than that, he was attracted right back.

Casting him another sidelong look, she fell right into admiring everything so maddeningly unforgettable about him: his lean muscles, his golden skin, the charming smile he beamed her way when he caught her watching. She remembered the touch of his hot tongue on her naked nipple, and as if he did, too, his smile widened.

He was too damn good at this.

Scowling, she jerked her focus back to the cutting board and almost wished she hadn't hurried home on Friday night after they'd returned to his house from the restaurant. While it had allowed her to break free of him at a crucial moment, maybe if she'd stuck around some new plan would have occurred to her. As it was, she was now stymied as to how to handle the situation.

Stuck.

Without a single idea of what to do about the man she wanted as a reference, not a lover.

As he opened the sliding glass door to step inside, she kept her gaze on the golden yellow triangles of pineapple she was piling into a bowl. The one thing she had going for her was how well she kept her distance from other people. Until she came up with a better plan, she'd pretend there was a wall between herself and Jay.

The problem with that, of course, was that he didn't see the same imaginary bricks she was so busy cementing together. He came into the kitchen and so far into her personal space that when he reached around her for a coffee mug, the damp underside of his bare arm slid against her shoulder.

She jumped just like when he'd put his hand over her mouth Friday night—at times her instincts would balk at a man's sudden moves—and then shuffled left so that she had more air.

"Nice weekend, cookie?"

Small talk. She could do that, though she wasn't good at it. "Sure. Spent a few hours at the martial arts studio working on my black belt, taught a self-defense class at the local Y, then polished all sixteen pairs of my steel-toed boots that *you* won't let me wear to work."

He leaned back against the countertop, regarding her with a lazy gaze. "Oooh, scary. But you're a better chef than you are a storyteller. I'm betting you actually caught up on your backlog of cooking magazines, pampered yourself with a pedicure, then watched some sappy chick flick on Lifetime while you practiced your new hobby."

Her You Make Me Blush painted toenails curled into the soft soles of her flat sandals. "It was *Pulp Fiction* on Spike TV, I'll have you know, and what makes you think I was knitting?"

He lifted the little pile of needles and yarn she'd forgotten she'd left on the opposite counter. Eleven skinny inches of knitted rows dangled. "What the hell is this, anyway?"

At the moment, Nikki didn't have a clue. As she became more facile with the activity, though, she'd found it soothing to continue stitching row after row until what had started out as a swatch was something . . . well, something else. "I'm making you a tie," she lied.

The horror reflected on his face was delicious. Maybe she had a way to put him off after all.

She smiled at him, so saccharine it was sure to leave an aftertaste. "You'll use it, won't you? That's the kind of thing I particularly appreciate in a man—if he wants me in his bed, that is."

The doorbell rang, signaling the arrival of the *NYFM* staff and Nikki blessed their promptness. She liked leaving things between herself and Jay just like this—him speechless and her secretly smug.

He passed her on his way to the entry, snagging a shirt he'd flung over a chair. Then he strode back, and snatched up her knitting again. With a thoughtful look on his face, he wound the length around his strong wrist.

His gaze caught hers. "Sure, cookie. I'll be happy to use this as a 'tie.' It'll come in handy when I knot your hands to the headboard before administering my patent mind-blowing orgasm."

Evil man.

Because he left her like that—him blatantly smug and her secretly . . . thrilled.

No!

Because he was so not going to be administering any orgasms. So not. And he was never going to tie her down—that was certain.

Still, she appreciated the buffer the incoming staff of eight presented. They filled their plates in the kitchen, then lounged around the living room and spilled onto the deck. After the group ate, they congregated for business talk with cups of coffee while Nikki cleaned up and put the leftovers away.

Their meeting finished about the same time she did, and most of the group went onto the sand to kick around a soccer ball. The lone female in the group, a scrappy-looking woman with a freckled face and short wisps of black hair, came back in the kitchen for more of the cheddar and cayenne crackers Nikki had baked over the weekend and served with paper-thin slices of deli meats.

"Do you give out your recipes?" the staffer, Michelle, asked, munching on a handful of the cheesy bites.

"Sure. When it comes to cooking, nothing I know is confidential."

"Good. Because then maybe you'll also let me interview you for a piece I'm writing about the behind-the-scenes of a busy restaurant."

"That's not what I do now," Nikki pointed out.

"General background stuff is all I'm looking for. It's a 'through my eyes' article. I've lined up a few days at a top-tier kitchen next week."

Nikki eyed the small woman. Scrappy, yes, and she supposed working with a bunch of guys at *NYFM* had prepped her some, but . . . "Kitchens have a very male-dominant atmosphere."

Rolling her eyes, Michelle jerked a thumb toward the soccer players on the sand. "You think the dudes out there don't forget I'm female at least four times a day? I've been told enough jokes about the farmer's daughter and her hoo-hah to fill that ocean out there."

"In a restaurant kitchen, they'll *never* forget you're a woman."

"Aaah." Michelle took one of the stools drawn up to the kitchen bar and pulled out the other, indicating Nikki should sit. "Come on, sister dear, dish."

Sister. Nikki didn't have one of those or really any close girlfriends either. She thought of Cassandra and the dress she'd borrowed and would have to return soon. Before Friday, she'd not once shared someone else's wardrobe.

"Nikki?"

She topped off both their cups of coffee as she thought how to explain. "A restaurant kitchen is part locker room, part artist's studio, and probably a lot like a pirate's ship where women were considered bad luck. Plates go out the door as fast as multilingual curses fly about the room and if there's a glitch—and there's always a glitch—it's certain to be your fault."

Michelle's eyebrows rose. "Every time?"

"On occasion, the men might begin by blaming the new guy or the new pans or the customer who was stupid enough to order the squash when they should know it's not cooking up right that day." Nikki shrugged. "But in the end, it will be the fault of the woman in the kitchen."

"And the penalty is . . . ?"

Nikki studied her cup. "What makes you think there's a penalty?"

"The expression on your face."

"It's not so bad." She glanced up at the woman, then back at her coffee. "You get kind of used to it."

Michelle frowned. "Yeah? Used to what?"

"Insults. Intimidation. Sex."

The other woman choked. "*What*?"

"A kitchen is small, no matter how many work in it or how many it's expected to serve. The space between the ovens and the stoves and the prep areas are close. Very close. Tick off another chef and he'll take four of your six inches. He'll bump you with his body, he'll press his groin against your butt as he passes, he'll find a way to brush his hand against your breasts half a dozen times during your shift."

"Sounds like some dates I've been on."

Nikki laughed. Sometimes you had to. "It's worse, though, because the sexual aspect is a tool. He uses sex, but not because he wants your body. What he wants is your discomfort. What he wants is to feel power over you."

In the awkward quiet that followed, she considered banging her forehead on the granite countertop. This was why she didn't do the girl-gab thing. The way Michelle's gaze was sliding away from hers to a point over Nikki's shoulder shouted she'd made the other woman more than a little uneasy.

"TMI," she said, grimacing. "Sorry, Michelle. Too much information."

A different voice responded. "'Shelle, your ride's leaving." Jay's voice. Jay, who Nikki realized now was that focal point that had snagged Michelle's attention.

The brunette couldn't slide off her stool quick enough. With thanks to Nikki and Jay, she and the others were gone.

The surf was loud in the awkward vacuum left behind. The legs of Nikki's stool scraped against the floor as she got to her feet and started to busy herself about the kitchen. Without giving Jay a glance, she could feel him standing there, staring at her.

Outside, seagulls screeched, berating each other like Nikki wanted to do to herself. She was supposed to be putting walls between herself and Jay and now, she feared, she'd unwittingly given him a window.

For a man who liked things simple, Jay decided he couldn't have stumbled across something—someone—guaranteed to complicate his life more than Nikki Carmichael. She was bustling about the kitchen, wiping countertops that were already spotless and adjusting canisters that were standing shoulder-to-shoulder like soldiers. All the while obviously tightening that armor she wore around herself as if she were expecting a firefight.

He should walk away and refuse to engage.

After a weekend without her, he'd decided to do that very thing. He'd reconsidered the plan of pursuing her for a little romp in his bed. Out from under the influence of her unbalancing blue-and-green gaze, he'd decided once again to back off—it would be the simplest solution, after all.

But then she'd sent him that sidelong look as he'd come in from the water and he'd immediately started thinking with his other brain. The one that liked her gaze on his body. The one that wanted to know *her* body well enough to fit her for a custom wetsuit.

"I would have thought you'd have put your black belt to use," he said to her now, though he suspected her martial arts skills were as imaginary as his in ocean-gear design.

She didn't pretend not to understand as she rearranged the salt and pepper shakers. Salt on the left, pepper on the right. Pepper on the left, salt on the right. "Karate kicks tend to break crème brûlée cups as well as kneecaps. Restaurant owners aren't happy with broken chefs or broken crockery either."

When Jay had brushed against her earlier in the kitchen, when she'd nearly jumped out of her skin and then tried warning him off with her big talk of self-defense and black belts, he'd wanted to laugh. But now, understanding why she was so skittish around him only made her that much more tempting. It was reasonable for her to be wary, given the way other men had used sex against her. It made sense that she jumped when he got too close. But what was so damn intriguing was that Nikki never quite jumped completely away.

His blood ran hotter thinking the attraction was just that strong—and it made him want to make love to her with such finesse and to provide her with such pleasure that she'd overcome her prejudice against his gender.

She turned away from him to play the shell game with a set of spices and he noted her back was stiff enough to serve as a picnic table. Oh, yeah, her armor was buckled tightly in place.

"I'd plow my fist in every one of their faces if I could," he said.

She didn't spare him a glance. "I can take care of myself."

Which went without saying, of course. He hadn't thought for a minute that she'd welcome the sentiment because it didn't take a genius to know that his cookie didn't want to appear capable of crumbling. No tears and trembling lips for this woman—she'd scratch before she cried.

So sympathy was wasted on her . . . and was no way to get her into his bed.

"I want you anyway."

She paused now and gazed at him over her shoulder, a feminine sneer curling her upper lip. "Has anyone ever told you you're incredibly spoiled?"

He pretended to consider. "One of our centerfolds. May 2006, I think. I suggested a rainbow-colored thong and a fan that looked like a butterfly. She wanted yellow panties and a peacock feather."

"Let me give you some free advice," Nikki said. "No real woman—or woman who retains her real body parts, that is—wants to hear about your uncooperative cover bimbos."

"They're not bimbos! They use their modeling fees to pay college tuition."

"Yeah. For the College of the Casting Couch."

He grinned. "In any case, cookie, all this resistance of yours has the competitor in me itching to go a round or two."

"Even Rocky Balboa couldn't hold onto his champ status forever. So give up, Jay. The truth is, I believe I'll find it infinitely more satisfying to be the hiccup in your uninterrupted winning streak than just another warm body in your bed."

He moved so fast that before her mermaid eyes could widen he had her in his arms.

"Wha—"

"Shanna. Coming up the deck steps."

"But—"

"A deal's a deal, remember? For a month you agreed to at least look like that warm body in my bed."

Nikki tried to peer around his shoulder, but he caught her chin between his thumb and fingers and lowered his head.

"Don't," she said.

"I won't. This is just for show." Except already he could feel her skin heating like a fever beneath his hand. And despite her big talk, her body was leaning into his as if she couldn't help herself. He gathered her nearer, his forearm pressed against that dip at the small of her back so that their bellies were pressed close.

Apparently close enough for her to feel his aroused response. She frowned. "Jay . . ."

His mouth was just a whisper from hers. "Don't worry. I'm not going to try taking this any further. I understand now about your sexual hang-ups."

Everything that was soft about her stiffened. "What?"

"Sexual hang-ups. Sexual block. Inadequacy. Whatever you want to call it."

He'd never thought of green as a color that could burn, but it was keeping up with the sudden, laser heat of her blue eye. "It's what I want to call you," she retorted. "And that's completely mistaken. I'm not hung up, damn it, or blocked, or the least bit inadequate in any way."

"But those men in the restaurant kitchen. How they treated you—"

"Is part of the job. I coped."

"By closing yourself off." Jay held his breath, waiting for the pinch of guilt he surely deserved. When sympathy hadn't worked, he'd figured baiting her might, and it looked as if he'd been right. "By being unwilling to indulge in your own desires."

"My desire for *you*, I suppose."

He slid his hands to her waist then dragged them a few inches upward, hearing her sharp intake of breath as a shiver shook her body. "Is that part of your coping mechanism? To pretend you're not reacting to my touch? To pretend you're not curious about what it would be like to be with me in my bed?"

Nostrils flaring, she placed her hands on his chest and shoved him back. He gave her space, then gaped as she reached for the bottom of her stretchy T-shirt.

"You make it sound like I'm afraid." In one quick move, she drew it off and threw it to the floor. "Since Shanna is obviously not coming inside, it's time to prove I'm not afraid of sex or of you."

He took another step back as she slipped out of her sandals and then put her hands to the snap at her waistband. "Nikki . . ."

The beautiful monster he'd created wasn't listening. She was breathing hard—if she was a dragon there'd be flames—causing her plump breasts to rise over the cups of her bra that was printed with tiny daisies. It was a hell of a pretty sight to behold, and only the abrupt shucking of her jeans could have drawn his eyes away from it.

But she did that, pushing down her pants and then stepping out of them to reveal the creamy curve of her hips and her long legs. Daisy-printed panties made him want to roll around in fields of Nikki-scented skin. And though she was covered by more fabric than made up most bikinis on the Malibu beaches, he still couldn't catch his breath.

"Well?" One eyebrow—the one over the green eye—rose in a challenge as she regarded him from his place four feet away. "Who's afraid now?"

So this was it. He'd baited her to the point of having her. Right now. Right this minute he could lead her to his bed and plant himself in the very center of her summer morning. It would be as simple—and, oh, how he liked simple—as that.

His cock was standing at attention, clamoring to get on with the plan, reacting like the randy adolescent that was all he'd ever expected of it. That was all, maybe, that he'd ever expected of himself.

Ouch. There was a thought that pinched.

And Nikki looked ready to take her own hefty twist out of him. "Well?" she said again, a hand on her hip.

Well, shit. He'd pushed her into half-nakedness, working with that exact suspicion that she'd want to prove she didn't lack anything—which would give him the chance to prove to her that a man could use his sex only for pleasure.

Her pleasure.

That was suddenly damn important to him, but Tricky Nikki would never make it so easy.

Clamping down on his inner horndog, he stepped forward and took her into his arms. He squeezed his eyes tightly shut, yet held her loosely, gently, enjoying the seductive brush of her bare back against his inner forearms, of his cheek against her temple as he breathed in the faint vanilla scent of her hair.

His mouth found hers and he kissed her, kissed her sweet, not dirty like he wanted to, taking his time to savor the softness of her mouth like that first day in his entryway. He'd been amused by his reaction to her then, but it shook him a little now, and he used the unsettled feeling as reason to restrain his impulses.

The Jay he knew wanted to slide down her body. He wanted to catch the edge of her bra with his teeth and yank it over her breasts so he could suck at her nipples. But that wouldn't be enough. The Jay he knew wanted to go down on his knees and deflower her pussy. He could see himself hooking his forefingers in those pretty daisy panties to slide them to her ankles while placing soft kisses on the inside of her thighs. He wanted to breathe in the scent of her arousal and taste the flavor of her wetness.

But that wasn't going to happen . . . yet.

"Well?" she said again, when he lifted his head.

"Well, I'm just not that kind of man," he told her. "I insist on dinner first."

"Dinner?" She blinked. "I've cooked you dinner every night."

"I mean a dinner someone else cooks. A date."

"A *date*?"

She was unsure and wary again, and he knew it was because he wasn't reacting the way she'd expected to all the attitude she'd been throwing at him. *He* wasn't sure why he was reacting this way either. Why wasn't he taking immediate advantage of what she'd offered?

Though he didn't want to think too hard about it, he couldn't ignore the answer. The fact was, Jay wanted to get close to Nikki before he got inside of her.

Nine

If you're a kid in Southern California, somebody—
whether it's you or your parents—throws your hat in
the ring and I think everyone had a commercial or
two.

—DANNY BONADUCE,
ACTOR AND RADIO PERSONALITY

Shanna trudged through the sand from Jay's house to hers,
trying to put the image of him and his private chef out of
her mind. But it was there despite her best efforts: the way
he'd scooped the woman against his body, the way he'd
cradled her to his chest, the way he'd been focusing on her
with a single-minded intensity that only made Shanna . . .
yearn.

That's what she wanted. As she approached her mid-
thirties, she felt less solid, as if parts of herself could be
scattered by the ocean breezes. To be safe, she wanted a
man—Jay—to gather her close and keep her in one piece.

To make her whole again.

Or maybe for the first time ever.

The sole of her shoe found a strand of half-buried, rust-
colored kelp. As she trod upon it, one of the attached grape-
sized bladders popped, just like what kept happening to her
Jay-and-Shanna-forever fantasy.

Inside the security fence enclosing her father's marble
palace, she settled on one of the stiff chaise lounges, listening

to the sound of the surf battling the rush of water over the pool's three-tiered waterfall. Maybe she should go into town to see if Rico, her stylist, had time to blow out her hair. Or she could call her massage therapist to check if he had a last-minute cancellation.

Or maybe she could give up men forever.

What had they ever done for her anyway—shiny hair and rubbery muscles excepted—besides disappoint and diminish her confidence?

Plenty of women were happy without a man. She could be one of them.

Shanna slid lower on the lounge and stared unseeing across the pool, contemplating a new kind of life. She was a blonde because everyone knew men liked blondes best. Her generous C-cups were thanks to what men wanted, too. A friend of hers had augmented all the way up to Ds to please her man, but in the end he'd deserted her anyway, leaving her with a closetful of shirts that wouldn't button across the chest unless they came paired with maternity waistlines.

The denizens of fashion design needed to share a few beers with their breast-obsessed brothers, Shanna concluded. Maybe then they'd add "Augmented" to the usual size scale of Small, Medium, and Large.

In her new life, though, the one where males mattered not at all, she could eat more, highlight less, and never wonder at what age collagen injections became a *Glamour* "do."

The wind shifted direction, drawing her hair across her eyes, and as she fingered it away, she noticed movement at the property next door. One of the massive and snarled bougainvillea bushes between her house and the next was waving and shaking, as if sending out signals by semaphore.

Curious, she hurried through her gate and down the beach toward the old Pearson place. There, a man was half-buried in the bougainvillea beside the back deck, his head and shoulders embedded in the massive bush and only his denim-covered butt and long legs visible.

"What are you doing?" she asked.

A voice cursed—it sounded like a curse, anyway—in muffled Spanish. The leaves shook some more and blossoms drifted onto the pale gray deck like scarlet snowflakes. There was another curse, and then the man backed out of the tangle of green leaves, red flowers, and nasty thorns. He turned to face her, his hand cradling something to his chest—an orange marmalade kitten.

It was Jorge Santos, holding the small creature as close as she'd wanted Jay to hold her, before she'd sworn off men.

"Ms. Ryan," he said, nodding.

"Shanna," she corrected, her gaze on his scratched brown hand and the creature that was struggling to free itself from his grasp. "A new friend?"

He grimaced as its claws sank into the thin cloth of his workshirt. "She thinks I'm the enemy, I'm afraid. I've seen her running between Jay's place and this one. I thought I could find her a better home with my niece. But she's not going along with the idea."

As if to prove him right, the kitten gave another all-body squirm and broke free of Jorge's hold. Tiny paws bolted down his leg and the animal disappeared into the bush.

Hah, Shanna thought. So young, and yet already the kitten had decided she didn't need a man. Smart. Smarter than Shanna had ever been.

The rejected rescuer sighed, then muttered something unintelligible.

"What's that?"

"Nothing." He shook his head, as if ridding himself of frustration. "And how are you? How is your project coming?"

A flush of embarrassment crawled up her neck. Her project. He was looking over at the Pearson house now—the house she'd claimed a few days before she wanted to rehab. The house he'd encouraged her to work on herself.

But she didn't know how to work. So she'd done nothing

more since then other than moon about Jay and contemplate getting him back.

"I, um." Her hand lifted and then fell to her thigh. "I haven't had a chance . . ."

"Well, good." He smiled at her.

"Good?" She'd forgotten how very white his teeth were and how very dark his eyes.

"Then you haven't had a chance to buy any brushes or scrapers."

"No."

"I brought some from home." He gestured toward a cardboard box sitting on the deck. "I thought . . . I thought I could help you get started."

Surprised, Shanna took in the mishmash of tools he'd indicated. Brushes, rollers, other things she couldn't identify. They weren't new, but items that had been used, and more than once, judging by the multicolored layers of splatters left on wooden handles.

She swallowed. "I couldn't . . ."

"Of course you can accept my help. I'm offering it."

What she'd started to say was she couldn't paint. That she didn't know how. That she couldn't do anything, actually, if it required more than an in-depth knowledge of cocktails and the latest issue of *People* magazine.

"Get your keys," he said, his voice brisk, as he crossed to the box and hefted it into his grasp.

She stared. There it was again, that manly, possessive stance that kept calling out to her. Though it was just an ordinary cardboard box he was holding, it still struck Shanna like an arrow through the heart. Jorge cradled the tools against his body like he'd cradled the kitten, like Jay had cradled his chef, like Shanna wanted to be cradled in order to keep whole.

Before she'd given up on men, that is.

"Go get the keys," he said again.

Was it because she was weak? Was it because she didn't know what else she could do without being out-and-out rude? For whatever reason, Shanna found herself retrieving the keys, all the while telling herself that taking a man up on his offer of aid didn't equate to taking up with the man himself.

Not that she thought Jorge wanted her.

And not that she wanted him back.

Back at the Pearson place, she dithered again. Really, she should thank him politely and then reject his services, but man of action that he was, he was already spreading a dropcloth and then opening a paint bucket to pour a creamy yellow river into a shallow pan.

"Do you like the color?" he asked, turning his gaze on her.

The paint looked like summer sunshine à la mode and would brighten the dingy living area walls. "Yes," she admitted, though instantly regretted the word. She should have said she hated it, she realized, and thus put off this little work event he was orchestrating. But, she thought quickly, she had a way to save the situation.

Not that she'd admit to giving up on men. Instead, she'd merely confess she didn't know how to work the paint roller or even where to start. Her ineptitude would drive him in the same direction every other man who'd known her had eventually taken—far away.

He put a brush in her hand. "You cut, and I'll roll."

Cut what? And with a *brush*?

The questions didn't come out of her mouth fast enough. Before she could express them aloud, a little smile crossed Jorge's mouth and he recovered the paintbrush from her and then dipped it into the can. As he ran it along the wall, he outlined the molding of the doorjamb. "Cutting," he explained. He smiled at her again, that white flash creating deep slashes in his tanned cheeks.

Ignoring the little tingles prickling her skin, Shanna looked away from his handsome face to the line of paint he'd just made. Truly, it looked so easy. How could she possibly claim it was beyond her abilities to attempt?

Her self-esteem wasn't *that* low. And shouldn't a woman determined to boot men out of her life be able to make some simple improvements on her own?

Careful not to make contact with his skin, she took back the paintbrush and continued moving it alongside the door molding. It required more concentration than she'd expected to keep it steady, but she focused on the job and almost forgot the person working nearby.

Except he smelled like a man, even over the odor of the paint. It wasn't an expensive, designer scent—God, she'd sniffed enough of those at velvet-roped L.A. nightclubs, always mixed with the sharp bite of liquor and the lingering earthiness of luxurious leather bucket seats. Jorge Santos, by contrast, smelled like plain soap and masculine shampoo and it was so wholesome and . . . dependable that she couldn't stop herself from drawing it deeply into her lungs.

Then he started talking in that deep, slightly accented voice. He spoke of a mother and sisters and his extended family living in a small village outside of Mexicali. Of the grandmother who made the best tamales in the universe and of his grandfather, who had recently taken to wandering away from home and forgetting who he was and how to get back to the house.

"So far, a cousin or a great-nephew or one of my aunts has quickly tracked him down," he said, worry furrowing his brow, "but soon we're going to have to convince my *abuela* he needs a more secure situation."

Shanna looked up from the paint can she'd just dipped her brush into. "You mean *you're* going to have to convince your grandmother."

That incredible smile dug dimples in his lean cheeks again. "What makes you guess that?"

"Because you strike me as the responsible older sibling everyone expects to handle every problem."

That smile flashed again. "Guilty as charged."

She went back to cutting around the window she'd moved on to. "Oh, it's not an accusation."

"Ah. From one who knows the weight of responsibility, then. I recall that your father put this house project in your lap."

And it was the only thing Shanna's father had ever asked her to do for him. And only because if she didn't do anything about it—which he probably suspected would happen—it would mean nothing more than a slight delay in his grand master plan of destroying this warm, unpretentious dwelling in order to build something on scale with his blockbuster ego.

A sting of tears surprised her. Why did she keep crying around Jorge Santos? But she had to blink, and blink again, as her hand faltered and she realized she really did care about this place. She wanted to bring it back to its former, comfortable-in-its-own-skin glory. She thought of that photo in the hallway, of her arms opened wide to embrace the world.

She'd been comfortable in her own skin then, too.

"Ooops," said Jorge, as he came up behind her. "Let me get rid of that paint drip for you."

Blinking, she realized that her hand had trailed over the enameled molding, leaving a wide streak over the white-painted wood. Jorge's arm snaked around her to wipe away the new paint with a rag.

She spun and shifted to get out of his way, but found herself trapped between his chest and the window behind her. They both froze.

Despite the prevailing, raw smell of new paint, she could still detect his own soapy scent. She could see the masculine, close-shaven line of his jaw, his dark eyes, with their spiky fringe of blacker-than-black lashes.

Jorge was staring at her mouth.

Those tingles broke out afresh, starting at her neck and then tumbling down her spine, her thighs, the backs of her knees. They were female tingles, a female reaction, a female-to-male response.

And she'd decided to boot men out of her life.

His lips lowered toward hers and their gazes caught. She

couldn't look away, she didn't back away, even as she tasted his first kiss. In the black of his pupils, she saw her own reflection, and it was what kept her feet glued to the floor.

How could she turn away from him? She couldn't. Not when through him she could see herself for the very first time in a very long, long while.

Inside Malibu & Ewe, Nikki passed the time waiting for Jay by starting on an ambitious—for her, anyway—project. Per Cassandra's advice, she wound a rubber band around one of her needles as a reminder to increase the number of stitches every other row. She'd just put a slip knot on the other needle in preparation to start her kerchief, when the adjacent sofa cushion bounced as the yarn shop owner dropped down beside her.

"Found it!" she said. "It was hiding away in my supply closet. But I think the purse is perfect with your outfit."

She dangled it in front of Nikki's face. It was an evening-sized square, knit in pale blue and with a feathery fringe in the same color around the top. Natural wooden beads interspersed with white shells were strung together to create the short handle.

Reaching out, Nikki played her fingertips through the light, funky fringe. "A purse, too? And on top of my one-of-a-kind, designer T-shirt."

Cassandra tucked the purse between them. "I hope you have as much fun wearing it on your date as I did making it."

Nikki grimaced. "I'm thinking of telling my date I've changed my mind." Or found it. What stupidity had prompted her to agree in the first place? Jay had thrown out a dare, she could see that so clearly now, and she'd fallen right for it, determined to show him she wasn't afraid of men, or sex, or even dinner dates.

Her touch almost maternal, Cassandra patted her shoulder and then adjusted the top she'd created for her from a simple, tie-dyed, "just in case" T-shirt Nikki carried in the back of her car.

The process had been quick, but amazing. One moment she had a plain boring tee, and the next Cassandra had scissored and tied and threaded to create a collarbone-clearing, cap-sleeved garment. The back view made it really something. She'd cut away the fabric from shoulder blades to waistline, and using strips of leftover material, laced it up the back like a corset, cinching it to her ribs yet still leaving a lot of bare spine showing.

The blue and white matched the purse and also went well with Nikki's white, calf-length linen skirt. A pair of flat, white leather sandals would make walking easy on her knee.

It was getting better, thank God. Without the constant rush of a restaurant kitchen and within the smaller confines of Jay's, the swelling had subsided and the pain had lessened. She still sensed its inherent weakness, and wasn't anywhere close to signing up for those martial arts classes she'd bragged to Jay about, but it gave her confidence that she could go on with her life without the operation the orthopedic surgeon insisted was necessary. She couldn't do the surgery.

First, because of that little hospital phobia she'd developed following her mother's sudden death. And second—

"Penny for your thoughts."

Blinking, Nikki's focus shifted back to Cassandra. "My thoughts? Oh. I was thinking about my mom."

Cassandra's hand smoothed her shoulder again. "She died about ten years ago, is that right?"

"Thirteen." Nikki shifted away from the touch and concentrated on her knitting. "But that's way in the past."

"If you'd ever like to talk . . ."

Embarrassed, Nikki shook her head. "No, no. You've been so nice to me already. I don't understand why"—not any more than she understood why she'd come here for wardrobe help again—"but I do appreciate it."

Cassandra cleared her throat. "I, um, felt a kind of connection when we met. Maybe because we . . . we grew up in similar circumstances."

Puzzled, Nikki glanced up. "Really?"

The other woman flushed. "Well, not exactly." Her fingers twined in her lap and then she straightened them out to press at imaginary wrinkles in her khaki trousers. "Um, Nikki—"

The loud rattle of the bells attached to Malibu & Ewe's front door interrupted. Three women burst inside.

With a slight grimace, the shop owner checked her watch. "Tuesday Night Knitters' Club."

"That reminds me," Nikki remarked, "I've been meaning to tell you I received some advertising from your shop before I started with Jay. I don't know how your marketer targeted me—I've never been into crafts. But it's a weird coincidence, huh?"

"Um. Yeah. Weird coincidence." Glancing down, Cassandra ironed her pants once more with the flat of her hand. "Nikki . . ."

The bells rattled again, causing Cassandra to jump. She looked over as more women entered the shop, then back at Nikki. "Maybe . . . maybe we can talk about this later?"

"Sure." Though Nikki didn't quite get what else there was to say. Maybe her obtuseness was due to her dad's detachment gene showing up again. It had rendered her unnaturally ungood at girl chat. So instead of attempting to join in, she listened to it as others arrived and situated themselves on the couches.

A new mother, baby nestled next to her, was having trouble with lining the diaper tote she'd knitted.

A gray-haired lady complained about her latest haircut and seemed to take it out on the cat bed she was creating for her mother-in-law's favorite feline.

A younger woman was surprised by the group's communal reaction of horror when she said she wanted to knit her new guy a sweater. "It's a curse," one expert proclaimed. And a well-known fact that the relationship would surely be finished before the boyfriend sweater.

The legion of true-life examples trotted out by the knitters only ended when a beautiful celebrity entered the shop and plopped her skinny body on an ottoman then set to work on a baby bootie. Nikki might have thought herself delusional except her sofa neighbor introduced Nikki to the striking beauty as Oomfaa—short for One of the Most Famous Actresses in America. The nickname was conferred upon her by the rest of the group, the woman explained, after a *Malibu* magazine piece on the store used that vague reference to preserve the A-lister's anonymity.

Oomfaa flashed Nikki her trademark blinding smile and continued plying her needles. As a rat-a-tat clackety-click filled the room, it struck her that twenty industrious knitters made a noise not unlike a stage full of tiny Irish step dancers.

A noise that abruptly cut off when the door's bells rang again and Jay stepped into the room.

All heads lifted and turned his way. Twenty pairs of eyes took him in.

Only Jay Buchanan could handle the all-female regard with such aplomb. There was the merest hesitation and then he strode forward, wearing a grin as blinding as Oomfaa's had been earlier.

Nikki found herself on her feet and in full retreat as he continued his confident advance. As she backed out of the knitters' circle, her shoulder bumped into Cassandra's, stalling her sudden need to escape.

Clutching her knitting to her middle, she spoke out of the side of her mouth as Jay paused to greet the first of the women. "Tell me you have a back exit."

"You're really changing your mind about tonight? What's the big deal? You said you two were an item."

Nikki kept her eye on Jay and went for the shortest explanation. "We don't suit."

"He didn't appear convinced of that last week on the restaurant dance floor."

It wasn't the time to talk about lesbian charades and Nikki in bed with twins. "Think about it. Me and Hef Junior together? That sunstruck example of male sexuality and *me*? He belongs with someone as . . . as shiny as he is. He belongs with someone like Oomfaa."

And he was currently kissing Oomfaa, smug, charming bastard. On the cheek, but still.

" 'Belongs'? You're looking for long-term, then."

"No!" It wasn't about that. She knew she wasn't any good at keeping anyone around. Not family, not friends, certainly not lovers. But everything had come so easy for Jay and she still had her noble purpose to consider. Someone had to say no to him. "He's only pursuing me because I'm the one who resists."

And he was coming toward her now with a conquering light in his eyes. She shuffled back another step.

Cassandra touched her shoulder. "You're afraid of him."

"No." Nikki whipped her head around. "Heck no! I'm not afraid of any man."

And then *the* man in the room was there, standing beside her. He wore a pair of soft, bleached jeans sans the usual holes and frays that would normally go hand-in-hand with denim that buttery. His mint green shirt was oxford cloth, the usual style, but it didn't look usual on him, unbuttoned to show the strong column of his tanned throat and rolled to reveal his powerful forearms.

It reminded her of his annoying, early-morning habit of near-naked kayaking. Of his bare, rippled torso and his inguinal ligaments she ogled every morning.

"Cookie," he murmured. His hand slid up her back, bumping over the strings of her "corset" T-shirt to reach the smooth skin between her shoulder blades.

To prevent a shiver of reaction, she clenched her stomach muscles hard, then narrowed her eyes at him as she iced her words. "Good God, could you get more obvious? I know you're copping a feel to see if I'm wearing a bra."

He smiled and leaned down to kiss the side of her mouth. His wandering hand slid to her butt. "And checking for panties, too." He cupped a cheek.

She swatted his hand away, but heat still sprinted down the backs of her legs as wetness rushed between her thighs.

This was what she would be afraid of, if she was afraid of anything.

For the last twelve years, she'd had to nurture her sexual responses, babying the tiny, smoldering blazes that so rarely ignited inside of her. She'd close her eyes and conjure visions in her head, picturing an anonymous man pleasing some woman—always some *other* woman. Maybe it was strange, but like blowing on embers to start a real fire, it had worked well enough to attempt intimacy a time or two.

With Jay, though—with Jay it was different. Jay *was* the fire, and his touch, his smile, the press of his mouth against her cheek could start the burn.

It was unfamiliar, okay? And it was natural to be uneasy with the unfamiliar.

Or afraid of it.

No. She wasn't afraid of anything.

As if he sensed her uneasiness, Jay frowned, and tucked his hand under her chin to tilt her face to his. He looked into her eyes. His fingers were warm, and his thumb absently stroked the soft underside of her chin.

"Sink or fly," he murmured, shaking his head. Then his voice strengthened. "Are you okay?"

No. Because as she dropped her lashes to get away from his piercing gaze, one of her visions popped into her head. But it wasn't an anonymous couple in some anonymous, private peep show. She saw herself on the stairs at Jay's house.

I look into your eyes and don't know whether I'm going to sink or fly.

Then, in her mind, it was Jay. Jay gathering her—Nikki, with her wavy hair and her sprinkle of freckles—close. In an instant, she was melting against him, candle wax to his flame, her face flushed, her mouth already opening for his kiss.

More heat pooled at the juncture of her thighs and the flesh there throbbed. Her eyes flying open, she tried scurrying back, but he tightened his hold on her chin and bent to press his lips to hers.

"Cookie," he whispered against her mouth. "I can't wait to get you alone."

What would happen then? Her stomach jolted at the thought, at what it would be like to have free access to that golden chest that had been fascinating her from the very first day. How would the hard parts of his body feel rubbing against the wet heat of hers?

She shivered and his head lifted as he took her hand. "I thought we could have a private picnic at my house . . . I ordered a basket for us and it's already in my car." Like a starstruck zombie, she let him lead her five feet toward the front door.

Then her errant self-preservation stepped in. Yes, he could melt her into a puddle of want. And yes, she'd stripped down in his kitchen the day before in a reckless, sexual version of "bring it on."

Still, any woman with sense, even one like her who wasn't worried about the state of her heart, would remember she was working for the man. If tonight ended in his disappointment, would it affect him recommending her for future jobs?

She could refuse him, citing her career.

That was the ticket.

Nikki dug her feet into the floor of Malibu & Ewe. "Jay—"

The front bells sang out again. Fern and her sullen boyfriend, Jenner, ambled into the shop. He had the girl caught tightly against him as they moved. Nikki wondered if she could breathe.

"There you are," the girl called out to Jay. "Your cell's not working."

He grimaced. "Our famous Malibu reception."

Nikki already knew about this. The proximity of the Santa Monica Mountains on one side and the Pacific on the other made coverage spotty, at best.

"Well, I'm checking in like I said I would." She fiddled with the hair hanging over her shoulder. It fell in a pinstraight, gleaming mass that all but covered her neck and half of her double-layered tanks. A tiny skirt, the size of Nikki's palm, hung from her prominent hipbones to the top of her thighs.

This was the *responsible* cousin?

The cousin the family thought could take care of herself?

Maybe Nikki was projecting. And to be honest, the outfit wasn't any more outrageous than what other girls around town wore. But the boy's possessive hold on the teenager had Nikki's stomach hopping again.

Jay glanced from Jenner to his cousin. "I thought you were spending the night with Marie."

"I am. But first I'm going to a . . . uh, get-together at Zuma." She glanced at her boyfriend, then back at Jay's face. "Jenner will drive me over to Marie's house after the beach closes at ten."

The lanky boy tossed his head to move his long hair out of his eyes. "Sure I will. After the par— I mean, get-together. Just a few friends, a bonfire, you know. We're going to roast marshmallows."

Riiiight, Nikki thought. Surely Jay wouldn't fall for that one?

But he nodded instead of protesting. "Okay then. Have fun."

Jenner spun as if he might be attacked by yarn cooties at any moment. The quick movement caught Fern by surprise, and she slid out of the boy's grip, her hair flying back as she turned to catch up with him.

They were out the door in the space of a breath.

Jay's hand tightened on Nikki's. "Shit. Was that what I thought it was?"

It wasn't her place. None of this was her business. That girl wasn't Nikki twelve years ago, caught in the clutches of a controlling, older boy and her own emotional turmoil. "What did you think it was?"

"A hickey, damn it. A hickey on the side of her neck."

Nikki's eyes had caught the bruises on the girl's wrist.

"Is it too late to play the grown-up card?" he asked, looking down at her.

"Not if you are a grown-up."

"Shit," Jay said again. He tugged her in the direction of the door once more. "Change of plans. We're taking our little picnic to Zuma."

Nikki found herself going along without a protest, her plan to avoid tonight's date taking off on the ocean breeze. With a sigh, she realized she was now more concerned for Fern than she was for herself.

Ten

How would you like to stand like a god before the crest of a monster billow, always rushing to the bottom of a hill and never reaching its base, and to come rushing in for a half a mile at express speed, in graceful attitude, until you reach the beach and step easily from the wave...?

—DUKE KAHANAMOKU,
INVENTOR OF MODERN SURFING

Zuma was a mega-beach, two miles long and 500 feet of sand between the road and the water. Dozens and dozens of volleyball courts were strung near the parking area that was itself bigger than most California beaches Nikki had ever visited. As it neared sunset, Jay pulled in, passing carloads of sunburned Angelenos heading out. They found an empty space and he reached into the back of his Porsche to pull out a large picnic basket.

"I hope you have something tasty packed in there," she said as they hurried across the blacktop toward the wide expanse of sand. "Kiwis and Evian won't satisfy me, unlike those breasts-on-a-stick that you usually date."

He ignored the dig, which wrote volumes about his preoccupied state as he scanned the vicinity. "All I know is I better find a girl, a party, and something grilling pretty damn quick."

The grim note in his voice had Nikki's insides twitching again. If Jay was worried, then she . . .

Then she didn't have to worry at all. Fern's situation wasn't her business. Fern's life wasn't a replay of hers.

He glanced over at Nikki. "You think I'm overreacting?"

She thought she wanted to keep her opinions to herself. Given what happened yesterday, when her conversation with Michelle had revealed more than she'd intended, zipped lips seemed a safer way to go. If she spoke up, she might speak of too much, and she liked her secrets safely buried.

"I—"

His hand on her arm halted her words. "Thank God. There she is."

There was all of it—gathered around a concrete fire ring just down the beach. The girl, the looks of a party, and grilling, though Nikki couldn't tell from here if it was weenies or even those marshmallows Jenner had promised.

Jay grinned, looking as relieved as she felt. He blew out a long breath. "Good. Now we can take ourselves to a more private place."

"No," she said quickly. Public places would keep clothes and secrets safely in place. "We should keep an eye on them a while longer." Her gaze cut to the scene down the beach.

He looked back toward the twenty or so teenagers, his eyes narrowing as another five or six joined the group. A girl in a shoestring bikini shrieked in mock fear as a boy chased her across the sand. A pallet was thrown onto the fire, sending up sparks. Someone turned up a boom box so that rap music pounded the air like fists.

"I don't know." Jay shook his head. "Fern'll kill me if she spots us."

"We can plant ourselves on the other side of the lifeguard tower."

Jay gave her a sharp look. "Spy much?" But he headed off in the direction she'd indicated.

She moved slower. The sand was soft and deep, and churning through it wasn't easy on her knee. With Fern secure, Nikki's reluctance about the whole evening and all the danger attached to this "date" was returning.

He had selected a patch of sand and was already opening the basket when she reached him. "What's with the snail's pace?" he asked.

Letting her gaze wander to a wet surfer emerging from the water, she shrugged. "Now that I'm out of the hetero closet, I'm taking my time checking over all the hot guys."

A long arm slung around her shoulders and he gave her a brief, companionable hug. "Damn. I'm going to miss the old days when we could troll for girls together. How much fun was that?"

She didn't dignify the remark with a response, just watched him proceed to shake out a checked tablecloth and spread it on the sand. Once she chose her spot on it, he sat close, and poured something from a flask into a blue plastic cup that he handed over.

He poured another for himself, then set down a platter of cut vegetables and another of fruit. Next he dug out a fat votive candle, lit the wick, and anchored it into the sand nearby. "Aren't you going to taste your drink?"

Nikki brought the cup under her nose and sniffed. A very dry Pouilly-fumé. "Isn't alcohol banned on the beach?"

He leaned back on his elbows and crossed his legs at the ankle, the picture of a man at home with seduction. The smile he sent her way made her clothes start to smolder at the edges. "Let's break some rules, baby."

Like the one that said no smart cookie of a chef would get involved with the guy she was cooking for? She frowned, suddenly irritated. "Hasn't it occurred to you that in the real world you wouldn't give me a second glance?"

"What world is that, again?"

"The one where you spend your days in a downtown office peopled by adolescents who look like grown men and tits and asses that somehow manage to walk and talk . . . though certainly not both at the same time."

His eyebrows rose. "You have a real thing against women who take off their clothes for a living, don't you?"

She refused to let the comment sidetrack her. "But instead you're stuck all day in your Malibu house where I'm in your kitchen and you're confused—"

"Like you were about your sexual identity?" He sipped from his wine.

"You enjoy the food I cook, so—"

"I want to eat you. I'll go with that."

She threw a strawberry at him, though her aim wasn't any better than it had been at high school softball. "Jay, don't—"

"Make you think about it?"

His voice lowered but she could still hear every word over the shush-shush of the incoming waves and the pulse of the rap beat down the beach. "C'mon, cookie. Imagine how it will be. For an appetizer, I'll start with that soft spot behind your left ear. You know about my sweet tooth and I have a feeling your skin is going to be extra sugary there. I'll lap at it with my tongue, then give it the slightest suck until I feel you shiver. Next on the menu is that sleek curve on the underside of your breast. I wonder what will happen to your nipples when I take the tiniest of bites—"

"Stop."

"And wait until I tell you what I'm planning for that curvy little backside of yours."

This time her aim improved and the baby carrot bounced off the end of his nose.

He rubbed at it with the back of his hand. "Hey!"

"That kind of talk might work with . . . with . . ." She had trouble articulating when her mind was spinning with images and her body was prickling in the places he'd mentioned as well as some he hadn't. "With . . . with . . ."

"Those breasts on sticks," he interjected helpfully.

"Aarh!" She threw up a hand in frustration. "You're impossible."

"Not for you. For you, I'm available." He sat up and took a sip of his wine, eyeing her over the rim of his cup. "Unless, well . . . You're not holding out for true love, are you, cookie?"

"Oh, please." She rolled her eyes at him. Cassandra had asked a similar question earlier and it rankled even more now.

"Just answer the question. It's not like I think it's a bad thing."

"Then why aren't you? Why aren't you holding out for true love?"

"I'm thirty-two years old and my mom, sisters, aunt, and cousins have at least that number of theories. Go ahead and pick one."

"What do your father and uncle think?"

"That I need another beer and we should turn up the volume on ESPN."

She had to laugh. "All right. So expound on these theories your female family members hold."

"Hmm." He topped off her wine and then his own. "Current thought is that I'm like a certain kind of rodent. A weasely kind of thing if I remember right, but not a weasel."

Nikki laughed again. "I think I'd like the women in your family."

He snorted. "Remind me never to introduce you. But the fact is, I really can't blame them for the idea, because it comes from an article published in *NYFM* last year."

"I must have missed that issue."

The air was cooling as the sun slipped lower. She pulled the sweater she'd brought with her around her shoulders and didn't edge away when Jay shifted closer to block the breeze.

"It goes like this," he said. "There are two kinds of these rodents. One quickly finds their mate and bedded bliss, so to speak, and from then on identifies sexual pleasure with that particular individual. The other variety likes to do the wild thing, too, but unlike their cousins, the way their brain processes the intimacy and orgasm hormones is different. They apparently don't have the same receptors, which means their enjoyment isn't heightened or even affected by their partner in the deed."

"Any weasel will do?"

"So the research says."

"That explains a lot of men I know."

"In this case, Wanda and Wally Weasel Type 2 operate exactly the same way. Both genders cheerfully pursue their one-night stands."

"Huh." While she didn't bond with anyone—man or woman—easily, she wasn't an indiscriminate sex-seeker, either. But the reasons for that were something less to do with brain receptors and more with memories she'd buried very deep. "So, Wally, what else do you have in that basket?"

He drew it close to rummage around inside. "I'm not exactly Wally, at least that's what my family's females hope. When it comes to humans, the idea is that it's not so black-and-white as bonders and nonbonders. Some persons, though, may be born with fewer receptors than others."

"Say, like you."

"According to my mom and Aunt Annie." He handed her a sandwich that looked like smoked turkey and cheese on a crisp baguette.

"The man of few receptors," he went on, "likely considers all this love business the stuff of Ephron screenplays. Then comes a day when our unattached bachelor discovers the one with whom the hormone release of intimacy and sex finally reaches those diminished receptors of his. For the first time, our man fully experiences the effect of a serotonin, dopamine, and oxytocin cocktail. He'll never want to let go of the sole female who provides that euphoric high."

Nikki took a bite and chewed, wondering what it would be like to introduce such a man to those feelings. Every time they had sex, the bond would only grow and his attachment would only strengthen . . . A hot shiver wiggled under her skin.

Jay looked at her over his own sandwich. His smile was sly. "So when you think about it, I'm actually disabled. As a matter of fact, you should take pity on me because the receptor-impaired need their comforts. You'd be doing a poor guy like me a favor by taking me to bed."

Her focus snapped back to him, golden and gorgeous. Or, as he put it, pitiable, disabled, and receptor-impaired. His seductive smile widened.

"You are so full of it." Irritated, she tossed her plate to the tablecloth and shoved him over. But he made a last-minute grab and brought her down with him.

She stared into his laughing eyes. "Did you make that whole thing up?" she demanded.

"No, no, it's all true, or at least as far as my foggy recollection goes. And you should have seen your face. For a minute there you looked ready to do it with the next confirmed bachelor who walked by. You were feeling so warm and fuzzy I could have fixed you up with the biggest horn-dog in Hollywood."

Not that she'd tell him, but the only man she'd been thinking about getting warm and fuzzy for was Jay.

The jerk.

Hef Junior.

Her boss.

And all those thoughts flew out of her head as he speared his hand in her hair and drew her lips to his. She was going to protest, any moment, but his tongue was cool and tart in her hot mouth and his hand had snaked under her sweater and then under the corset lacings of her T-shirt. He palmed that hot shiver once again racing up her spine. The kiss went deeper.

He shifted, and then his knee split her legs. Her skirt was loose enough that she could part them for the hard muscle of his thigh. His other hand left her hair and smoothed down to find the curve of her butt. He caressed her there, pressing down as his knee rubbed in suggestive counterpart.

The move wasn't subtle, but neither was her immediate response.

Her body flamed. The throbbing place between her legs turned wet again, as if that would put out the fire. Everything spun away but Jay's kiss, Jay's hands, Jay's long, hard body against hers.

A raucous cry from down the beach pierced her haze of smoky lust. Reality descended like an upturned pail of water.

Nikki scrambled back, breaking Jay's hold on her. She found her feet, felt the brisk slap of the ocean breeze, took a deep breath of cool common sense.

Then glared at him. "We're on a public beach!" That was supposed to keep clothes and secrets safely in place. And lust under control.

He took his time sitting up, rubbing his thumb against the edge of his mouth. His lower lip gleamed wet in the flickering candlelight. "Not my smoothest move," he admitted.

"We should go," Nikki said. Another scream from down the beach drew her eyes that way. The flames in the teenagers' fire ring were leaping higher, and even from here she could tell the party was rowdier than before. A third feminine shriek had her insides twitching.

Jay glanced in the same direction and grimaced. "She won't be happy if she catches me, but I better check on Fern again."

"I'll do it." The walk would clear her head and lower her body temperature. Though she was trembling, her skin felt hot to the touch. "You pick up the food and I'll be right back."

She didn't want to think about what would happen after that. So she focused on the group down the beach, realizing even before she'd reached it that the number of partygoers had tripled in size. The music was as loud as before, and some of the kids were dancing. Girls gyrated, facing each other in little knots. Despite the fast tempo, couples swayed in slow motion, plastered together like they were having sex on their feet.

She smelled beer and the sticky sweetness of wine coolers. Skirting a sleeping bag, she noticed an entwined couple was snuggled inside. As she passed, the boy reached for a tall can of malt liquor half-planted in the sand.

A cold slick of sweat burst over Nikki's skin as a few feet away she saw another boy, backlit by the fire, pour a stream of liquid from a Boda bag into a girl's mouth.

She rewarded him with a voluptuous kiss.

He palmed her breast and she laughed, pushing him away. He pushed her in return and she ran, him taking chase.

Nikki wiped her forehead with the back of her hand and squinted through the smoke. Where was Fern?

A trek through the center of the party zone didn't bring her any answers. She wound her way through more dancers, and then around a circle of young men playing drunken catch with a football. It was an older crowd mixed in with the younger, she noticed, but there was still no sign of Jay's cousin.

Finally, Nikki moved to the dark perimeter of the gathering, hoping some distance would give her a better view. No familiar, girlish figure. She shuffled back, preparing to turn away and report her lack of success to Jay.

But a hand clamped heavily around her upper arm. "You can't leave now," a man's voice said. She was turned in one quick movement.

Nikki stiffened. "I—" But her protest was stifled by strange, cold lips that tasted like dark beer and garlic. The man's hands squeezed her shoulders and when she tried yanking away, they only bit harder.

With that, years fell away. She was fifteen. So young. Stupid. Sad.

Another dark party. Other drunken guests. Other hands biting, other lips that were too hard and then too wrong.

You can't go now.

You can't leave me like this.

Give it to me, baby.

You owe it to me, baby.

A hand clamping her breast. A palm over her mouth to stifle her protest. Biting pain between her thighs. And the last tears she'd ever shed, colder than snow, colder than death, trickling from the corners of her eyes to her temples and into her hair. Until then she'd thought sex was a way for him to make her feel loved. Now she knew it was a way for him to make her feel less.

A strangled oath brought her back to the present. She was on the beach and on her feet, the stranger's kiss over. No one was touching her breast. There was nothing between her thighs. But a sick dread still held her in its thrall. Fear tasted like blood in her mouth and her skin jittered, the old memory continuing to crawl across it like spiders.

"You're not Connie." The hulk of a young man who'd caught her was staring down at her, his eyes blinking with the rapidity of a strobe light. His hands still held her shoulders, but now Nikki realized they were holding her upright. "Shit, lady. You're not Connie."

She didn't stick around to introduce herself. She broke free of him, if not from the past still swirling like dark smoke in the air, and ran back the way she'd come, her breath loud in her ears, her knee stabbed by fiery pains. But that didn't matter, not when she was trying to outrace the years and all that she'd promised herself she'd leave behind. Nothing would have stopped her until Ventura, maybe even until Oregon, but then another man's hands found her shoulders and caught her up against him.

Jay. She knew him instantly. Jay. Jay. Jay.

Nikki flung her arms around him and buried her cold face in his warm throat.

"Cookie. Nikki. What's wrong?" His embrace was firm and his chest wide. He was keeping her as close as Connie's guy had, but this was different. So different.

Jay bent his head and pressed his cheek to hers. He smelled so good, like one of the slick, scented inserts between the pages of *NYFM*. His touch was as gentle as his voice was urgent. "Nikki, tell me what happened."

And she did. The words she'd never told another soul. They crept out of their burial plot at the back of her mind like creatures from the dead, covered in dirt and rattling like bones. The truth came out, yet still she found a way to detach herself from it, if only a little.

"He hurt her. She didn't want him to, and she told him no, but still, still, he hurt her."

Eleven

In his kitchen, Jay made his crappy version of coffee. He didn't think Nikki would notice it anyway, not after he dumped some whiskey in her mug to disguise its bitter taste. With the half-and-half in hand, he slammed shut the refrigerator door with his elbow, rattling the relish jars and beer bottles inside. As violent as the action was, it didn't do a thing for his vicious mood.

Damn the woman! Each time he thought things between them were going to be simple, she scrambled them up.

He glanced over to where she was sitting on the couch in the living room, before the fire he'd lit to warm her up. His eyes closed. Hell, at least he should be truthful. The person he was mad at was himself, because he couldn't get his feet to move backward like they usually did when a woman made things complicated.

Instead, here he was, hovering: lighting a fire, wrapping a blanket around her shoulders, making Irish coffee—the kind of things that made him uncomfortable when a lover was doing them for him.

She'd wanted to head to her own home once they'd left the beach, but he'd even gone so far as to pocket her keys to keep her near. What had happened to the Jay Buchanan who'd written to his fellow men that he'd given up on women?

More important . . . so much more important . . .

What had happened to Nikki?

He took the heavily doctored coffee into the living room and pressed the hot mug into her hands. She took it without a flash of her usual smile and that bugged him, too. Christ! He didn't need this. Inhaling a breath, he told himself he'd get the story out of her and then take her home himself.

She pursed her lips—he looked away—to blow across the top of her coffee, then ventured a sip.

"Feh!" The mug landed on the coffee table in front of her with a clunk. She glared at him. "Are you trying to poison me, Buchanan?"

A grin broke over his face as he fell for it—as he *almost* fell for it. Though he wanted her to be her usual prickly self, he couldn't fool himself about it no matter how hard she tried. Those blue and green eyes, usually so clear and bright, looked as dulled as beach glass.

Dropping to the coffee table to face her, he grabbed the coffee and pressed it on her again. "Drink damn it. You look worse than it tastes."

"I noticed you didn't serve yourself any of this swill," she grumbled, but he watched until she took another healthy swallow.

"I'm drinking my whiskey straight tonight." He wasn't drinking at all, knowing he was going to get back in his car and drive her home ASAP. He didn't need booze affecting his driving ability or softening his resolve.

Get her story and get her out, Buchanan.

Her next swallow gave him the go-ahead to his plan. "Now, Nikki—"

"Are you sure Fern's okay?"

Nice try. But he surrendered to the stall. It wouldn't last

long—he wouldn't allow it. "I told you. While you went on your odd little adventure down the beach, God graced my masculine beauty and charm with cell reception. I got through to Fern *and* Marie's mother, though that was admittedly a home landline, so I didn't tax the Almighty as much as I might have. My cousin left the beach bacchanal earlier than expected and was watching a *Veronica Mars* marathon with her friend when I called."

"Bless your beauty and teen detectives," Nikki murmured, then took another sip of the medicine he'd made.

"Speaking of which, I called the cops when you were in the bathroom."

Her gaze flew to his face. "Nothing happened."

"Uh-huh." *Right.* "Not to you, maybe, but that beach party was trouble waiting to erupt."

Nikki sat back on the cushions. "You're right. And you were right to call the police."

Jay leaned forward and placed his elbows on his knees. "Why didn't you think of it?"

"I told you. Nothing happened out there to me."

"I caught you in my arms after you were tearing down the beach like the devil was after you, cookie," he said. "I know what I know."

Her body, shaking as if buffeted by an arctic wind. Her heart slamming against his chest like it wanted out of hers, until he made her swear on all that was sacred, including Julia Child and Rachael Ray, that she wasn't physically hurt.

When that hadn't cracked a smile, he'd been forced to clamp down on his own rising panic. A panic that he'd yet to get control over. He had a writer's imagination, and he needed the details before he resorted to making them up himself.

"Cookie—"

"You know, I hate that nickname."

"Learn to live with it." Like he was having to learn with this new turn to his life. Christ, he didn't let himself get personal enough to lift the hood of a woman's car, and now he wasn't going to be able to sleep until he probed Nikki's past.

"'He hurt her,'" he repeated back, remembering it word-for-word. "'She didn't want him to, and she told him no, but still, still, he hurt her.'"

A log in the fire popped and they both jumped. Jay closed his eyes and pinched the bridge of his nose. Crap. Damn woman had him on edge and he was *never* on edge. He liked his relationships casual, simple, and for God's fucking sake, unbonded. But now he was soaking up Nikki's tension like a frickin' sponge.

She put down her mug again and ran a hand through the tangled mass of her hair. It waved in matching agitation to their moods. "It's really no big deal."

He threw his head back and made a sound that was part snort and part sigh. "What a disappointment you are. Here I thought you were different. But no, now you're going all girly on me. I hate that. 'No big deal,' you say, and I'm supposed to read your mind and correctly interpret that to mean you're mad I've forgotten your birthday, or the anniversary of the hour we met, or your favorite ice-cream flavor."

She stared at him. "You're the one who insisted I wear pink. You're the one who nixed my commando boots. You're the one who's made me hide my soul-deep devotion to Ellen DeGeneres."

His eyes narrowed. "And you're the one who isn't so funny that I'm going to lose the point here, cookie." She wasn't moving from the couch, but all the same, she was scrambling. Why couldn't he just let her off with her bullshit and leave it at that?

But he'd held her to him, her heart racing against his, her cheeks so cold she'd scared the hell out of him. His arms crossed his chest as he quoted once again. Damn his good memory. "'He hurt her. She didn't want him to, she told him no, but still, still, he hurt her.'"

A moment passed. Then Nikki looked down at her lap,

looked up. "Okay. Fine. Here's the thing. In high school, I had a friend."

He let that sit for sixty seconds, then pinned her with his glare. "And I was voted Prom King and Most Likely to Sleep With the Playmate of the Year. Friends and admirers galore. Move on, cookie."

"I just had a bad moment, okay? At that party tonight, I was remembering something about my friend." Beneath the yellow blanket his grandmother had crocheted a million years before, one shoulder lifted and fell in a shrug. "We . . . we were at a party. People were drinking. I lost track of her for a while. I thought she was with her boyfriend. She had a boyfriend—did I mention that?"

"At party with a friend. Check. Friend with boyfriend. Check."

Her throat moved as she swallowed. "A *boyfriend*, Jay. A close boyfriend."

God, it was going to be morning before he squeezed this story out of her and got her home and finally out of his hair. "Okay. *Close* boyfriend. Meaning they engaged in sexual relations, I suppose."

"And . . . and . . . my friend didn't think it—the sex—was all that it was cracked up to be."

"Oh, bummer. Because teenage boys are so well known for their technique."

"But he told her it was how she proved her love—and how he showed his. So how could she change the nature of the relationship?"

"Uh, 'no'? Or, 'Gee, I'm not happy with how things are'?"

Her hand lifted. Fell. "But there's the problem. Some people don't take 'no' for an answer."

Ah, fuck. Of course, Jay had thought it might be something like this. He'd wanted the details because he hadn't wanted it to *be* this. His eyes closed. "How old was your friend?"

Shit. *Friend*. There was a crock of crap.

"Fifteen."

She hadn't even hesitated before slaying him. The damn woman had gone straight for the jugular. Fifteen. Fifteen-year-old Nikki with a boyfriend she'd been sleeping with within a year of losing her mother. And then, one night the son of a bitch hadn't taken no for an answer.

There was a special jail cell in hell for bastards like that, right?

Then he remembered Nikki's general jumpiness. The way she sometimes skittered away from him if he came up on her from behind. The near-violent reaction she'd had that time he'd placed his palm over her mouth. It all made sick sense—and made clear that the night her Romeo hadn't taken "no" for an answer, there'd been more coercion involved than "pretty please."

Now *Jay* felt sick.

Ignoring the riot in his gut, he shot to his feet. "We've got to go now. I need to drive you home."

She straightened, too, his grandmother's sunny throw falling off her shoulders. "Only to my car—I left it at Cassandra's shop."

"I'll drive you to your place. You've been drinking bad coffee. And didn't I hear you tell Fern you have a fish? I need to bring you home safely to your pet."

She laughed a little, but the sharp sound cut. "It's plastic, Jay. You wind it up and the fish circles around the bowl. I don't need to feed it. It doesn't even know I'm gone."

He stared at her. *He* was gone. He was a goner. Because despite all his single dude instincts, right now he could not let this blue and green–eyed woman, this *bruja*, go home to an empty apartment and a plastic fish. Not tonight.

Shit. Damn. Fuck. What was the bet he'd made with Jorge? It didn't matter. He'd fallen under her spell.

Temporarily, anyway. For this one night.

She made a little sound of protest as he settled back on the couch beside her. He kept to his side of the cushions. "Shut up," he said, "and now tell me exactly what happened out at Zuma."

She huffed out a frustrated sigh, then gave in. "Oh, fine.

This young man on the beach . . . he . . . he grabbed me and kissed me. That's why I spooked."

Jay refused to look at her. "Should I go find the SOB and beat him up?"

"No. It's kind of funny, now that I think of it. He sounded appalled when he realized I was a stranger. He'd mistaken me for someone named Connie."

"I don't mistake you for anybody." It was the uncomfortable truth. Jay couldn't seem to dismiss her from his mind like all the other women who had come before. Settling back against the cushions, he propped his feet on the table in front of them.

There wasn't a chance he was going to sleep tonight, not with all that was rolling around in his head. And he didn't think Nikki truly wanted to be alone after her scare or flashback or whatever the hell it was that she wasn't being entirely truthful about. Her *friend*.

Christ.

Leaning to his left, he snapped off the light beside the couch. The room dimmed to flame-gilded shadows. Outside the bank of windows, the spotlight on the roof illuminated the lacy-looking surfline.

He slid lower and set his head against the back of the cushions, then rolled it left to take in Nikki. In profile, she looked so damn vulnerable and so damn sweet. His chest ached. "How do you feel about waiting for sunrises?"

Her back stiffened. Her head whipped toward his. *Uh-oh*, Jay thought. She was going full prickle. What had he done now?

" 'Waiting for sunrises'? Is that what we've come to?" She stabbed a finger at him. "I don't think so, buddy. Instead, I think we're going to have sex."

Twelve

The only abnormality is the incapacity to love.

—ANAÏS NIN,
AUTHOR

There was no need of defibrillators with Nikki in the room, Jay decided, his mind spinning. She'd just startled the hell out of him.

And she continued to stare him down. "Well?"

He pushed his hands through his hair. "I thought we were having a tender moment here, God damn it." So he sounded more aggrieved than understanding, but for pity's sake, she'd knocked him on his ass.

Again.

"Tender? You're looking at me with pity. You're afraid to touch me just because I had a bad moment on the beach tonight."

"Nik—"

"I'm not some victim, you know."

He tried to keep the sarcasm out of his voice. "Not like your young friend in the past."

The eight inches separating them evaporated. "She isn't a victim any longer either."

He groaned in frustration. "I thought you were against us having sex!"

"That was before I learned that you'll lose interest after our one-night stand, Wally Weasel. I figure one bout in your bed and then I'll be free from your attentions. I can go back to making you delicious meals while wearing my favorite mannish footwear."

He resisted the urge to search for hidden cameras. MTV's practical joke series, *Punk'd*, had ended a season or two ago and he didn't know of one on the current television schedule titled *Single Guy Seared By His Own Stupid Words*. "Look . . ."

She drew her knees onto the couch and edged even closer. "What's the holdup? Don't you want me anymore?"

He'd *never* wanted to want her, damn it! Not only had he sworn off women, but she made him crazy with her abnormal eyes and her abnormal attitude. In his experience, women didn't want just one night with a man, and even though he'd been looking his whole freakin' lifetime for someone who'd take just such a casual approach, now that he'd found her . . .

Now that he'd found her . . .

"I like it fast," she said. "And you don't have to worry about finesse."

I like it fast.

Don't worry about finesse.

Now that he'd found the woman his buddies wrote to *Penthouse Letters*—all lies—about . . .

"I want this, Jay."

Now that he'd found this exasperating, confusing, infuriating, fascinating bundle of contradictions that was blue-eyed and green-eyed Nikki Carmichael, he couldn't move a muscle. Jay Buchanan, man-about-town, more important, man-who-knew-his-way-around-women, was scared shitless.

The fact was, she'd been betrayed by men—most recently in restaurants and before that at fifteen years old when some butt-ugly, dick-for-brains, cowardly boy had hurt her. Had hurt Jay's private chef.

Oh, God. He recalled every dumbass thing he'd ever said to her.

Chef with benefits.

She'd been traumatized by sex in the past and from the first he'd placed sex squarely into their business relationship, just because it amused and entertained him. How shallow was that?

Maybe she really *was* a witch because she seemed to be reading his mind again. "Jay Buchanan," she said. "If you don't make a move on me right now, I'll never again make you my barbecued ribs."

She swept her hair off the side of her neck, holding it away in one fist so he was looking at the fragile shell of ear, the skin so transparent that the firelight shone through it, making the pink flesh glow. The one earring in the rim winked at him, yet another temptation. "Didn't you say you were going to start here?"

Christ. Suddenly his vision did something like the cameras in a crime show, his focus ch-ch-changing in little bullet sequences, getting closer, tighter, until he swore he could see the blood moving under all the delicate, female, sweet Nikki skin.

Her whole body was quivering, he noticed, moved by just the tiniest of tremors. He could almost smell the bravado rising in the air along with her vanilla-based perfume.

"Baby," he said, his voice as soft as the touch he placed on her free hand. It was cold. "You don't have to prove anything to me."

She squeezed shut her eyes and yanked her hair farther from her pretty neck. She bent her head to offer him a clearer shot at her smooth skin. Her voice hardened. "You said you wanted to start here."

His heart stopped beating. Sometimes being a storyteller was a bitch, because it not only made him an observer, but gave him the skills to connect the dots and create a narrative that fit the evidence before him. And now

Nikki's response was killing him, killing him, because the tale this evidence told was that she *was* hell-bent on proving something—but to herself, and she was trusting him to help her accomplish it.

And who was Jay Buchanan for any woman to trust? He'd never stayed with one long enough to buy anything but thanks-for-the-boink gifts. He'd messed with Shanna next door and then messed her up, too.

"Cookie," he murmured. He didn't know where to start, what to do, how to approach the situation. *What if I screw this up?*

It was a hell of a question for a man who'd always considered himself an expert at this particular game.

But there was all that exposed skin from Nikki's ear to her collarbone. It called to him, made him hungry to taste it, and he almost smiled, thinking of the *NYFM* article last month that had explored the current wave of vampires in popular entertainment. Maybe he understood, now, what those fictional descendants of Dracula were all about.

He bent to put his mouth on the pulse at her neck. Her skin was cold here, too, and he moved his mouth over it to warm it before tasting with his tongue.

Nikki jerked, and he reassured her by squeezing that cold hand under his. Cold skin, cold hand . . . God, he wasn't really going to do this, was he?

Because what if I screw this up? This time the question screamed at him.

But then she leaned closer, her body language talking, asking for him to touch her again with his tongue, and he did, running it along the rim of her ear, then flattening it against that sweet spot behind it. She gave another little jerk, and then she was leaning even closer, her hand losing its grasp on her hair so she could catch herself on his shoulder.

This hand was warm. The one under his warm now, too.

Nikki was heating up. Despite everything, she was heating up for him and his body tightened, his cock going hard and I-can-do-this ready in two slamming heartbeats. He pulled her across his lap, so that her fabulous ass was cradled against his hips and her mouth was right where it should be—just a breath away from his kiss.

Her lips parted as he lowered to them. He noticed her eyes were still squeezed shut, but then he closed his, too, and slid his tongue into her mouth. Key to lock. Warm to wet. Take to give.

Oh, hell, he thought, groaning to himself even as the kiss went deeper and the pleasure of it rolled down his spine. This wasn't time for poetry. This was time to give Nikki a safe place and safe partner with which to demonstrate she was no man's casualty.

His hand splayed against her back, feeling her silky skin in between the strings that held her stretchy shirt together in back. When he slid a finger beneath one of them she sighed, and he took that as a good sign.

More good signs followed: the way she wiggled in his lap as he traced the crisscrossed lacings with a lazy thumb, the way her hand tightened on his shoulder when he pushed up into the cushion of her tush, the way she sucked on his tongue as he tried to back off for air.

Okay, the way she sucked on his tongue eliminated his need for air. He grunted, goaded to grinding his lips against hers like he wanted to grind his hips between her thighs—and then she moaned. For a second it scared him—had he scared *her*?—but quickly he saw she was still warm and flushed and pliant against him.

The sight—that sign of continued trust—struck him somewhere north of his raging hard-on. Maybe it was perverse of him, but at this moment he could only think how thankful he was for all his many and varied sexual experiences. Because surely he'd learned something along the way that would help him out here. That would help him make this good, very good, for Nikki.

Another moment of wallowing in that wet and luscious kiss, and then he finally managed to lift his head. Drawing in the O_2, he watched his hand edge around her side to her breast, where he thumbed the nipple that was peaking against the soft cotton of her shirt. It tightened even more at his touch and he glanced at her face, at her closed eyes and the worry wrinkles between her brows.

Worry?

"Baby, is this good?" He knew it was, because she was arching into his hand, yet still, that concerned expression pricked him. His thumb circled the hard nub, then slid away.

She made a little sound of protest.

"I won't touch you where you want me most unless you talk to me."

A gleam of light showed between her lashes and her lower lip slid out in her trademark sulky frown. "*You* talk too much."

"Some of us can accomplish two things at once."

"Not your cover bimbos."

"Damn." He shook his head. "I'm not doing my job if you're still thinking of other women." His hand roved to her sleek back again and to the bow that was at her waist. He yanked it free and started unlacing the corset ties of her top. "How about I loosen things up?"

He pulled the fabric completely from her body. At the sight of her naked breasts, the material slipped from his hand to the floor. Firelight flickered over her creamy skin and warmed the peachy-pink color of her stiff nipples. He had to touch, and as his hand reached for her, he saw it tremble.

Startled by the sight, he stilled, trying to wrap his head around a man shaking so hard just at the idea of such a rudimentary move. But then she gulped a breath, pushing those sweet handfuls closer to him and he went all-guy, giving up the thinking to another part of his anatomy.

And that throbbing part of him was only sending one thought chugging through his bloodstream. *Taste taste taste.* His hand curved beneath one soft breast, plumping it for his mouth. He bent his head and touched the velvet berry in the center with the tip of his tongue.

She gasped, pushing that bud against the rasp of his

tongue and he obliged the silent request by closing his lips around her nipple and sucking her into his mouth.

God. His belly clenched, lust striking a match inside of him. Driven forward by the fire, he sucked harder, pushing her nipple against the roof of his mouth to caress it with the flat of his tongue. Nikki's hands flew to his hair.

Jay froze, cold caution dousing the sudden blaze of heat that had overtaken him. Did she want him to stop? Had he frightened her?

Instead of letting go though, he merely eased up, holding her gently in his mouth as he breathed in the scent of her skin—vanilla and heat. Her fingers relaxed and he started sucking again, not so wild, but not letting up either. His second hand shifted to her other breast and he indulged, there, too, running his thumb over the hard crest and rolling it between his fingers.

Then he switched places, plucking her wet nipple with his fingertips while taking the other into his mouth. This time he kept his suction slow and steady, but ratcheting up the pressure at intervals until he was sucking as hard as the first time and she was moaning with the pleasure of it.

When he lifted his head, his belly clenched again. Her nipples gleamed in the firelight and she must have licked her lower lip because it was wet, too. God. He kissed that little pillow, running his tongue over it until she opened for him.

Her trust was blowing his mind.

And now he needed to see how much further it would go. With hands on her shoulders, he laid her back on the cushions. Her lashes were dark crescents on the flush-pink of her cheeks. He rubbed at that bothersome worry line on her forehead with his thumb.

She caught his hand, and eyes still closed, brought it to her mouth. She kissed the pad, and something inside him jerked tight, pulling his heart toward his throat. "Cookie, cookie, cookie," he said, his voice rough. "You have some lethal moves."

She made a little sound—a laugh? a protest?—but then

turned voiceless as he pulled his hand from her mouth to draw his damp thumb along the waistline of her skirt, an inch below her belly button.

Her muscles quivered, and her bottom shifted on the cushions. "I've been wanting this since the first moment I met you," he said.

"No way," she whispered. "The first moment you met me you wanted to go back to bed."

"With you."

"That came later." Her hips shifted as he traced that line across her belly again. "After I made coffee."

"You make me sound so easy," he complained, locating the zipper at the side of her skirt. It made a little hiss as he slid it open.

He saw a sliver of her eyes again between her lashes. "But are you hard, Jay? Are you really hard?"

What she was asking was obvious. He slid her skirt off her legs and tossed it to the floor. Silky green panties covered her pussy, and he stared at the magic vee while he yanked off his shirt. Then he insinuated himself between her thighs, loving the feeling of them widening for him. He pressed his jean-covered cock to her sweet spot and rocked.

"What's that tell you?" he asked.

She sighed, her legs opening more. "That I'm not your pity . . . you know."

"The only pitiful one has been me." He smoothed his palm up the inside of her thigh, pulling it up and out so it rested against the back of the couch. "Thinking for so long you wanted Rosie O'Donnell instead of me."

A smile flickered over her mouth and he bent his head to taste it. The kiss went hot and deep, one of those day-long things that he didn't remember giving to or getting from any other woman but Nikki. It made heat roll down his spine and then spiral around his ribs, constricting his chest until he couldn't breathe.

He tore his mouth from hers and then, laughing at himself, dove for another taste of the same. He palmed the sleek skin of her inner thigh, then snaked his forefinger beneath the elastic leg opening of her panties. She was wet.

Oh, thank God. She was swollen and hot and very, very wet.

He kissed the corners of her mouth, then her chin, then he dipped lower to bathe each nipple again. Nikki was flushed and panting and he had to chuckle when she yanked him up by the hair so that they were chest to chest once more. She rubbed her breasts against him, twisting side to side.

The scent of vanilla and the creamier fragrance of her aroused sex rose in the room as his head fell back and he slid his finger into her body. It was a tight fit as her inner muscles clamped on his intrusion and he stilled, looking quickly to her face. As before, her eyes were closed.

Her lip pushed out in that irritated pout. "Jay, Jay, I want to feel more of you."

He rubbed his chest against her body, circled his finger inside her snug channel. "Right here, cookie."

"Right *now*. I told you I like it fast."

Since she couldn't see him, he rolled his own eyes. "Nik—"

"Look, sometimes I'm a little slow to warm up . . ."

He was pretty sure she was smokin' now.

"But then when I want it, I want it."

Safe place, safe partner, he reminded himself with a sigh. "Your wish is my command." He would do it her way. And since there had to be steam coming off his own skin, he pushed away to shuck the rest of his clothes. From the back of the drawer in the coffee table, he pulled a stash of condoms from a cardboard playing cards case. A bachelor's trick in a home often visited by family.

Rolling on the rubber, he glanced over and saw she'd somehow dispensed with her panties. The only thing between him and heaven was a little thatch of golden-brown curls, and the sight sent more flames licking over his flesh.

He lowered himself to her body again and her arms came around him. Her palms swept along his back and he shuddered against the soft touch. Her knees lifted and he slid farther into the cradle between her thighs.

"Now, Jay," his chef with benefits ordered. Her hands pulled on his hips.

And Christ, what was he waiting for? Lifted on his elbows, he placed his cock at the entrance of her body, and let her arousal bathe the throbbing head for a moment. "Ah, cookie, this feels so good." Then he bent his head for another kiss as he let his weight carry him in.

The fit was tight at first—too tight. He shifted back, shifted in, and this time she opened to him on a gasp and a groaning sigh that sent an answering arrow of heat rocketing up his spine. Her hot inner walls closed around him and his cock pulsed against the wet, velvety tissue as he breathed through that first blaze of pleasure.

But there was more to do. His hands cradled her face as he took up a gentle rhythm. He watched Nikki's expression—those eyes of hers still closed, that worry line still present—but the deeper flush across her cheekbones and her clutching hands gave away her growing excitement.

She bit her bottom lip and lifted her hips to his, fueling the lust inside him. He tamped down the urge to move with more speed and more roughness by mentally chanting his new little mantra. *Safe place for Nikki, safe partner for Nikki. Safe place for Nikki, safe partner for Nikki.*

Even with those words at the forefront of his mind, his hips pistoned, each stroke driving deeper. Nikki's legs twined around his hips, her inner thighs sleek and hot against his skin.

He gritted his teeth, holding on.

Safe place for Nikki. Safe partner for Nikki.

The words rolled around in his head, but desire was having its way with him, driving him toward release. On his next downstroke, he nipped at her bottom lip and she jerked upward, seating them together that last crucial bit. They groaned together.

The heat between them burned. Nikki was breathing hard now, her eyes squeezed so tight there was a fan of

lines at each corner. That unease poked at him again, jar-
ring him out of his rhythm. He glanced down, saw the flush
of pre-orgasm spreading across her pretty breasts.

Her nipples were hard and bright, making him so hungry to come that he could barely breathe. "Oh, this is so
good, baby. So good. Are you close?"

Her eyes squeezed tighter. "Yes. Yes. Almost there. Go,
um, go on ahead."

His hips hitched again. Jay stilled for a moment, then
shit, it dawned on him. She thought he'd been prepared to
take his pleasure and leave her behind.

"I can help you, baby." He was feeling more than a little
annoyed. What kind of selfish dude did she consider him?
"I was planning on doing my part here."

"Huh?" Complete confusion.

Oh, geez. Like missionary alone could easily get a girl
off. Though he'd figured it out himself years ago, *NYFM*
ran articles on sex every month and at least six times a year
busted that myth. And yeah, that was a men's magazine,
but didn't women ever talk amongst themselves? Say, during that knitting night thing?

Surely some grandmother type, while stitching a lace
cap or something, could take it upon herself to expound on
the benefits of clitoral stimulation?

Though still embedded in Nikki's sweet, hot pussy, he
lifted to his knees. Her thighs fell open. He brought two
fingers to his mouth, licked the pads, then stretched them
toward the swollen button that needed a more direct touch
to send her flying.

Her eyes still closed, Nikki clenched around his cock.
"Jay?" Her voice sounded strained and she tightened on
him again. "*Jay*?"

His hand halted as more pieces of the puzzle sorted
themselves. The closed eyes, the desperate body language,
not to mention the expression she wore that was more like
someone getting through something, rather than someone
getting off.

"Baby. Nikki. Do you know how to come?"

"What?" Her eyes opened to the merest slits. "Yes. Of course."

Liar.

"Do what I say." He lifted her hand to her mouth. "Wet your fingers."

She hesitated.

He touched them to her lips. "Wet your fingers."

Her pink tongue emerged and his body reacted, pushing forward with a shallow thrust as the twin sacks between his legs tightened. He swallowed his groan. "Wetter. Stick out your tongue and get them really wet."

Watching her do as instructed was punishment for any prior bad acts, he swore to God. He panted through it, and when two of Nikki's fingers gleamed with moisture, he drew back, then pushed himself into her body at the same time that he brought her hand down to her clitoris.

She gasped. Her body arched. He thrust again as he directed her fingers. A circle. A short stroke. Another circle.

Another thrust.

Oh, God. It was incredible. Unbelievable. The memory of every damn sexcapade in his past faded against this—of feeling Nikki, of tutoring Nikki, of watching her face as the pleasure moved beyond good to better, to soooo damn close.

That's what she was saying with those little sounds from the back of her throat. *So close.* And he lapped up every passionate noise and every amazing change to her face, free to watch her like a freakin' voyeur because he could, because she had her eyes squeezed shut again.

It was oddly freeing to realize he didn't need to worry about keeping his cool, even as the top of his head was getting ready to blow from watching this woman learn how to get herself off with his help.

He pulled out of her, all the way to the tip, mesmerized by the wet gloss of her arousal on his shaft. Then he moved in again, watching her body swallow him as his dark, big hand made her smaller one play again with that upstanding bud at the top of her cleft. His spine tingled as his balls drew tight.

"Jay?"

Oh, Christ. She wanted to talk? He didn't have any words left, not when it was all he could do to keep himself from exploding right this instant. Yet he found his voice. "Cookie."

Okay, just the one word.

"*Jay?*"

And then he smiled, because he realized what she wanted. "Go ahead, cookie. Go ahead and come."

And he pulled out again and then moved deep, his gaze trained on her face. She quivered, lifting into his thrust, and as he watched her body start to tremble, her eyes flew open.

His cock erupted. His heart shook like an earthquake. The hand that wasn't on hers grasped the back of the sofa to ride out the rocking and rolling world and all the while he was conscious of not only the incredible, screaming pleasure, but that blue and that green pair of *bruja* eyes.

I don't know whether I'm going to sink or fly.

When it was over—minutes? months? later—as his heart continued to thunder, he pulled away and turned her on her side, making room for both of them on the couch. She wiggled against him and he slid his fingers, still damp from her, against the warmth of her flank. She sighed.

Contented?

God, he hoped so. God, he hoped he'd given her what she needed.

Safe place. Safe partner.

But now that it was done, now that his blood was still running like a drug through his veins, he had to wonder whether Nikki was safe at all.

For him.

Thirteen

I cried on my eighteenth birthday. I thought seventeen was such a nice age. You're young enough to get away with things, but you're old enough, too.

—LIV TYLER,
ACTRESS

Fern tossed the steaming brownie from hand to hand, cooling it before biting it in two. It melted on her tongue and bathed her back molars in grainy chocolate before she swallowed it down. Even as she popped the other half in her mouth, she was already reaching for a second straight out of the pan.

Beside her on the bed, Marie was closing her eyes in dreamy appreciation of the undercooked dessert they'd pulled out of the oven ten minutes too soon. "The gooiest ones in the middle are my favorite," she said. "Better than sex."

"Really?" Too late, Fern realized she'd spoken the question out loud.

Marie's eyes widened and her hand paused, a brownie halfway to her mouth. "You and Jenner?"

The *Veronica Mars* marathon they were watching on TV switched away to commercials and Fern pretended to care about the latest hair remover. After all, she wore short shorts.

With her French-pedicured big toe, Marie nudged Fern's ankle. "You can't leave it like that. I figured . . ."

Fern shook her head, still watching the long-legged girl on the screen dance under a disco ball. The guy watching her spin looked as if he wanted to lick her bare limbs like a Popsicle. *Eww*.

Marie wasn't letting the subject go. "Not with *anyone*?"

Again, Fern shook her head, then pinched her thigh as punishment. Stupid self. How could she have been so careless as to give that much away?

Except she wasn't careless. She never had been. That was part of the whole problem. Now that she was feeling just a little bit careless and a whole lot reckless, there wasn't a single Two Shoe available to discuss it with—at least not one who she could talk to about the subject of sex.

Marie might have to do.

She sent the other teenager a sidelong look as she reached for the pan again. "What about you?"

The girl waved her brownie, scattering chocolate crumbs on the paper napkin she'd spread over her lap. "Sure. I had a boyfriend at the end of last year. He moved in June, though. Las Vegas."

Fern picked up her own napkin and started pleating it into an origami shape she thought she remembered learning in fourth grade summer day camp. "Jenner wants me to sneak out and meet him tonight."

An hour ago, Marie had braided her hair into a dozen dark tails and now the rubber-banded ends flew out as she whipped her head toward Fern. "Tonight?"

The brownies no longer seemed so irresistible to Fern. Her stomach twisted, protesting the chocolate rush—or at least that's what she told herself it was protesting—and she pushed the pan closer to Marie. "I haven't decided."

"He's gorgeous," the other girl said, digging free another chewy square. "And there's plenty of other girls willing to give it up to him if you won't."

"Marie!" Fern frowned. "Didn't you outgrow that

argument freshman year? We don't give it up for a guy just because if we don't, we'll lose him."

"It's true, though." Marie peeled off a piece of the brownie's shiny top and then licked it off her thumb. "Guys are like that."

"Not all guys—"

"Yep. Pretty much all guys. Think about it. You're a raging male hormone. On the one hand, you have that nice girl with her legs crossed tighter than a pretzel. On the other, you have that nice girl who isn't holding out for . . . what are girls holding out for anyway?"

"Nice girls don't—"

Marie looked up. "Just because a girl has sex doesn't make her a slut."

"I know." Fern thought she wanted sex, and that wasn't so much different than actually having it, right? They'd read about former President Jimmy Carter in Advanced Placement U.S. History last year. He'd shocked the American public by admitting he lusted in his heart for women other than his wife.

Okay, so Carter was president like a hundred years ago—not a hundred, but way before Habitat for Humanity became the look-at-me-hammer charity for rock stars and rappers—but people probably still considered that heart lust thing this close to doing the deed itself.

So if what she felt in Jenner's arms was what she thought—well, there was no sweet-faced Rosalynn to keep Fern from taking her lust out of the four-chambered organ in her chest and putting it into real action.

There was no Rosalynn, but there was Emily.

Fern closed her eyes, trying not to think of her best friend. Normally, she'd never take such a step like this without her best buddy's full and serious consideration, but nothing about Em was ever going to be normal again.

Fern's mom said that wasn't true, but her mom hadn't seen Em's lank hair or the weird fortress of books she'd built on the tables on each side of the bed in her room.

Fairy tales, Harry Potter, a slew of Nancy Drew mysteries that had once been her mother's. The rest of Em's summer, apparently, was going to be spent rereading all her favorite children's books.

While maybe the rest of Fern's summer was going to be spent finding out what it was to be a woman.

She looked up at Marie. "Didn't we become women when we got our periods? Didn't they tell us that?"

"They should have told us not to buy any more white jeans," Marie grumbled. She was close to finishing half the pan of brownies. "Hey! Maybe that's why I have the munchies. I'm expecting a visit from my 'little friend.' "

They both started laughing. "No one calls it that anymore, do they?" Fern asked.

"My mom does." Marie made a face. "But only in front of my dad. And now that you're horribly cruel enough to make me remember, that *is* exactly what she said when I had my first magic moment of cramps. She told my dad I was a woman now. Where was that hole in the floor when I needed it?"

"So, was she right? Or is it having sex that makes you a woman?"

And what about Em? At home with her unicorns and witches and Nancy's mysteries: Was she a woman now?

"I'd rather have sex than my period, that's for sure."

"But you'd rather have brownies than sex," Fern pointed out.

Marie stilled, going silent for a moment. "It's true. Do you think there's something wrong with me?"

Fern laughed at Marie's aghast expression. "I don't think so. Maybe there was something wrong with your old boyfriend."

Maybe he hadn't awakened Marie, and then continued to keep her from sleeping night after night with thoughts of what could be. Jenner had done that to Fern. One of the four Two Shoes had come to Malibu for the summer, ashamed that she was almost happy to get away from Em, but not expecting any more than lazy days and nights at the beach. At home, she'd dated on occasion. Been kissed more than once and felt that wild rush of blood around her body when a boy hesitantly stroked her breasts.

But nothing before had ever lit her up like Jenner's touch. Everything about him was rough—his hands, calloused from beach volleyball, scraping along her sunburned shoulders; the metal grommets in his boardshorts poking into her belly when he rolled on top of her on the sand; those biting kisses he hid beneath her hair.

It should have been something she backed away from. Good-girl Fern had been born with warning flags that shot up whenever necessary. But Em was good, too, and she'd possessed those exact same warning flags, and they hadn't saved her from danger. Maybe this time Fern needed to fling herself toward her fears as a test—a test to make sure she could save herself if it came to that.

But right now, Jenner's kisses didn't feel like something she needed to be saved from—that was the most amazing thing to her. All those tepid touches from high school boys who smelled like Tommy Boy cologne and Speed Stick deodorant couldn't compare to one moment in Jenner's arms. What happened there was indescribable, when their skin was hot, their swimsuits cold and wet, his mouth burning like a beach bonfire on hers.

He could make her crazy with wanting more: kisses, touches, *everything*. He could slide a finger up her knee toward her thigh and her legs would turn to rubber. He could press her hand over the hard length of him beneath his pants and she didn't think it was gross—instead she wanted to know what happened next.

The fact was, *he* wanted what happened next, and Marie was right, she'd probably lose him and all that he represented if she didn't soon say "yes."

She glanced over at her friend, who looked about twelve with her hair in those silly braids and chocolate on her mouth. "Will you cover for me if I go out to meet Jenner?"

"You wouldn't rather make another pan of brownies?"

He'd been angry when she'd told him she didn't know if

she could sneak out to meet him tonight, and that passionate display only made her heart pound harder. She didn't know exactly why.

When they were kids, she and her cousins would sit at the table after a family dinner was over and see who could hold their palms the longest over the candle flames. Fern had run to her mother way before the others were finished with the game.

She wasn't running anymore.

Jay woke, in one instant aware of the sunshine on the other side of his eyelids and the empty spot on the other side of his bed. His hand groped over the barren sheets anyway.

None of Nikki's body warmth lingered, and at the discovery, some emotion rushed into his chest. It should have been relief—he preferred waking up alone, even after spectacular sex. It couldn't be alarm—Nikki wouldn't have gone far . . . would she?

But then whatever you wanted to label that weird emotion leached away as the blessed aroma of brewing coffee reached him. If she'd run, it was only to his kitchen. He smiled to himself and stretched his toes toward the end of the bed, and let his mind wander.

It didn't go far either. It stayed right where he was and imagined Nikki returning to the bedroom, carrying a cup of his favorite java and naked as the day she'd come into the world. His hand slid down to his morning erection and he rubbed over his hot skin, envisioning the imminent possibility of A.M. sex.

Then he laughed out loud. When had Nikki ever fallen in with his plans? He'd bet a hundred bucks she'd gotten up and made coffee as his chef, not his lover, and would expect him to get his lazy ass out of bed to sample it.

Still, she had to be looking forward to that moment as much as he was. She'd taste like coffee and toothpaste—his, and he oddly liked the idea of that—when he kissed her.

Would she melt against him or try to keep her cool? He couldn't guess, and that made him grin wider.

Unpredictable, prickly, sexy as hell. That was Nikki. Last night he'd half-carried her to his bed and she'd fallen back to sleep the moment her head hit the pillow. He'd walk over leftover barbecue coals before he'd admit it out loud, but even as horny as he'd been again, he'd let her stay in dreamland, merely putting his nose against her shoulder to breathe in the scent of her skin.

Christ, even to himself that sounded dangerously sappy.

And only made him want to breathe in her scent once again.

He sure as hell wasn't going to rush out to the kitchen though, he decided, opening his eyes and casting a look at his bedside clock. He'd lie in bed at least another fifteen minutes, follow that up with a leisurely shower, and *then* he'd venture outside the bedroom to take a gander at Nikki's morning-after attitude.

In seven minutes he was in jeans and a T-shirt. He didn't waste time locating shoes before he bare-footed it out of the bedroom and started down the hallway. The coffee smelled just that enticing.

Yeah. The coffee.

Okay, fine. He was curious about Nikki's reaction to their intimacy of the night before. Concerned even, now that his brain was becoming more alert. That was only natural, right? Every time he went to bed with a woman there was that possibility he'd made a big mistake—no matter how hot the mambo had been.

Look at Shanna.

Nikki was nothing like Shanna.

The drunken debacle that was his single stupid interlude with Shanna was nothing like what he'd had with Nikki last night.

Shit! He halted, sudden airlessness forcing him to lean against the wall. That unfamiliar, unnameable feeling was filling his chest again, making it hard for his lungs to move. Alarm?

It felt more like freakin' panic.

With a wet-dog shake of his head, he got his feet moving again. Coffee and a clue about how Nikki was reacting would surely get his equilibrium back.

Voices from the kitchen had him pausing once more. Nikki. Nikki and Cassandra. He moved again, and then hesitated at the far end of the living room, close enough to see and hear the women, but far enough away that he escaped their notice.

Nikki was at the cutting board, giving him a side view. She must keep an extra set of clothes somewhere in his house, he thought. He took in her cropped jeans and the plain white T-shirt that clung tightly enough for him to appreciate that sweet little sway in her back that he'd—damn it all—left untouched the night before. He could only see the profile of her face, but she seemed cheerful enough.

That whatever-you-wanted-to-call-it loosened its vicious grip on his breathing as he continued to study her. Her wavy hair was contained in a cotton bandanna she'd tied beneath the sun-and-brown mass at the base of her neck. The ocean-green color contrasted with the warm pink of her cheek. It would match, he knew, the unforgettable color of her left eye.

"So you grew up knowing you were the product of artificial insemination?" Nikki asked, her attention still on the mango—his favorite—she was slicing.

Jay watched her lips move with each word and he remembered the soft feel of them under his, the heat hidden inside her mouth, the sweet touch of her tongue against his. At the memory, an echo of that euphoric high he'd felt last night seemed to thin the blood in his veins. His head took an odd spin, and he put his hand on the back of the couch to steady himself.

Cassandra was talking now. She had knitting needles in her hands, but for the moment they were still. Jay told himself he wouldn't have eavesdropped if it wasn't something she'd already revealed to him before—and if he wasn't so damn dizzy. ". . . never thought of keeping it a secret any more than she thought the two of us required a man. To her, it was more a matter of feminism than family. She wanted to prove we two women didn't need a man."

A smile flashed over Nikki's face. "Makes you wonder what she would have done if you were born a boy."

The knitting needles started clicking. Cassandra bent her head and Jay studied her profile, blinking. There was something . . .

"I wondered for a long time if I had a brother," she said.

"What?" Nikki glanced over her shoulder at the other woman. "Your mother had another—"

"No. The sperm donor. When I was a kid, I often wondered if one of my classmates, or maybe a little kid I saw being pushed on a playground swing was really my half-sibling, because another woman had also used that same donor."

"I used to imagine I was the princess of an exotic country who'd been adopted by my parents in order to save me from a dastardly plot to overthrow the royal court. There was more than one long summer afternoon when I expected an envoy to come and retrieve me to my rightful throne."

Cassandra laughed a little. "I see. So, you didn't feel you entirely . . . belonged with your mom and dad?"

Nikki's shoulders gave a little shrug. "Doesn't every kid at some time or another? After my mom died, well, my dad wasn't very demonstrative and I took a short but self-destructive path, hoping to belong to someone—anyone. Bad mistake. After that I learned to be independent. Parents, siblings, who needs 'em? I have myself, my cooking, my fish."

Her plastic fish. Jay tightened his grip on the sofa. She was doing it again. Killing him. He knew all about her need to belong and how hellishly that had worked out for her.

His Nikki, so independent because who she should have been able to count on had not been there for her. His Nikki, who didn't even know that she needed . . . she needed . . .

Not him.

She wasn't "his."

What had happened last night, he reminded himself, was

nothing more meaningful than dozens of other nights he'd experienced. She was not any more special than other women with whom he'd scratched that same particular itch.

He hoped to God Nikki understood that, but if she wanted to turn it into something bigger and brighter, well, he had practice in making clear it had been nothing more than Wally Weasel's drive for nonspecific-woman sex.

Even if that meant he was destined to lose out on that morning repeat he'd been hankering for. Striding for the kitchen, he was determined to set things straight.

". . . I'm not the only one curious about possible brothers and sisters," Cassandra was saying. "Donor sibling registries are cropping up on the Internet, and it's not that hard, with a little digging, to discover—"

She broke off as Jay rounded the breakfast bar.

"Ladies. Good morning." His voice sounded clipped and he kept his eye on the prize—Nikki. He steeled himself for her reaction. If she cuddled up to him, he was going to be firm and set very certain boundaries.

Her swift glance at his face revealed nothing. Neither did her silent move toward the coffeemaker. In seconds, he had a mug of coffee in hand.

And she was back to her mango. "I'm sorry, Cassandra. You were saying . . . ?"

"Um . . ." The other woman rose to her feet, sending Jay an odd look. "I think I'd better be going."

"Oh. Okay," Nikki said. "I'll walk you to the door." Strolling past him, she followed Cassandra toward the entry.

Leaving him barefoot, barely caffeinated, and alone with his morning-after anxiety.

Nikki wasn't cuddling up to him.

Nikki wasn't making more out of the oh-good-God-wasn't-it-incredible they'd done together last night.

Nikki wasn't doing a single thing that set his alarm bells ringing.

And the fact that it bugged the shit out of him that she didn't made them finally start to clamor.

Fourteen

Nikki dawdled on her way back to the kitchen. Maybe by the time she returned to her half-made fruit salad, the bachelor by the coffeemaker would have taken himself away.

But there he was, looking more golden and gorgeous than one man had a right to be. His hair hung over his brow as he frowned down at his coffee.

"Careful, handsome," she said, breezing past him. "Your face might get stuck in that ugly expression."

The legs of one of the bar stools scraped against the floor as he seated himself. She sliced through the middle of a cantaloupe and gutted it onto a paper towel. Then, taking a breath, she turned to face him.

Leaning against the counter, she gripped it with both hands. "I could go for balls this morning. What do you think?"

His head jerked up. His gaze slammed into hers. "Huh?"

"Balls? I'm in the mood."

"*What?*"

She snickered, doing her best to be that tough babe she only wanted him to see. "*Melon* balls. Get your mind out of the gutter, dude."

"That's not where my mind's been playing, cookie," he retorted, his eyes narrowing. His thumb gestured over his shoulder, toward the sofa. "It hasn't had to go that far."

The blush crawling up her neck was *not* allowed to make it as far as her face. "Oh? Well then, I'll go ahead and give you good marks on your performance. Thanks and all that."

He stared at her. " 'Thanks and all that?' That's it? That's what you have to say?"

Putting one hand on her hip, she heaved a big sigh. Okay, so he'd given her the first orgasm of her life, but she couldn't let him see how deeply the memory of it was imprinted on her brain. He wouldn't want to know the brand he'd left on her and how she savored even the faint soreness between her legs.

"You're not one of those, are you?" she asked. "A rehasher?"

When he didn't answer, she continued on, babbling as if she knew what she was talking about. "Fine. I'll play Monday morning quarterback with you. That's what all your *NYFM* readers would call this, right? Sure, some of the plays could have gone more smoothly and the defense didn't do their job until late in the eleventh inning, but the offense was a well-practiced machine, showing the benefit of its many years of experience in the big leagues and deserving of its stellar reputation and many Super Bowl pennants."

He sipped at his coffee. "I hope you recorded all that for posterity in your diary, cookie. I might want to go over it again—you know, for those days when my ego needs to be stroked by such a sports expert as you."

"Oh, no. Sorry, but diaries are reserved for the diarist only—and her BFF, of course."

"Don't tell me—"

"Best Friend Forever." She whipped back around to go to work on the melon.

He was so annoyingly quiet that she didn't realize he'd moved until she felt his hands mold her hips. "Who is your BFF?" he said. His warm breath stirred the small hairs at her temple that had escaped her bandanna. "Who do you let get that close?"

"You shouldn't sneak up on a woman wielding a knife," she warned, willing her feet to root in the floor and her spine to stay as straight as steel. It was difficult, when everything female he'd found so deep inside of her now flared again and was insisting that she move back and nestle against the comfort of his body and heat of his sex. "As a matter of fact, why don't you go about what it is you usually go about doing and I'll call you when your breakfast is ready."

"I don't have anything that needs to be done."

"Yeah? Well then, Narcissus, your reflection is probably lonely. Go give your mirror some company."

His fingers slid up to her waist. "Narcissus? Wasn't he cursed to fall in love with his own beauty because of his callousness toward his lovers?"

Nikki couldn't keep still any longer. She slid away from Jay's hands and edged toward the refrigerator. "I didn't mean it like that."

"What did you mean it like then?" He grabbed her elbow and turned her, pushing her back against the brushed steel of the appliance and pushing his hips against hers. He was aroused, his erection pressing against the pad of her sex.

Immediately, she softened everywhere, getting warm, too warm. The skin south of her navel started to throb. But they'd had their one-night stand! She was supposed to be back in her metaphoric combat boots this morning. She pressed her palms to his chest, struggling to think, and to think of something to make him back away. "You're . . . you're scaring me."

"Liar." He crowded closer, his gaze dropping from her mouth to her throat. "I can see your pulse racing, cookie."

She could *feel* her pulse racing, driving the urge for another round of sex through every cell of her body. Last night she'd insisted on doing it because she couldn't bear him viewing her as a victim. *Never let them think you're weak.* But this desire presented different dangers.

"Hef, honey—"

"Stop that." His eyes narrowed. "Don't make it like that."

"Like what?" She was desperate here, desperate to remember that last night's intimacy didn't connect them in any way that she couldn't easily break. "Like what was it to you?"

He opened his mouth. Closed it. Took a breath, then backed away. "Damn it," he muttered.

A chill rushed across her skin at the loss of his heat. She turned to open the refrigerator and then stared at the shelves, trying to remember what she was after.

Peace. That's what she wanted. A little peace and space to absorb the fact that she wasn't necessarily a frigid freak, doomed to fake orgasms for the rest of her sorry life. The truth was, she wanted to fling herself into Jay's arms and kiss his face a thousand times for giving her something no other man had . . . and that she'd never been able to give herself.

It didn't take a genius to determine why sex had been a struggle in the past . . . but knowing the source of her hang-ups and overcoming them were two separate things. However, she couldn't let gratitude fool her into imagining a bond neither of them wanted.

So just to be on the safe side, she planned on never touching him again.

"Nikki—"

"Go away, Jay." There was little fight left in her right now.

From behind her, she felt the air move and then he was playing with her hair. Goose bumps rolled down her neck as he twisted a piece around his finger—ominous image, that. Nikki pressed a forearm over her tightening nipples, desperate for him not to see how sexually defenseless she was to him.

"Nikki . . ."

Weak Nikki. Weak Nikki who turned into his body and lifted her face. It was an invitation to a kiss, she knew that, he knew that. His hand slid to the small of her back and pulled her closer as his mouth came down—

—and the telephone sitting on the nearby countertop rang.

The brash sound brought common sense crashing back. Nikki made to move from his hold, but his hand tightened on her even as the other reached for the receiver. "We're not through," he said.

But they were! They were!

He held the phone to his ear. "Hello?" As he listened, his hand slipped off her back.

Relieved of his touch, Nikki quickly stepped away.

"She's not? You're sure? When?"

At the sharp note in Jay's voice, Nikki stepped back to him, reaching out to grasp his forearm. "What? Who?"

He was off the phone after two more terse sentences. "Damn it," he said. "That was Marie's mom. Fern isn't there. According to Marie, she left last night and didn't return."

Nikki's stomach twisted, images of the beach party unspooling in her mind. "Do you think she went back to Zuma?"

"Doubt it. I guarantee the cops were on their way to breaking that up."

"Oh, God. *Jay*. What could have happened? Where could she be?"

"You're white as a ghost." He pulled her into his arms and she rested her cheek against the steady thump of his heart. "Don't think the worst."

"There was booze at that party. She could have been drinking."

His arms tightened on her. "Fern wouldn't do that."

"What if Jenner wanted her to?" Nikki knew her voice

was rising, but she couldn't seem to calm herself. "What if he handed her the drinks in order to loosen her up? Some of that stuff, you have to know, Jay, some of that stuff is tasteless. They mix it with Gatorade or fruit juice and then . . ."

"Fuck." Jay pushed her away and looked down into her face.

Nikki could see he didn't want to believe her. "I know what it's like. I know how a girl can get caught up trying to please the boy who makes her feel like someone special."

"*Fuck*." His fingers tightened on her upper arms, stopping just short of pain as his voice rose. "Damn it, Nikki, is that how it started? Is that what happened to . . . to your 'friend'? Her Romeo got her drunk as his idea of foreplay?"

"It doesn't matter what happened then. Fern matters now."

"Both of you matter. Then. Now." He spun away from her and shoved his fingers through his hair. "I don't know how to do this. I don't know what 'this' is."

Nikki ran a soothing hand down his back and tried calming her own concern. "It's worry over Fern. Let's think—"

"Worry over me, why?" Fern's voice.

"*Fern*." Both Nikki and Jay whipped around to face the teenager. Wearing a pair of baggy pajama bottoms printed with smiling seashells and a matching short-sleeved tee, she was staring at them, her hair pillow-tousled.

She blinked, then headed for the counter where she nabbed a piece of mango to pop into her mouth. "What's the matter with you guys?"

"You were supposed to spend the night at Marie's," Jay ground out, the muscles beneath Nikki's hand tight.

"I came back."

"Without telling Marie or her mom."

Fern shrugged. "Whoops."

Jay's spine snapped straighter. " 'Whoops?' That's all you have to say? And how'd you get here in the middle of the night anyway?"

"You're not my father." The teenager focused on the cutting board and scooped up another piece of fruit.

Her cousin's voice lowered and lost any semblance of its usual laid-back style. "But I'm in charge of you and I won't hesitate to call Uncle George if necessary. I don't care that your parents are on their anniversary cruise with mine. Got that? You answer my questions or I will call your father."

Fern's gaze jumped to Jay's. "You wouldn't—"

"I will." His face was grim. "How'd you get here?"

After a tense moment, her eyes dropped and her shoulders slumped. "Jenner, okay? He picked me up at Marie's and then brought me here."

"I'm going to talk to that kid—"

"Don't." Fern looked more desperate than defiant now. "Please. I'm not seeing him anymore. We broke up last night."

"Oh, Fern." Nikki's hand slid away from Jay as she took a step toward the teen. "Are you all right?"

"I'm fine." She turned to open a cabinet and pull out a mug. "Even better if you'll show me how to make one of your famous mochas."

Nikki stared at the bruise just peeking from beneath the sleeve of the girl's shirt, her stomach clenching. But Jenner was out of Fern's life now, she told herself, so she swallowed her concern and moved to start the drink.

Scowling, Jay stayed planted in the middle of the kitchen, his arms crossed over his chest, necessitating that the two of them walk around him. Finally, Fern slanted him a glance. "Get out of the way, Jay. And what's with all the third degree, anyhow?"

"Somebody's got to be the adult."

"Well, that wouldn't be you," Fern scoffed.

"Gee, thanks."

"Admit it," the girl continued. "You're the family's Peter Pan."

He jerked back. "What?"

Fern spooned whipped cream on top of her mocha. "You heard me. The boy who never grew up."

Nikki busied herself with the rinds of fruit, though she couldn't miss the curse he muttered under his breath as he strode for the back door. The slider slammed behind him.

Four seconds later he was back, his feet shoved in a pair of ratty deck shoes that usually spent their day on the back porch. "I'm outta here." He grabbed his car keys from the abalone shell on the counter.

"But breakfast—"

"Don't worry about it. This morning I'll be getting mine in Neverland."

Then he was gone again. Fern wandered away shortly after that. Nikki stood alone in the kitchen, breathing in the quiet.

She was supposed to be glad, she thought. She'd wanted to be alone this morning. Except the two cousins had left her with a half-prepared breakfast and enough emotional leftovers that guaranteed her anything but peace.

Jay realized speeding off in a huff didn't make him appear any more adult, but for God's sake, the women in his house were making him nuts. They'd turned his comfortable bachelor pad on Billionaire's Beach into an active minefield of indecipherable reactions and insulting accusations.

Peter Fucking Pan.

He noticed that Nikki hadn't leaped to his defense. No, sir. She'd just stood there, her crazy-making eyes glued to the countertop while his cousin—his teenaged cousin—stripped the skin off his bones.

No wonder he'd made his escape to Neverland . . . uh, farther north in Malibu. But hell, it wasn't so much different from that imaginary world, when he thought about it. The near-fantasy natural surroundings, the surfers who were obvious stand-ins for both the Pirates and the Lost Boys, the dozens of Mermaids wandering the beaches in their bikinis and flip-flops.

He rolled down his window and let the salty breeze mix

with the air-conditioning, his head bursting with all that had happened in his first hour of the morning.

Nikki's nonreaction to their night before.

Their fleeting concern over the missing Fern.

His chef delivering a blow to his heart: "Some of that stuff, you have to know, Jay, some of that stuff is tasteless. They mix it with Gatorade or fruit juice and then . . ."

His snot of a cousin finishing him off: "You're the family's Peter Pan."

Christ. No wonder he was desperate to escape that house. More caffeine and male companionship were what he required to restore order back to his life. To regain the simplicity he craved.

He pulled into the parking lot of Gabe's café a few minutes later. At this time of day, late morning, it was too early for the mixed-sex lunch crowd. Now, the patrons were most likely to be all-male—day laborers eating *almuerzo* because they started work at dawn, or starving surf dudes just in from their first go at the waves.

The coffee he ordered at the counter came quick and its heat burned his palm through the foam cup. He inhaled the bitter scent and the greasier one of the fish and chips the guy in front of him had purchased. Then he turned toward the L-shaped seating area, looking for an empty spot among the crowd of occupied white plastic tables and chairs.

"Jay!" The voice's gender was already an unhappy prospect. But when he looked in its direction, he couldn't avoid Cassandra's come-hither wave. "Over here."

Putting a polite mask on the beast he felt inside, he threaded his way toward her. Maybe she just wanted to say hello.

Yeah. Because that's just the way his luck was going. Everything his way, and it wasn't going to take an act of Congress to get Nikki back into his bed tonight.

Wait—was that what he wanted? Nikki for more than just one night?

But that wouldn't simplify anything, he knew, and he shoved the notion from his mind as Cassandra gestured to the chair beside hers and shut the laptop that had been open on the table. "Keep me company," she said.

He shrugged, accepting his fate. Why not? Sure, she was female, but he'd always found her one of the more restful sorts. And that's what he needed. A few quiet moments to get his head together.

She smiled as he settled into the plastic chair and moved her own steaming, capped cup away from the table's edge. "I didn't get to say much to you earlier this morning."

"You looked as if you had places to go and people to see."

"People I thought to see, anyway. I'm hoping to catch up with Gabe here this morning. It's his usual payroll day. But . . ."

"But?"

With both hands, she pushed her long fall of hair over her shoulders. "But Gabe has an annoying habit of going AWOL."

Another voice joined the discussion. "AWOL assumes I have someone I'm required to report to."

Ah, the person in question. Both Jay and Cassandra glanced up, and Jay couldn't help but wince. The other man looked like a walking bender: His black hair was uncombed, his dark, five-o'clock shadow would have been edgy two days before, but now, paired with rumpled khakis and a half-buttoned shirt, he looked like Bogey's better-looking, taller twin, just off *The African Queen.*

Gabe flopped into the chair on the other side of Jay and reached a long arm across the table to grab Cassandra's cup. He threw back his head to take a swallow, then snapped it forward again, his eyes bugging as he slammed the drink to the table. "What is that?" he choked out. "Surely we don't heat and serve lawn fertilizer."

"Herbal tea. I brought my own bag over from the shop. You provided the boiling water."

Cassandra's smile beamed sunshine, but it seemed to hurt Gabe's eyes. He squinted and half-turned his face away. "Damon," he yelled in the direction of the counter. "Bring me a quart of coffee, will you? Black and bitter."

"Just like your mood," Cassandra said, her voice as sugary as her smile was warm. "How fitting."

"We can't all be vegan and virtuous, Froot Loop," he retorted. "Christ, what the hell's wrong with you? Your cheeks are too rosy and your hair's too damn shiny. And can't you give all that smiling happiness a rest?"

His mood lightening, Jay sat back. Maybe it was perverse of him, but the battle of the sexes didn't feel so life-and-death when he watched others engaged in it as well. Hell, maybe he could take some tips from Gabe and handle Nikki just as he handled Cassandra—which was not at all, and while wearing a bewhiskered scowl.

Except Cassandra didn't appear the least put off by her landlord's ill-temper. "You promised to meet me at the Chamber of Commerce meeting last night. You weren't there."

"That was last night? No. Last night was Tuesday. Your meeting is Wednesday."

"And this is Thursday. Gabe, did you have a blackout or something?"

"No!" His scowl deepened and he looked around him, as if getting desperate. "Where's my coffee?"

Jay curled his own cup close to his chest. "I'm not sharing."

Cassandra leaned across the table. "And I'm happy to inform you you're now the chairperson of the parking committee. As those things inevitably go, in your absence, you were elected."

The other man's head swung back to pin her with his bloodshot gaze. "God damn it, Cassandra. You put my name in, I'll bet. That's not fair."

"Don't blame me. I'm the one who sent you a reminder e-mail." She shrugged. "It's not my fault you bury yourself."

"I'm not six feet under—not yet anyway, and when I go, I'm starting to think of taking you with me." He yanked her laptop toward him and flipped up the top even as she made a strangled sound of protest. "And you didn't send me an e-mail. I'll prove it."

Just then, Gabe's quart of coffee arrived. It distracted him from Cassandra's computer and as she half-rose to reclaim it, the screen bloomed with a photo of Nikki. Without thinking, Jay grabbed the other woman's wrist to stop her from shutting it down once again.

He heard Cassandra's nervous clearing of her throat. "I, um, took some pictures with my cell phone at the restaurant opening. You know, I thought I might use them to, uh, advertise the shop or my dress designs or, um . . ."

Jay barely heard her. His attention remained focused on the screen as a Nikki slide show started. It was that damn dress, he decided, that made it impossible for him to look away. He'd never fully appreciated the back view, and he could see it in this shot, one in which she was standing beside the glass wall and gazing out over the ocean.

Her hair tumbled to her shoulders, a riot of sun-shot brown, and then there were the delicate wings of her shoulder blades that his gaze bumped over on its way to that intriguing sway at her back. God! How had he missed that last night? He wanted nothing more than to bare it for his touch—to give it a raunchy roll with his cock as he sucked on that innocent spot on her nape so often left naked by her little-girl-gone-grown-up braids.

She didn't know how horny that innocuous hairstyle rendered him.

That photo dissolved too soon and another emerged. It was Nikki and he on the dance floor, their gazes locked together. He could remember that moment, his gaze focused on her mouth and how tempting her just-tongued lips looked. How ready for his kiss. In his mind that instant morphed into one from last night, when he watched her body claiming his wet cock, sliding inside her as she came.

It was back, that buzz in his blood, that incredible, druglike high he'd found when her orgasm had triggered his. No lay had ever been better for him, no matter how quick or lazy or downright dirty. No bed partner, no woman had ever fascinated him, touched him, fucked him like Nikki had.

The dance floor photo faded and he found himself reaching out for it, his fingers slipping back to the tabletop as the next one materialized. It was he and Nikki again, the two of them leaving the party, his arm around her shoulders.

Her bound to him . . . where she belonged.

And then it hit him. The euphoria he found in her body. The panic when he'd woken and she was gone from his bed. The way she had of making him so freakin' crazy.

This was it.

It.

What he'd never really understood. What he hadn't truly believed in until this moment. He couldn't have been more blown away if he'd come downstairs on Christmas morning and found a red-suited fat guy spreading presents under the tree.

His breath backed up in his lungs as he realized what had happened. Damn it.

Damn it!

Those receptors in his brain had finally opened up and he . . . he was in love with Nikki.

Prickly, independent, not-even-certain-she-liked-him Nikki Carmichael.

Could it be true? Could it be as simple as that?

That his life would never, ever be simple again?

The photo faded. The next was Nikki alone, a close-up shot that did justice to her unusual blue and green eyes, the cut of her cute nose, the red of her mouth, and the jut of her stubborn chin. Apparently Cassandra had Photoshopped the image, because now the color leached away, turning Nikki's face to stark black-and-white and giving Jay a new perspective of her looks. With his attention not so riveted on her mouth or her unusual eyes, there was something about her . . .

Something . . . familiar.

Oh, shit.

Oh. Shit.

Scattered snatches of conversation shifted in his journalist's mind, coming together in a story that he couldn't ignore or dismiss. Slowly, his gaze lifted from the screen to Cassandra's anxious face.

He scanned her chin, the shape of her bottom lip, the arch of her eyebrows. "She's your sister," he said. "Nikki's your sister."

"Donor half-sibling," Cassandra whispered. "And Jay . . . Jay, you have to promise me . . ."

He wasn't going to like this, that was a given. Just as he didn't like knowing he'd fallen head over his ass in love for the first time in over thirty years, just as he didn't like that the woman he'd fallen for was a crazy-making female who couldn't even have both eyes the same damn color like everyone else. He could never let Nikki know, he decided. He could never let her find out what she'd done to him.

"Promise me, Jay," Cassandra said. "Promise me you won't tell Nikki."

Oh, hell. And now he really didn't like the fact that he had a second secret to keep from her.

Fifteen

You must be a Lotus, unfolding its petals when the Sun rises in the sky, unaffected by the slush where it is born or even the water which sustains it!

—SAI BABA,
INDIAN RELIGIOUS FIGURE

Shanna was drowning. Her heavy limbs took her down through the saltwater that filled the Olympic-sized pool, down toward the tiled coat of arms her father had ginned up from an ancestral legacy as deep as a sheet of Kleenex. The heated water stroked like silk against her skin and she reveled in the calming sensation. Closing her eyes, she spread her arms wide and embraced the fall, sinking into the serene moment.

A muted, liquid crash made it through her water-deafened ears. Her eyes flew open, but there was only a riot of champagne bubbles in her sight and then the hard grasp of a hand on her ankle. She gasped, inhaling water, as instinct made her fight the strange touch dragging her upward.

She breached the surface, coughing and sputtering, to face the one who'd manhandled her and still continued to hold her with a firm grip on her upper arm. Jorge.

"Wha—" She couldn't get out a whole word before the coughing took over again.

His Spanish sounded more like Anglo-Saxon curses. In

two long-armed strokes, he towed her to the side, then cradled her into his arms to mount the steps.

She was plopped onto a lounge chair and a beach towel was wrapped around her. When she looked up, the sun was behind him, turning him to a dark, threatening figure.

"How could you?" he demanded.

Water was still streaming into her eyes. How could she what? She coughed again. "What are you . . ." It took her a minute to catch her breath. ". . . talking about?"

"What were you trying to do to yourself?"

Relax? Revel in the warm water and sunny day? But then she thought how she must have appeared to him, spread-eagled and drifting downward. She coughed once more to rid herself of the last of the water. "It's just something I used to do as a kid. Give myself . . . give myself over to the water, I guess you'd say."

Jorge released an explosive sigh and moved so that the sun was no longer directly behind him. "You frightened me."

"I guess." Shanna took in the sight of him in his drenched work uniform of khakis and a Santos Landscaping shirt. "You need to dry off, too."

He tried waving her away, but she rose from the lounge chair and, skirting the heavy work boots he'd managed to unlace before diving in for her, went inside to find fresh towels.

She scooped up a double-wide beach towel, then scurried to one of the downstairs guest baths for something smaller for his hair. As she started to hurry back, her wet feet lost purchase on the tile and she reached out to stop her slide. Her flailing hand caught the medicine cabinet over the sink and the door popped open, tumbling items from the shelf into the sink below.

Making a face, she stepped carefully back and began returning the sundries to the cabinet. Two kinds of sunscreen, a bottle of acid controller, and then another, almost full bottle of oxycodone prescribed to her mother. Shanna frowned at the painkiller for a moment, remembering that it had been mislaid on Robin Ryan's last visit to the Malibu house. *So here's where it had landed.* She tucked it beside the Pepcid, then reached for the small box now lying alone in the bottom of the porcelain sink.

A convenience pack of condoms.

The back of her neck burned and she hastily shoved it away, glancing over her shoulder to make sure Jorge hadn't followed her into the house.

The last thing she wanted was for him to find her fondling prophylactics. They'd shared that one kiss while painting at the Pearson house, and then he'd stopped by this place earlier in the week "to check on how his workers were doing," but he'd spent more time with her than with the men trimming the hedges.

He'd kissed her then, too.

But she was trying hard not to think of where that was leading. Like a few moments before when she was floating in the pool, she was trying to enjoy the moment instead of worrying about what lay ahead.

For the last few weeks—months? years?—the future had seemed so empty to her. She'd latched on to Jay, hoping he would fill her void, but that relationship had drifted away like dry sand in a stiff breeze.

Returning to the pool with her stack of towels, Shanna promised herself she wasn't so desperate that she would think of Jorge in any but the most here-and-now sort of terms.

And here-and-now he was, looking soggy and more than a little self-conscious as he dripped, still fully dressed, onto the pool deck. Shanna tossed him a couple of the towels and used a third to wring out her wet hair.

"Do you want me to see if I can find something of Dad's for you to wear?" she asked. "I'm sure there are sweatpants upstairs."

He shook his head. "I'll be all right." He started to blot his clothes.

"That's not going to work very well," she advised him.

"At least take off your shirt so we can spread it out to dry."

Though he halted his ineffectual blotting, his hand merely hovered over the buttons at his throat. His hesitation puzzled her.

"I won't look," she said, smiling a little to show she was joking.

"Promise?" he muttered.

Unsure if he was kidding now, she half-turned as she fashioned her long towel into a below-the-armpits sarong. He'd already seen her modest black bikini, of course, but his discomfort was making her uneasy. And too aware of her near-nudity.

From the corner of her eye, she saw him fling the wet fabric toward a woven-backed chair where it landed in a heap. She crossed to it herself, tsking a little, and spread it out across the seat. Then she turned to him. "You'll never get it—"

The word "dry" didn't make it off her tongue. Instead it stuck there like a postage stamp, as she took in the sight of Jorge, half-naked. Oh, wow.

His chest rippled. Beneath fine-grained, dark golden skin, there was a wealth of working-man muscle. And to keep it all from being too extraordinarily beautiful, the dark tattoos scattered across his flesh gave him an edge no amount of Method acting would lend to even the most leading of Hollywood's men.

"They're gang tattoos," he said, his voice abrupt. "Most of them, anyway."

They certainly weren't the colorful illustrations you saw at the mall or the gym. The tribal armbands the big-wave surfers had inked around their biceps and the Disney characters adorning their girlfriends' ankles looked nothing like the raw black images sprinkled on Jorge's chest and upper arms.

A primitive thrill shot up Shanna's spine as she drew closer to him, intent on getting a better look. It was the same thrill, she realized, that she'd felt years ago when she'd gone with some friends to a Native American powwow at a desert reservation east of L.A. That day, the primitive beat of the drums had created inside her this exact combination of excitement and dread.

Jorge's gaze was on her face, she could feel it, though her own couldn't break away from the canvas of golden skin in front of her.

A tombstone adorned one heavy bicep. RIP, it read, and then two dates. Whoever it memorialized had died at 17 years old. On the opposite arm was a sombrero leaning on a machete that was dripping blood.

Other symbols, stylized letters that were an acronym she didn't recognize, an Aztec Indian head, and an intricately drawn sun decorated the right side of his chest and belly. But over his heart at slight center-left—she blinked, trying to believe her eyes—over his heart was the profile of a woman's face.

Her face.

Could it be? Was that her head and torso in profile, a replica of that old advertising for Decadence candy bars? It certainly looked like it was, with her chin tilted back, her hair flowing down her neck, her eyes closed as if she was savoring . . . or anticipating . . .

Shanna watched her hand reach out. Slowly, slowly, as if it might disappear if she moved with any speed, she placed the pad of her forefinger against the image.

Jorge's muscles flinched beneath her touch, but the tattoo remained. Her gaze lifted to his.

"A decade ago you were like . . . a . . . a pinup girl for me and my friends," he said.

His friends? His gang? She could feel his heartbeat reverberating through her hand. "You take pinup pretty seriously, I guess."

"Yeah." He tried to catch her hand in his, but she moved it then, drawing her fingertip away from that tattoo, over the brown nub of his nipple, down to his bands of abdominal muscles, toward the wet waistband of his pants. As she watched her hand travel lower, desire rose inside of her like the volume of those powwow drums.

She hooked her finger over the edge of his khakis, and drew him closer to her. "I . . . I don't know what to say."

At the Pearson house the other day, she'd seen her reflection in his eyes. Now she was on his body, inked onto his skin, and she could only think how much she wanted to be *in* his skin. Her own flesh shivered.

In the moment, she reminded herself. In the moment, yet in his skin. From the heavy-lidded, suddenly sexy look on his face, she thought he'd go along with the plan.

On their way to her bedroom upstairs, she remembered the condoms. She snagged them from the lower shelf, nudging aside that bottle of prescription pills and thanking heaven for the three-times-a-week housekeeper who thought of every eventuality for the potential houseguests who might visit.

In her second-floor room, the long windows caught every ray of sunlight, making it warm despite the humming air conditioner. Shanna flipped on the lazy overhead fan and then dropped her towel to the white carpet. Jorge moved toward her as if he was fighting molasses to reach her side.

Or maybe that was just his technique, because he kept it up like that, everything slow, every touch measured, every minute drawn out to its full sixty seconds. At some point they made it to her white sheets and she admired the strength of his body and its tanned contrast to hers.

The fan ruffled his hair as he leaned over and touched her with hands that were calloused and lean but that could whisper over her skin as if her flesh was as fragile as those transparent bougainvillea blossoms next door. She remembered him holding that sharp-clawed kitten and wondered why it had worked so hard to get away.

She wanted him to touch her, hold her, forever.

No! Not forever, but for now. This moment. This *loooong* moment in the heated room that smelled now of his soap and of her body's sexual perfume.

This moment became the next moment and the next and the next and the next. The condom was unwrapped, Jorge was still unhurried, and then . . . and then . . . moment upon moment upon moment until Shanna and her quiet, edgy, exciting lover came undone.

Afterward, she rested her head on his shoulder and traced that tattoo of herself. Her fingernails were short and natural, for the first time in years, thanks to her work next door.

"What were you thinking when you had this done?" she wondered aloud.

His hand slid over her hair. "I was young. At that time I wasn't big on thinking. As you can tell by the trouble those tattoos symbolize."

"Is that why you keep them? To remind you of the trouble you left behind?"

He laughed, and rubbed his chin against the top of her head. Her hair caught in his already-rough beard. "I keep them because I'm afraid of the pain I'll be in when getting them off."

Shanna frowned, trying to determine how she felt about Jorge ridding himself of her image—or of him being inked with it forever.

Forever! No, that didn't sound like in-the-moment language. Not at all.

Jorge's hand swept over her hair again. "I lied," he said softly.

She turned her head, propping her chin on his warm, hard chest to look at his face. "About what?"

"I remember exactly what I was thinking when I had the artist tattoo you over my heart. That's the woman, I told myself, who will be my wife and carry my babies." He smiled, as if indulging the young man who he once had been. "Dumb, eh?"

She was dumbfounded. And dumb as well. Mute. Because she couldn't think of a single thing to say in return, not when her mind was only filled with images of things she suddenly wanted more than anything she could remember in a long time. Images she couldn't put out of her head. Shanna as a man's wife. Shanna, the mother of a man's babies.

Jorge's wife. Her stomach growing big with the child that would be their future.

That would be a kind of forever.

Sixteen

When Nikki heard the back door of Jay's house slide open it was too late to jump from his couch and hide the signs of what she'd been doing. So she stayed where she was, her butt on the cushions, her gaze on her knitting needles, her ear cocked toward the television and the show playing there.

Scrambling up would only make her appear undignified, agitated, or both, and she was determined to restart her relationship with Jay as something calm and—finally—completely professional now that they'd released the sexual tension that had infused their previous encounters.

With the house empty for the last several hours, she'd made that her new plan. Except now that she was no longer alone, the way he was just standing there, staring, made her nervous. She didn't look at him, but she didn't need to, she could feel his gaze. It rolled across her skin, and in response, each of her tiny hairs stood at anxious attention. Her fingers slipped, and she dropped a stitch.

Swallowing a curse, she fished it back onto the needle,

then shot him a glance, unable to stand the charged quiet a second longer. "What? *What?*"

So much for dignity.

"Just doing a quick systems check," he said, his voice calm. "And I'm operating on the same wavelength as I was at Gabe's this morning."

Puzzled, she sent him another glance. "Well, uh, good for you."

He laughed, though it didn't sound as if he was much amused. "Anyway, what's up, cookie? Is that some new method of food preparation I haven't heard of?"

"Hah-hah." She adjusted the bag of frozen vegetables draped over the knee she'd propped onto pillows on the coffee table in front of her. "You said you don't like peas, so I thought you wouldn't mind if I put the ones I found in your freezer into service in another capacity."

"I like them better now that they're giving me an excuse to check out so much of your bare legs."

She resisted the urge to yank on the hem of the mid-thigh skirt she'd changed into an hour ago. The short length was for practical, not prurient reasons, surely he could see that. It made the cold compress process easier—not to mention how it saved her from having to shuck a pair of pants anywhere near where he lived and breathed. That was part of history now—and better left there.

Jay took a seat on the coffee table beside her foot, facing her. He tweaked her big toe. "I didn't hurt you last night, did I?"

"What?" Her face burning, her hands stilled on her knitting even as she registered a delicious twinge at the tender space between her thighs. "No. Of course not. My knee is an old injury."

"Yeah?"

"I taxed it last night rushing away from that beach party, and then this morning after you left I went for a walk on the beach while I was waiting for the bread to rise. I twisted it in the sand." She was usually more careful, but once she'd kneaded her dough into submission, her head was still teeming with memories that hadn't yet cleared. "In a few minutes I'll be good to go and can finish the dinner prep."

"Don't rush." He switched seats, taking a spot next to her on the couch.

Did he notice how she inched away from him? She hoped he'd get the hint.

His shoulder nudged hers. "What kind of injury is it?"

"ACL." Edging away again, she figured that brief answer would be sufficient. He was a guy, and damage to the anterior cruciate ligament was a common injury among pro football players, she'd learned from her time in the waiting rooms of orthopedists.

"Damn that defensive line," he said, proving he knew exactly what she was talking about. When an athlete, say like a running back, took a hit that caused him to pivot in a direction different from his planted feet, the trauma could damage one of the ligaments connecting the femur and the tibia. "Tell me you at least made the first ten yards."

"It was the game-winning touchdown, actually. The crowd's reaction was insane."

He chuckled. "Nice to know you went out in a blaze of glory, cookie. I wouldn't doubt it for a minute."

Nice to know she could bamboozle him when she wanted. Twelve years ago, it hadn't been a blaze of glory but a blaze of pain—followed by that life-altering lesson in what could go wrong when you got too needy.

"Not a complete tear, then?" he asked. "Since you haven't had surgery."

"Mmm." He knew more than most, darn it. A complete tear, when the ACL was actually severed, almost always required reconstructive repair. Without it, her doctors said, a person's activity level should only be limited to walking and "maybe" golf. She hated golf.

But she loved working in restaurants, and cooking full-time for one was more strenuous than eighteen holes on a three-par course. Every orthopedist she'd seen had recommended a surgical procedure that wasn't just of the two-teeny-holes-and-get-up-in-an-hour variety. What she required was a reconstruction of the knee that meant opening it up and harvesting part of her patella tendon as a replacement for the severed ACL. Then there was the drilling into bone, the grafting, and the stapling it all back together, followed by an overnight-or-two stay and weeks of limited mobility. Months of physical therapy.

For a woman who was scared spitless of hospitals since her mother's death and who was without the human support system to make it through a lengthy convalescence . . . well, she was living with her bum knee.

As well as with the ridiculous attraction she *still* felt for the man beside her, apparently. He'd eased closer, his upper arm against hers and the fabric of his jeans soft against the naked flesh of her good leg.

She shivered.

He glanced over. "Cold?"

"Um, yeah. You know, the ice . . ." She was getting good at this fibbing stuff. Because he bought it again, going so far as to drag that crocheted throw folded over the sofa arm across the two of them.

Her needles stuck in the blanket and he obligingly reached under it to help her untangle them.

She gasped, and pulled her knitting free. "Do you *mind*?"

"What?"

Oh, he was so bad at the innocent look. Or just so bad, period. "That's, um, my *thigh* you're playing Pat the Bunny with."

He grinned. "Darn. Bunny wasn't the animal I was going after."

Squirming, she adjusted her needles and ball of yarn to avoid his laughing, charming, *knowing* eyes. Damn man. Did he enjoy flustering her? Did he know she was definitely *not* interested in him any longer—despite whatever her pounding pulse and clenching . . . bunny were saying? What an ego rush he'd get from that!

But Jay was not going to know he still held residual

power over her. It was supposed to be a one-night-only thing, and she was going to stick to the rules they'd tacitly agreed upon.

Maybe he was of the same frame of mind, because he suddenly switched subjects. "What are you making there?" he asked.

A fool of herself, she worried, despite the neutral turn to the conversation. Between the stupid blanket and his maddening closeness, she was hot and her skin so sensitive. When he breathed, it caused the sleeve of his T-shirt to brush against her bare arm, making sure her goose bumps got goose bumps.

And her breath, she didn't have enough of that. She was supposed to be putting last night behind her, but memories of the way he'd felt against her, the way he'd kissed and touched her, kept stealing into her head and under her skin and then robbing all the oxygen from her lungs.

He had to know.

He couldn't know. She couldn't let him know.

She just had to find her famous detachment.

Jay grabbed the dangling end of her piece of knitting and wiggled it to get her attention. "So what is this?" he asked again. "Are you knitting something special?"

"Well . . ." She looked down at the rectangular swatch. There was still that kerchief to complete, but she was playing with this yarn instead, its color the exact down-to-business blue of Jay's eyes.

"Because I could use a sweater," he said.

"No!" The word rushed out of her mouth, too loud and too fast, and she cleared her throat and tried again. "No, I'm not up to sweaters yet."

Not to mention that little piece of conventional wisdom she'd learned at the Tuesday Night Knitters' Club. The Curse of the Boyfriend Sweater, she remembered the women calling it. No guy lasted for the length of time it took to start and finish such a labor of love.

Though, hey, she was used to that, she mused. No one

stuck by her. Certainly pro-bachelor Jay wasn't interested in that, anyway.

"All right," he said. "I give up." In another sudden mood change, he grabbed the needles and yarn from her hands and tossed them on the table. "I'm done trying to warm you up the slow way, cookie."

Startled, she looked over at him. "What?"

But his only answer was to capture her chin in his long fingers and hold her like that as he closed in for a kiss. His mouth was hot and impatient, but she found she was impatient, too, and she opened her lips so he could sweep his tongue inside.

He groaned, as if she'd offered food and he hadn't eaten all day. Her body trembled and he drew her closer, the frozen peas sliding off her knee as he turned her into him.

It was last night all over again. Jay surrounding her with his touch, his taste, his relentless maleness that overpowered her senses. She closed her eyes and let herself be taken up and taken over.

Then he tore his mouth from hers. "Damn."

She jerked back. Damn was right. She knew better than this. She'd made a plan this morning. Calm and professional. Her face burned and she started to babble. "Sorry, sorry. We had rules, didn't we? An agreement it was just the one night?" Her hand went to her mouth.

He snatched it away and swooped in for another hard kiss. "Damn, cookie, Fern just came in the front door."

"Oh." Oh. Thank goodness his hearing was better than hers. She leaned over to retrieve the fallen peas, taking the wool throw with her.

Jay snatched it back, arranging it over his lap and then hers. "Need a little, uh, camouflage."

When Fern wandered into the living room a few moments later, they were two grown-ups, feet propped on the coffee table, watching television together.

The teenager glanced at the screen, then gave them a sharp look. "*Pants-Off Dance-Off?*"

Nikki stared at the TV, finally focused on it, and then froze. A guy who looked more suited to sitting behind a computer monitor was stripping to an old Bon Jovi tune while the music video played behind him. When he was down to a sunken chest, knobby knees, and a pair of green knit boxers, she found her voice. "Urp."

The bleat seemed to galvanize Jay, who looked equally stunned. He made a hasty pat of the cushions, then lifted up to produce the remote from beneath him. "Nikki's favorite show," he said, as he flipped his thumb and a news channel took over. "But, cookie, I'm sorry. I require something more stimulating."

Fern regarded them for another moment. "You guys are so weird." Then she turned toward the stairs and disappeared.

They looked at each other. "*Pants-Off Dance-Off?*" they said together.

Nikki managed to glare at him. "Remember, that's my favorite." She whacked his arm. "Thanks a lot."

Laughing, he captured her loose fist. Then he slid lower on the sofa cushions, her hand still in his. "Hey, I'm rehabilitating my rep, here. Wouldn't do to be Peter Pan in the morning and a voyeur of geek stripping in the afternoon." He kissed the top of her knuckles. "Now settle down and put your head right here."

"Right here" was his shoulder. He patted it again, his expectant gaze trained on her face.

She wanted her hand back. Her sanity. The way things had been before she'd ever met him.

Like when sex had left her as cold as the peas on her knee?

"Jay . . ." Surrendering, Nikki flopped back on the couch and didn't protest as he pulled her into place against him.

"Nikki . . ." he mimicked in a gentle voice. "Just shut up."

And she did. She didn't know why—well, she knew why, and she also knew it wasn't her best idea—but she let herself lean against his body. When was the last time she'd had someone else to hold her up?

The newscaster droned on about gasoline prices and other economic indicators. Outside the blanket covering their laps, Jay held her one hand in the loose grasp of his. And though Nikki was a bit too warm and a bit too aware of him, she found herself relaxing against his body.

But this was Hef Junior, and so she should have known the restfulness wouldn't last. Under the daffodil-yellow throw, his free hand brushed her bare leg.

She automatically moved away.

He, naturally, moved in again.

Her gaze cut sideways. His was glued to the TV. A finger wandered higher.

Nikki gulped. "Jay—"

"Shh," he said, still looking at the screen. "I'm interested in this."

But a few seconds later, she had to wonder what "this" was that interested him so. The man, the naughty man, was drawing designs on her upper thigh with his forefinger. Tic tac toe, dirty words, maybe even calculus equations, she didn't know. She couldn't think. The plan she'd come up with that morning evaporated in the heat of renewed lust.

Her heart was slamming against her chest, and surely he could hear its thundering beat, but he stared straight ahead as he caught at her inner thigh and drew her good knee up and over his hard leg. The hem of her skirt went along for the ride, hitching high, nearly to her hips.

She made another *urp* sound again, but the newscaster was onto baseball scores now and Jay was watching the highlights with half-closed eyes as he approached third base. The pad of his forefinger played with the elastic edge of her panties.

Nikki flashed hot and chills rushed down the inside of her legs. If he moved an inch, he'd know everything his touch did to her. "I don't think, um . . ."

"Oh, lighten up and let's play, cookie."

Play. Of course that's what he wanted, nothing more

scary or permanent than a game. She shouldn't be afraid of something like play. And she wasn't afraid of . . . anything. With his hand so close to her throbbing center, all she could think was what was wrong with recreation and why was she fighting it so hard?

Except . . . "Fern."

"That's all up to you, cookie. If she comes downstairs, I'll look like I'm just sitting here watching TV, while you—" She gasped as his finger took a quick foray beneath the elastic and he smiled, smug and male. "While you can either look innocent or wicked. Your choice."

Innocent or wicked? Her choice?

She had no choice. It was all deliciously orchestrated by Jay, by his stealthy, nimble fingers. They went farther now, sliding away from the crease of her thigh to toy with her through the dampening fabric of her panties.

Her breath moved in and out of her throat and her face burned. This was crazy. And exciting. The hidden, under-the-covers aspect of it made her feel like she was seventeen and playing with her daring boyfriend in her parents' living room.

Just something else she'd skipped, like those movie-theater and at-the-prom kisses.

Two of Jay's fingers traveled higher, then slid under the waistband of her underwear to dip shallowly into the softening center of her body. She was so wet there that it sort of embarrassed her, except that she saw a little smile of satisfaction come over his face. He drew the moisture up, stroking it over and around the soft layers of her sex, though missing the one magic spot he'd made her touch the night before.

She wanted to moan, squirm, heck, suck on his tongue, but he was acting avid television viewer and she was aware of Fern, who could come tromping down the stairs at any time.

One long finger slid inside her body. Deep.

She went rigid, swallowing her groan, but her muscles clenched down on him as he circled and plunged again.

The slight soreness only, perversely, made his intrusion more exciting. Her flesh throbbed and she whimpered with the naughty delight of it all. "Jay . . ."

There was a flush high on his cheekbones and his jaw hardened as he glanced over at her. His eyes glittered as they cut her way. "Shhh, baby. Innocent, remember?"

But she couldn't feel anything but wicked as he slid another finger inside her. Her hips lifted into him, desperate for him to thrust deeper, to take her higher, to touch her *there*.

He glanced over again. "Pull up the blanket, cookie. You're distracting me."

Oh, God. She looked down to see her hard nipples poking against the thin fabric of her bra and T-shirt. Her fingers trembled as she covered herself, and he nodded, his gaze lifting to her face.

"Good girl," he whispered, then rewarded her by sliding his whole hand into her panties so he could push deeper inside her and brush across the top of her sex with his thumb.

She jerked into his touch, even as she tried to hold herself to the cushions. He stroked there again, and her womb twitched, her inner muscles tightening on him with the same pressure as the pleasure that was squeezing like a belt around her hips.

This was dangerous, wasn't it?

Play, she could hear Jay's voice in her head, gentle, casual, charming. *Play*.

He was watching her now, and she went hot from her collarbone to her pubic bone, so hot she had to close her eyes, too. His fingers were still inside her, and only his thumb was moving, strumming her like an instrument, fooling with her body that was straining, straining for her second-ever orgasm.

"Touch yourself, baby," he said. "Do it for me."

Her skin blazed, but her hand moved slowly under the blanket. His thumb moved to make room for her.

"That's right," he coaxed. "Touch yourself and make it happen."

She wanted to. She had to. She did.

Oh, God.

The climax washed over her, through her, toppling any leftover concerns, and she held on to it as long as she could, gripping his fingers with muscles that shook with the sharp, sweet bliss of peaking satisfaction. She wasn't any teenager getting a furtive thrill, but a woman who had been denied for too, too long.

Her breath was still caught somewhere between her chest and her throat when she heard clattering footsteps on the stairs. Without looking at Jay, she jackknifed out of her slouch. His hand drew away from between her thighs, though he slid a warm palm along her leg as he sat straighter on the cushions.

When Fern entered the living room they were both seemingly engrossed in entertainment news. Nikki struggled to gather her thoughts together. Oh, man. Her "professional" plan was blown to smithereens, but she had to recoup *something*. She had to come up with a way to equalize things between herself and Jay.

Tuning into the broadcast, she recalled that noble, holy purpose she'd struck upon the first day they'd met. He had to learn that every woman wasn't a complete pushover when she came up against his playboy charms.

"You have Hollywood connections, handsome," she said, inserting a sugary wheedle into her voice. "Can't you somehow connect your favorite lesbian girlfriend with the object of her affections? Especially since we've just learned she's in town shooting a new music video?"

Jay sent her a look. "This Madonna fixation of yours has got to stop."

"Why?" She batted her lashes at him, copying a move she'd seen Cassandra make on Gabe. "When she makes me so," her mouth silently finished the word, just for him, *hot*.

His eyes darkened. He half rose from the couch, her hand already squeezed by his. Now this was more like it. He seemed as turned on as she had been moments before. If what they had wasn't professional, at least it could be power-balanced.

Fern reminded them both she was still in the room. "You guys are so weird," she pronounced again. "I'm going to meet Marie. I'll be back at seven."

The front door slammed shut behind her.

Within the next breath, she and Jay were scrambling for his bedroom. When he saw her limping, he swung her up in his arms and she shrieked.

And then again, as he tossed her onto the bed and followed her down.

"We have to be done by seven," she said, breathless.

"I'm a journalist," he reminded her, his mouth already on her neck. "I work best with a deadline."

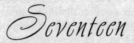

Seventeen

Life loves the liver of it.

—MAYA ANGELOU,
WRITER

And it was just like that between Nikki and Jay for the next several days. Sneaking around Fern to revel in sizzling exchanges wherever, whenever they could. Again, just like two high schoolers who couldn't get enough of each other, they traded luscious kisses behind the screen of the pantry door, they trailed fingers over each other's hot skin while parked in the shade of the lot at the grocery store, they shared an ice-cream cone and it felt as intimate as sleeping on the same pillow.

Nikki didn't spend another night because there was a teenager in the house, not because of any rules they'd set or time lines they'd established or plan she'd made. She didn't think of any of those when they made sweet, hurried love while his cousin went to the post office or when they drew out the pleasure during the evening hours Fern spent at the movies.

Though Nikki was admittedly out of her element, she didn't let herself consider how each moment in his arms bonded them in a way she'd never before experienced. She only thought of how each moment was so erotically sweet.

And it was just another thrilling one when he came up behind her in the kitchen as she sat on a stool, de-stringing snap peas to add to a cashew chicken salad. His hands cupped her shoulders and he bent down to kiss her jaw.

"Mmm," he whispered against her skin. "I love vanilla."

Her nipples tightened and she clenched her thighs together, holding the instant pleasure in. She had to hook her heels more securely on the rungs of the stool so she didn't slide into a puddle of want at his feet.

It took her a moment to steady her voice. "That's not what you said yesterday when I refused to climb a ladder onto the roof so we could, as I think you so elegantly put it, 'do it on the shingles.'"

"I said I'd put a blanket over them. And I was in a state, cookie. The cleaning lady was running the vacuum, Fern was watching TV in the living room, and I was desperate to have you."

Jay Buchanan desperate over a woman? Never gonna happen. But she let the statement lie. "Still," she turned to frown at him over her shoulder. "You made fun of me for only wanting what you call 'vanilla' sex."

He nipped her bottom lip. "It's because of all your teasing talk about your strap-on. I'm sorry, though. I'll let you tie me up and torture me later."

She raised an eyebrow and pretended tepid interest instead of giving away the cinnamon-hot longing that stabbed through her at the idea of being alone with him and with enough privacy to do everything from vanilla to spicy in his bed. "Is Fern going out tonight?"

"No. Actually, I am. I just took a call and now I have to meet a guy in Century City for drinks."

"Oh." She turned back to her snap peas. "I'm scheduled to clean my fishbowl tonight, anyway." It was the second thing that came into her head and she went with it, since claiming she needed the time to wash her hair sounded even more lame.

Jay spun her around to face him. His smile was full of boyish charm and the certitude of a man who always got his way. "Don't go home, cookie." His voice was soft and sounded like sinful persuasion. "Stay here until I get back."

As sweet as these moments were, she didn't want him thinking she depended upon them. And as exciting as it was to be with him, she told herself she missed the familiarity of her silent condo and the security of her solitude. "We've been tucked in each other's pockets for days, Jay. There's nothing wrong with a night off."

His thumb stroked across her cheek and a corner of his mouth hitched higher. "But I like your pocket, Nikki." His voice lowered to a husky whisper. "It's so pink and pretty and wet and once I work myself inside it grips me like a hot, greedy little fist."

Oh, God. Her spine melted and she felt liquid heat rush to the very place that he was talking about. That's what she got for getting involved with a man who used words for a living. He was so good at using them on her. She licked her lips, trying to stay strong. "Now, Jay . . ."

He wiped the moisture off her lower lip with that maddening thumb, as the gleam in his eyes turned crafty. "Stay for Fern, then. I don't like leaving her alone at night."

Oh, he knew so well how to get to her. Since her breakup with Jenner, the girl had stuck closer to home yet stayed so quiet that it wasn't easy not to worry about it. Even for Nikki, with her keep-your-distance DNA.

She sighed. "Well, I've been meaning to work on the menu for the anniversary party."

"Fern could help you with that. She should. It's for her folks, too."

When Nikki had agreed to take this position, the big event at the end of the month to celebrate the anniversary of the double wedding of Jay's parents and that of his aunt and uncle had seemed like a perfect opportunity to make useful contacts. She'd known she'd need them to make a go of this new solo career. But she hadn't been thinking, lately, of any of that.

Maybe because her knee was so much better, despite last week's tweak in the sand. She was even beginning to believe she could safely tap into her emergency surgery fund if she found herself between positions.

But for now there was this position, and this golden man with his sexy body and coercive hands, who was so near-impossible to refuse. "Please, cookie." He tucked a lock of hair behind her ear. "Later I'll show you how grateful I can be."

Her body throbbed at the low, seductive promise in his voice. "All right. I'll be here when you get back," she said, throwing familiarity and security to the wind. Though this ongoing involvement with Jay had taken her outside her comfort zone, she was managing.

"You'll be able to reach me on my cell," he said. "Anytime."

Nikki frowned at him, disliking such assurances. "Oh, get over yourself. Anything that comes up, I can handle on my lonesome."

Except that the house seemed too quiet without Jay, she admitted as the dusk settled over the beach outside. Refusing to clock-watch, Nikki sat on the living room couch and doodled on a notepad while Fern flipped through a magazine.

The girl's cell phone rang. She pulled it from the front pocket of her hoodie, checked the readout, then thumbed the side button that cut off the ring. Two minutes later, the phone sounded again. Two seconds after that, Fern turned off her phone altogether and shoved it under a cushion.

Nikki stared. Severing the ties of teenage communication was a drastic measure, if her brief experience in Fern's proximity was anything to go by. The tight expression on the girl's face told the same story.

But Nikki wasn't getting involved. Fern wasn't her relative, and anyway, when it came to forging bonds of feminine sisterhood, Nikki was out of her element there, too. Fern could keep her confidences.

Leaning forward, she dropped her notepad on the coffee table and picked up her knitting. Her no-set-purpose piece was growing longer, and though she still had no idea why she continued with it, the repetitive action soothed her.

From the corner of her eye, she saw Fern retrieve her phone and power it on again. In seconds it rang, and in seconds Fern had reperformed the whole shut-it-down-and-shove-it-away routine.

Nikki opened her mouth, shut her mouth, opened it again. A white flag waved in her mind. Fine, she'd pry a little. "Someone's sure intent upon reaching you."

Fern stared at the glossy pages on her lap. Then she blew out a sigh. "It's—"

The glass on the back door rattled, startling them both. Nikki's head whipped toward the sound, and her heartbeat spiked. A figure in dark pants and a dark sweatshirt stood on the back deck, faceless in the dusk.

Instinctive fear rose from that burial plot in the back of her mind, but she stood up to it, putting her hand out to Fern as she got to her feet. "Stay right there."

But the teenager was already moving, her magazine sliding off her knees and to the floor as she rose. "It's Jenner. That's who's been calling my cell."

Identifying the threat didn't calm Nikki's jangling nerves. "You don't have to talk to him," she said quickly. "You didn't answer his phone calls."

"I was being stupid. I'm not going to let him believe I'm running away from him."

Never let them think you're weak, Nikki's inner voice agreed. But as Fern brushed past her she had to fold her fingers into fists instead of reacting to the strong urge to latch on to the girl's hood and hold her back. Though she'd told Jay she could handle whatever came up tonight, this was none of her business. This was not her concern.

Still, she followed Fern to the doorway and stood there as the girl eased open the glass.

"I need to talk to you," the boy said, his voice harsh. He held up his cell phone. "You're not picking up."

Nikki's stomach shrank in on itself, shying away from Jenner's angry tone.

"I'm answering now," Fern said, tossing her hair over her shoulder. "What do you want?"

The boy's gaze flicked toward Nikki. "To be alone. Let's go up to your room."

Fern seemed to sway back, but then she held steady. "Outside."

His tone turned cajoling. "*Fern,*" he said, his hand reaching across the threshold to slide around her neck.

She ducked away from his touch and pushed past him onto the deck. From there she took the steps leading to the beach. Nikki hurried toward the open slider, but Jenner slammed it in her face and strode after Fern.

The barrier of glass reminded Nikki of her place—on the outside of whatever was going on with Fern and Jenner. But she didn't move away from her front-row seat. As the dusk darkened, her gaze stayed glued to their forms.

It was like a silent motion picture, and she didn't need text breaks to read the story. His entreaty. Her refusal. His more passionate plea and her more emphatic shake of her head. He opened his mouth again, but she turned toward the house and took a step.

His hand closed around the girl's upper arm.

Nikki's fingers shot to the door handle.

Fern shook away the touch, then trudged through the sand.

Halfway back to the house, he caught up with her, grabbing her elbow. Then he spun her around and shook her. Hard.

One moment Nikki was inside Jay's, still feeling unsure and out of her element. The next she was barefoot on the sand, racing toward the couple.

"Let her go!" She startled a seagull that had been roosting on the beach, and it rose up with a raucous cry, wings flapping. She came to a stop near the teenagers. "I said, let her go."

Jenner jerked his gaze toward Nikki. "Get lost."

Fern yanked on her arm. "Jenner, leave me alone."

He shook her again, his expression fierce. "Not until you listen. Not until I have my say. You owe it to me."

You can't leave now.

You can't leave me like this.

Give it to me, baby.

You owe it to me, baby.

Nikki's skin iced over as those old words echoed in her mind. A sick dread shot through her blood and she thought her muscles might be frozen, too, but they were working, moving, taking her through the thick sand. She grabbed Jenner's hard forearm. "Let go of Fern."

His gaze didn't leave the girl's face as his free hand lifted. With the flat of his palm, he gave Nikki's shoulder a brutal shove. She stumbled back, then fell on her butt, her knee twisting as she hit the sand.

The hard fall disturbed the past she tried so hard to keep buried. It crawled into the open again, dirt clinging to its ugly form. She looked up at the boy and he morphed into a different one. Nikki was young again, and the looming figure was older, stronger, selfish. His needs first, her needs less.

Nikki less.

She felt again the nauseating pain in her knee that had robbed her breath and then recalled those hands, their touch no longer coaxing and familiar but drunken and mean. Her clothes shoved aside, his fly opened. Him pushing inside of her, while she lay paralyzed by shock and hurt, the booze she'd swallowed earlier not enough to dull her awareness of what was happening. When she'd opened her mouth, he'd clapped his hard palm over it.

Sick with shame, sick with fright, sick with the revelation that her neediness for love had opened her to this risk, she'd swallowed her screams.

But not now, she thought, dragging herself back to the present. It was different now. She was different. Now she wasn't paralyzed. Now she wasn't voiceless. She couldn't be, not with Fern in danger.

Funny and sad, she realized in a flash, that this, *this* was her element.

Nikki sprang to her feet like she should have done twelve years before instead of staying low and small as she had then. She'd felt so afraid and alone, but now she wasn't either of those. "No!" she yelled, louder than the high-pitched whine of anxiety in her ears. "*No!*"

She leaped to reach the couple in one bound. "Stop!" With both hands, she grasped the boy's arm, and with all her strength wrenched, pushing down on his elbow while pulling up on his wrist to break his grasp.

It worked. Fern stumbled back as she was freed and Jenner rounded on Nikki. "Bitch," he spit out.

Fern ran backward toward the house, her movements clumsy but quick.

Nikki wasn't running anywhere. "That's right," she told the boy, adrenaline pumping into her system until she felt seven feet tall and Superwoman invincible. "I'm the biggest bitch from your baddest bad dream. And it's only getting worse. I'm going inside and I'm going to call the police and then I'm going to call your parents. And if I ever see you around this house, if I ever see you around Fern, if I ever hear that you've touched her, well, I'm a chef, which means I'm trained with knives and perfectly willing to try an adaptation to my recipe for buffalo balls in béarnaise sauce."

The stupid jerk sneered, but he was moving off. "You're crazy, you know that? Crazy."

Nikki caught sight of Fern, halted on her path back to the house. Suddenly getting to her was much more important than preventing Jenner from getting the last word. Ignoring the shrieks from her knee as well as the curses from the retreating boy, she hurried to the girl and grabbed her hand to hustle her inside.

Behind the locked back door, Nikki sank into a chair at the kitchen table and watched Fern do the same. Adrenaline still flooded her bloodstream, and she felt good, hella-good as a matter of fact, that she'd stood up to that bully. As she'd told Jay, she could handle whatever came up. All by herself.

But there was still more to be confronted. She sucked in a breath and kept her voice calm. "Fern, did Jenner hurt you?"

The girl's head shot up, then she pulled her sleeve off her shoulder and inspected the faint red marks on her upper arm. "No," she said, covering herself back up. "I just bruise easily."

"I mean other times." Nikki forced herself onward. She could do this. She'd faced Jenner, right? And she would do whatever else she must. "Other times did he make you do things you . . . you didn't want to do?"

The girl's face flushed and she trained her gaze on the tabletop in front of her. "Other times he did things that made me want him. But he's mad because I broke up with him instead of—" Her hand lifted. "You know."

Nikki silently released the breath she'd been holding. "Instead of having sex."

"Yeah." Fern's mouth barely moved.

"Well, he won't be bothering you anymore." She'd make sure of it.

A smile flickered over the teenager's face and she glanced up again. "Buffalo balls in béarnaise sauce?"

"A guy who treats a girl like that deserves nothing less."

Fern went silent again, and her fingers reached for the zipper pull of her hoodie. She toyed with it, running it up and down in short, nervous bursts.

Nikki started to push herself to a stand, thinking to make tea or hot chocolate. Thinking she'd weathered the event and done more than okay. That hella-good feeling resurged.

"My best friend, Emily, was raped last May."

Sinking back to her seat, hella-good transforming into horror, Nikki stared at Fern. "Oh." Oh, God.

"She was visiting her brother at college and he took her to a party at one of the frats. They went different ways and she . . . well . . ."

"Oh, Fern." The last of Nikki's adrenaline leached away in a whoosh.

More words tumbled out of the girl's mouth. "I didn't want what happened to make me afraid like she is now. I wanted to prove I could take the most dangerous boy I know and handle him. That way . . . that way I could prove to myself I wasn't vulnerable like Em."

Nikki slumped against the back of her chair. What should she say? She was out of her element all over again. Her mother hadn't lived long enough to set an example for this kind of discussion. Nikki didn't have girlfriends either, who might have provided practical experience she could draw upon. Should she tell Fern that all women were vulnerable?

Should she say some women—Shanna came to mind— gave too much of themselves in order to have a man? Should she say that it was better—safer—to give little to them and expect nothing in return? Is that what she was doing with Jay?

She hoped that's what she was doing with Jay.

Before she could formulate an answer, Fern was talking again. "I don't want to give up on males altogether, though."

Two weeks ago, giving up on males altogether pretty much summed up Nikki's own strategy.

"So I guess I'll just keep my eyes open," Fern continued. "*Be* open, but wait for one I can trust with . . . with me. What do you think?" Her gaze met Nikki's.

She didn't know how to respond to Fern's question or even the ones in her own mind. But she'd promised Jay she could handle anything that came up. Her fingers itched to call him, but wasn't she independent? Capable all on her own? And anyway, she doubted he'd be any better at honest romantic advice than she.

"I think . . . I think . . ." Cassandra. Her image leaped into Nikki's mind. It was Tuesday, wasn't it? Knitters' Night— make a connection, make a friend! For the first time in her memory, being surrounded by other women sounded comforting, not uncomfortable. Much better than being alone.

She stood up, putting all her weight on her good leg. "I think we should go to Malibu & Ewe."

At her first step, her right leg buckled. Nikki grabbed the table, pain slicing through her knee as if the ligament was being severed all over again. Oh, God, oh, God. Oh, *no*.

"Nikki?"

The concern in Fern's voice helped her push back against the pain. She breathed slowly, then took another experimental step, limping to make it easy on her now-throbbing knee. Her purse and an elastic bandage were only a few feet away.

"We'll take your car, okay?" she told the girl.

She couldn't drive. She could only hope she was correct, that there'd be comfort available at Cassandra's shop. Because right now being by herself wouldn't cut it. It would only make her panic more about the extent of the new damage to her already injured knee.

Eighteen

A bachelor never quite gets over the idea that he is
a thing of beauty and a boy forever.

—HELEN ROWLAND,
WRITER

Jay drove too fast along PCH. He told himself it was because he'd found the house empty and he was worried
about Fern. The call he'd managed to make to her before
the lousy Malibu cell reception broke up should have been
reassuring. She and Nikki were fine. Together.

At Malibu & Ewe.

Cassandra had made him promise not to tell Nikki about
their sibling status, and he'd taken the easy route, as ever,
and agreed. It was simpler for the yarn shop owner to find
her own way through that thorny patch. He had no idea
how Nikki would react and he had enough trouble dealing
with her himself.

Dealing with how he felt about her.

Which was another reason he was in a hurry to get to the
yarn store. A couple of drinks, a rare steak, and a bull ses-
sion with one of his oldest friends, now headquartered in
NYC, had gone a long way to putting this . . . thing with
Nikki in perspective.

Love. Shit. What the hell did he know about that? The

fact was, her long legs turned him on, her *bruja* eyes be-
witched him, her hot, melting center was just the perfect,
snug little pocket he'd called it. Combined together with
the absolute glee he felt at her surprised reaction each time
she achieved another big O—well, those were the ingredients of a recipe for powerful lust.

Nothing more.

When he saw her tonight, he'd have his perspective in
place and be able to view her as the summer fling she was—
as clean and sweet as vanilla and mango, as spicy and satisfying as her jalapeño-laced homemade guacamole.

But a summer fling all the same.

The parking lot shared by the café and Malibu & Ewe
was more than half-full, even though Gabe's place closed
at eight. That meant a roomful of knitting women, but he
didn't let the prospect hitch his stride. The sooner he saw
Nikki, the sooner he'd have his world ordered the old,
comfortable way. In the number-one position, a solo Jay,
free of cumbersome emotions that threatened his happy
male autonomy.

He rolled his shoulders and twisted his neck, palming
his jaw to give the adjustment an extra oomph. Screwing
his head on straight would come just that easily, he promised himself. One look at Nikki and he'd realize he was
back to the good ol' days of sex sans emotion.

A figure flitted through the door ahead of him, and he
recognized the thin figure of Oomfaa. At first she'd objected
to the nickname, but in the way of small towns everywhere,
there'd been no escaping it.

New York could have Uma. Malibu had their Oomfaa.

He was on her heels as the door swung shut behind her.
He caught it in his hand so it didn't make a sound as he entered the shop. None of the women looked up from their
projects.

It was larger than the groups he'd seen gathered there
other times. Women filled the couches, a couple of ottomans,
as well as a dozen folding chairs that Cassandra had pro-
duced from somewhere. He didn't see Nikki right away,

but Fern was at the back of the shop, her fingers running over the colored yarns in the built-in bins.

He smelled coffee and something else that had him thinking Nikki had brought a loaf of her lemon almond bread along for the ride. He sucked in a lungful of the delicious, nutty scent and God, didn't that just explain away the last of the ridiculous "in love" business. He had a jones for her food, and added to everything else, it had made him jump to the entirely wrong conclusion.

Oomfaa was standing outside the knitting circle, her canvas bag full of knitting gewgaws held against her chest and a funny little smile on her face. The others kept chatting around her, oblivious to the actress and whatever piece of news she was eager to impart.

Yeah, he could tell she was raring to spill some juicy tidbit, that was for sure. She was an actress, not a card player, and no one would be asking her to a celebrity poker table anytime soon.

Finally, she gave a little flounce. Jay hid his smile, because Oomfaa wasn't often overlooked and she didn't handle it well.

"Everyone!" she called over the sound of needles and chitchat.

Everyone's noise took a moment to peter out. When it finally did, a woman shifted and he caught a glimpse of Nikki's earth-and-sunlight hair from her place on a low cushion. The rest of her was hidden by the arm of a sofa and one of the chairs.

Jay stayed where he was by the door. Not that he was worried about seeing her, because, of course, he now had his reaction already sorted out. But he was loathe to break into the all-female ritual when for the first time it seemed as if Nikki was content to be in the middle of it.

Oomfaa continued with her stand, too, waiting for the dramatic moment when all eyes were on her. Show-off. But that was as much a part of her as gossip was part of small-town Malibu.

"I just heard the news!" Oomfaa finally declared.

Jay smiled again. Yeah, he was right on the money.

"I just heard," the actress continued, "that Cassandra had a visit from her sister!"

Oh, shit. His smile died.

From the center of the circle, Cassandra rose, her face pale. "No. Oomfaa . . ." Her head swung in Nikki's direction, then quickly jerked away. "Oomfaa . . ."

But Oomfaa was as lousy at picking up on nonverbal cues as she would be at reading the flop. "Cassandra, when were you going to tell us?" she demanded. "I had to hear it from your accountant, who heard it from, well, I don't know who he heard it from, but the news is traveling around town. We should be celebrating the fact that you found your chef. Your donor sibling. The one whose mother used the same sperm donor as yours did. The one you sent that Malibu & Ewe invitation to. Nanette? Nicolette? What's her name again?"

Another figure rose.

"Nikki," Cassandra whispered, turning her way.

Oomfaa's face brightened. "That's it. Your donor sibling's name is Nikki!"

Cassandra's donor sibling had found her feet if not her voice. Nikki was on the move now, weaving her way free of the knitting circle. Jay immediately noticed that she was limping heavily. His gut clenched, biting hard on the sudden concern that filled his belly. As she came closer, he saw her face, her eyes wide with confusion and surprise and . . . fear?

He found himself striding toward her. Her sandals stuttered to a stop as he stepped into her path. "Jay," she said, blinking a couple of times. "Jay." Her hand lifted. Fell.

She moved forward again, but one of her legs seemed to buckle beneath her. At her gasp, he caught her in his arms. Her vanilla scent invaded his head, but its sweetness couldn't counteract the empathetic pangs that had invaded his body.

"Jay, let me go," she said, her voice urgent. "I need to get out of here."

"Sure, cookie," he answered, even as his arms tightened

on her. Her body was trembling and it seemed to shake his bones, too.

Christ, he hurt. He hurt because she did.

Oh, God.

Her confusion was his confusion. Her distress, his. Her pain, his.

So much for his return to all-male autonomy. A rare rib-eye, a baked potato, and a couple of beers couldn't transform the truth, he realized.

This was his love in his arms and he couldn't rationalize that away any longer.

He helped her toward the door, sending a glance back at Fern. She nodded, mouthed "Marie" and shooed him off with a sweep of her hands.

"Jay, let go of me." Nikki tried pulling free of him.

He wrapped her more tightly against his body as he helped her out the door. "Let me take care of you, baby. Let me take care of you."

Nikki wasn't going to get rid of him, Jay promised himself, no matter how many times she reiterated, "I can take care of myself," as he drove her home to her apartment in Santa Monica.

"You can't put pressure on the accelerator to drive yourself," he said, trying to sound sensible and not stubborn as he followed her directions through the quiet streets. "Now, if you'd just agreed to stay at my place tonight . . ."

She mumbled something.

He looked over. "What's that?"

"Pain meds. Anti-inflammatories. I have my prescriptions at home."

He was glad to hear that, but once she'd had five minutes alone in her bedroom, he started worrying again. "Do you need my help?" he called through the closed door.

"I can take my own clothes on and off, Jay."

He swallowed his retort that it was more fun when he did it for her. Now wasn't the moment for that kind of talk, and then all thoughts of getting her horizontal for sexual purposes flew from his mind when she hobbled out of her room. She had a skinny-strapped tank top above, but below she wore a pair of ratty sweatpants that gave evidence that her knee problems were ongoing—the right leg was cut off at thigh level. Jay saw that her knee was swollen to wince proportions.

"Ah, cookie," he said, grimacing. "What can I do to help?"

"Nothing."

He shoved his hands through his hair. "Nikki—"

"Okay, okay. The bag of peas in the freezer and a bottle of water." He trailed her to a reclining chair where she settled in and propped up her leg. "Help yourself to anything you want in the kitchen," she added.

On the way there, he took a look around her apartment. There wasn't much to see. Though the fridge and freezer were well-stocked—no surprise—the rest of her place looked as if she'd used the same decorator responsible for some dreary chain of temporary executive suites.

Perhaps the thought telegraphed to her as he settled the frozen vegetables on her puffy knee, because when he dropped onto the narrow, thin-cushioned couch nearby, she glanced over. "I know it doesn't look like much." She shook out some pills into her palm. "I bought most of the stuff at a sale of secondhand hotel furniture."

"Ah." That explained its bland lines and boring colors. It didn't clarify why she'd chosen them as her own surroundings. The only Nikki thing about the place was the lingering notes of her personal scent. "But I thought you'd at least cover the bare walls with your collection of Melissa Etheridge posters."

"You haven't seen my bedroom." She swallowed down the pills with several sips of the water from the bottle he'd set on the small table at her side. Now he noticed the fishbowl at her elbow.

The sight of it felt like a fist to his chest. "You really do have a plastic fish." Anonymous furniture, empty walls, a fake pet. Nothing that attached her to her environment, let alone to anything living and breathing.

"What? Yeah." She set down her water and let her head rest against the back of the chair. Her wince as she adjusted her right leg stole his breath.

Shit, it had to hurt.

"How'd you do that?" he asked. "How'd you injure it again?"

Nikki's spine jerked straight and she almost knocked over her water bottle as she jackknifed in her seat. "Oh, my God. Fern. We left Fern alone. How could I have forgotten?"

Alarm chilled his blood. "Forgotten what?"

Five minutes and a phone call later, he'd calmed them both. That scrawny little excuse of a male adolescent was going to be sorry he was born, but that was another night's agenda. For now, Fern was safe at her friend Marie's and Jay believed her promise to stay put.

Nikki slumped back in her chair and her eyelids drooped. The meds were doing their thing, he suspected, glad she was getting some relief. When she was sleepy enough—soon, he suspected—he planned to tuck her into bed.

And make a place for himself right beside her for as long as she'd let him stay.

"No, Jay," she said. "I'll be fine by myself."

"Christ," he complained. "Stop reading my mind."

"I'm reading the way you just kicked off your shoes and then made yourself more comfortable on my couch cushions." Her eyes blazed open, the blue and the green unbalancing him again.

But he was growing accustomed to it, and they were so beautiful that he was beginning to think he'd willingly teeter for the rest of his life.

"I don't need a keeper," she said.

"For tonight, how about a friend?"

She stilled, then glanced away. A long moment passed. "Do you think it's true?"

He figured he knew what she was talking about. "I don't

know, cookie. We can call Cassandra. I'll bet she'd even come over—"

"*No*." It was in her voice now, that fear he'd seen on her face at Malibu & Ewe.

He didn't understand it, but he didn't press. "All right."

"I think it's true." Her gaze flicked toward him, flicked away. "The other morning at your house, she came over and told me all about being conceived through artificial insemination. I didn't think much about it at the time, because Cassandra is one of those friendly, girly types who talks about everything—I think I know her SAT scores and the name of her first boyfriend—but she also mentioned donor siblings and how the Internet could make it fairly easy to locate them."

"Would your parents have kept from you that kind of information?"

Instead of answering, she dipped inside the fishbowl and scooped out her pet. A few cranks on the winder and she let it free again, her gaze focused on its manic plastic fins. "I can see them not saying anything," Nikki finally answered. "My mom once mentioned fertility issues, I think, but she wouldn't have wanted me to feel anything other than 'normal,' so might have kept quiet. My father . . . maybe my mother would have made Dad promise not to tell before she died? Or was he embarrassed by the situation that he was himself infertile? I don't know. That I wasn't his biological child could explain why he was so . . . so cold."

She looked over at Jay, her pretty face blank. "I don't remember a time that he touched me, you know. Not even at my mother's funeral."

Oh, hell. His hand crept up to his chest. How did people navigate this damn love thing? Her bad knee made his throb. The dents in her heart made his own ache like the devil.

He shoved up from the couch and reached her in two strides. It only took a moment to lift her up and then into his lap as he took her place in the chair. His hands were careful as they replaced the fallen bag of peas and then they were gentle as they cradled her to him.

He buried his nose in her hair and inhaled her scent as her head lay heavy on his shoulder. Their breathing synchronized and it was the oddest damn thing, but he felt his heart growing bigger, expanding like the volume during the chorus of some cheesy hair band's rock ballad.

Could he live like this? Could he live *with* this? Maybe if he ran now, he could save himself from whatever these feelings for her were doing to him.

Her whisper sounded over the voice in his head urging escape. "Why do think she didn't say anything? Do you think Cassandra recognized me that first day and then decided she didn't want me to know about our connection?"

Oh, no. Oh, God. His arms tightened around her reflexively. "Of course not." He managed to choke out the words, though there was a vise of emotion closing hard around his neck. "I can't know what Cassandra is thinking, of course . . ."

Nikki's back straightened, and she turned in his lap so she could look at his face. There was a wrinkle between her eyebrows and her bottom lip was pushed out, doing that thing that was supposed to be a frown. "You knew, didn't you? Before tonight. You knew that Cassandra and I are biologically related."

Fate must be laughing her—of course female—ass off. When it came for Jay's time to fall, he'd taken the dive for a woman who was all unsettling and at least half-psychic. "I . . . I . . ."

The wrinkle on her forehead disappeared as her eyebrows rose in question. "You . . . you . . ."

Thirty-two years old. Experienced with women. An editor of a national magazine. A journalist who'd met all sorts of people in the pursuit of a story. You'd think he'd have learned self-preservation along the way. But he discovered he couldn't lie to those beautiful, mesmerizing eyes.

"I found out a few days ago," he admitted, his muscles

tensing. She was going to throw his ass out now. Cut him loose, shut him down, slap his face, at least metaphorically, if not in reality.

On the same night that he'd truly accepted that he was in love with Nikki, Nikki was going to show him the door. His mind raced, thinking what he could say to soften her. What he might do to persuade her to give him another chance.

"Oh," she said, settling back against him. "I understand perfectly. I wouldn't have wanted to get involved either."

The knife, the knife he knew she didn't even realize she'd wielded, slid deep between his ribs. The cruelest cut was the one that made clear she expected so damn little of him.

Nineteen

Fear makes strangers of people who would be friends.

—SHIRLEY MACLAINE,
ACTRESS

Days later, Nikki limped around the Malibu kitchen. The next afternoon was the big anniversary party and with her knee bound in an elastic bandage and with plenty of breaks to give it rest, she was managing all right. Jay wasn't happy with the arrangement, but he wasn't happy about her moving around at all.

"I'm going to get a butt as big as Texas if you keep this up," she'd told him the night before as he'd come into her living room carrying bags of take-out—greasy hamburgers and fries. "Not to mention what this kind of food will do to your heart."

He'd sent her an odd look. "My heart is my problem. Now your butt . . . that's my problem, too. And my biggest problem with it is that it's all covered up when I thought I told you before I left that I wanted you naked and willing as soon as I got back with the food."

"Seriously, Jay, I don't like someone doing things for me. I don't need it."

He grinned, ignoring her complaint. "You like

someone—me—doing things *to* you, though. So cut me some slack, cookie."

They'd eaten dinner, he'd uncovered her butt along with all of her other body parts, and she'd very nakedly and willingly let him, well, "do" what he wanted.

When it came to sex, she still let him melt her at will and on demand. She followed his sweet, persuasive suggestions, blushed at his raunchy orders, and went eagerly into every new position he introduced, in each case relying on him to make the experience something worthwhile.

God, he'd probably hate that, knowing she was thinking of Jay Buchanan as Old Reliable. A cold chill broke over her skin. She should hate that, too—she did hate that, as a matter of fact, because it wasn't smart to be considering anyone so steadfast. Including Jay Buchanan.

Particularly Jay Buchanan.

Behind her, she heard the sliding glass door to the deck open. "Hey, Hef Junior," she called over her shoulder, her voice purposefully light. "Remember *101 Dalmatians*? I was just thinking you reminded me of that movie's ancient, long-eared bloodhound."

"It's me."

Cassandra's voice had Nikki spinning around on her good leg. The other woman stood in the doorway, wearing a knee-length full skirt of thin cotton and a lacy tank top she surely had crocheted. Both hands gripped a large, woven reed basket.

"What are you doing here?" Nikki asked.

Cassandra hesitated a moment, then came closer, holding out the item she carried. "I brought something for you. A peace offering. My version of a plate of baked goods or a bowl of fruit." She set it on the counter near Nikki, then backed away.

Inside was a pretty jumble of different balls of yarn—their colors bright and their weights as varied as their shades. A pair of hand-painted knitting needles stuck up like chopsticks. Just as tempted as she was by the fresh produce at a farmer's market, Nikki reached out a finger to test the different textures.

Cassandra had tied a bow made of a glittery knitted strip around the handle, and Nikki decided that's what she could do with the mile-long swathe that she continued to work on. Of course, she'd have to hope someone was looking for ribbon to wrap an SUV or maybe a real elephant.

She touched the loop of the bow. "You didn't need to do this."

"I would have brought it earlier, but Jay warned me off."

Nikki frowned. "What?"

"He said he didn't think you were ready to talk to me."

Her temper rose. Damn him. He had no right making decisions for her. Though their sexual affair was hot and heavy, she didn't want him looking into her head. They weren't that close, and she'd make that clear to him as soon as she finished this with Cassandra. "He should keep out of my business."

The other woman blinked at her vehemence. "He seems to care a lot about you."

"In a superficial kind of way," Nikki insisted.

Cassandra tucked her hair behind her ears. "Anyhow, I came to apologize. I'd shared with the other knitters some particulars of my, uh, situation. But I didn't plan on the way the revelation was sprung on you the other night."

Nikki lifted a shoulder. *Never let them think you're weak.* "I was surprised, I'll give you that."

"I'm sure you've put two and two together about how it came about. A few months ago, I started some sleuthing on the Internet. I found you, and sent you that advertisement, hoping to entice you into the shop."

"Picking up the phone wasn't an easier option?"

Now it was Cassandra's turn to give an uncomfortable shrug. She looked down at her feet. "The thing is, I wanted to get a look at you first. It felt weird to call a stranger out of the blue with that kind of news. 'Hey, we're both products of the same sperm donor.' And then when you came in the shop that first time . . ."

"You recognized me," Nikki remembered. "Without even knowing my name."

"Because of what I know about our father."

"Not that. Not father." She'd had a father. Maybe he hadn't been a particularly warm or happy or honest one, but she couldn't erase him from her life like that. He'd taught her important lessons—like standing on her own two feet because she couldn't count on others to stick around and prop her up. "Sperm donor."

Cassandra acknowledged the point with a nod. "Right. Well, he was a medical student when he donated. In the early days of artificial insemination and sperm banks, it was a common practice for the men in medical school to make extra money that way."

"Doctor, huh? Maybe that explains why I don't mind deboning chickens."

Cassandra gave a little laugh. "Maybe you're right. He's a surgeon now. And he has eyes like yours. It was in the records. One blue and one green. When I saw you, that's how I knew."

"Okay. Well, mystery solved. And thanks for the basket."

Cassandra didn't pick up on her dismissal. "When I actually met you that day, I had second thoughts about making contact. I realized it might be selfish of me and that you could be perfectly happy not knowing the truth about our biological relationship. So I kept quiet and continued my inner debate." She continued standing where she was, looking miserable.

That wasn't Nikki's problem. She turned back to the countertop where she'd been threading vegetables onto skewers.

Cassandra cleared her throat. "But now that you do know, are there any questions—"

"No." Then Nikki took a breath and turned around again. "Okay. Yes. Is there any medical history I should be aware of? My mom died of cancer, so I already have a concern on that score."

"No. At least nothing he reported as a young man. He doesn't live far from here and from what I've learned about him now—"

Nikki signaled "stop" with her hand. "I don't want to hear more."

"Okay. Okay. I respect that." She swallowed hard, then brought her hand to her lips as if to hold something back.

Oh, God. Tears. Nikki bit down on the inside of her mouth. She *so* wanted Cassandra out of her kitchen. She'd never asked for this . . . this entanglement, and she wasn't going to get drawn into its web.

She was better on her own. "Listen, you'll have to excuse me now. I'm helping Jay throw a big party for his family tomorrow and I have a lot to do before then."

Behind that unmoving hand, Cassandra's head nodded.

Nikki's stomach clenched. "Maybe this is all a mistake, have you thought of that?" she asked, desperate to cut off the emotion welling in the other woman's expressive eyes. "We're nothing alike. Not really. You knit. I cook. Your . . . your hair is longer. You talk. You cry."

There were definite tears spilling over Cassandra's bottom lashes. Nikki crossed to the tissue box on the counter, yanked a few out, then pressed them into the other woman's free hand. "Here," she said, her throat tightening in annoyance. "I'm sorry, but I'm really beginning to doubt your whole story."

Cassandra laughed behind the tissues. "I can understand why. At this moment, I wouldn't want to be my sister either."

Her sister.

Nikki hadn't really considered that very much. During the brief moments she'd allowed herself to think over the situation the past couple of days, she'd used the time to review her childhood. While her father probably had not been an affectionate man by nature, that she was the product of artificial insemination using another man's sperm likely explained his very palpable detachment—she wasn't even his child! It also meant she hadn't genetically inherited her keep-your-distance DNA from him as she'd always assumed. But that only proved when it came to temperament that nurture had its sway over nature.

So . . . sister?

Well, Nikki didn't need one.

She steeled her spine and looked Cassandra straight in her now-dry eyes. "Look, you seem very nice, and it's . . . it's nothing personal, but I don't need anyone—a donor sibling, a sister, whatever you want to call yourself—in my life."

"There's something more—"

"But I don't want to hear anything more. I'm sorry. I just don't. I'm not one of those people who gets close to others. Do you understand?"

"I can understand if you don't like me."

"No!" Nikki's chest tightened on that aching thing that was thudding inside of it. This is what she didn't want. The ache, the hurting. She didn't want to experience the pain when bonds were broken. And they always, ultimately, did break. "It's not you, it's me."

Cassandra laughed again, though it lacked humor just like the first time. "Have you been reading articles in Jay's magazine?"

"I'm serious." And the mention of *NYFM* gave her a way to explain it. "There are two kinds of weasels, you see. Those that socialize naturally and find it easy to make attachments with others. That's you. Then there's another variety, a variety like me, that do better on their own, independent of close relationships. I'm Weasel Number Two."

Cassandra just looked at her. "You're going to make me cry again, little sister, comparing your pretty self to a rodent."

Not just sister. *Little* sister.

All at once, Nikki's chest constricted tighter, shutting air from her lungs. Her face felt hot and both her knees seemed ready to give out on her. She looked away, blinking rapidly, wondering whether she could make it to the phone and dial 911. For some reason, she was without air.

As black dots did somersaults at the edge of her vision,

Jay was suddenly by her side. He pulled a stool toward her and lifted her onto the seat. He said something to Cassandra about Nikki's knee injury, and the other woman finally, finally left her kitchen, Jay at her heels.

Nikki was finally, finally alone again.

But still scared as hell, especially when Jay returned to her and she allowed herself to be held against his chest. Leaning on him, she found her first free breath.

Jay prowled the anniversary party, nodding greetings, smiling social smiles, and accepting the compliments that came his way. Yes, his parents and aunt and uncle had been surprised. It *was* a beautiful day. A wonderful event.

None of which made him happy. His month with Nikki was coming to an end and worry gnawed at the edges of his inner peace—worry that she was going to disappear from his life without warning. It didn't help matters that he'd wanted just that, many too many times, when it came to other women he'd invited into his bed.

What goes around, comes around.

Karma's a bitch.

Those two little nuggets kept echoing in his head, and he couldn't figure out a way to silence his mental voice. So he settled for sticking close to Nikki, as if that would ensure she wanted to be close to *him*.

In the kitchen, he found her directing the servers they'd hired for the day, and he waited nearby while she finished her instructions. Another disquieting note: She was dressed in her chef armor again.

He suspected those checked pants and that starchy jacket were her attempt at neutralizing her appeal to him. But the joke was on her this time, because the genderless outfit only fixated his attention on that ultra-feminine sweet spot at the back of her neck bared by her braids. The skin there was fine-grained and pale, as sexy to him as the sleek texture of her inner thigh or that delicate flesh on the inside edge of her hip bones.

"Come out of the kitchen and enjoy the party," he coaxed, as the servers left the kitchen with trays filled with skewers of vegetables and fruit. "Mingle."

The roll of her eyes was in her voice. "As soon as forty-plus people eat, drink, and be merry."

"Nikki—"

Two cool hands suddenly covered his eyes. "Guess who?" a woman asked in sultry tones.

He swallowed his inward groan. The voice wasn't immediately familiar, but he recognized the roundness of female breasts against his back. The fingers clung to his as he peeled them off, but he shook them loose and turned to face the woman, hoping Nikki was too busy to notice.

Because it was one of those cover models she so often used to poke fun at him. "Stephanie," he said. "You're here."

Duh. But "glad you could make it" or "I'm so happy to see you" might have sent the wrong message to the braided chef behind him.

Stephanie Nichols, dressed in a short, clingy dress the color of orange sherbet, didn't seem to notice his lack of a warm welcome. "I wouldn't miss your parents' party." One step of her stiletto sandals and she was pressing a friendly kiss to his mouth.

Almost before it was over, he was turning in the direction of the death rays he felt sure were being aimed at the back of his neck. And there she was, the ray-beamer, not two feet away. "Nikki," he said, holding out his hand to her. "Come meet an old friend."

Instead of touching flesh to flesh, she slapped a napkin onto his palm. "Lipstick, handsome," she whispered sotto voce, tapping her own mouth. "Don't want the ladies around here to get the idea you're taken."

"But I am taken, cookie," he murmured, narrowing his eyes and pulling her forward by the elbow. "Stephanie, meet Nikki."

The other woman's gaze jumped between their faces. "Your . . . ?"

"Chef. For the time being," Nikki answered. "And I really need to get back to it. If you'll excuse me?"

She slipped from Jay's grasp before he could anchor the eel to his side.

For the time being.

Yeah, she was preparing to run out on him, he was sure of it.

Stephanie's eyebrows were raised and speculation was written all over her face, but he didn't have any more time for her. He started edging toward Nikki. "You can find your way to the folks?" he asked the other woman.

"Sure." With a long look over her shoulder, she headed toward the deck.

He headed toward his chef. With benefits, and she better not be forgetting it.

She shot him a quick glance. "Month? Year?"

Brat. "The December 2005 issue. I grew up with her brother; he's one of my best friends."

Her lip curled. "So she used her connections to get the cover."

"Actually, I didn't know anything about it until she had the job."

She busied herself pulling a baking sheet holding three foil-wrapped loaves out of the oven. "Next you're going to tell me she has her master's from MIT."

"Stanford. And it's just a bachelor's degree in biology."

The scent of buttery garlic wafted through the air as she unpeeled the foil to check on one loaf. "But of course, as cover bimbo, more important was her past experience with plastic surgery."

Jay ran his hand along his chin. "I'm pretty sure they're real."

"*Riiiight.*" She refolded the foil and bent to shove the pan back in the oven.

"One hundred percent sure."

Nikki froze, then straightened to face him. An oven mitt shaped like a lobster poked out from under an elbow as she crossed her arms over her chest. "You're shattering my illusions."

"That she's not stupid, that sometimes they're real, that not every model sleeps her way to a photo shoot?"

"That you wouldn't lie about sleeping with her in order to make your life easier."

He pulled her by the lobster claw toward him, so that her starchy shirt scratched his softer one. He linked his hands at the small of her back. "Are you going to make life hard for me, cookie? I'm really hoping not."

"I don't understand you, Jay."

"I was with Stephanie before I ever met you. And, for the record, she broke it off."

"Really?"

"All right, I wasn't exactly writing Dear Abby about my lovesick woes after it happened, but the fact is, we dated for a while, and then we didn't. We're still friends."

Yet Nikki had a point. Not coming clean about it would have been simpler. And wasn't that what he always was after? Keeping things uncomplicated? But he'd already discovered that lying to those blue and green eyes was damn difficult, and if what he wanted with her was a relationship, then honesty—

A *relationship*?

Was that what he wanted?

And an inner voice answered him quickly: He wanted it all.

The knowledge was like a California temblor inside of him. He took a steadying breath, even as he acknowledged that he had to make it the same for Nikki. He must shatter her illusions. He must shake her up. He must rock her world, because that's what it was going to take to break down her self-sufficient, I-don't-need-anyone attitude.

"What are we doing here?" she whispered. "Why are you with me? Why are you with me and not with one of them?"

Her honest beauty, his former shallowness. He couldn't

find fault with her doubts. "Nikki," he said. "Because not one of them *is* you."

A flush warmed her cheeks. "Jay . . ." She leaned into him.

He had her! It was relief, not triumph, and God, wasn't that a bitch.

Like karma.

Like what goes around, comes around.

He lowered his forehead and touched hers.

"Jay! Jay, I need to talk to you."

He stiffened. This new voice he recognized instantly. Shanna. "What's up?" He held Nikki's gaze with his own.

He felt his neighbor enter the kitchen. "I'm sorry to interrupt, but this is an emergency."

Nikki eeled out of his hold again. "I have things to do."

Damn, now checking out Shanna's face, it looked as if he did, too.

With a sigh, he turned to her. "What's the matter?"

Her high heels clacked on the floorboards as she backed into the relative privacy of the dim, narrow hallway, and with another sigh, he followed her. "I'm looking for Jorge," she said.

"What? Your sprinklers aren't coming on when they should? Weeds invading the potted pansies?"

"No." Her hands made a nervous slide down the silky fabric of her party dress. "He . . . he was going to be my date, but he didn't show up at the time we agreed upon."

Jay stared, not sure what surprised him more, that Shanna was dating the man she considered her gardener, or that she'd been stood up. "Jorge gets straight As in responsibility. If he really wanted to be someplace, well, he'd be there."

Too late, he realized how that came out. "I mean—"

"I know what you mean." Shanna backed farther down the hall, toward the front door. "You're saying he probably didn't want to be with me after all."

Oh, damn. That wasn't what he meant to say, and yet Jay didn't know how to make this right—or even if he could. It wasn't that long ago that she'd been making up excuses to see him. Many times over in the past six months she'd called him, needing an escort to this event or that party. Perhaps she'd just transferred her fixation to Jay's friend and Jorge wasn't any more interested in being involved than he had been.

Before he could do anything about determining the truth or repairing the damage, she was gone.

And cad that he was, he was relieved, because he could return to Nikki and work on cementing her to his side.

Except she wasn't in the kitchen.

In the empty space, he instead saw her as she was the day before, facing her half-sister and wearing an earnest expression.

I'm Weasel Number Two.

The kind that did better on their own, she'd said. Independent of close relationships. The words had sent those icy goose feet trekking down his spine then, and they did now, too. *Where the hell was she?*

He shot out of the kitchen.

His skyrocketing pulse fell as he saw her offering a tray of hors d'oeuvres to his parents. Trying to get his cool back, he ambled over to join them as his dad was popping one into his mouth. Jay slid his arm around Nikki. "Mom, Dad, I don't think you've had a chance to meet my girlfriend."

His father choked.

His mother's eyes rounded, but that might have been due to anxiety over her husband's health. Jay was forced to step away from Nikki in order to thump his dad's back. Even then, he still kept an eye on his chef, and a good thing, because he caught her arm with his free hand as she started to sidle away.

Damn woman. "Don't go," he ordered.

"I can't do the Heimlich with my hands full."

His dad waved. "I'm . . ." He coughed. "Okay." Two more coughs and then he managed a smile for Nikki. "Just surprised that Jay . . ."

Too late, Hugh Buchanan realized that perhaps "surprise" wasn't the best sentiment to express. *Gee, thanks, Dad.*

His mom jumped in to smooth the moment over. "Surprised that Jay . . . that Jay . . . that Jay . . ."

Christ, could his parents make it any clearer that he'd lived the life of a confirmed commitment-phobe? Nikki would never believe he had the least bit of long-haul in him. With a sigh, he took the tray from her and placed it on a nearby table. "This is Nikki Carmichael. Nikki, my mother and father, Ellen and Hugh Buchanan."

They exchanged handshakes, and before Nikki could get away again, he snagged his sisters, and then his aunt and uncle, in order to make those introductions as well. "My girlfriend," he said each time and as his relatives hid their astonishment at the term—with more or less success—he could sense her growing bewilderment.

Which only contributed to his own unease. He linked his fingers with hers to draw her closer to his side as she suffered through his sisters' inevitable nosiness. She shot him an uncomfortable look, but he wasn't sure if it was because of his possessive touch or because she had to respond to his sister Susan's probing questions.

"I don't know exactly why I turned to cooking as a career," Nikki said.

"You must have learned your love for it from a mother or grandmother," Susan asserted. "A family tradition kind of thing."

"No." Nikki tugged on the hand holding hers, signaling her need to escape.

Jay squeezed her fingers. "Enough of the third degree, Sue. She doesn't have to know exactly why she makes meals for other people."

"It's the connections," his mother said. "That's obvious."

Nikki stopped pulling on his arm. "What?"

"Look around you." Her gaze drifted to the crowded deck and the guests chatting, drinking, eating. "Or think about a restaurant. Chefs know food creates connections. By combining colors and flavors you bring people together, Nikki."

And wasn't that a revelation, Jay thought. Self-proclaimed independent Nikki, making meals and making bonds.

Making him have hope that she wanted that for herself.

He held onto the idea for the rest of the afternoon. Through the party, the toasts, the cleanup. Finally, he walked his parents to their car, and waved at Fern as she went home in the backseat of her parents' sedan.

Leaving him with his chef, who he hoped wanted him as much as he wanted her in his life.

But she'd disappeared.

His heart plummeted. Damn it! He couldn't take his eyes off her for a second!

He ran to the back door, scanned the deck, the beach, and then craned his neck to search the alley between his place and Shanna's. But the lights were out next door and he couldn't detect any movement in the shadows. He sped toward his room to grab his keys, intent on tracking Nikki down. They were going to have this out tonight. He was going to make clear he wanted more . . . that he wanted—

His feet skidded to a halt in the doorway.

His chef with benefits was emerging from the attached bathroom, wrapped only in a dark green bath towel that skimmed the top of her thighs and turned one of her eyes emerald. Her shoulders and throat glowed pink and damp. When she stepped closer, the edge of the terry cloth lifted and he glimpsed the sweet, seductive cleft between her legs.

He jerked his gaze away. It wasn't smart to be sidetracked by that. Feelings came first this time, and he had to get his out before anything else.

"Jay," she said, her husky voice beguiling. Bewitching.

He swallowed. "What?"

From the top of his dresser, she lifted a coil of fabric and ran it through her fingers. He stared at that long blue ribbon of knitted yarn she'd been working on for days. The thing had to be eight feet long now. "I finished it," she said, bringing it to her cheek. She caressed her rosy skin with sensuous strokes.

He followed the movement with his gaze, unable to look away. "What . . . what is it?"

"I think I finally decided," she said, drifting closer. In a blink, the item was looped around his neck and she pulled on the two ends to draw him closer.

"Nikki—"

"Shh," she said, her mouth getting nearer.

But he had a plan. An agenda. Something to do before they slipped between the sheets. Something that had to do with feelings, with wanting her to want him. But all that was being left behind as his mono-tasking male brain jumped the rails and took off on an entirely different track.

The sex train set off at full speed.

Ah, well, he thought as her tongue touched his. At least he could be certain she wanted his body.

Shanna had left the party next door before sunset, but as the day darkened, she didn't bother turning on the lights. Artificial incandescence wouldn't change the gloominess of her mood.

Jorge had grown tired of her.

Like every other man who'd been in her life.

Opposite the white leather couch where she was slumped was a white wall. A huge mirror was hung there, one with a heavy, ornate frame. But her position on the cushions was so low, she wasn't reflected in the glass.

Or she'd lost her reflection, just as she'd lost Jorge.

She remembered that day she'd seen herself in his eyes, finding herself there. Then that other day, when he'd found her in the pool and she'd found herself imprinted in his very flesh. He had given her substance.

Something to hold on to.

Some*one* to hold on to.

But now she was alone again. By herself. A former party girl who'd only been famous for her notoriety, and now Paris Hilton had eclipsed her once-infamous reputation. Hell, the younger woman had received a prison sentence.

Shanna was behind bars, too, though, stuck in this cold house, jailed within herself—the worst of all possible cell mates.

The thought made her stomach churn, and it hurt enough to get her off the couch, though she couldn't find the energy to make the stairs to her bathroom. Remembering the acid reliever she'd found in the medicine chest in the downstairs powder room, she headed in that direction. At the bar, she paused to pour herself a vodka tonic—long on vodka, light on tonic. A girl needed something with which to wash down the pill.

She didn't bother trying to meet her own eyes in the mirror over the sink. There'd be no one there.

The contents of the medicine chest were as she remembered them. Except the convenient condoms were gone, now stashed in her bedside table, which left a box-shaped hole between the Pepcid and that prescription bottle of oxycodone.

Shanna swallowed the whole of her vodka-plus-little-tonic, studying that empty space that was so like the emptiness in her chest that was so like the emptiness of her life.

The vodka buzzed like a lone summer bee in her system, so she wandered back to the bar and poured another tumblerful, hoping a whole hive would join in. With the glass half-empty, she topped it off again, then drifted back to the medicine cabinet for the acid controller.

Her fingers reached for the plastic bottle. *Oops,* she realized, as she lifted it from the shelf. She'd grabbed the oxycodone instead. But hey, she told herself, it could stop her stomach pain, too, right?

At the bar again, she lifted the crystal decanter. Instead of filling her tumbler, she tucked it in the crook of her arm and wandered with it and the prescription bottle to the window. From here she could see the little house next door that she'd been working on. The porch light was on. She stared at it, and could see moths circling.

She was drawn to it as they were.

Outside, she paused beside the pool for another swallow of vodka. Juggling the decanter, its top, and the prescription bottle proved to be too much and the oxycodone tumbled to the ground. Her mother's arthritic hands made her request lids without tamper-proofing. The pharmacist must have left this one loose, because as the bottle fell so did the pills.

Shanna kneeled to gather them up, which also required setting down the decanter. With the medication cradled in her two palms, she couldn't lift the vodka from the pool deck. Damn.

She looked at the dark water, remembering that feeling of sinking into it, of giving herself over to its warmth and weight. Nice. Giving over sounded so, so nice.

Without more thought than that, she tossed one handful of oxycodone pills into her mouth, then washed them down with a swallow of vodka. The second mouthful was as easy as the first.

Tucking the pill bottle into the pocket of her jeans, she took herself and the decanter next door.

Twenty

During *What Ever Happened To Baby Jane?*, I knitted a scarf from Hollywood to Malibu.

—JOAN CRAWFORD,
ACTRESS

It was Nikki's last chance.

This afternoon, watching the interplay between Jay and his family, between Jay and his family's friends, between Jay and they-were-one-hundred-percent-real cover bimbo, she'd been brought up short by how very different they were. How what they had together couldn't last—or last much longer.

He was the supreme insider. Mr. Well-Connected, Mr. Most Popular. She was outside all loops, unfamiliar with family ties, un— Well, not exactly unlovable maybe, but unable to open a path to her heart. That was okay, though. As a Weasel Number Two, she didn't do the love thing. And loving Jay, Mr. Most Likely to Seduce the Female Masses, would be disastrous.

He deepened the kiss and she tightened her grip on the long scarf, pulling him even closer. His hands brushed her shoulders and then pushed the towel to the floor. As her belly met the hardening erection behind his pants, his palms slid to the small of her back.

Nikki moaned against his mouth. He'd provided her a job transition and sexual satisfaction. Now she wanted to use him for just one more thing.

Leaving the knitted material looped around his neck, she went to work on the buttons of his silky shirt. When she brushed bare skin, one of his hands wandered between her legs, but she hastily reached behind and returned it to her waist, even as the flesh between her thighs heated and went wet. When Jay touched her like that, he owned her response.

But nobody, *nobody* owned Nikki.

It was time to prove that. It was time to prove that just as she was able to receive sex now, that she could give it, too.

She was going to make it so good for Jay that she'd be able to walk away from him, smiles on both their faces. Then the balance of power between them would be equalized forever—and she'd be whole like she hadn't been since she was fifteen years old.

His shirt slipped off as she pushed him toward the end of the bed. The backs of his legs hit the edge of the mattress and he went down, his fingers creating a trail along the backs of her thighs that her goose bumps finished for him at her ankles.

Eyes at half-mast, he let her go to work on his pants and soon he was naked, too, except for that Jay-blue length of yarn she'd knitted. It was nearly long enough to bind him like a mummy, but she wanted more access to his skin than that.

She clambered onto the bed to press against his side. He brushed her hair off her forehead with his hand. "How's your knee, cookie?"

His concern gave her a sweet little shiver. "This is not about my knee." She pressed a kiss against his raspy chin, then another on the side of his neck.

He groaned, his fingers sliding along her scalp. "Come up here and let me give you a proper kiss."

"I don't want a proper kiss." Her mouth found his nipple

and she rolled the tip of her tongue across the tiny, hardening point.

His back arched, pushing his hot skin against her lips. She sucked.

His free hand closed around her upper arm. "Nikki, God."

Leaning over his chest, she found his other nipple and swirled her tongue around the areola. "*Bruja*," he whispered. "Get up here." His hand tried to drag her toward his mouth.

"No," she said, shaking her head as she pulled back to sit on the mattress. "You keep your hands to yourself, handsome."

"Can't. Can't not touch you."

She loved the guttural tone. But he wasn't getting his way this time. This time it was her way, her choice, her power.

His response.

Her hand brushed the length of scarf and she pulled one end, sliding it from behind his neck. "What are you doing?" he asked, as she positioned his wrists together and rested them on the flat of his stomach.

"What does it look like I'm doing?" She wound the fabric around and around, creating a soft set of bulky handcuffs.

"Hey, wait," he protested. "I believe I called this kinky game first."

"You talk too much. Haven't I told you that?" Still, she was amazed at his cooperation. Not every man, she suspected, would cede control like this. "It's time for you to shut up and take what I'm going to give you."

He grinned. "You should have put it like that in the first place."

Her gaze jumped to his. "You're so bad."

"I love it when you frown. Come up here." His tone cajoled, laughter danced in his eyes, and she could tell he wasn't really letting her have her way. Instead he was trying to talk her into what he wanted. "Let me bite that pouty lower lip."

She sucked it back. "I do not pout."

"Only when I complain about your commando boots. But right now I could sing hosannas to some thigh-high leather and a bustier, the pink tip of your breast between my—"

She bent, and the rest of his blather was lost on a choked-in breath as she took the head of his erection into her mouth. Her tongue circled the ridge of flesh before moving to the smooth skin of his shaft. Her gaze drifted to his.

"Shutting up now," he whispered. "Quiet as a mouse. Noiseless as a nematode . . ."

She sucked him deeper, sucked hard to take the flavor of him into her body. Her tongue painted passion along his slick skin.

His body shuddered. "Silent as surrender."

It was what she wanted. Him taking, Nikki giving. It was what she needed, and she couldn't damn the man for the suspicion that he understood exactly that. He understood women.

So many times he'd understood her.

The palm of her hand brushed up his hair-roughened thigh. He twitched at her touch, then his thighs parted to give her access to the round, cooler warmths at the base of his shaft. She cupped them in her palm and then moved her mouth to suck lightly at their baby-soft skin.

"Nikki," he whispered. "Cookie. God, you're good at that."

The praise was like an aphrodisiac. Like warm chocolate running through her veins. She slid against his body, cuddling closer so that her nipples pressed against his flank and then she slid her good knee over one of his thighs to hold him still for her ministrations.

Someone was moaning—oh, it was her—as she rubbed her breasts against the hot skin of his leg. She ran her tongue up and down the glistening shaft of his erection and then pressed a smacking kiss on the very top of the swollen head. From the corner of her eye, she saw his fingers flex, as if he had to move even though she'd constrained him.

She licked another path downward, then up again, stopping when she saw the droplet seeping from his body. Her gaze jumped to his, saw the burn there, that was all for her. No, *from* her.

I did this. I do this to him.

Power shot through her as she reached out her forefinger to claim his body's tear. "Wet," she whispered, looking at her fingertip, then at him. "Wet, like me."

Holding his gaze, she sucked her finger into her mouth, savoring his taste against her tongue.

"Enough." He reared up, his arms breaking free of her yarn chains in one swift movement. Before she could pull her finger free of her lips, she was flat on her back and Jay was leaning over her.

"Hey," she said, pushing against his chest. "Hey, this isn't . . . that's not . . ." The last words were lost against his lips.

Lost in his kiss. All of her, lost.

He lifted his head as her hands slid to the mattress. "My chance now, cookie."

"But . . . but . . ." The words died. Surrender was so sweet and she'd proved her point, hadn't she? He'd trusted her enough to let her truss him up and she'd tasted how far she'd taken him, how far her power over him could take them both. It wouldn't hurt to let him have his turn.

He made her muscles gelatin in a matter of seconds. His mouth traced her ears, her jaw, the length of her neck. He had passionate revenge on her breasts, not stopping until she was lifting off the mattress and begging him for . . . something.

Then he turned her over. He was silent a moment. "That ass," he finally said, running his palms over both round curves. "I've neglected that ass for much too long."

His fingers kneaded her there, and then moved upward, massaging the small of her back and then the muscles across her shoulder blades.

Her eyes closed in sensuous delight. "Jay . . . what you do to me—"

She shrieked, startled by a nip on the apple of her bottom. Jerking her head from the pillow, she glared at him over her shoulder. "What are you doing?"

"I'll make it better." He covered the sting with a sucking kiss.

Her heart stuttered. "Are you . . . did you . . ."

At a matching place on her other cheek, he nipped again, then sucked. She jerked, unsure if it was pain or pleasure buffeting her senses.

"Twin hickeys on your ass," he said, his voice smug. "Beautiful. And our little secret."

Outrage wouldn't come. Only more heat, more wetness, more want that ached and pulsed between her thighs. "*Jay* . . ."

She moaned as something round and cool rolled down her spine. The scent of citrus reached her nostrils. "What are you doing now?"

"Putting one of the lemons you left on the table here to good use."

"I needed the counter space in the kitchen." Her bottom was still throbbing from those heated little marks, but that firm, smooth fruit was confusing her nerve endings. She squirmed as he rolled the lemon firmly down the bumps of her spine and then horizontally in the dip at the base. "I thought a bowl of fruit was more manly than flowers for your bedroom."

"That's me, manly man." The lemon made another erotic trip over her back. "I always see you rolling lemons like this. How come?"

Her face burned. She forced herself not to squirm again. "To . . . to release the juice."

His hand froze. The lemon pressed hard into the small

of her back, and she clenched her bottom muscles in reaction, setting those silly hickeys to throbbing again.

"Is it working?" he asked, turning her over to face upward again. "Are your juices released?"

"*Jay.*"

"Nikki?" One of his eyebrows lifted as he waited for her response. When she stared up at him, silent, his mouth kicked up. "Okay, then, I'll just have to find out for myself."

He grabbed up the abandoned length of scarf. Her heart tripped. Maybe he could see it in her eyes, because his face went serious and there was a sexual hardness to it that he usually disguised with laughter and charm. With a slow movement, he reached for her left wrist.

She couldn't help but stiffen. Being held down, feeling forced in any way, this fear was the final legacy of her old experience, no matter how much she wished it away. One look at Jay's intent face, no longer playful, told her he knew exactly how nervous this made her.

"I trusted you," he said. "Show me you trust me, too."

Shivers ran hot and cold over her skin. Though they'd never discussed that what she'd claimed happened to her "friend" at that drunken, dark party had really happened to her, she understood Jay knew the truth. He'd known it from the first. So what was he doing?

Oh, God, she knew what he was doing.

She'd thought taking over would give her back what she'd lost. He thought the same . . . that if *she* gave over to *him*, she'd get herself back. If he took the power and gave her only pleasure in return, all the while allowing her no way to escape him . . .

Would it work? She only knew she couldn't display her panic, not even now. *Never let them think you're weak.*

Watching her face, he wound the scarf around her right arm then fastened it over her head to the headboard. A long tail trailed free on one end, an even longer one on the other. Threading the longer tail beneath her naked back, he didn't smile. His chest moved up and down with heavy breaths as he tied her left hand to her left ankle, bending her good knee so that her heel met her hand. The rest of the scarf dangled from this new knot.

She inhaled a test breath as she pulled on the fastenings. He'd tied her firmly, but she realized now that as his gaze ran over her flushed skin it was passion, not panic, that drove her thrumming heartbeat and pounding pulse.

"Jay," she whispered. "Look at me. I'm okay."

"Yeah, baby. I'm looking. But we're not done yet."

He moved over her and she arched for his kiss, but he ignored her proffered body to grab the end of the scarf attached to her right wrist. Leaving plenty of play between them, he tied it to his left one.

"What?" Her heart slammed against her breastbone. The skin covering her belly jittered. "*Why?*"

His free fingers snatched up the extra length attached to the knot on her left. He wrapped it around his right wrist and used his teeth to yank the fastening tight. Though there was enough free fabric between them that his hands could roam freely, the two of them now were—

"Attached," he said, satisfaction glittering in his eyes. "Both of us tied up, Nikki. Tied together. Connected to each other."

No. *No*. She wanted to say it out loud, but the sound she made was half-wordless plea, half-moan. This wasn't what she wanted!

This was what she was truly frightened of.

Connection.

Words, arguments, refusals struggled to form inside her, but they didn't coalesce beyond mere whimpers. And then he went further. Then he kneeled between her thighs and pressed the knee of her bent leg toward the mattress. Opening her to him. Opening her body that was attached to his, opening it to his gaze. His fingers separated her folds, holding them apart so that the most secret, inner part of her was exposed to him. Even when so vulnerable, heat washed over her and more liquid rushed to the place where he was looking. It trickled wetly onto her thigh.

She felt his eyes on her there, avid with desire, and then his mouth found her, kissing her in a way so erotic and intimate that she could only whimper again.

Oh, *God*. He was melting her with every swipe of his knowing, expert tongue. Her heart started slamming against her breastbone as he kept up the amazing, experienced torture. His tongue thrust inside her. "*Jay*."

He didn't let up, instead drawing closer so that the looped ends of the Jay-blue scarf brushed like gentle fingers against her inner thighs. Endless rounds of goose bumps chased after previous sets of hot-cold chills as she yanked on her wrists so she could do something . . .

Push him off?

Pull him closer?

Retreat?

Advance?

But his knots held firm, held her as much as fear had imprisoned her so long ago while her muscles tightened in expectation of climax. But could she let go when Jay held her down like this? When she'd been powerless before, there'd been pain, but now there was only warmth, his wet tongue meeting her wet flesh, the liquid sounds of his taking in her pleasure loud enough to make her blush. Instead though, they only pulled the tension tighter, as she was reminded of the lush sweetness of fresh summer fruit.

Ripe.

Ready.

Bursting.

"Jay." Her voice was urgent. "*Jay*."

His gaze jerked to hers and his tongue jumped to her clitoris. Oh, oh, oh. She was close, so close, her flesh tingling, throbbing beneath his wet mouth. But orgasm seemed just out of reach. Every other time they'd been together, in the crucial final instants Jay had always coaxed her to touch herself. So smart he was, letting her own the moment of sexual release.

Letting her keep a part of herself from him.

But with her hands tied . . .

Her body writhed against the sheets, and those crazy hickeys made their presence known with a renewal of their exotic sting. A bit of scarf tickled the crease between her thigh and torso as his lower hand reached down and a finger pushed inside.

Her womb clenched, her inner muscles clamping down on the masculine invasion.

Heat flushed over her skin as her female body reveled in the demand. Oh, God.

His hand moved in counterpoint to his mouth. Filling her, stimulating her. Stimulating her, filling her.

Oh, good.

Nikki's eyes stung. She blinked rapidly. This was too, too much. "I'm going to scream," she said quickly. He had to let her go or . . . or something was going to happen. "Untie me before I scream."

He lifted his head, his mouth glistening, his eyes unconcerned. "Go ahead, it'll only make me hotter."

"No." He needed to let her go now. If it wasn't a scream, some other, dangerous thing might come out of her mouth. "Please."

"Trust me," he whispered, his breath hot against her thigh. "Let go."

Bending his head once more, Jay licked a hot path over her throbbing flesh. Three fingers worked their way into the wet place where she ached to be filled by him. Her hips shot up.

That scream, those tears, the unsayable emotions she wanted to hold inside her continued to bubble dangerously. Her head thrashed on the pillow, and her cheek encountered cool, citrus smoothness. The lemon.

She remembered it against the heated flesh of her back. In her mind's eye, she saw another Nikki-Jay tableau, his tanned hands rolling it near her round behind, with the twin hickeys burning there. A deeper, almost painful yet exquisite thrust of his fingers brought her back to the present. Her shoulders pressed hard into the mattress as she arched. And then accepted another swipe of his tongue.

Another drive of his hard, long fingers. His mouth moved down the slick flesh between her legs then up again to her clitoris. One light, teasing circle, and then he took it between his lips and sucked.

Her body convulsed against his mouth. She opened her mouth—to scream, to cry, to declare things that should never be said—and in the last second she remembered that lemon against her cheek. Turning her head, she managed to bite down on the fruit, first tasting its clean oil and then its bitter pith. The flavors slid down her throat as her body shook with wave after wave of frantic contractions.

Then the lemon was gone and it was Jay she tasted as he covered her body and kissed her. Ah, but not just the taste of Jay. It was Jay and herself. Still attached. Connected.

Dangerously bonded.

He groaned as he ground his hips against hers and his sex filled her body.

Another attachment.

Connection.

Bond.

He murmured against her lips. "Take me. Have me."

She tilted her hips to meet him, to open herself to his body and to his passion. And with a last wild thrust, he went over, his release as violent as hers. He whispered against her ear as his heavy, sated body pressed down damply. "Love me."

Love me.

The two words broke her heart.

It cracked like a raw egg—she found out it was just that fragile. In those post-orgasmic moments, all sorts of pent-up emotions spilled out: blame, shame, guilt, fear, loneliness, but there was no way to fill it up again without taking in Jay's scent, Jay's warmth, Jay's command. "Love me."

She wouldn't. She didn't.

Instead, she resisted with everything she had, even as her body complied with his movements, letting him turn her against him, two tethered spoons in the damp drawer of his bed.

He nuzzled her hair.

She tasted the lingering acidity of the lemon at the back of her throat and took it as the final signal she'd been waiting for. Closing her eyes, she felt Jay press a gentle kiss near her ear.

She'd always known the end would be bittersweet.

The telephone on his bedside table woke Jay. Bleary, he blinked, turned, squinted at the clock beside the ringing receiver. One fucking A.M.

"I'll get it, cookie," he mumbled over his shoulder. Then his head rolled left, his whiskers scratching the cool pillowcase. Christ. The other side of the bed was empty.

He snatched up the phone. "Nikki? Baby?"

The sound of a blurred voice did that creepy goose waddle down his spine. "'s me. Sh'nna."

Sitting up, he shook his head, trying to will alertness. "Shanna? Is Nikki with you?" Putting out a hand, he discovered the sheets on her side were stone cold.

"No. No one. No one with me."

"Crap," he muttered.

"No one wants me."

He rolled his eyes. "You're drunk, Shanna. Go to bed. Sleep it off. You'll have a hell of a hangover in the morning, but them's the breaks." In the last few months she'd called like this at least a dozen times, her voice thick with booze or tears or both. Leaning over the side of the bed, he found the hem of one pants leg and snagged it, reeling in the garment to get to his cell phone.

"Not jus' drunk."

He ignored Shanna's reply. Where the hell was Nikki? Why would she run off in the middle of the night? Fuck, he'd known he should have talked to her before having sex, but . . .

He looked down at his wrists. Somehow she'd untied the scarf without him waking. And she'd unknotted herself, leaving not even a thread of yarn behind.

Damn it, damn it, and double damn it.

"Took pills, too," the voice slurred again through the line.

"Say again?" He was staring at his cell phone screen, annoyed—not panicked, no, not that, not yet—that it showed not one missed call, not one voice mail message from the woman he'd just tied up and trusted.

Damn it, he *had* trusted her! And she'd run out on him!

She'd run out on the man who was contemplating compromising his simple, confirmed bachelorhood.

A chill wafted over his skin. *Compromising his bachelorhood?*

"Took pills. Mom's. Oxy . . . Oxy . . . thing."

The chill on his skin froze over. "What?"

"Oxy . . . vodka an' oxy."

"*What?*"

"Don't wanna die," Shanna said. "Was dumb to wanna die."

Oh, Christ. His gut clenched. "Shanna. Shanna, sweetheart. Where are you?"

"Nex' door. No. Nex' door nex' door."

Oh, God. "I'm calling nine-one-one."

"No!" Panic sharpened her voice. "No p'lice. Dad. Public'ty. Gossip."

"Shanna." His mind raced, understanding she didn't want the tabloids in on the story, but Christ! "Where are you?"

"Nex' door nex' door. Call . . . call Smitty."

Adrenaline focused his mind. "Smitty" was their old pal, Thomas Smith, now Thomas Smith, M.D., who headed one of Malibu's twenty-six licensed detoxes-by-the-sea—nearly one for every mile of coastline. "Nex' door nex' door . . ." He remembered now that her father had bought the place on the other side of Shanna's marble palace.

"I'm coming, sweetheart," he said, already thumbing through his cell's address book for Smitty's number. "Stay put."

It took a few minutes, but he got to Smitty. He convinced Shanna to hang up so he could dial her back on his cell phone, and he managed to get dressed while keeping the slurring woman talking. Then he ran out the back door, nearly tripping as he spied that long blue scarf abandoned on the floor.

Like a signpost to lead him to Nikki? Or like a river on which the love of his life had sailed away?

His mouth went dry, so he said the vow inside his head. *I'm coming for you, too, cookie. No way am I letting you go.*

Twenty-one

You make me want to be a better man.

—JACK NICHOLSON,
ACTOR, IN *AS GOOD AS IT GETS*

Though for the time being, Jay's silent promise was long on feeling and short on follow-through. In the light of an overhead fixture, he found Shanna in the living room at the old Pearson place, sitting on the floor with her back to the wall. Holding his breath, he pushed wide the double doors to rid the place of the acrid stink of new paint mixed with spilled booze.

"Dropp'd it," she said, her hand making a feeble wave at the shards of a crystal decanter spread across the scarred hardwood near her feet. "Didn't want more."

"Good." Jay checked his watch. How long had Nikki been gone? How long before Smitty arrived to take over as white knight? "You've already had too much."

"Here, take 'em," Shanna said, fishing under one hip. She held out a plastic bottle. "The oxy. The oxy . . . whata-macallit."

As Jay snatched the pills from her hand, a few rattled against the plastic, and his stomach roiled again. He glanced down at the label. Oxycodone, she was right about that. "Jesus, Shanna. What were you thinking?"

"Wasn't anything—wasn't anyone—without Jorge."

He hunkered down beside her. "You don't need Jorge. You don't need any man to be someone."

She nodded. "Know that. Now. Not then. Not next door. But here . . ." Her hand waved again.

Jay glanced around. He'd peered inside the dirty windows a few times when walking down the beach, and the junk that had been stored inside and out on the deck then was gone. The paint was fresh and the glass of the French doors polished. "You had the place fixed up."

"Me. I fixed it. Fixed it myself."

Surprised, he looked over at her. She held out both hands and he could see her fingers were denailed and paint stained her cuticles. "*You* did the work?"

She nodded. "Almost all me. Paint. Hauled garbage. Left the photos, though."

"Good." He had no idea what photos, but that didn't matter. She was half-lucid and Smitty had said to keep her talking. "They're nice photos."

"I'm in 'em. Happy photos. Happy me. Happy here."

"Great." He checked his watch again and let his mind leap back to Nikki. Why the hell would she have left after that spectacular bout of sex? *How* could she have left after that spectacular bout of sex?

Damn, it made him want to tear out his hair. He knew he should have had it out with her before they hit the sheets. So it was his own damn fault that she was gone, but that didn't stop him from being pissed off at her.

Worry always pissed him off.

As soon as Smitty showed, he was on the hunt. To find answers, to find her.

Except then Smitty showed, and shit, Shanna suddenly showed a resurgence of her previous fixation on him.

"Stay with me, Jay." Smitty was going to take her to his clinic where he said they'd pump her stomach and then feed her activated charcoal to absorb any leftover toxins.

She'd be there at least for the next few days so they could monitor her for liver damage, and assess her emotional needs as well.

Her hand lifted toward him in entreaty. "Don't leave me, Jay."

Hesitating, he stared at her thin, outstretched fingers.

Stay with me.

Don't leave me.

Women had said similar words to him before, and he'd closed his ears to them. Going in, he'd always reasoned, they'd known he wasn't the staying type. He was a leaving kind of man.

Meaning he'd always opted for the charming smile and the speeding feet when words like that reached his ears.

Stay with me.

Don't leave me.

But the one saying the words now was Shanna, his childhood friend. Shanna, his careless fling.

What a mess he'd made with that.

A mess he'd love to walk away from now.

And he had himself to consider, didn't he? Nikki to find.

Damn it, where was she? How could she have done this to him? Instinct he'd never acknowledged or been in touch with before told him he had to find her, and find her fast, before she walled herself off from him.

Shanna's voice broke through his anxious thoughts. "Jay?"

He closed his eyes and rubbed his palm over his face, trying to think clearly. To think of himself and what was best for him. What was best for Hef Junior, the randy adolescent inside himself, Malibu's selfish bachelor who had never once looked over his shoulder to acknowledge any hurt he'd left behind.

When he opened his eyes, it was to realize that it was time, finally, to grow the hell up. At whatever the cost to himself.

"I'm right here, Shanna," he said. "I'll stay with you as long as you'd like."

Hours later, she was as pale as the clinic's sheets. He was seated on a chair beside her bed, his hands trying to warm one of her cold ones. Her pale eyelashes fluttered against her cheeks.

"Tell me again," she murmured. "Tell me again how I don't need Jorge."

He squeezed her fingers. It wasn't the first time he'd repeated the words. "You don't need Jorge. You don't need any man to be someone."

A smile lifted the corners of her chapped lips. "That's right. When I went back to my house tonight—the little house, did I tell you I'm buying it? I told my father my plan and he sputtered, but I was adamant—I realized that if I could redo that house and if I could stand up to my dad, well, I could be comfortable in my own skin. I could be woman enough to live without a man in my life. Even Jorge."

On the heels of her words, the man in question ran into the room. His clothes were rumpled, his boots dusty, his face unshaven and bristly. *"Madre de Dios!"* he exclaimed. "What the hell is going on?"

Smitty showed up next, his ponytail flying behind him. "Shanna, he said Jay left a message on his cell phone about where you were. We couldn't stop him at the desk."

Her eyes were wide, darting between their faces until they landed on Jay. He shrugged. "I called him. Told him on the off chance he might want to know."

"Might! Might want to know!" Jorge followed that up with a string of Spanish that had Jay a little concerned about where his head might end up before the morning was over. "I had to race to Mexicali—"

"Your grandfather?" Shanna lifted onto her elbows. "Was it your grandfather?"

"Sí, sí. Before dawn yesterday morning he goes missing and no one can find him. I think I can get there, get back for your party, okay, maybe a little late . . . but the *pobre* cell phone service across the border means I can't tell you

where I am. Even once we find my grandfather and settle him back in the house safe and sound."

"The landline—"

"I don't *know* your landline number, I don't have any cell reception to call it with anyway, and even if I could have gotten through to U.S. information—which I finally did—your father has it unlisted!"

It was the longest, most impassioned speech Jay had ever heard his friend make.

As if it was all too much, Shanna collapsed back to her pillow.

"*Shanna.*" Jorge rushed toward the bed and Jay made way for him by ducking out of his chair. The other man dropped into the seat and took Shanna's now-free hand. "*Pobrecita*, I'm so sorry. But how could you have done this?"

"It was stupid. *I* was stupid."

"How could you imagine I don't love you? That if something happened to you, it wouldn't kill me, too?" Jorge's accent thickened as feeling filled his voice. "How could you not realize I couldn't go on without you? That I wouldn't be anyone without you?"

Jay shuffled back, embarrassed by the other man's very Latin, very emotional outburst. He almost held his breath, just like he did when he got in an elevator with someone who was sneezing. Shit like that might be contagious.

Shanna was smiling at the sap, though. Some color had returned to her face. "You'd go on without me, you know you would."

"No, no—"

"Shh." She reached out to put her hand over his mouth and he held it against his lips for a kiss. "Tell him what you told me, Jay."

Jay started. "Huh?"

She nodded at him. "Tell Jorge what you've been telling me."

Ah. He looked over at his friend, meeting the dark eyes that seemed wet—God, the other man wasn't near tears, was he? "What I've been saying, Jorge, is that you don't need any man to be someone."

"What?" Jorge's brows slammed together. "Of course, I don't need a man. You know damn well I'm straight."

The drama of the scene must be upsetting Jorge's thinking processes. Jay laughed. "What I mean is, I've been telling your woman that she doesn't need any man to be someone."

Still looking confused, Jorge turned to Shanna. "But you want me, yes? You love me."

"Of course. I do." She caressed his whiskery cheek with her palm. "But a woman can be happy without a man. I could live without you."

"But I don't want to live apart." Jorge's face registered alarm. "You must marry me. You must say yes."

Christ. Marriage?

Jay took another step back. The man was going all out here. But Shanna's smile was tender, and if happiness was a color, it was that dawn-pink staining her cheeks. "Yes, yes, I'll marry you. But the point is— Oh, I'll explain it to you later. Right now, I need a kiss."

Grinning, Jay took that—finally—as his cue to leave. He could turn his attention to himself now. And to his chef with benefits.

Smile dying, he recalled with a chill Shanna's almost-last words: *A woman can be happy without a man.*

Did that include Nikki?

Summer's end was nearing, and as Nikki inched her way up PCH it was clear from the multitude of cars around her that everyone wanted to spend it at Malibu, while all she wanted was to be out of the place. Still, she'd had to make one final trip beachside, even though she was careful not to glance at Jay's house as she passed. By now he'd probably woken to find her gone, and as much as she knew he loved her coffee and though she expected he very much enjoyed the sex they'd shared, in his heart of Hef Junior hearts, she figured he was glad she'd made the first move and left him.

"Love me," he'd said last night, the ass. No wonder women followed him around like hungry cats after the smell of salmon. When a golden-haired, silver-tongued professional bachelor like Jay Buchanan whispered "love" in a bed partner's ear, who could blame most for not detecting the distinction between "love you" and "love *me*?"

Even she had almost fallen for it, and though she'd drawn herself back from the brink, her heart had still suffered. Damn man. If she ever came across him again, she'd give him a piece— No, she never wanted to come across him again.

A sudden red light made her stomp on the brake pedal. *Ow. Ow ow ow ow ow.* Pain radiated in a sharp sunburst from her injured knee, and though the A/C blasted like an arctic wind, sweat popped on her forehead.

Yesterday had proven to be the end of something else, too. The self-concocted myth that she could make a private chef career despite her bum joint was now officially debunked. Whether it was the result of Jenner's shove and her fall, or just the accumulation of wear-and-tear despite the more relaxed kitchen work of late, the swollen size of her knee and the pain it was producing testified to the truth.

She'd lost her last hope to continue a culinary career.

Shoving that thought from her mind, she turned into the driveway shared by the café and Malibu & Ewe. There were a few cars clustered around the eatery, but it was much too early for knitting shop hours, just as she'd planned it.

Limping toward the front door with a basket under her arm, she breathed in one of her last breaths of Malibu summer. There was ocean in the air, of course, and the delicious, greasy smell of Gabe's fish and chips. She'd been attempting to wheedle the recipe for the batter from him, but so far without success. He seemed the sort of man well-armored against female sweet talk.

Even Cassandra could rarely get any emotion out of him besides annoyance . . . or outrage.

Nikki bent to place her burden on the welcome mat outside the door to Malibu & Ewe.

"Little sister," Cassandra said from behind her. "This is a surprise."

Making a face, Nikki took a long time straightening up and then turning around to confront the other woman. She'd so hoped to ditch and dash. But now she was caught, and Cassandra was playing the little sister card again.

It wasn't going to get to her, Nikki promised. It wasn't. Not when she was here to break her last ties to Malibu.

Her eyebrows lifted to emote a very casual interest. "So how much younger *am* I than you?"

"Two years." Cassandra stepped around her to lift the basket from its place. "What do we have here?"

"A parting gift, I'd guess you'd say. There's those knitting books you let me borrow earlier in the month and a few other things I thought you might enjoy."

"Your creations," Cassandra said, peering into the basket with its plastic-wrapped packages.

"All vegetarian. Some muffins, two kinds of cookies, and a container of vegetable chowder. It's frozen, and will keep for weeks."

"Thank you." The yarn shop owner drew out a set of keys from her pocket and unlocked the door to push it open. "Will you come in for some tea?"

Nikki stepped back, swallowing her wince at the answering twinge in her knee, and shook her head. "I'm going. I have to get back home."

"I thought you had a few more days with Jay."

That wouldn't be wise. "I'm cutting out a little early."

"Another job lined up?"

Nikki shook her head. "It turns out I'm not going to be cooking for a living anymore."

Cassandra stepped into the shop, flipped on the lights, then threw a glance over her shoulder. "That means I'd better try these cookies ASAP if they're my last chance at

Nikki's cuisine. Come in and have some tea. Except for the food, I won't bite, so you don't have to be afraid."

Old habits answered for her. "I'm not scared."

Cassandra smiled. "I didn't think so."

So that was how Nikki found herself on one of the cushiony couches, her bad leg propped on an ottoman, idly winding a skein of yarn into a ball. Cassandra had shown her how a couple of weeks before.

Nikki dropped it into her lap when the other woman pressed a mug of tea in her hand. She sipped, then resisted the urge to spit the stuff out. "Oh, God. I'm starting to sympathize with Gabe. That stuff is vile."

With a graceful flutter of her calf-length skirt, Cassandra settled on the couch across from her. "You get used to it."

"No." Nikki slid the mug onto a nearby table and pushed it well away. "You get used to taxes. To putting gas in your car. You're not supposed to have to get used to something you introduce to your taste buds unless it stops raging disease or cellulite from forming on your thighs. I know of some excellent herbal blends, heck, I can even put together one myself that's got to be a thousand times better than this."

"Which doesn't sound like a woman no longer interested in the culinary world."

"I didn't say I'm not interested in cooking. I've loved my work with food." She retrieved the yarn ball to resume winding. "The chance to put together different colors and textures and tastes . . ."

"Well, then why—"

"It doesn't matter." Answering the big "why" question meant revealing her weakness—and she wasn't thinking about her damn knee for the moment. With the yarn still in her hands, she rose from the couch. "Anyway, I have to, um, get on . . ."

"With Jay's lunch?"

She didn't want to think about him either. "No, no. I told you, I'm leaving Malibu. I'm leaving the job with him. I've got to go home and get, um, back to my, uh, fish."

"Fish?" With a wave, Cassandra dismissed that excuse. "That doesn't sound pressing. Sit back down."

Nikki stayed where she was, but smiled a little. "You're bossy. No wonder you're the oldest."

"But I'm not." Her gaze was direct. "I'm in the middle."

"What?" Stunned, Nikki dropped back to the couch. "There's . . . there's someone else? You didn't mention that before."

"You asked me not to tell you any more, remember?" Cassandra picked up a pair of needles and some yarn off the couch beside her and started clicking away. Nikki had no idea what she was making, but it combined the colors of blue, green, and peach.

Nikki frowned when Cassandra didn't continue. "Well? Tell me now. There's another one of us?"

Us. *Us*. She hadn't been part of an "us" for years. Since her mother died. That thing inside her chest—that broken thing that Jay had smashed somehow with his inventive lovemaking and his oh-so-cavalier "Love me" last night— made itself known, the broken pieces rattling painfully in her chest cavity. She rubbed her breastbone. How could she leave here before knowing it all? "Tell me everything, Cassandra."

"There's three of us. Three girls. From what I can gather, our . . . well, the man who provided the sperm withdrew the rest of his specimens from circulation sometime after your conception. Donors have that option. Maybe he rethought his participation in the program or maybe he married and was starting a family of his own." She shrugged, her eyes on Nikki. "Who knows?"

All right. Three. Three sisters. For some reason, the notion of donor siblings was getting harder to dismiss. "Why'd you do the research, Cassandra? And why now?"

The other woman's gaze dropped to her nimble, moving fingers. "Last year, my mother left for a two-year trip backpacking around the world."

"Wow. Adventurous."

Cassandra flicked her a glance, smiled. "She had me ten

years before TV's Murphy Brown decided to raise her baby by herself and caused a popular culture uproar. So, yeah, to not only raise a child alone at that time but to intentionally conceive it that way too—well, that tells you exactly how adventurous my mother is."

Nikki frowned. "I didn't think how uncommon it would have been in those days."

"My childhood had its interesting moments, that's for sure, though Mom did her best. When she left last year . . . well, the hole I'd felt all my life widened." Cassandra's cheeks flushed pink. "I was more lonely than ever."

Nikki protested. "But you have so many friends! And it's clear you make them easily." *She* was the one who kept her distance from people.

"Still . . ." Cassandra shrugged, her knitting fingers stilled. "I was always hungry for something else. For those biological connections."

Hungry. The word struck an uncomfortable chord. Last night, when her heart had leaked so many long-dammed feelings, she'd acknowledged for the first time a painful sense of aloneness. But hunger . . . was that why she cooked? Was she always trying to concoct something that would fill the emptiness that she'd lived with for so long?

Squirming at the idea, she stared down at her hands, noticing how securely they'd wrapped that single ball of yarn. It was like she was, turned in on itself, tightly wrapped, and so different than what Cassandra did with the same material. There on the other couch, she was creating, connecting, knitting together disparate colors and textures to make something beautiful and functional.

Like a family.

The thought slid into Nikki's mind with the ease of an omelet exiting a well-greased pan. She swallowed, looking away.

The problem was, a family could be there one day and gone the next. Like her mother. Like her father, who had never really been there for her at all. It was dangerous to attach with anyone in such a close way. She'd learned that. She *knew* that.

Wanting more had only hurt. She'd learned that at fifteen.

And since then, wanting more was what always made her afraid.

The ring of a phone startled them both. Cassandra rose from the couch to pick up the phone near the cash register.

"Hello? Oh. Jay."

Jay.

At his name, a dozen fractured images of him shuffled through Nikki's mind. His ocean-wet chest. His lean hand reaching for the coffee mug. The amused glint in his eyes. That charming, laughing smile on his face . . .

She'd miss those.

She'd miss him.

His teasing, his laughter, his touch. Oh, God, his touch.

Him. All of him.

For the rest of her life, she'd remember Jay as the man who had returned her sexuality. For the rest of her life, she'd remember him as—

She'd remember him for the rest of her life.

"You're looking for Nikki?" Cassandra's voice broke through her thoughts.

Nikki's gaze jumped to the other woman's, her eyes widening. What? Shaking her head and waving her hand, she tried signaling that Cassandra shouldn't give her whereabouts away.

What was he up to? Nikki had been so sure he'd be glad she'd left without an awkward good-bye, let alone an embarrassing scene. But now he wanted to find her?

"She's not at home? You checked, you say, and she's not there?"

Oh, my God! He'd gone to her place? Nikki stood, wondering if she should flee the yarn shop, too.

What was wrong with the man? He was a Weasel Number Two, endlessly horny, easily distracted, and never persistent with one particular mate. Scientific studies proved he shouldn't be chasing after her!

"Does he think I have something of his?" she whispered, just loud enough for Cassandra to hear.

"Does she, uh, have something of yours?" Cassandra repeated. She listened, then nodded. "Okay, sure, I understand that's between the two of you."

There was no two of them! Nikki would have stamped her foot for emphasis, if it wouldn't possibly have hurt her knee and if Jay might not have suspected something if a weird thump sounded through the phone.

But that was the whole reason why she'd left while he was sleeping. She wanted to get away clean and quick, before all his sweetly erotic knots and sweetly tempting words—*take me, have me, love me*—actually emotionally tied her to him and made her believe in something as impossible as the "two of them."

She hadn't wanted to fall in love with the man, because she didn't fall in love, of course. And because it would be stupid because he would never love her back, and because, oh, God, and because she'd already done it, she realized. She'd already gone ahead and fallen in love and it was such, such, such a damn disaster.

With a silent moan, she collapsed back to the couch. She'd wanted to escape before she had to acknowledge it to herself, but there was no escaping the fact now that when he'd broken that shell around her heart, somehow he'd ended up finding his way inside it, too.

Cassandra ended the call. Then she looked over at Nikki, her expression concerned. "I hope I handled that the way you wanted me to."

"Yeah." She placed her hand over her eyes, then rubbed it down her face and looked at Cassandra. "I've never had anyone cover for me like that before. Thanks."

Cassandra's smile flickered. "It's what friends do for each other. And sisters."

Oh, God. There was that, too. She was not only disastrously in love, without a job, and being stalked at her own home by the man she most wanted—and most wanted to avoid—but there was this whole sibling thing now, too.

How could her life be such a mess? And how was she to clean it up when she could barely walk to the bathroom and back by herself?

"I don't know what I'm going to do," she whispered, not meaning to speak the words aloud.

But Cassandra heard them, and hurried to the couch beside her. She took Nikki's hands and held them with both sets of her own talented fingers that knew how to make something out of nearly nothing. "I'm here for you. Just say what you need."

Nikki shook her head.

Cassandra squeezed her fingers. "We liked each other from the beginning. Admit that. And I'm your sister."

Her connection. Her family. Her sister.

"Tell me what you need," Cassandra insisted.

Between Nikki and other people was a chasm that had been dug twelve years before—maybe even longer ago than that. How could she breach it? How could she trust making a connection across it that could be so swiftly severed—leaving her more alone than ever? The idea terrified her.

"Little sister," Cassandra whispered. "What is it I can do for you?"

Nikki looked up. Blinked. For the first time, she saw the other woman's resemblance to herself. It was in the shape of her eyes and in the shape of her mouth, especially when she said those two words. Little sister.

The decision wasn't conscious. It came straight out of her vulnerable, newly broken heart. "Cassandra, I need help."

Twenty-two

Life itself is the proper binge.

—JULIA CHILD,
CHEF

The bells attached to the door of Malibu & Ewe rang out a warning. A warning Nikki didn't bother heeding as she stayed at her place in the tiny kitchen, laying out her home-baked cookies on a platter. Someone had likely arrived early for Knitters' Night to ensure their place on one of the couches. It was the end of September, and Cassandra said this time of year put panic in the hearts of those with holiday projects.

The place was certain to be crowded with crafters anxious about completing their kids' Christmas stockings or their glittery shawls for New Year's Eve.

Heavy footsteps trod across the floorboards. Nikki's fingers paused. Gabe, she decided.

"Hey," she called out. "Cassandra dropped me off and then went on to the store for more coffee. So you're free to enjoy one of my caramel brownies without any of her cracks about your failing health or your poor eating habits."

The footsteps found their way to the open kitchen door.
She glanced up, a smile—

Dying, right there on her face. Just like she was doing
inside, her stomach shrinking to the size of a kidney bean.
Because it wasn't Gabe's heavy footsteps she'd heard, but
Jay's. Jay Buchanan, close enough to touch.

"Cookie." His grim gaze took her in. "You're looking
well."

Her hair was too long, lighter, too. She touched it self-
consciously and then shoved her hands in the pockets of
her long skirt. With all the time she'd been spending in the
sun at Cassandra's house, she knew she was tanner than
she'd been before. And thinner, but that was because—

"Aren't you going to say I'm looking well, too?"

She cleared her throat. "You look like, um . . ."

"Crap," he finished for her. "Don't bother starting a
new trend by trying to spare my feelings, Nikki. I do have
mirrors."

He appeared leaner, too, she had to admit. His hair was
scruffier, there was a couple of days' worth of golden stub-
ble on his chin, and the shadows under his eyes said he'd
been staying awake nights—writing or . . . ?

The bean that was her stomach hardened as she thought
of Jay laughing down at some other woman lying in his bed
at that sunny house. But he wasn't laughing now.

"I would have cleaned up a little for you," he said. "But
when my spy network passed on that you'd been spotted
here, I couldn't take the chance that you'd go chicken on
me and fly the coop again."

"I'm no chicken," she said, frowning at him. But flying
the coop sounded pretty fine right now. She *had* taken a
chance coming to the yarn shop tonight, even though she'd
never imagined Jay caring where she was anymore—
whether it was Malibu or Manhattan or any point in between. Their fling had been over a month ago. Still, seeing
him again made her poor heart feel freshly wounded. "And
I didn't realize you had any spies."

"Give me a break, cookie. You're aware how people

around here love to talk. And I think it's interesting that
you tried so hard to make sure no one spilled where you've
been hiding the last four weeks."

Cassandra had known, of course, and consequently Gabe.
And though she'd never really expected Jay to be concerned about her whereabouts for any longer than it took
an ego prick to heal, she'd sworn them both to secrecy. "So
who told you I was at Malibu & Ewe?"

"Oomfaa saw Cassandra drop you off." He took a step
closer.

Instinct shuffled her back. Her knee gave a tiny twinge
at the movement, but she ignored the sensation and forced
herself to freeze. *Never let them think you're weak.*

Even Jay.

Especially Jay.

"We have some unfinished business, cookie."

"Our business was finished a month ago. Sorry I left a
couple of days early. I returned that part of my paycheck.
I'm sure I prorated it accurately."

"I'm not talking kitchen business."

She swallowed. "Well, you can't mean *bedroom* business," she said, trying to sound as tough babe as she could.
"Or if you do, it's only because I broke it off before you did."

"I wasn't ready for it to end," he ground out.

So it *was* that. She'd bumped up against his ego and he
wanted her to pay for the little scratch. Okay. She'd let him
let her have it and then he'd go back to his swinging lifestyle
and she'd go back to finding a way to live without the professional bachelor she'd fallen so hard for.

He returned to the doorway and leaned a shoulder against
the jamb. All he needed to do was take off his shirt and it
would be like a dozen times in his kitchen—God, she'd
missed his company—the way he'd stay near as she made
coffee or chopped vegetables for a salad. He'd filled so easily those empty spaces and too-long silences in her life.

"We didn't get to talk like I wanted to," Jay said.

Fine. Apparently he had a practiced buh-bye speech that
put a period on all his affairs. She gestured with a hand and

steeled her spine for the belated rejection. "Go ahead, say whatever you need to."

"I want to know how you got so strong."

Cold washed over her, followed by a scalding burn. "I don't know what you're talking about."

"We both know what happened when you were fifteen, Nikki. You used to flinch away from my touch, but you held your feet to the floor more times than you didn't. That couldn't have been easy."

There was a whine of anxiety in her ears. She didn't talk about this with people. And she'd expected a standard breakup speech, not a breaking-into-her-head discussion. "I didn't want to be a victim forever," she heard herself say. "I figured out why I'd gone looking for what I did when I was fifteen. I'm sorry for that little girl. But I grew up since then. That's not me anymore."

"Some parts of her still have to be you."

"No," she said. "I used to have trouble with sex, I'll admit that. But you know that's not true anymore."

"It's not just the sex, Nikki. It's the way you won't allow your emotions out either."

Her hands made fists in her pockets. Why did he make that sound like a failing?

"Isn't that what every man wants?" she demanded. "A female in his bed who makes things simple and undemanding? One who takes the relationship just as casually as he does? That's the whole premise of your latest series in *NYFM*, if I recall correctly. 'In Search of the Perfect Woman'—one who looks at the opposite sex just like a man."

"Funny you should mention that . . ."

The bells on the front door rang out again, and then Cassandra's voice sounded. "Hey, Nikki, do you think you could give me a hand for a minute?"

She glanced over at Jay. "Would you mind helping her? I want to finish with these cookies."

He gave her a hard look, but did as asked. She waited only a heartbeat before scurrying out of the kitchen and heading for the nearby stockroom and its convenient back door. If he wasn't going to leave her alone, then she would leave herself. Her hand was closing around the doorknob when his dry voice found her.

"Bock bock bock bock bock bock." His poultry impression was atrocious. "I called the chicken thing, and look, cookie, I was right. You're flying the coop."

"I'm not afraid of anything!" Too late, she heard her words and all that they gave away. Exasperated, she swung around to face him. "Look. You weren't supposed to still care about where I am or what I'm doing. Out of sight, out of mind, right, Hef Junior?"

"Right. It wasn't supposed to be this way for Hef Junior. But for Jay Buchanan, ah, that's entirely different, cookie."

"Different how?"

"Different in that though I got exactly what I was looking for—that sexy, breezy, no-sloppy-emotions-necessary female—she turned out not only to be the perfect woman but also the perfect one with whom I want to spend the rest of my life."

Uh-huh. Yeah. That anxiety whine was back in her ears but she wouldn't let him know. Instead, she gritted her teeth and made for the doorway. "Let's go handsome," she said, pushing past him and heading for the open area of the shop. "You've won me over. I'll go for another romp in your bed, then you can break up with me, and all will be right with your world."

"Oh, baby, you're working so hard you're killing me again."

She was in the shop when she faced him. While she was vaguely aware the room was filling up with knitters, she didn't let that stop her. "Working so hard at what?"

"Never opening up to anyone."

She hated him. She did. Yanking up her skirt so it revealed her to mid-thigh, she put on display her newly scarred knee, her jointed brace, the way her right quadricep had withered from lack of use. "I opened up myself just fine, see? I opened myself up to a fine orthopedic surgeon who opened up my knee and did the best he could with the

damage that occurred when I was fifteen and that I'd in-
flicted on myself since. I opened myself up to Cassandra,
to my sister, who took care of me when I freaked before
going into surgery and who took care of me afterward—
doing everything from getting me to the bathroom to getting me to the physical therapist. So don't talk to me about
not being able to open up, damn you."

"Oh, God." His eyes closed, and he rocked back on his
heels, as if she'd wounded him. "Cookie, I would have been
there for you. I want to take care of you. I want to take care
of you always."

No man had ever been there for her. No man had ever
taken care of her. It was dangerous to start believing one
could!

The volume of chatter from the knitters in the room could
no longer be ignored. She glanced over, and noticed they
were all gathered around the table centered between the
couches. Cassandra caught her eye. "Little sister, come take
a look at this."

She glanced back at Jay. There was a new expression on
his face, something maybe like fear, and it was so surpris-
ing that she stepped toward him, concerned. "Jay? Jay, are
you okay?"

He smiled a little, but with none of the seduction or
charm that she remembered. "That's it. You've just proven
to me that I've finally grown up and gained some smarts.
No matter what, no matter what happens, you're the best,
cookie."

"Nikki, come here."

This time she followed Cassandra's direction. She headed
toward the klatch of knitters and they made a place for her so
she could see what was on the table. "It's a page proof," Jay
said, coming up behind her. "For next month's dead-tree
version of *NYFM*."

It wasn't glossy like a magazine page, but the layout
and the font were the same as she'd seen in *NYFM*. The
headline read, "In Search of the Perfect Woman." Her

photo ran beneath it, something taken at that restaurant opening because she was wearing Cassandra's eye-popping dress. Next to her picture was one of Jay. Stamped over his face, the words "TAKEN" in red.

Taken. *Taken.* In print!

"I was getting desperate to find you, Nikki," he said, his breath stirring her hair.

Desperate? Jay Buchanan desperate over a woman?

"I was counting on this to flush you out."

He'd listed a cash reward for tips leading to her . . . oh, God . . . leading to her marriage to him.

Taken?

Desperate?

Marriage?

The blood drained from her face, then filled back up, leaving her flushed and hot. Nikki's heart felt weightless as she slowly, slowly turned to confront Jay. This man had been desperate to find her the last four weeks and now she could see each lonely hour on his face. Jay Buchanan, this beautiful, golden, worried-looking man wanted her. Wanted *her.* Her heart bobbed around in her chest as disbelief gave way to effervescent delight.

Taken.

Marriage.

. . . And a reward?

She had bills piling up, despite her emergency surgery fund, and Oomfaa, who'd tipped Jay off to her whereabouts, got paid more money per movie than Cameron Diaz.

Nikki licked her lips. "What would it take for me to get that reward?"

The look of apprehension on his face fled. Suddenly, smug replaced the tired lines. She should hate it—no, she shouldn't. Because smug and arrogant and confident were as much Jay Buchanan as everything he knew about her. It would be a challenge to keep him on his toes, but really, who else had what it required to do it? From the beginning, it had been her noble—no, holy—purpose.

"You know what it will take, baby. Accept me. Accept and believe and *trust* that I love you. That I will for the rest of our lives."

Oh. Yeah. He *did* know her.

She looked at the knitters surrounding her, noticing how closely they stood to each other, at how closely they stood to her in her time of need. New friends. Cassandra, her eyes tearing up, rubbed Nikki's shoulder in that maternal way she had, and to Nikki, it was the touch of her own mother, of all mothers.

And so it wasn't just the love she saw on Jay's face, but the strength she gained from her teary-eyed sister, as well as the others who stood around her, that provided her with the ultimate courage. She remembered thinking about telling Fern that some women gave too much of themselves to be with a man. And then there was her, who always gave too little in order to protect herself. With the feminine support she felt from this small crowd, maybe she could give everything, and trust her heart, like her body had always trusted Jay.

"I want to take care of you, Nikki," he said, his voice gentle. "I love you."

Heartbreaking. Heart-mending. He'd done the first and was accomplishing the second. He'd healed so much of her.

"I—" she started. But love was the expected word, and in her case, not really the most important one. She'd share it with him later, privately, when there was nothing between them but skin. Now she counted on him to know her well enough—and, oh, he did—to realize how momentous her next words really were. She held out her hand to him, because being the one to reach out at this moment seemed important, too. "I need you, Jay."

Tears stung her eyes. When his fingers closed over hers, so strong, so male, so understanding, Nikki cried.

He brought her flush against him and whispered in her ear. "Dry your eyes, cookie. No sense getting blotchy when I've got Madonna booked for the wedding."

And Nikki laughed while the tears flowed.

Epilogue

The web of our life is of a mingled yarn, good and ill together.

—WILLIAM SHAKESPEARE,
PLAYWRIGHT AND POET

Three weeks later

Nikki sat shoulder-to-shoulder with Cassandra at Malibu & Ewe, in expectation of another blowout crowd. After the public resolution of her romance with Jay during Knitters' Night, Tuesday evenings in the shop were more popular than ever. It didn't seem possible that they'd find a way to top that spectacle, though.

She frowned down at the yarn and needles in her lap. "Are you sure about this? Do you really think I'm ready?"

Cassandra nudged her good knee with her own. "More important, do *you* think you're ready?"

"Well, it's not a boyfriend sweater. And for a fiancé, everyone says the curse doesn't apply."

"You should probably take off your ring anyway, in case it gets caught in the yarn. I'll sacrifice and wear the big rock for you tonight."

"Um, no." Nikki laughed and looked down at her left finger. It *was* kind of a big rock, but Jay had picked it because he said he wanted to weigh her down in case she tried running from him again.

That so wasn't going to happen.

She'd started a new trend and given him an engagement ring, too. No sense in putting off reinforcing that "taken" status, was there? Without hesitation, he'd agreed that what was good for the goose was good for the gander.

God, she loved the man.

"You're going all teary again," Cassandra warned. "Do I have to break out the Kleenex box?"

"No—"

But she was already pressing something into her hand. It was white and soft, and threaded with a thin, pink satin ribbon. "A garter!" Nikki said, recognizing the lacy band. "You knit a garter."

"It's never too early to start on the traditions."

Delighted with the pretty thing, Nikki impulsively leaned over and kissed the other woman's cheek. The tears were in Cassandra's eyes now.

The bells on the door rang out. They both quickly looked over, maybe equally eager to keep these new emotions in check. The long-legged stranger walking into the shop provided quite the distraction.

She wore expensive clothes. Nikki didn't recognize designers, but she did recognize wealth, and this woman was dressed like authentic big bucks. Her pants outfit wasn't the usual eclectic, casual Malibu chic, but something more classic. The woman herself was a classic. It was hard to determine her age, not with her caramel-colored hair sleekly pulled back at her nape to reveal a pair of diamond earrings that were tasteful but glittered as expensively as the rest of her.

She hesitated a few feet into the shop, then came a bit closer to Nikki and Cassandra. Close enough to reveal the color of her eyes. Blue and green.

Beside her, Cassandra stiffened. Then she popped from the couch cushions like a jack-in-the-box. "Hello, hello," she said. "Welcome. I'm Cassandra Riley, the owner of Malibu & Ewe."

"Hello." The blue and green–eyed woman gave a small smile and then her gaze shifted past Cassandra to Nikki.

Cassandra noticed the direction of her gaze. She half-turned. "And this is Nikki, Nikki Carmichael, my—" Her voice broke, and her face flushed.

"Her sister," Nikki finished for Cassandra. She smiled for both the women, but her gaze was fixed on the blue and green eyes that she usually only saw in her mirror. "We're sisters."

Turn the page for an excerpt from the next book
in the Malibu & Ewe series by Christie Ridgway . . .

Unravel Me

Coming soon from Berkley!

Twenty minutes after learning a most startling piece of personal news, the facts had yet to sink into Juliet Weston's mind. The entire drive from the yarn shop by the beach to her home in the Malibu hills, the information had kept a certain distance. Now, as she peered through the heavy dusk to watch the garage door of her new-to-her house lift in silence, the information still merely hovered overhead. Her Mercedes eased inside, its purr lighter even than the touch of her shoe on the accelerator. She let herself into the shadowy house—out of practice with even the most innocuous kind of night life, she'd forgotten to leave a light burning—and set her keys in the abalone shell she and Wayne had smuggled back from their honeymoon in Italy. An ordinary act on such an extraordinary evening.

She should be grateful to feel so unmoved, she decided. Her detachment gave her time and space to deal with this complete surprise.

Without bothering to switch on the nearby lamp, she wandered into the kitchen that overlooked the flagstone

deck and pool that stood between the main house and the guest cottage. The cabinets, the sink, even the butcher block island just a handspan away seemed as remote to her as the stretch of Pacific Ocean that was her view beyond the pool. As it had been since Wayne's death, she felt separate from everything, buffered from reality by the grief that lay so thickly around her. It was as if layers of goosedown muffled her from the rest of the world.

Still staring out the windows at the pool beyond, still wrapped in the numbness that had surrounded her for so many months, a question whispered through her mind. *Who am I?* Heartbroken widow, of course. But beyond that . . .

"Who am I really?"

At the same instant she voiced the question, a light flashed on outside. Startled, she jerked, stumbling back so she had to catch herself from falling by slamming her hand onto the butcher block.

Some idiot had left a knife there, a small one that the same some idiot had used to cut up an apple earlier in the day.

It cut *her* now. Without thinking, she lifted her forefinger to her mouth, her attention shifting out the window again.

The pool lights were glowing, turning what had been dark waters into a tranquil turquoise lagoon. The sight made her breath catch in her chest; it was that beautiful in contrast to the indigo darkness of the now-descended night.

And then the surface rippled, the lagoon invaded, the tranquility shattered.

A man was in Juliet Weston's pool.

Her finger was still bleeding. The blood was salty on her tongue, giving an earthy flavor to a further realization.

A *nude* man was in her pool.

She should turn away. At least, shut her eyes.

Instead, she found herself staring at the naked, novel sight.

Against the turquoise light he was a dark silhouette with an aquamarine outline running along the edges of his body like veins of neon light. He was tall and lean, his shoulders wide, with strong arms that reached out as if to gather life closer to himself with each stroke.

He swam away from her, and as his long legs fluttered with lazy kicks, she detected the shift of muscles in his rounded buttocks, the muscles tightening to create a scoop on the right, then a scoop on the left. She watched, fascinated at how every movement, how every line of that big body exuded power. And sex.

Sex?

Embarrassment flooded Juliet's face with heat, but something was suddenly burning inside her, too, burning so hot that her protective goosedown was at risk of catching fire. And then it did. As her gaze stayed glued to that masculine specimen of sinew and skin, she could feel her muffling layers flame, blaze, and then fall to ashes at her feet. Her flesh was left behind, still clothed, but hypersensitive to the gentle scrape of silk against its surface. It left her hyper-aware of that swimming man, turning now.

Coming toward her. Inexorable. Inevitable.

Climbing the steps, climbing out of the pool, his all-male nakedness part threat, part magnet.

His right foot breached the deck. His left.

Her heart expanded, pounded against her chest wall. *Get back!* her instincts screamed. *Get away!*

Air rushed out of her lungs. She leaped in retreat, even as she knew he couldn't see her through the darkened windows. Her hips crashed into the square butcher-block table, shoving it along the terra-cotta pavers with a piercing screech. The knife clattered to the floor, followed by the shallow wooden bowl that held the rest of the ripe red fruit.

Thump thump thump thump.

Apples rolled unevenly along the floor, noisy as the feet of the children she'd never have.

One darting glance showed that the dark figure had frozen, but then it thawed in an instant and made a dash for

the kitchen door. The door that was the only thing keeping the two of them apart.

It was wrenched open. The overhead light blazed on.

Juliet resisted the urge to hide from him. What good would it do?

She kept her gaze steady on his face, not glancing down, not letting him realize that she realized that his big male body was dripping on her floor. His big, dripping, naked male body.

He didn't acknowledge his nakedness, either. Instead, he stared, his gaze running over her. She felt it like a hand, his hands, big like he was, strong and sinewy. Goose bumps rose in the wake of that imaginary touch. Her breasts tingled inside her bra, and again her face burned.

"You're bleeding." His voice was rough but he reached toward her slowly, one of those hands lifting in her direction, heavy veins standing out on the back of it. The dark hairs of his forearm were plastered against his tanned skin and drops of water still moved along his muscles like a man sweating after hard work . . . or after making hard, satisfying love.

Forgetting her cut, she put her hands over her eyes, appalled by the direction of her thoughts. Shocked by the heat of a flush on the back of her neck, by her swelling breasts, by the sensitive pinpricks that rose on the flesh inside her thighs.

The air in the room shifted, so she supposed he was moving, but for a man so big, he was graceful and silent. She'd never noticed that about him before.

"Juliet." Closer now, his voice. "Juliet, honey."

Honey. When was the last time a man had murmured an endearment to her? This man had never. This man must be rocked to the soles of his size twelve feet—God, somehow she'd even noticed his feet and made a determination of their size!—if he was talking to her like that.

And touching her like this. Because he was peeling away one of her hands. The hurt one. Like a coward, she only squeezed her revealed eye tighter shut.

His palm cradled her fingers. The calluses of his skin made an erotic scratch along her knuckles. "You've hurt yourself. What happened? Did something frighten you? Did some*one* frighten you?"

You. Me. She had no idea which was more accurate. But she did know she couldn't pretend she wasn't standing in her kitchen with a naked man for any longer.

Her heart still whomping inside her chest, she opened her eyes. Oh. Not naked. Not naked any longer.

He was staring down at her, a line between his black brows and concern in his blue eyes. Around his neck was the strap of a butcher-style apron. It was printed with yellow lemons and green leaves. It barely covered the flesh between his dark nipples and its ruffled hem hit him at midthigh.

She remembered buying it at one of the boutiques in the Malibu Country Mart, thinking it would look cheerful hanging in her kitchen. Wrapped around him, it should have looked ridiculous. The sight should have made her smile, if not out and out laugh. Instead, she could only think that on the other side of the apron he was—no, don't go there.

Too late. His first-class buttocks were back in her memory, that vision of him as he churned naked through the water. His muscles flexing, creating a tantalizing scoop on the right, scoop on the left.

"Oh, God." She put her free hand to her forehead.

One corner of his mouth ticked up. "I know, I know. I'd be ready to thank the Lord, too, if someone presented me with such primo blackmail material. If I let you take a picture, will you tell me what's going on?"

"I have absolutely no idea what's going on," she answered, with all honesty. Her voice came out a little rusty, and his fingers tightened on hers, like a brief embrace. "Not beyond the fact that there's a man dressed like Rachael Ray in my kitchen."

One of his eyebrows winged up. "So *she's* the one they call 'The Naked Chef'?"

"No." She rubbed her forehead again. "No. It's . . . oh, it's all so complicated." So completely unexpected.

"Not so bad. Nothing we can't fix with a Band-Aid."

He was looking at her cut hand again. While all she could think of was that what really needed fixing wasn't going to be helped by something to be found in her medicine cabinet.

Because something momentous had just happened to her tonight. Something inside of her had woken up, or perhaps it was *she* who had woken up, likely a delayed reaction to the astonishing news that had been revealed to her at the yarn shop. Right now Juliet Weston didn't feel like herself, which made sense, after all, since she'd just discovered she really wasn't who she'd always thought.

But the why of this current situation didn't matter, not when the what was so clear to her. The what—*oh, God*— was this: Her protective layers of grief were gone and she had a sudden and raging sexual attraction for the naked non-chef standing on her tiled floor, holding her shaking hand. He affected her just that much. Her whole body was trembling in reaction to him.

Him. Noah Smith.

The man who worked for her. The man who had tended to her dying husband. The younger man. The younger man who was, for all intents and purposes, her closest companion.

He shouldn't go back to her, Noah thought, pulling on jeans and shoving his feet in a pair of ragged running shoes. He should stay in the cottage and mind his own business, leaving Juliet to whatever it was that had spooked her earlier in the evening.

But hell, before finishing college and attending three years of law school, the Army had schooled him long and schooled him well on keeping focused on the mission. And his mission—but no, not his obsession, damn it—was Juliet Weston.

For her—no, for the *mission*—he'd done some things, and then not done some others that were secrets he expected to take to his grave. He didn't regret a one, but he was now bound to her in a way she didn't know. That's why when he'd heard the strange sounds from her supposedly vacant kitchen—she'd said she was going to be gone for a couple of hours—that he'd rushed in wearing nothing more than his protective instincts.

Probably scared the bejesus out of her; a big, wet body decorated by only an infantryman's meat-tag tattoo. Naked Noah.

Except he couldn't say she'd looked at him with any particular awareness then or before. From the cool, pleasant manner she always exhibited, he supposed she considered him along the lines of a convenient piece of furniture.

While she'd never struck him in the least like a chair or a table or a desk.

Just another reason to keep to his side of the pool.

He glanced out the window to assure himself all was well. There was no reason to go back over there. To her.

Except a stealthy figure was just now creeping over the wall to position itself outside Juliet's kitchen windows.

Christ! What now? Kidnapper? Peeping Tom? Didn't matter. His Army training said OP-FOR and he was going after this particular opposition force with everything he had.

Noah was through his door and across the flagstone deck before the intruder could take another step.

"Hey!" he yelled, grabbing the stranger by his shirt collar to yank him around. "What the hell do you think you're doing?"

The lights from the pool glowed greenly on the other man's face. He was in his late twenties, early thirties maybe, dressed in jeans, the cotton shirt that was crumpled in Noah's fist, and lightweight hiking boots. Two cameras hung around his neck. Noah twisted the shirt collar tighter and the guy stumbled closer.

"What are you up to?" Noah demanded again.

"Easy, easy," the stranger said, not attempting to fight Noah's grasp. "I'm a friend of the lady's." He gestured back toward the kitchen windows. "She invited me over."

"You and your cameras?"

"She . . . she asked me to take some pictures." The stranger's voice was low, his smirk suggestive. "You know."

Noah didn't want to know, but hell, he had to find out, didn't he? "Juliet?" He pitched his voice louder. "Juliet!"

The fixture over the back door flipped on and then she stepped out, hesitating there as the light turned her caramel-colored hair to a deeper gold. When Noah had blasted into the kitchen earlier, it had been hanging straight down, but now it was pulled away from her face. It looked damp around the edges as if she'd just splashed water on her skin. The lashes surrounding her amazing eyes—one green, one blue—were spiky with wetness.

She blinked as she gazed at the two men. "Noah?"

"Is this a friend of yours?" he demanded, not easing his grip on the other dude's shirt. "Did you invite him over?"

Juliet blinked again.

Shit, Noah thought. Maybe she had. For God's sake, she'd been a widow for eleven months and her husband had been dying for many, many before that. It would be natural to want companionship, and there was no reason to be pissed that if she wanted a man she hadn't turned to him. She was the quintessential uptown girl and officer's wife, while he, after all, was the hired help, the enlisted guy, the piece of furniture from across the pool. But did she have to torture his imagination by wanting pictures, too?

Because God, imagined freeze-frames were overtaking his gray matter. Juliet out of her conservative slacks and sweater and into a black teddy, lace playing peekaboo with his gaze so he glimpsed a shell-pink nipple here, the crease that separated her long legs from her hips there. Now a backside shot, Juliet peering over the creamy, elegant blade of her shoulder, the sweep of her spine leading to the taut hump of her ass. One set of ruby-tipped toes in the air.

Trying to banish the thoughts, his eyes closed and his

hand tightened on the photographer's collar. He barely recognized the grating sound of his own voice. "Well?"

"I've never seen him before in my life."

"I've never seen her before in my life."

Juliet and the stranger spoke together. Noah's eyes popped back open. "What?" Loosening his grip a little, he shook the man he held. "I thought you said she invited you over."

"I thought she was somebody else!"

Noah's eyes narrowed. "You forgot your friend's address?"

"She used to live here, anyway. I know this used to be her house."

Puzzled, Noah stared at the guy for a long minute.

"Oomfaa," Juliet put in quietly. "Remember, Noah? She owned it before I bought it."

Oh, Christ. The Realtor had revealed that "One of the Most Famous Actresses in America," who was referred to only as Oomfaa by the Malibu community to help retain her privacy, had lived here before Juliet moved in. Which meant that the guy with the cameras was likely—

"Paparazzi," he said with disgust, letting go of the man's shirt and shoving him away at the same time. "I hear they guarantee celebrity sightings at the Malibu Starbucks. Get lost."

The man shrugged his shoulders and pulled on the placket of his wrinkled shirt, the camera cases clicking together with the movement. "Wrong. Now the best spot is The Coffee Bean & Tea Leaf. But I'm looking for Oomfaa in particular. Do you know where she moved? I heard she's for sure in Malibu."

Noah rolled his eyes. "As if I would tell you."

The guy slid his hand in his front pocket. "There'd be money in it for you. I sell my stuff to that website—I'm sure you know it—celeb.com. I pay for tips that pan out."

No surprise that he'd offered the sleazy bribe to Noah. No one would consider for an instant that golden girl Juliet would do something so crass as give up the 411 for

a couple of bucks. But Noah? Ah, you could hone a hungry boy into a warrior. You could take the G.I. bill and use it and his B.A. and J.D. degrees to polish him to a mighty sheen. But still, still, those in the gutters of the world recognized a former fellow dirt dweller.

"I don't want your money," he said, shooting a glance at Juliet, wondering if she'd be surprised by his refusal. They both knew that the actress had moved just a few homes away.

The paparazzo followed his gaze. After a heartbeat, his pose went from casual to alert. He pivoted to face Juliet fully. "Wait a minute. I *do* know you."

When his hands moved toward his cameras, Noah wrapped his fingers around the straps hanging from the guy's neck. "No pictures. Don't even think about it."

The photographer pointed his forefinger at Juliet instead. "You married America's Hero."

That's what the media had dubbed General Wayne Weston: America's Hero. With his Hollywood looks, his West Point education, and his well-documented bravery, he'd been a military man that the populace—and more importantly, maybe, politicians on both the right and the left— could be proud of. When he'd retired, the world assumed he was going to run for public office. The highest office.

And win.

"They called you the Deal—"

Noah's hand jerked to the other man's throat. "That's—"

"Okay," Juliet interjected. "Let him say it. And let him go."

Shit. He gentled his stranglehold, but didn't completely ease off. "Juliet . . ."

"Then I'll say it for him. They called me The Dealbreaker."

Shaking his head, Noah dropped his hand. Why she wanted to repeat that, he couldn't fathom. As a sort of penance? Because it was true that when the general had married his very much younger wife, both of the parties had dropped him like a hot political potato. Where before

they'd been courting him to run on their ticket, now they couldn't back away fast enough. Rumor had it that when he'd mentioned his wedding plans to a woman thirty years his junior that the national committees had said the bride was out or their support was gone.

Wayne Weston had chosen marriage.

The media and the people hadn't taken very well to losing the presidential contender that made them so very proud. But had they blamed the hierarchies of the parties or even their hero himself? Hell, no. They'd blamed Juliet.

"Then they called me the Happy Widow."

Every muscle in Noah's body clenched. He hated that part of the story most of all. He'd been there in the last months of the general's life and in all the months since. Not once had Juliet been happy.

Not goddamn once.

But because she hadn't been at Wayne Weston's side in his last hours, unfounded, anonymously sourced rumors had been swallowed by the hungry-for-content twenty-four-hour media machine, to be regurgitated into cruel sound bites like the Happy Widow. And here, right beside Noah, was a representative of that slanderous, libelous, salacious fourth estate.

Hey, he thought, cheering a little. *And I've been trained to kill.*

"You'd better leave," he told the man in a low voice, deciding even a dolt like this one deserved a warning. "Now."

The guy was smart enough to shuffle back.

But Juliet intervened once again. "Celeb.com, you said? Don't they have a companion TV program in the new fall line-up?"

"Well, yeah," the photographer replied, shooting Noah a wary look. "Celeb.com on TV. You a fan?"

"We happy widows have to fill our hours somehow," she answered, without a hint of irony in her voice. "Maybe they'd like to do a piece on the general's book."

Noah rocked back on his heels. It all made sense to him now. General Wayne Weston's autobiography was hitting

the shelves four weeks from now. Juliet wasn't above chatting up a slimy paparazzo if it might gain attention for her late husband's book. Noah knew Juliet was fiercely committed to the hope that the general's life story in his own words would repair the damage to his reputation that had been the result of his marriage to her.

Christ. Noah rubbed his chest. He really wished he hadn't left the cottage now. He hated seeing her like this—because it made him worry that what she wanted so badly wouldn't come to pass.

"How about if I take a couple of shots of you?" the photographer asked.

"Now?" Her hand went to her hair.

"Sure. Why not? I'll bet people would like to know what you're up to." He jerked his chin in Noah's direction. "And *who* you're with."

The light over her head showed clearly the flush shooting up Juliet's slender neck on its way to color her face. "That's not . . . we're not . . ."

Yeah, Noah thought. *I'm the furniture. The enlisted guy. The hired help. Not good enough for her, and I know it.*

Her gaze flicked to his face, then jumped away. "Noah is . . . Noah was my husband's assistant. He helped Wayne as . . . as my husband declined. He helped him dress, helped him with his meals, helped him with the book he was writing."

Noah refused to let any feeling show in his expression. He'd helped the general in ways that Juliet would never know about. In ways that she would never thank him for if she ever found them out.

Which she never would.

The paparazzo shrugged. "None of that means you two aren't an item."

Juliet was shaking her head, her cheeks still bright pink. She glanced over at Noah again, and licked her lips.

God, he thought, staring at her mouth. *She's so effing beautiful, sometimes it hurt to look at her. And maybe it*

hurt a little more to see her total rejection of him as a romantic interest.

Of course, they were miles apart and he accepted that. And he also knew her well enough to realize it would be difficult for her to verbalize this to some dumbass from celeb.com. With a sigh, he stepped closer to the photographer.

"Listen, bud, the lady said we're not . . . intimate or whatever the hell you're getting at, and that's a fact. She's . . ." He ran out of steam, and just lifted his hand to where she stood under the light, glowing golden, like a dream. "She's . . ."

"Too old for him," Juliet said.

Noah froze. He was hearing things, right? There was water in his ears from his swim. Because he *knew* Juliet Weston. Of the many things to keep them apart, the *very* last thing that would ever stand in the way was . . . was . . .

He moved his head to stare at her. She couldn't have possibly said . . .

But then she said it again. "Noah's younger than me."

All right. He hadn't left the cottage and come back to her after all. Instead, he'd fallen across his bed and then into a deep sleep, dreaming.

A really odd, odd dream.